LOVE'S CRE•SCEN•DO

RAE LLOYD

Cover Design: K.B. Barrett
Editing: Steph White (Kat's Literary Services)
Proofreading: Vanessa Esquibel (Kat's Literary Services)

www.raelloyd.com

Dedication :

This is for everyone who is a Myles or has a Myles in their life.

TRIGGER WARNINGS

This book contains references to explicit sexual scenes, homelessness, on-and-off page drug use, drug addiction, drug overdose, on-and-off page sexual assault, including a brief mention of on-page rape, on-page murder, a brief mention of pregnancy loss, parental abuse and abandonment, off-page death of a parent, and on-page dealing with grief. Please read with care to your mental health.

I sat with my anger long enough until she told me her real name was grief.

— C.S. Lewis

Chapter One
I'm Not Okay by Citizen Soldier

0:01   SD   3:01

The first time I saw her was on a cold, miserable day in September. She was wrestling with a backpack in the pouring rain. Her long, dark, curly hair was plastered to her head as she shoved something into the bag and then, almost violently, zipped it up. She stood there for a moment, rain dripping off her face, sweatshirt soaked through, her frustration apparent on her face. Then she flipped her hood up and began to trudge her way across the street, toward the park, and out of my view.

The second time I saw her was in the same spot, six weeks later. I had returned to the middle of the busy outdoor mall to busk as it was almost Halloween, and the tips were sure to be good with so many shoppers out and about. She was standing outside the local coffee shop, Kafe, wearing her green and brown apron, smoking. She wasn't enjoying it. At least it didn't look like it. She wasn't standing calmly, lazily tugging on the cigarette. No, she was huddled over it, sucking it down as quickly as she could, almost looking like she had to, but didn't actually want to. It was the saddest smoke I had ever seen in my life.

The third time I saw her, she finally saw me. It was the night before Thanksgiving, and I was singing in the same area again. She was leaving Kafe with a group of people and was holding her apron in one hand with her overstuffed backpack in the other. Her hair was a mess of waves around her, cascading all the way to her waist. She was laughing at something one of her friends had said, yet she turned when she heard the sound of my guitar. Her gaze caught mine, and I was startled to see how blue her eyes were. They looked even brighter in contrast to her olive-toned complexion and long, dark lashes. I kept singing and strumming on my guitar, keeping my face impassive as she studied me. Her friends began to make their way toward the parking lot, yet she walked over to me, standing very close to the speaker, seemingly unbothered at having the music blaring in her ears. I sang the last notes of the song and then went quiet, letting the guitar rest loosely in my hands against my knee.

"I like that song. You have a good voice."

Oh, her voice had a rasp to it, and it sent tingles down my spine.

"Thank you." I dipped my chin at her. She glanced at the money strewn in my guitar case, then reached into the pocket of her threadbare coat and pulled out a crumpled five dollar bill. She bent slightly at the knees and placed it gently on top of the other money.

"Thank you," I said again. She nodded, biting her bottom lip between her teeth.

"Do you know the song "Something in the Orange" by Zach Bryan?" she suddenly asked.

"I've heard it." I nodded.

"Can you play it?" She gestured to my guitar.

I shocked myself by saying, "I can learn the chords and play it for you the next time I see you."

"I work right here," she offered, jerking her chin in the direction of the coffee shop.

"Then I'll be back," I told her. She gave me a slight smile and then turned to follow her friends. It was the most words I had voluntarily spoken to another person in a long time.

AFTER WATCHING HER WALK AWAY, I counted the money in my guitar case. One hundred twenty-one dollars. In this life, that was not bad for a six-hour day. I shoved the money into my pocket and gathered up my guitar, mic, and speaker. On my walk back to my van, I stopped at a food cart and got myself a shawarma with extra hummus and fried onions. I ate it for the rest of my walk. As I approached the lot where my van was parked, I noticed a couple of guys in hoodies standing in front of it while their friend was trying to remove my hubcaps. The adrenaline in my blood got pumping immediately. I placed my guitar down gently on the grass and then shouted, "Get the fuck away from my van!"

They looked up, surprised, as they hadn't heard me coming. When they saw it was just me, one guy, against the three of them, they grinned and kept working.

"Mother fuckers, I said get the fuck away from my van," I called out again as I ran full speed toward them. The one trying to jack my hubcap stood up, holding his tool in his right hand.

"Boy, back up," he said menacingly. I didn't slow down as I ran up to him and knocked him out with one punch to the side of his head. I turned to his friends as their guy fell to the ground.

"Let's go. Who's next?" I all but growled. They took off, leaving their friend behind, unconscious and bleeding from his face.

I could still feel the adrenaline coursing through my body, but I forced myself to walk slowly as I went back to retrieve my guitar. I double-checked that my tires and hubcaps were still intact, then hopped into my van and pulled out of the parking lot just as the remaining offender started to stir. It felt good to be able to defend myself. I felt the thrill of it thrumming through me as I drove.

EVERY NIGHT, I parked my van near the gym where I had a membership and worked out for two hours till I exhausted my brain and my body and depleted every bit of pent-up anger inside of me. Tonight was no exception. When I was done, I took a scalding hot shower, reveling in the way the water pounded on my back. When I got out, I put on a pair of clean sweatpants and a sweatshirt. Then I took out my razor to clean up my short beard. I had never grown a beard before and had been surprised to find that it grew out in a mix of dirty-blond and light-brown shades. After trimming my beard, I dried my hair that had grown out so much that I had begun pulling it back into a small man bun. I figured I was less recognizable now that I had grown my hair out from the usual buzz cut I had sported my entire life. I didn't mind it, as anonymity was now a priority of mine. Once I packed my belongings back into my gym bag, I went to the little coffee area they had set up with free drinks and protein bars. I made myself a hot chocolate, stirred my amino acids powder into it, and then grabbed two protein bars for the road. Once I was back in my van, I ditched my usual routine of staring at the photo in my wallet until I wore myself out enough to fall into a fitful sleep. Instead, I sat in my makeshift bed, learning the chords to the song my wild-haired stranger had requested to hear me play.

I didn't return to the outdoor mall for three days. I didn't want to go back until I knew the song backward and forward. I almost didn't go at all because I couldn't figure out why I was being stupid. I had avoided people for over a year now, and for good reason. I had seen plenty of beautiful women, so many of whom had thrown themselves at me. I had never even blinked in their direction, and suddenly, this curvy girl with a mess of curls had me learning a new song and setting up my mic and speaker outside Kafe again. I saw no sign of her for the first half of the day, so I played my usual playlist of songs and collected a decent crowd around lunch. This area was bougie. I knew this group well. One didn't stroll around shops that sold designer clothes and bags on a random afternoon in the middle of the week if you didn't have stupid money. I knew that women with stupid money usually had husbands who were never home who were giving them said stupid money. These women liked to watch the overly muscled pretty boy with a strong jaw, bright green eyes, and dirty-blond hair play guitar. I knew this because they said it out loud as if said pretty boy couldn't hear them. I also knew if I looked at them from under my long lashes, giving them a smolder and a slight smirk, the tips would be plentiful. Many times those tips came with a number on a paper, which I always threw away. Women like that would use you and discard you like the trash they thought you were.

I WAS FINISHING up the last chords of the song "All Eyes On Me"
by Bo Burnham when I saw her. She was wearing her green
apron again and a sorry excuse for a coat, which belied how cold
it was outside. I watched her light up a cigarette and take a long
inhale before exhaling in a cloud of smoke. I saw her see me.
She grinned and pushed off from the wall she was leaning on. I
didn't smile back as I watched her walk over in her black,
scuffed Doc Martens look-alike boots and wide-legged cargo
pants.

"So you finally learned the song, huh, music man?"

She was so blunt it startled me, and I felt a sizzle of something spark in my blood. I was so used to feeling angry all of the
time that I couldn't name what this different emotion was.

"It's Kian." I pulled my beanie further down on my head and
watched, waiting for a flicker of recognition to pass over her
face. But to my relief, it didn't. She just continued to observe me.
So I stared back.

"You gonna play?"

Again, her direct tone surprised me.

"Maybe." I gave a noncommittal shrug.

"My break is over in five minutes."

I humphed and leaned over my guitar, placing my fingers on
the frets. I didn't look at her for the entire song, but I put my
whole soul into it. When I finished and looked up, she was grinning. She has a dimple, my brain noted.

"You're really good, music man," she told me. *I know*, I
thought. But I didn't say anything.

"Coffee?" she asked.

"What's that?"

"Do you want a coffee?"

She had some sort of frenetic energy to her. It felt like she
could never be tamed. Maybe it was her hair giving me that vibe.

The cold air had caused all the little hairs around her hairline to frizz up, giving her a bit of a halo.

"Um, sure."

"Be right back."

She was gone in a whiff of coffee grounds, nicotine, and something else that I couldn't place.

TEN MINUTES LATER, she came back with a large cup of hot coffee, which she handed to me as she said, "Take Your Time, Sam Hunt."

"Huh?" I gripped the coffee cup, warming up my cold fingers with it.

"The next song I want you to play for me." She tossed her insane hair over her shoulder as she turned around to walk back to her job.

"How much do I owe you?"

"A song," she called back without turning around. I felt my mouth try to smile, but I reached up to smooth my mustache and stop my lips from curling up. I wasn't sure what was happening, and I wasn't sure if I liked it.

THAT NIGHT IN THE GYM, I boxed out my frustration barehanded until my knuckles bled. No one from home would recognize me with my six-pack, ripped arms, and muscles bulging from my shoulders. My old self was thin, wore round-rimmed glasses without a prescription, and the only calluses I had on my fingers were from playing guitar. This version of me had turned myself into a fighting machine. I knew why—I just didn't want to think about it. So in order to shut off all the noise, I worked out until my body broke—night after night. Tonight, I went even harder than

usual. I was especially annoyed at myself because something
hummed in my blood when my mystery girl was around. The
hairs on the back of my neck had stood at attention when I caught
a whiff of her natural scent. The muscles in my stomach had
clenched when my fingers brushed against hers as she handed me
the coffee. I hated my body's response to this objectively beautiful
woman. It had been so long since my body had defied my orders
to live the lonely life I had curated for myself, and I didn't know
what to do with this tug-of-war going on inside of me. On one
hand, I wanted to go back to my home in my van and obsessively
learn the Sam Hunt song that had been requested of me, and on
the other hand, I wanted to pack up shop and drive as far away
from temptation as I could. I had chosen this permanent vigil, and
I couldn't be distracted. I hadn't been until now, and I wouldn't let
anything get in the way of it either. They say time heals all
wounds, but I was determined to keep mine open and bleeding.

I didn't go back to her for over a month. Instead, I made my
way deeper into town to sing and play music near the bars at
night and by the town square during the day. This area was
where the college kids hung out, so the tips weren't as generous
as they were by the mall with the horny housewives, but I did
okay. I had no major bills—mainly gas and food. I didn't even
have a phone number right now; I just connected my phone to
local, free Wi-Fi when I wanted to. I was singing "Dependent" by
Keenan Te when a group of drunk, college-aged girls gathered
around. They threw a few twenties into my guitar case.

"Do you take requests?" one of them called to me. I nodded, shifting on my stool. They all giggled, and I heard snippets of them commenting on my face and body. One said a little bit too loudly, "I bet his beard will get dirty when he goes down on me."

I kept strumming and didn't let my gaze rest on any of them for too long. I wouldn't know; I hadn't gone down on a girl since I had grown my beard. I flinched at my own thoughts. One of the girls, with a long braid resting down her back, walked closer to where I sat. Her cheeks were flushed from the cold, and her lips were done heavily in red lipstick. This was my usual type: tall, thin, blonde, and compliant. A glimpse of dark curls and a rounded ass flashed in my mind's eye. I blinked to brush away the unwanted thoughts that were harassing me.

"Do you know the song 'In The Stars' by Benson Boone?"

"Oooh, good choice, Sasha!" Her friends clapped gleefully and turned to me to see what I would say.

"I know it," I said gruffly. Sasha blinked at me prettily and took a fifty-dollar bill out of her pocket. She dropped it in the case and then looked at me expectantly. Shame flooded my system. Sasha made me feel dirty. She reminded me of people and things that I wanted no reminder of. The shame quickly turned to anger, and I had to lean down to pretend to fiddle with the tuning machines to try to restrain myself. After taking a deep breath, I played the song without looking at her again. Sasha, with her red lips that would be sure to leave a rim of color on my cock. Sasha, with her blonde hair that would look so good wrapped around my wrist. Sasha, whose skin was pale enough to bruise just a little. With a huff of breath that turned into a cloud of smoke in front of me, I finished the song and then hopped off the stool to pack up. It was a little early for me to call it quits for the day, but I'd rather get dinner now and then go to the fight than be tempted by someone who would make me feel dirty when I was done with her. No, I deserved every bit of misery that was coming to me, even if a lot of it was now self-inflicted.

DINNER WAS A WHOLE ROTISSERIE CHICKEN. On a fight night, I always bulked up on as much protein as I could. I would go to the local grocery store and buy one of the small chickens sitting under the warmer in a plastic container. I would bring it back to my van and strip it all off the bone, then dip it into a chili sauce and eat it piece by piece until I was bursting at the seams. I kept doing it because it always worked. I hadn't lost a fight since I found this little town and joined their underground fight club. I didn't keep signing up to fight for the winnings, although the money didn't hurt. I kept coming back because it let me pummel another guy without the risk of going to jail. It was a safer place for me to channel all of my pent-up rage than out on the streets. I wasn't a boxer or a trained fighter. I was a singer and musician, but now angry enough to have learned how to use my newly discovered muscle mass and strength strategically.

TONIGHT'S FIGHT was being held in the basement of an abandoned church. The irony wasn't lost on me because the crowd that showed up to these fights wasn't exactly church friendly. It was a mix of hard-core boxers, their multiple girl-friends, and their girlfriends' crew which was usually made up of strippers and hookers. In attendance were also bookies, drug dealers, and rich men who made their money in suspicious ways —bored enough with their own lives that their excitement came from attending these illegal events to bet on a fight. I sat on my own as I wrapped my fists. Beau, who arranged the fights, was the only one who I interacted with. Everyone else knew to leave me alone. I took one more look at the photo in my wallet, then folded it back up and hid it under my jacket as I heard them announce my name. I was fighting a young kid tonight who had never lost a fight yet either. However, he wouldn't be winning tonight. That much I knew. I had nothing left to lose in life, and I fought like it. I walked into the ring, ignoring the crowd, the noise, the music, and the women screaming about how much they wanted me to fuck them. It was an even crazier crowd tonight, being that it was New Year's Eve. All I focused on in the ring was hitting as hard as I could, as often as I could, and reveling in the feeling of being one with my pain and my anger. Some would say that my behavior was unhealthy, but for me, it was a place where it was okay for me to be completely blinded by my anger and sadness. Once a month, during my fights, I was finally at peace with it.

As I WALKED into the ring, the young, cocky boxer with an obviously still-healing gash over his eye, a buzz cut, and a missing tooth sneered at me.

"They sent me a pretty boy, I see." He all but laughed. *Underestimate, bitch,* I thought to myself. But I said nothing. My silence generally unnerved my opponents. They hated that I wouldn't engage in their shit-talking. They got off on riling me up, and it wasn't very satisfying when I wouldn't react at all. The referee got between us to remind us of the rules, which in sleazy underground fights like this were basically don't kill each other. The bell rang and I felt my adrenaline and unbridled fury rise to the surface until my body was all but buzzing with it. It took me three minutes to get this undefeated boxer, who outweighed me by thirty pounds, down on the ground, bleeding profusely from where I had split his eyebrow. The crowd went wild. The ref lifted my arm as he proclaimed me the winner, and I barely reacted. Other than breathing heavily, I wasn't even moving. The constant tornado inside of me was hardly satisfied as I stepped out of the ring and returned to the other room to gather my belongings. Beau met me and slapped a stack of hundreds in my hand.

"I don't know why people bother to bet against you anymore." He cackled. I nodded wordlessly.

"Aight, bro, I'll text you the location next month." He knew I didn't talk much, so he didn't bother trying to drag me into conversation.

"Cool" was all I said as I zipped up my jacket and tugged my beanie back onto my head.

Tomorrow I will go back, I decided. And I'll play that damn Sam Hunt song.

The mother fucking cold was beginning to fully wear on me. I was no stranger to living on the street. I was twenty-five years old and had been off-and-on homeless since I was fifteen. But this winter had only just begun, and it was already destroying my confidence in my ability to make it through to spring with a good attitude. I thought longingly of the two remaining hand warmer packs in my bag, but I knew I had to save them for tonight and couldn't spare them for the walk to work. I gathered up my sleeping bag and stuck it on the side of the tent where Myles was still sleeping. At least, I hoped he was just sleeping. I shook his shoulder and said, "I'm going to work, My."

He grumbled, and I breathed a sigh of relief. He was alive.

"Watch my stuff," I told him.

He mumbled a "yup," but I knew my sleeping bag and my tent were always at risk of being stolen because as soon as he fully woke up, he would be coming down from his high and be out searching for the street pharmacist asking for another fix, leaving our stuff without supervision. All of my other belongings were in my backpack that I had slung over my shoulder. A backpack was easy to hide at work. A whole tent and sleeping bag? Not so much.

OUR TENT COMMUNITY was at the very edge of the park, where it backed up to a creek. The creek led to the highway, so for the most part, the town left us alone. It took me twenty minutes to walk around the park but ten minutes if I walked across it. Going across it meant walking through muddy or snowy grass, so most of the winter, I had to walk around the park so I could stay on the sidewalk. I always dreamed of moving somewhere on the West Coast. Living outside when it was warm most of the year would make my life one hundred percent more bearable. But I couldn't leave Myles, and Myles would never make it on such a long road trip. He'd end up running out of his stash and would go through withdrawals. As much as my dream was to have him be clean, it couldn't happen in a random town in Utah on the way to California. I also knew who he bought his supply from, and I knew it was clean. Out there, I would have no idea where to even start to find a safe dealer. I kicked a rock out of the way and scuffed up the front of my boot even more. Fuck. I was usually able to snap out of it. I was so good at seeing the glass half full and embracing the good parts of life, even in the suck. But this morning, the suck felt even suckier, so I indulged in a few moments of some *fuck this fucking life* thoughts as I walked toward my job at Kafe. I knew how lucky I was that I had gotten a job at such a high-end outdoor mall. The tips were great, the location was right near my tent community, and I got free drinks while working and 30 percent off food. It was also right near my gym. The gym I absolutely never worked out at but paid for membership anyway because I could shower there. They also let me rent a locker year-round, so I kept my spring and summer clothes and other important belongings in the locker. As I got to the center of the mall, I glanced around to see if my hottie music man was back, and I felt a twinge of disappointment when I saw that he wasn't. It was insane how hot he was. I had seen plenty of good-looking men in my day. I've even done some questionable things with quite a few of them, but I had never seen a man who was this smoking. He had always worn a big coat or flannel button-up when I had seen him, but I could tell that he was packing some serious muscle beneath his clothes. His face was all angles with a strong jaw covered in a beard that appeared both neat and full at the same time. His eyes were a piercing green, and the pain that laid beneath the surface intrigued me. His hair had always been covered by a beanie, but the part I could see was a mix of blonds and browns. And his voice, god, his voice. It was melodic and emotive. His range was insane, and the tone tickled emotion inside of me that made me feel happy and nostalgic at the same time. He reminded me of someone, but I couldn't figure out who. I sighed... thinking about him made me mad. I had asked for a song and he had failed to show up ever since. I know I had only barely met him twice, but I could have sworn beneath his somber face and his angry eyes that we had experienced some sort of connection. But it was obvious that music man hadn't felt it. Being part of the homeless community, I was used to people coming and going, but somehow, this one stung a little.

I GOT to work a few minutes early and went to the bathroom to straighten up. I had showered the night before and then braided my hair, so I let it out, and it swarmed around me in a mess of dark curls. My hair was all I had left of my mom, and I wore it with so much pride. I sprayed it with a detangling spray that one of my very part-time coworkers, Emmie, had brought in for me

the other day and combed the ends slightly. Then, I washed my
face and applied a bit of makeup. I may live outside but I had
pride in taking care of myself. I wasn't a girlie girl by any means,
but a little mascara never hurt anyone. I tied the green apron
with brown accents around my waist and then stashed my large
bag in the back room. I took a deep breath, shook off all the
sucky feelings from earlier, and went to join my coworkers for
another wonderful day of making coffee.

TWO HOURS INTO MY SHIFT, a gaggle of women came inside with
a rush of cold air following them, and I heard one say to the
other, "I would totally fuck that busker out there." Her friend
slapped a hand over her mouth and laughed.

"Maeve, oh my god, you wouldn't!"

I internally rolled my eyes. Just like I predicted when I first
saw them, they each ordered a matcha and a scone. The women
who shopped here were annoyingly pretentious, and sometimes
I wondered what they would do if they knew the girl making
their drink lived in a tent and occasionally peed outside. When I
finally finished serving them, I allowed myself to sneak a look
out the window to see which busker they were referring to. My
heart skipped a beat when I saw that it was Kian. It was time for
my break anyway, so I made two hot white chocolate mochas,
grabbed my coat, and went outside. I saw him see me. He didn't
acknowledge me other than a clench of his jaw as he kept playing. He was singing "Say Love" by James TW. I pretended that I
didn't care he had finally shown up a month later. I just put the
coffees down on the sidewalk next to me and cupped my hand
over my cigarette to light it without the wind blowing it out. I
took a deep puff in and let the nicotine hit my system. It was a
disgusting habit. An expensive habit. This, I was well aware of.
But I figured if I had to live outside, I could allow myself one

disgusting habit—a habit that helped keep my nerves calm and the hunger at bay. I always promised I'd quit, but I never did. I blew the smoke out and then glanced over at music man. He had finished the song and was staring at me. He said nothing, and I said nothing. We just stared. He finally broke first and started strumming the chords to "Take Your Time," and something inside of me warmed. I didn't get much in life, and I was okay with that and embraced that this was the hand I had been dealt. I had come to terms with all the shit that happened, and I found ways to not let it break my spirit. I didn't even let myself sit in shame for some of the things I had done. I had stolen when I was younger because the alternative was starving. I had agreed to give an on-again, off-again boyfriend a blowjob in exchange for a coat for Myles. I wasn't proud of it per se, but I knew who I really was and that I would not let those actions define me. They were part of my survival. I kind of let it go with the thought that I had to do what I had to do. But hearing him sing this song, knowing that he had learned it and came back to play it for me, goddamn if that didn't feel like a gift. I took one last puff on my cigarette, shook off the ash, and ground it out. I stuffed it back into my box so I could finish it later and picked up the two coffees. I waited till he finished singing to say, "I thought you'd pussied out."

He blinked in surprise. I knew I was loud. Blunt. Unafraid. I mean, I had lived on the streets for most of my adult life, so it made sense.

"I'm here now" was all he said.

"I can see that." I wanted to ask where he'd been, why he hadn't come back for a month, and why his knuckles were scabbing over, but I didn't. Instead, I held out the coffee, and he took it warily. I watched him take a sip.

"It's sweet." He stated the obvious. When he spoke, it sounded like he didn't talk a lot. His words were clipped and short. He didn't seem to be the kind of guy who felt the need to fill the silence. I liked that. I could fill the silence plenty on my own.

"It is sweet," I confirmed.

"What do I owe you for it?"

I squinted in the bright winter sunlight before looking back at him.

"'Burn The Ships' by for KING & COUNTRY. And don't wait a month to come back this time." I turned on my heel and began to walk away.

"What's your name?" I heard him call.

"When I see you again, I'll tell you," I called back. I didn't know what game we were playing, but I did know that I liked playing it.

The rest of the day passed in a whirlwind of coffee, sneaking looks at Kian out the window, and incessant worrying about Myles, which plagued me during my every waking moment. My every sleeping moment too. When I finished my shift, it was dark outside, and Kian was gone. I trudged over to the gym, said hello to the security guard, and went to hit the showers. Usually, I would only wash my hair once a week, but today, my curls had an incident with a spilled drink, and they were now hard and crunchy, so I had to wash it two days in a row. After my shower, I dried my hair the best I could so that it wouldn't freeze to my head overnight. Then I changed into my night clothes, which were made up of fleece leggings with sweatpants over them and a long-sleeved shirt topped by a sweatshirt. After zipping up my coat, I made the twenty-minute walk back home. I found Myles and two of his friends sitting outside our tent around their makeshift fire pit, which was crackling with warm, inviting flames.

"Hey." I smiled at them and ducked into the tent to put my backpack down. I had made thirty-seven dollars in tips, so I took my wallet out and shoved the bills inside. My money always got spent faster than I could make it. But I didn't let it get me down. I had enough for what I needed, Myles was alive, and a pretty boy played me a song today. It ended up being a good day.

I TOOK the two sandwiches that I had brought home from work out of my backpack and went back outside to join Myles by the fire. I unwrapped the first sandwich and handed him his food.

"Thank you, J," he told me with a grin.

"You got it, My."

We focused on eating our food before brushing our teeth with the freezing cold water from a bottle I had in the corner of the tent. Then I took the last of our hand warmers and shook them until they warmed up. I popped one into each of my socks and gave the other pack to Myles. They gave us some semblance of warmth while we slept.

I WOULD LIE awake listening to Myles breathing. I wanted my love to be enough for him to want to get clean, but I also knew his scars were just too deep. I knew too much had happened to him before he had become a part of my life that led to his current behavior.

My father had left my mother and me when I was fourteen. My mom had tried her best to get by, but by the time I was fifteen, we were living in our car with all of our worldly possessions in the trunk. We lost the car when I turned sixteen, but we finally got a spot in the women's shelter a few weeks later. Unfortunately, we left that spot behind a few weeks after that because my mom had started dating an old neighbor of ours who had a son two years younger than me. I had known his son, Myles, since I was young because we had gone to the same school until I was forced to drop out.

We moved out of the shelter and into their apartment. However, that only lasted for six months because my mom quickly found out that Paul liked to drink, and when he did, he would mercilessly beat his son. When we left, my mom took his son with us, and Myles became my brother. We had become close instantly. I had his back, and he had mine. I knew the worst part for him was Paul never even reported him missing. He just let him go, and Myles never heard from him again. We spent the rest of that year couch surfing, but no one wanted a struggling artist and her two teenage kids taking up free space in their home for too long. When we ran out of people to ask, we ended up back on the streets.

Myles never complained. He tried to keep up with school and never said anything negative about our situation. But I could see the pain in his eyes, and I wished I could do something to make it better. I still did. The year I turned eighteen was spent learning how to sleep with one eye open and assert myself so people looking for trouble would stay away.

At nineteen, my mom passed away from cancer, and it became just Myles and me against the world. We couldn't go back to the shelter because they would split us up, and at that point, Myles had started smoking weed and popping pills. I hated his need to check out, but I also knew that being beaten by your dad for years did irreparable damage, and he was coping the best way he knew how. The problem was that the people on the street needed the most healing, but healing was a privilege only given to some. Those with health insurance or money had access to a level of mental health assistance that Myles and I could only dream of.

When I turned twenty, I was desperate to get Myles off the

street and give him some semblance of normalcy. So much so that I compromised myself in the pursuit of it. I thought maybe I could get him clean if we lived a more "normal life." At the time, I had been working at a bar that was clearly in a seedier part of town because they let underage people serve drinks. One of the frequent attendees was an older man who patronized the bar often and paid way too much attention to me. I took advantage of it and quickly formed a relationship of sorts with him until I convinced him to let Myles and me move in with him.

The look on Myles's face when he had access to a bed and hot showers made what I went through worth it. I forced myself to ignore the extra tight grip the man kept on me when he held my hand out in public. I didn't protest if he didn't take no for an answer when he told me he wanted to have sex. I pretended it was normal when he laughed and hinted that his friends wanted to try out his live-in "whore" too. I told myself it was okay because he never actually hit me. He gave us plenty of food, money for bills, and, most importantly, a place to live.

For two years, I grinned and bared it as I slowly stashed away money. I either slipped twenties out of his wallet while he slept, used less of the grocery money than what he had left for us to shop with, or even stooped so low as to swipe pain meds from his medicine cabinet and sell them in the park. The irony of that was not lost on me. When I felt I had enough saved up, one night, when he was away on a business trip, I packed us up and we left without leaving a note. I rented us a bedroom in a long-term bed and breakfast.

At first, it was good—it was the year I got my job as a barista. I learned all things coffee and discovered I actually loved the creativity it took to make people their drinks. I was soon able to afford my first phone. I even got Myles clean for a three-month streak. Then it all fell apart. One night, I came home from work and found Myles high on something new and a man taking advantage of him. I had failed to keep my only family member safe, and it hurt more than almost anything else in my life had. I packed us up the next month, and instead of paying rent, I bought us a tent. In my mind, it made more sense to use my money toward therapy for Myles than on a room to sleep in when that hadn't even been safe.

FAST FORWARD THREE MORE YEARS, and we had gotten really good at living on the streets. Or at least as good as one could in these types of circumstances. Myles had detoxed in the hospital and had gone through multiple stints of NA meetings and seeing his therapist weekly. Those times were good because he was sober and clearheaded. Yet he would also be in enormous pain and get twitchy and irritable when he wanted to use. He, unfortunately, was not currently sober, and I worried for him constantly, especially since one of his friends had OD'd last week. I didn't know what he had taken, and I was scared it would find Myles. My goal for some time now was to save up enough for us to get a car or a van to live in. Maybe then I could get Myles clean for good, and we could finally move somewhere warm.

I SIGHED and rolled over to take Myles's hand. I was still happy somehow. After everything I had gone through, I felt at peace with my current situation. I knew I had always tried my best, never missed a day at work, and kept my head high even on the coldest days. I was grateful for my job. I was grateful my brother was still fighting his demons and not fully giving in to them. I was simply grateful that I had woken up to see another day. If all I had was my gratitude and my pride, so be it. I could deal with that. I leaned down and kissed his hand.

"Jessa," he whispered.

"What's up, My?"

He cleared his throat.

"If it gets me, I need you to promise me something."

"No..." I started. I couldn't understand how we had these conversations about his impending death when the solution seemed so obvious to me. Just stop using. I understood addiction in theory, having thoroughly studied it. I understood it in reality, having seen it most of my life. I understood it in practicality, simply understanding that it was a disease. But I still had a part of my brain that viewed the situation in black and white. Just stop. Save yourself. Don't let the drugs win.

"Jessa." He quieted me. The truth was, he was a special soul—I had known it the moment I met him. Kindness emanated from his brown eyes. He was quiet and unassuming, and he cared so much about people and animals. I would catch him helping frogs across the sidewalk to get closer to the water. Or feeding stray dogs. Or helping our tent neighbors light a fire. Or playing with some of the kids who lived in our community while their parents washed their clothes by the creek. I had never seen him get angry. Not once. He never stole to get high. He kept himself clean and presentable. I loved him with every fiber of my being, and as much as I held onto my gratitude and happiness, I also had a place inside of me that was full of anger for how unfair life had been for my brother.

"If it ever gets me."

I knew he was referring to his addiction, and I squeezed his hand.

"I want you to promise me you won't turn me to dust. I want you to bury me. I don't care where, but don't burn me. Okay?"

A sob got stuck in my throat.

"Don't leave me" was all I replied.

"Promise me." He wasn't giving up.

"I promise." My words hung between us, frozen in the chilled air. I felt him relax. Our fingers weaved together.

"Thank you."

Please don't leave me, I wanted to scream. But instead, I kissed his cheek and fell into a fitful sleep. Earlier, I had thought about how grateful I was that I had my brother, but the nagging thought that gnawed at me was, who really had him? Me or the drugs?

T he next day, I found myself sitting on my stool, strumming my guitar, pretending I wasn't uncomfortable with how much I was looking forward to playing the song she had requested and seeing the happiness on her face. I was also disgruntled when I admitted to myself that I was impatiently waiting to learn her name. I was playing my usual playlist outside of the coffee shop, sneaking looks at her through the window. I noticed that she smiled a lot, and every time she did, it put her dimple on display. Her long hair was held back by a large clip today, but wavy tendrils were escaping and making their way around her shoulders. I didn't like that I was noticing it. I didn't like that I had come back. I didn't like that I wanted to know her name. Being here and exchanging names felt like it may lead to something. Interest perhaps or even possibly time spent together.

I had spent so much time mourning the damage that came from caring about another person that I was shocked to find myself sitting here waiting for her. It could endanger everything

I had worked on to lead me in the exact opposite direction of what I was doing right now.

I didn't even know what I was doing right now other than watching her step outside, her thin coat flapping in the wind. Her hair was out of its clip now, and it was floating around her like it was dancing. I allowed myself one slow perusal of her body. She wasn't tall, maybe five-four or five-five, and she was curvy in all the right places. I could imagine myself grabbing a handful of her thighs, letting them jiggle just slightly as I ran my hands up to her trim waist and then weighed her sizable breasts in my palms. *I bet they'd spill over my hands*; the thought barreled through my brain, and I flushed. Calm down there, boy. I shifted uncomfortably in my seat, willing my sudden and inappropriate erection to deflate.

"Hi!"

She felt like the sun, I realized, exuding warmth made up of sass and happiness rolled into one. What an exotic combination. I had never met anyone with her energy before. I nodded but didn't respond, not trusting my voice to sound chill just yet. She extended her hand to give me one of the coffees that she held, and I backed away from it.

"I haven't sung your song yet." I explained my hesitation. She laughed, and the sound sparkled inside of me.

"Take a sip, at least," she encouraged me. I begrudgingly took the cup from her and brought the rim up to my mouth to taste the drink. The flavor of hazelnuts exploded in my mouth.

"It's a hazelnut hot chocolate!" She beamed. "It's a secret menu item, but I wish more people would discover it. I blend mocha sauce with steamed milk for the hot chocolate portion and then add a few pumps of hazelnut syrup, which basically makes it taste like Nutella in a cup." She paused to take a sip of her own drink, and I watched as she closed her eyes to savor it. I could see clearly that this was not just a job for her. She seemed to genuinely find joy in making coffee. I think I might love that about her. Feeling uncomfortable from my unbidden thoughts again, I glanced down at the cup in my hand and saw that my fingers were covering some letters. I turned the cup till I could see what she had written. It was the name Jessamine written in a loopy script. I raised my eyebrows and looked at her.

"You're giving me your name before I play the song too?" Wow, that was a lot of words in a row for me. I smirked at myself. She hugged her arms around herself as the wind picked up.

"You showed up." She sounded grateful, but for what, I wasn't sure.

Her lips were full, and when she smiled, I got a glimpse of her white teeth. The top two were slightly overlapping, and it fit the little I knew of her personality perfectly.

"So now that I gave you my first name, what's your last name, Kian?"

I sighed.

"How about this? I have a two-questions-a-day rule, and I can always plead the fifth on a question. Okay?" I began to strum her song on my guitar in the background of this seemingly innocent conversation, yet her question weighed heavily on my chest. She giggled, unaware of my turmoil.

"Okay, question one, what's your last name?"

"Let's stick to just Kian. Okay?" I winced.

"Are you running from the feds, Just Kian?" she joked, giving me a look from over her coffee cup.

"What's your second question, Jessamine?" I asked her as I firmly avoided answering that question as well.

"My friends call me Jessa."

"I'm not your friend yet," I corrected. Her blue eyes flew to mine, and we stared at each other over my use of the word *yet*.

After a moment, she asked bluntly, "Am I allowed to know how old you are?"

"I'm turning thirty this year." To this, I acquiesced some true information.

"I'm twenty-five," she informed me, freely offering up tidbits about herself without me even having to inquire. "When's your birthday?"

"Ask me tomorrow when your two questions renew," I quipped. Oh look, funny Kian was back, I noticed. I hadn't seen him in a long time.

"Well, technically, I asked two but only got one answer, so your terms and conditions are kind of flawed, music man."

She was so quick with her witticisms, and I envied the careless way she talked back to me, as if nothing ever really bothered her. It was quite the opposite with me. Almost everything has bothered me lately. Apparently, I was back to *music man* as well. I didn't answer; I just sang my slowed-down acoustic version of "Burn The Ships." I found her staring at me as I sang the lyrics.

Could she tell how much the words meant to me? I had shuddered when I first sang them in the safety of my van. She blinked and broke the moment as I finished singing.

"Thank you," she murmured. "You choose the next one tomorrow."

"I'll find something," I promised. She didn't say goodbye, she just walked away, back to work, seemingly forgetting about me already. My past self was so used to my women in heels, delicate chains on their ankles with perfectly done toes. Yet her chunky black boots hit differently, and by the way my pants tightened at the crotch, clearly, I didn't mind it. I took another sip of my coffee and looked back at her name. Jessamine. It rolled beautifully in my mind. It sounded like a symphony to me. I turned the cup again and noticed that she had written something else along the bottom,

"You look hot today, music man."

My cheeks and my heart hurt as I grinned, this time unable to stop it.

Not much later, I quit earlier than usual as the afternoon wind turned to snow. I slung my guitar over my back and glanced back over to where Jessa stood behind the counter frothing milk. I wondered where she lived and if she needed a ride home. Would the snow get bad? I cleared my throat to also clear my mind and remind myself that caring was dangerous. Without another look, I trudged off back to my van. I stopped at a Caribbean restaurant to pick up my favorite oxtail soup. I usually would take it to the van to eat in my preferred silence and solitude, but something had shifted inside of me today. Tonight, I surprised myself and chose to eat my dinner at a table, albeit alone, inside the crowded restaurant. Although I did keep my beanie on and my collar flipped up, hoping no one would recognize me. I dipped the crusty slice of French bread into the soup and had to hold back a moan when the pungent flavors hit my taste buds. I literally licked my fingers and broke off another piece of the bread. When the bowl was empty, I leaned back, feeling warm from the soup and from my interaction with the sweet spitfire that was Jessamine.

When I left after finishing dinner, the snow had picked up considerably, and I briefly contemplated just hunkering down in the parking lot of the restaurant for the night, yet I knew I had to drive to the gym. As much as the soup and the girl had tempered me, my flame of anger was still there, and it needed its nightly outlet. I parked, then grabbed my gym bag from the back of my van and made my way in. After changing into workout pants and a tank top, I wrapped my hands and went to the boxing bag, where I proceeded to beat the everloving shit out of it. About an hour in, I heard a guy from behind me say, "Yo, are you all-natural?"

I turned to look at him, breathing heavily.

"Huh?"

He gestured to my body where my muscles were bulging, my chest was drenched in sweat, and my veins were overly pronounced.

"Do you take steroids or, is this all-natural?" he repeated.

I didn't look at myself much. I obviously didn't have a full-length mirror in my van. The area I worked out in didn't have a mirror either, so the only place I ever got a glimpse of myself was in the changing room. Even there, I didn't spend much time staring. Yet I was obviously aware of how intense I looked in a tank top. My arms were jacked, so much so that they couldn't rest fully flat to my sides. My stomach was etched, every part of my six-pack was pronounced. My back was bunched with sinewy muscle, and my chest was well-defined. Was I natural? Of course I didn't take steroids, but I had built this body from sheer fury. My anger had led me here night after night, building a body that could protect the people who mattered to me. Never again would I be caught unawares and weak. Fuck with me and literally find out was my life's motto.

"I don't take anything," I grunted in response.

"Damn, bro." He was impressed. I wish he'd be quieter, as he was causing people to stop and stare. The fewer eyes on me, the better was a newly adopted goal. I shifted away from the bag.

"Have a good night," I murmured.

"Ya, bro."

I jogged to the showers and stripped. I wondered if Jessa would like what she saw. At the thought of her, my cock jumped to attention. I wanted to rub one out to my imagination of her soft, curvy body, but I couldn't. My body was disrespecting me.

That was all. I wiped the water out of my eyes and leaned against the wall of the shower as the weight of my frustration overtook me. What the fuck was I even doing anymore? My self-imposed exile was weighing heavily on me tonight. I stood in the hot shower, ignoring my penis, until the water ran cold.

BACK IN MY VAN, I searched for a song to sing to her tomorrow. As much as my angry side didn't want to go back, the rest of me felt drawn to her, like iron to a magnet or a compass to the north. If my friends could see me now, they would laugh.

"Bag her, Jace," they'd say. I flinched at the sound of my first name in my head.

"It's not that deep. It's just some pussy," Ash would tell me. "Stop being a little bitch about it."

I reached into my wallet and took the picture out. It had been folded and unfolded so many times it was starting to wear away at some points. I stared at it, trying to force my soul to hurt again and stop getting distracted. I felt my chest clench at the sight of the photo. It did hurt. But more like a throbbing bruise than the usual gaping, bloody wound.

"Fuck!" I shouted into the empty air around me. Why had it started to hurt less? How could I have let it begin to fade away? I picked up my guitar and my notebook, and I angrily wrote a new song until I was so tired I couldn't even see straight, and the voices had quieted out of sheer exhaustion. I fell asleep with ink smudged on my hand. It had been a long time since I had done that, and the reason why was not lost on me.

I WOKE UP LATE. I knew it was late because my stomach was rumbling from hunger, and the sun hung heavy in the sky. I hopped from the back seat to the front and turned the van back on so I could get the windshield wipers going to wipe the snow off. It had snowed a lot last night, but I could see that the roads were relatively clear. I ate a protein bar for breakfast as I drove toward the outdoor mall. I would be better off busking near the ice skating rink today because people would be gathered there, and the tips would be plentiful, yet I found myself parking near one of the popular clothing stores. Then I clambered into the back of my van to get changed into fresh clothes. I made a note to stop at the laundromat as I was running out of boxers. I was humming the tune to my new song as I set up my mic and speaker, so I was startled when I heard her voice behind me.

"Late start, music man?"

I felt my groin stir, and I willed it to settle down before I turned to look at her.

"I had a late night," I confirmed.

"What's her name?" Jessa's cheeks flushed pink, and her tone sounded teasing, but I could hear the subtle inquiry as well.

"I was writing a song." It felt like I was telling her a secret.

"Can I hear it?" She sounded so excited that I immediately knew I would be singing it to her, although it was one hundred percent raw and unfinished.

"It's kind of rough around the edges." I settled onto my stool, noting the two coffee cups she held, and wondered what flavor she had chosen for me today.

"Aren't we all?" She was leaning against a pole now, watching me with her blue gaze. I noticed she was wearing that thin coat again.

"Aren't we all what?" I asked as I quickly checked the tuning on my guitar.

"Rough around the edges." She parroted my words back to me.

"Are you?" I inquired, watching her facial expression. She shrugged.

"Sometimes." She took a sip of her coffee and didn't say anything else. I began to strum the lilting melody that I had come up with and then I closed my eyes as I began to sing.

"They say it gets better with time
But time keeps pulling you away from me
And I admit I don't know how to be
As the pain hurts a little less
So time please give me back my mess

I know what to do with the agony
It shreds me
But it keeps my heart beating
To stop the pain from leaving

I don't want the hurt to soften
Just keep the ache (uh) hurtin'
I need it as a reminder
That you were once here

Don't heal my wounds
Cuz I don't know what to do
Without the shatter
Of my battered
Heart left after you

If hurt is all I have left
Then I'd like to stay bereft
So don't heal me, I'm not okay
Please, (time) I'd like to stay this way."

I NEEDED to play with the tune a little, move the arrangement, and add a second stanza to the song before I could record it. The thought quickly flickered as I remembered where I was. Old habits die hard; I grimaced. I looked up, feeling oddly vulnerable. Jessa's eyes were shiny.

"I hope you're not okay," she whispered.

Her words felt like a gift, an acknowledgment of the chaos of wanting to hold onto pain, being that it was the only thing I had left.

"That's just a little something I've been working on." I tried to sound casual and play it off like it was nothing. She caught on quickly and held up my coffee.

"Close your eyes and tell me what you taste." She sounded so gleeful that I agreed and closed my eyes. I held out my hand to take my drink, but my heart fluttered when I felt her hold the cup up to my mouth instead. I took a sip, and I could feel her waiting for me to react. A cacophony of flavors flooded my tongue, and I tried to focus on them as I swallowed. I opened my eyes to find hers focused on me, standing close enough that her hair almost enveloped my arm.

"It's like a cinnamon roll," I observed.

"Do you like it?" She seemed eager for my response yet very confident in how good she knew it was at the same time.

"I did. I do." I took the cup from her and took another sip.

"It's called a butterscotch. It's whole milk, caramel syrup, toffee nut syrup, cinnamon dolce syrup, and caramel crunch." She took a big gulp of her own drink and sighed around it. The sound went straight to my crotch.

"I'm gonna gain weight with these daily drinks," I joked.

"I doubt that." Her gaze lingered on what she could see of my body beneath my coat, and I remembered my question in the gym last night. It seemed I had my answer—Jessamine liked what she saw. I felt relieved somehow. I looked down at my cup to break up the awkward moment. She had written Jessa Bardot on the cup.

"Your last name or your middle name?" I asked.

"My last name," she confirmed.

"I like it," I told her.

"Me too." Her confidence was refreshing. It was so different from the tittering blondes I had known before.

"Thanks for the song, Kian." She walked away before I could even say goodbye. I looked to see if she had left me another message on my cup, and she had.

"I like that you came back," her messy handwriting had left around the rim.

Surprisingly, I liked that I had come back too.

Chapter Four
Break For You by Valley

0:40   SD   1:94

I wasn't a virgin, yet I had never been in love. I had fucked some guys for fun, some out of necessity, and unfortunately, some had been less than welcome. I winced at the memory. I was definitely not a virgin, but I was also far from a prude. Besides being twenty-five, I had also spent most of my life around questionable characters and in less-than-savory parts of town. It was not uncommon to hear people fucking through the thin bit of privacy the tents afforded. Sometimes, I'd even happen upon a prostitute working on my walk home. I was definitely not a stranger to the world of sex, but Kian made me feel like I was.

I HAD PARTICIPATED IN A THREESOME, been tied up, come on, and even fucked against the wall of a dance club, yet the hottest thing I could think of right now was putting that coffee cup against Kian's mustached lip. I had stood closer to him today than I had in our previous encounters and had gotten a whiff of his male aroma. I shivered at the memory of it. I wanted to hold his jaw and feel its strength beneath my hands. From what I could see, his hair was long enough to grab onto. Ugh, it made me want things. It was almost impossible for me to have a real relationship while living in a tent and caring for my brother, who was admittedly very easy to live with but was almost always high and was there all the time. But some semblance of a relationship was what I could feel myself craving with this mysterious man with the gut-wrenching songs. I barely knew him at all—that much was obvious, but I could feel an energy from him that my soul wanted more of.

I DIDN'T OFTEN LAMENT my lot in life. I generally accepted my situation, but at this moment, I wished things had gone differently for me. I would love to have a real bed to fuck him in. A kitchen in which I could sit on the counter, clad in just his shirt, while I watched the muscles in his back move as he made us pancakes. A bathroom where we could desperately fuck in the shower—me up against the wall, him in front of me rutting, one hand on my neck, the other holding my wrists so I couldn't move. I would love for him to leave marks on me—ones I would wear proudly the next day. I wanted it, and I didn't like wanting things that I couldn't have.

MAYBE HE HAD A SHITTY PERSONALITY, I thought, trying to convince myself why it was okay that I would never live out this pipe dream. The truth was he didn't smile much, and he seemed a little suspicious with his two-questions rule. Maybe he also had a tiny dick. I laughed at that one. He definitely doesn't have a tiny dick; who was I kidding? I looked out the window to see that he was surrounded by a crowd and was singing a song I could not hear. Damn, that beard would look good between my legs, that much I knew. But it could never happen. That much I knew as well.

I WAS FINISHING up my shift when I heard the bell tinkle above the door. I looked over and was startled to see Kian standing there. Alanna, my coworker, gave me a look. Everyone I worked with had seen me out there with him each day, and their tongues were already wagging. Alanna was convinced that he looked like a model. Eric, my boss, said he looked like a murderer.

"It's always the pretty ones, Jessa," he told me. I informed him that he watched way too much true crime and told them that they were both crazy and warned them to leave him alone. Kian walked up to the register. I hadn't seen him fully standing before, and I was startled to find him hovering well over six feet. His coat was unzipped, and I could finally see how much his shirt clung to the muscles on his body.

"Hi." I was almost uncharacteristically embarrassed with him here in front of me when I had spent the majority of the afternoon imagining him fucking me in every position possible.

"Hi." He smiled for the first time since I had met him, and I felt it zing through my body. Oh, he was even more beautiful when he was happy. I wanted to kiss away the pain he so obviously carried. Even more than that, I wanted to help him keep it since I had felt his sad desperation so clearly in his song.

"Do you want to order something?" I cocked my head, confused.

"N-no." He stuttered over that as if he was worried that it had been the wrong answer. He lowered his voice, seemingly aware that Alanna was standing by the sink, not even three feet away.

"You didn't give me a song for tomorrow," he said to explain his presence.

"Oh!" I was genuinely thrilled by him asking me to request a song. "I don't really know this band at all, but I heard this song the other day. Do you know 'Calico' by Pointing West?"

I watched his face go from open and curious to completely shut down.

"I won't sing that." He sounded stern, and he almost turned as if contemplating leaving. I reached out and touched his arm to stop him. He stilled instantly.

"Okay, never mind. It's cool. Will you sing 'Let Me Love the Lonely' by James Arthur?"

He nodded. Lips tight, eyes dark with something I couldn't decipher.

"Okay." I smiled.

"Okay," he repeated. We were interrupted by Alanna coming over, holding out a pastry bag.

"WE HAVE to throw out the extra pastries at the end of the day, so you can have these for free if you want." She was tall and blonde with a fuck-me mouth. I was curious how Kian would react to her. It's not that I wasn't confident in myself; I was. I fully embraced my perpetual tan skin tone, my curves, my ass, my thick thighs, and my double Ds, but I knew some guys preferred what Alanna had going on. The little, perky boobs, the big brown doe eyes, and the skin so pale that a small smack on the ass would show up red immediately. He didn't even blink in her direction.

"Thank you," was all he said, and then looked back at me almost immediately. I felt something warm in my heart.

"I'll see you tomorrow?" he asked. That was usually my question in regard to him since he was the one notorious for a disappearing act. I never knew if I would come out to smoke while his music filled the sidewalk or if quiet would follow me around all day. I nodded.

"I'm always here."

"Are you walking home?" he asked suddenly, causing me to go still. I wasn't embarrassed by my living situation, but it also wasn't something I was going to share with a guy I barely knew. So I just nodded again. Kian surprised me by immediately peeling off his coat. It was a thick, black down coat with the Canada Goose logo on the arm.

"Do me a favor and wear this." He held the coat up. I could see how built he was beneath his thin Henley. Images of his thick arms crowding me as he fucked me from behind clouded my vision. I needed to get laid because this was getting ridiculous, I reprimanded myself in my head.

"I have a coat." I was never one to actively look for handouts, but I also wasn't too proud to accept a gift either.

"This one is warmer," he simply replied as he leaned over and held the coat open, encouraging me to slip an arm into the sleeve. I did. It was big on me, and it was warm, like he had said. Was it the coat itself or was it because it had been warmed up by his body all day? He pulled me closer by the collar and reached down to zip me up.

"Oh." I was finally at a loss for words. I could feel myself slick up between my legs. This man had to be what sex looked like. If you googled sex, I imagined he would be the image that showed up.

"See?" He gave me another rare grin. I nodded, ignoring my raging hormones encouraging me to do naughty things to him.

"What will you wear?" I worried out loud.

"I have another one."

"At home?"

He paused, then responded, "Yes."

I nodded again.

"Okay. Well, thank you. That's very unexpected but nice of you, music man." I tried to lighten the mood.

"It's Kian," he murmured.

"I know." I winked. "Take your scone." I handed him the bag that Alanna had packed. He dipped his chin at me and then left with another tinkle of the bell.

I LET OUT the breath I had been holding the entire interaction and snuggled into the coat. It smelled of him—a mix of body wash, an outdoor scent, and something uniquely male. I put my hands in the pockets and found a guitar pick and rubbed it against my fingers. I wasn't sure what was happening, but it felt like it would be something that I would look back on fondly a year from now. After packing up dinner for myself and Myles, I grabbed my huge backpack and lit up a cigarette for the walk home. I decided to go to the gym in the morning instead of tonight because my shift started late tomorrow, and I wanted to do some laundry before work. The laundromat was next door to my gym, so I would put in a load, go shower, and come back to switch it to the dryer. The walk home felt shorter than normal. Was it because I was warmer than usual, or was it because a pretty man had played me a song today and made my heart happy? I wasn't sure.

MYLES WAS SMOKING a blunt outside when I got back. He had shoveled a path from the sidewalk to our tent and had melted most of the snow in front of it with the fire he had going.

"Sup, sis." He grinned.

"A guy gave me his coat today," I told him as my greeting and began to unpack the cheese, fruit, protein box, and the two sandwiches that I had taken from work for dinner.

"A guy?" he asked slowly.

"Yeah. He gave me this coat." I motioned to it. Myles looked up lazily from his food and blinked at the coat.

"That's really nice of him."

"Right?" I leaned back, looking up at the sky that was full of stars. The sweet smell of weed wafted over to me as I chewed my grilled cheese and watched the sky. Today was a really good day. Unexpectedly so, and I was grateful for it.

The next morning, Myles shook me awake.

"I'm going to get a haircut. The traveling barber is in the area today."

The traveling barber was a professional barber who owned a real barber shop, but once a month, he would come to the tent towns, as people called it, and would work a twelve-hour shift giving free haircuts. Rain or shine, no matter the weather, he was there.

MYLES LIKED to get up early and be one of the first in line. He also didn't like to leave me sleeping alone in the tent as not all of our community members were the most savory of characters.

"I'M GETTING UP." My voice sounded scratchy. My head was throbbing, and it hurt to swallow. Fuck. I couldn't afford to get sick. Not only did I not have health insurance since I opted out of the plan offered at work, but I also did not want to spend money at the doctor and miss work. We were probably a year out from having enough saved to get a car to live in, and I couldn't lose my stride now. I always said *we,* although Myles was struggling with his addiction too much to get a job, because we were a unit, and he was all I had.

I FOUND a bottle of acetaminophen in my backpack and swallowed the last two down with a swig of icy water. I layered my clothes, starting with a bodysuit, then a sweater, and then Kian's coat. I didn't have a lot of clothes, but I had enough to wear and still have some laundry to do. Some of the people living by the creek had no jobs and no income and literally lived in the clothes on their backs. I felt grateful to be in a bit of a better position than that.

MY BODY ACHED as I lugged my backpack through the park to the laundromat. I emptied the grocery bag of our meager items of clothing into the washing machine and then paid for a packet of laundry detergent. Then I walked over to the gym and took a very long and warm shower that helped soothe my sore muscles. My arms were tired as I took off the shower cap and undid the bun I had put my hair up into. As I dabbed on some makeup, I noticed there were bags under my eyes. What I wouldn't give for a warm bed right now. Normally I could make do in my tent during all sorts of weather but being sick in a sleeping bag in January sucked just a bit.

WHEN I WAS DONE in the locker room, I went over to the food bar and got myself a stack of buckwheat pancakes. Part of my membership included one post-workout meal. They never said I had to work out to get it. I laughed to myself as I soaked up the maple syrup with a forkful of pancake. When my belly was nice and full, and the shower had lulled my headache a little, I hauled my backpack back over to the laundromat to switch the wash to the dryer. As I walked in, I saw a very familiar face.

"Are you stalking me?" I felt weak, but I still had my sass intact. Kian's eyes darted up and met mine.

"Yes." He barely skipped a beat. Oh, so he's funny when he wants to be, I noted.

"Well, you're not very good at it. I caught you immediately." I found an empty dryer and began transferring my clothes.

"Maybe I wanted to be caught." The words looked like they slipped out his mouth unattended because he seemed to shrink a little when he finished saying them. Was he flirting? I wasn't sure, but I couldn't really focus on that with the fever I felt coming on. I smiled weakly.

"I would usually keep this going 'cause I'm so good at banter, but I'm just not feeling up to it right now."

He looked closer at me with worried eyes.

"What's wrong?" He stood as his washing machine beeped. I sat down on the bench and got comfortable as the dryer would take about forty minutes to finish.

"I think I'm getting sick." I shrugged. "I'll be okay. It's probably just a cold."

He fished around in the pocket of a coat that matched mine but in blue.

"Want a cough drop?" He was holding one in his hands.

"I'd actually love one."

His fingers brushed mine when he gave it to me, and I felt the touch all through my body.

"Thank you." I popped it in my mouth and watched as his eyes followed the movement of my lips.

"So when is your birthday?" I wasn't too sick for my two questions, especially since I hadn't asked any yesterday.

"June fifteenth."

"Ah, a Gemini," I announced.

"I don't know anything about zodiacs."

I pulled out my phone, googled male Gemini, and began to read, "This boy cannot stop moving! He is just so damn restless. Unfortunately, whatever he is doing at the time takes a backseat to what he thinks he could be doing. His brain is always a few steps ahead of his bod. Gemini men are usually big talkers, full of wit and wisdom and coolness. If he fails at something, well, look out because he will sink into a dark despair that is just no fun at all. This boy loves freedom, so no pinning down times and places and meetings; he wants to be free. Call him a Peter Pan—he'll never grow up. Women rarely come in as a high priority with this guy. But he's usually pretty bright."

My voice trailed off as he began to laugh. My brain stuttered for a moment till it realized that quiet, stoic Kian was belly laughing in a laundromat.

"What?"

"That's ridiculous." He guffawed. "First of all, who wrote that article? Because who says bod?"

I giggled at that.

"The article is definitely flawed because, for example, I'm definitely not a big talker. Second flaw is, if I'm with a woman, she is a massive priority to me."

I could hear the underlying innuendo of what else he meant, and I felt my legs tremble a bit at the thought of all the ways he could show his woman she was a priority.

"I think zodiacs are stupid. We all have our own personalities based on family, friends, and life's circumstances. I don't think it's because of the month we happen to be born in."

I nodded.

"Yeah, I agree. I am not a big zodiac girl either; I just know which month is which."

I was so tired, and my head felt so heavy. As my vision blurred, I saw Kian take off yet another coat of his and laid it on the bench.

"Why don't you lie down for a minute?" I heard him say.

"M'kay," I slurred and was out like a light a moment later.

"JESSAMINE." I felt a hand on my back, and I stirred. I wasn't used to waking up warm, and I hadn't heard anyone wake me up with my full name since my mom had passed. I blinked my eyes open and realized where I was.

"Hey." Kian's voice was so close to my ear that I could feel his breath against my skin.

"I'm sorry. I'm pretty sure I drooled on your coat. What time is it?" I sat up quickly and instantly regretted the sudden movement as a headache was drilling into my head with such a severe intensity that it hurt to even open my eyes.

"That's okay. I'm sure I've drooled on it plenty." The stiff, almost unfriendly musician I had come to know over the last few days was being gentle and attentive, and I wasn't sure what to make of it.

"It's eleven thirty."

"I start work at twelve." I loved my job, but a nine-hour shift with a fever and this headache felt daunting.

"I took your laundry out when the dryer buzzed."

I turned and saw that not only had he taken it out, but he had folded it and placed it back into the plastic bag.

"You folded my laundry?" I asked, feeling slow on the uptake and not used to people doing little things like that for me.

"I did," he confirmed. "I hope that's okay."

"You saw my underwear." I blinked.

"I did. I didn't mind."

I laughed at that, and he blushed.

"I just meant it didn't bother me. I mean to help you... not because..."

It was funny watching this man, who looked like he should be on a runway somewhere, stumble over his words with growing discomfort.

"I don't mind if you see them again. You know, to fold my laundry." I stood up, swaying slightly, and bent to heave my backpack up onto my shoulder. He flushed again but didn't respond.

"What do you keep in there?" he asked as he observed how heavy my bag was.

"Literally everything." I made light of it so he wouldn't realize how honest I was being.

"I'm stopping off somewhere first, but I'll be by later to sing your song," he said, holding the door open as I walked out, and the crisp air hit my heated face.

"I'll be there with bells on," I quipped, immediately regretting it as I said it. His eyes showed mirth, but his face remained impassive as he watched me walk away.

Chapter Five
Gravity by Matt Hansen

hy was her backpack so heavy? Why did I care? Why was I headed to the pharmacy to get supplies for a girl with a cold whom I had basically just met? A girl with some pretty provocative choices for underwear. My body heated at the thought of her lacy boy shorts and the red hipsters with a rip at the seam that said "Five stars. Would eat here again." on the ass. I was used to women who wore expensive thongs and then complained about their nonexistent panty line. There was something so refreshing about Jessamine and her ripped, *I don't give a fuck* underwear. The one problem was the men's clothing that I had folded along with hers. I had no right to be jealous. I didn't even want to be. I would much prefer to be following my own rules and living out my self-imposed prison of misery, but somehow, my interest in her had left reason behind.

I STOPPED at a CVS and went to the cold and flu aisle. I got a bottle of ibuprofen, a bottle of vitamin C gummies, a box of elderberry tablets, and a bag of throat lozenges. Back in my old life, I had to be healthy all the time, so these items were readily available to me, and I was well-versed in healing a sore throat. At the checkout, I added a chocolate bar and a bottle of electrolyte water. After paying, I made my way back to the high-end strip mall and awkwardly carried the bag, my guitar, stool, speaker, and mic to the area a bit past Kafe. I had discovered there was a sports bar on the corner, and there was nothing better than tips from happy, drunk sports fans as they listened to some of their favorite music. After setting up, I doubled back to the coffee shop and made my way inside. A man stood at the register, and Jessamine was nowhere to be found.

"Can I help you?" he asked.

"I'm looking for Jessa." I let my voice trail off so as not to say her full name in front of her co-worker.

"I sent her home," he responded, sudden interest gleaming in his eye. "She was running a fever."

"Oh." I felt disappointed, holding a bag of items that would have definitely helped her. "Where's home?"

Her co-worker suddenly seemed uncomfortable.

"Well." He fiddled with his phone for a second. "Who are you to her?"

I didn't even know.

"We've been getting to know each other." I tried to answer without sounding creepy.

"Are you the singer she's been talking about?" he asked.

She's been talking about me? Oh, my body liked the sound of that. I nodded.

"It's funny you're a singer; I had you pegged as a murderer. But ya know..." He shrugged.

"Wrong guy," I replied weakly.

"Alright, I'll tell you, but keep it to yourself, please."

Okay, things were feeling kind of weird.

"No problem," I assured him and braced myself for his answer.

"She lives in the tent town near the creek. If you follow the path into the park, you just keep walking along the side of the creek, and you'll eventually see it. I'm not sure which tent she's in though. I'm sorry." The sincerity in his voice showed how much he genuinely cared about her, and I appreciated that she had a co-worker like him.

"I'll try to find her. Thank you."

MY HEART FELT funny as I found out that happy Jessamine, who came across as so carefree, was carrying some heavy burdens of her own. Emotionally, I assumed, but also physically as I thought of her backpack. She told me she had everything in there, and now I understood that wasn't far off from the truth.

"NO PROBLEM," I heard him say as I left and another customer walked in. I went back to the bar, disassembled all of my equipment, and lugged it back to my van. Then I took the shopping bag and crossed the street. I found the entrance to the park easily and followed the path for about twenty minutes until a bunch of tents came into view. The area was clean for the most part. Some needles and condom wrappers were scattered in the bushes, and I felt apprehensive until I remembered what I now looked like and the damage I could ensue on anyone who bothered her. *Her.* The thought reverberated in my mind. Apparently, I felt protective over Jessa. That was interesting but not surprising to me at this point.

As I grew closer, I saw a younger-looking man standing

outside a red tent that was slightly larger than the others scattered around it. He looked up suspiciously when I approached. I could see from his pupils and the slight delay in movement that he was high on something.

"Hi, sorry to bother you, but I'm looking for Jessa Bardot."

"Who's asking?" He seemed fidgety and a bit restless.

"My name is Kian. We've been hanging out a bit at her work."

"You gave her your coat?"

I nodded wordlessly. I didn't realize how much she needed it, and now I was so glad I had the intuition to give it to her. I wasn't sure if I was about to face an angry boyfriend though.

"She's in there." He pointed to the tent with his thumb. "But she's pretty sick, and I don't know what to do." He worriedly ran his hands along the strings of his hoodie.

"I brought supplies." I held up the bag, and he looked relieved.

"Are you her boyfriend?" I asked, stepping closer to the tent.

"Brother." He almost interrupted me.

Ah, that explained the men's clothes in her laundry yet his lack of territorial behavior.

"My name is Myles."

"Nice to meet you." I held out my hand to shake his. He looked at me for a moment, seemingly taken aback, and then shook mine limply.

"Let me see if she's up for visitors," he said as he slipped into the tent. It made me sad how he said that, yet he was referring to a cold tent, not a proper home. I knew it sounded funny coming from me, the guy who lived in his van. Although mine was by choice, and I was sure theirs was due to circumstance.

I COULD HEAR the rumble of Myles talking, and then Jessamine's voice said something in response. Myles reappeared in the doorway of the tent.

"Okay, come in. Excuse the mess; we're redecorating," he said sarcastically. I couldn't help it, and I let out a burst of laughter. Myles patted me on the arm as I ducked my head to get into the tent.

"I like you already," he told me with a grin. My humor quickly faded when I took in what I saw in front of me. Jessamine was lying in a sleeping bag, a NY Giants hat on her head and a pair of gloves on her hands. She was trembling with chills.

"H-hi. Fancy meeting you here." She tried to give me a smile, but her teeth were chattering.

"Well, hi," I said gently. "I swear I'm not stalking you."

She tried to laugh, but it came out as a cough.

"A guy at your work told me where to find you. I hope that's okay. I brought goodies." I lifted up the CVS bag, and she nodded.

"Eric? Yeah, he thinks you're a murderer." She coughed again.

"Oh, he told me." I grimaced.

"Are you?" Myles asked. His eyes were rimmed red, but he looked relatively healthy otherwise.

"No, but I could be if I needed to be." I was dead serious.

"I mean, valid." Myles seemed perfectly fine with what I had just said. I sat down next to his sister and took out everything I had bought. I watched her wash two ibuprofen capsules down with the water. She laughed at the childish shape of the gummies but compliantly chewed a couple. She had never heard of elderberry, so we googled it on her phone so she could read how it helps the immune system. Twenty minutes later, she was looking a tiny bit less pathetic.

"So obviously, you can't stay here while you're sick." I broached the subject gently. Jessamine and Myles both looked at me.

"I mean, I can. I have," she responded. "It sucks, but we live here for real, and this is how it is sometimes."

"I know, but right now, you would definitely benefit from sleeping in a warm room and a comfortable bed. If you don't, you may never properly kick this thing." I knew I was acting like the worried dad, but I couldn't possibly walk away while she coughed up a lung in this freezing tent.

Myles nodded in agreement but didn't say anything.

"I know, that sounds amazing, but I'm saving up for a car, so I can't pay for a hotel room," she said regretfully.

"I'll get you a room." I fiddled with the car keys in my pocket, wondering how this would play out.

"No." She shook her head. "I couldn't let you do that."

"I insist. Can you walk to the parking lot of the mall, or are you too weak?"

"I can't leave Myles," she said in protest.

"He can come too." I looked over at her brother.

"I can't go anywhere." He looked ashamed but explained honestly. "I promised Jessa that I wouldn't buy too many pills at one time and only buy from this one guy over here because his product is safe. So I don't want to leave and then go through withdrawals before I can get back here."

I appreciated his candor.

"What are you on?" I asked him.

"Usually weed, perks, sometimes Xanax. Once in a while, he'll give me shrooms or Ketamine."

"I have a few Xanax left over from... Well, what I'm trying to say is if your sister is cool with it, I can give you a few to hold you over while you stay in the hotel. That way, you don't have to worry about feeling sick," I told him.

JESSAMINE LOOKED CONFLICTED. I could see that she was afraid to leave him alone, but it also felt wrong to actively give him pharmaceuticals. Myles pushed his shoe against the edge of the tent for a moment.

"Okay, but I'm worried they'll take the tent and our spot while we're away."

"Aight, I got this." I pushed my way back out of the tent and called loudly. "Hey, everyone, listen up!"

Heads popped out of the tents around us. People sitting outside smoking looked over at me.

"This is Jessa and Myles's tent and spot. They're going away for a couple of days, and if any of you take their stuff while they're gone, you will deal with me. Do you understand?" I made my voice louder and more menacing than was natural for me. I saw heads nod, and others eyed my muscles. I gave them all one last look and then went back into the tent, where I found Jessamine laughing.

"I doubt Larry is ever gonna ask me for a blow job again after you just scared the bejeezus out of them."

"He what?" I looked aghast.

"I mean, I've never done it." She defended herself dramatically. "He just likes to ask. Often."

"Ew, Jessa." Myles looked insulted for her. I picked up her backpack and swung it over one shoulder.

"This is fucking heavy." I looked over at her, not happy that she had to lug this thing around everywhere she went. She shrugged.

"I'm used to it."

I watched as Myles grabbed his own bag and helped his sister step out of her sleeping bag. He then rolled it up and placed it next to his at the side of the tent. The three of us slowly made our way from the park back to where my van was parked.

As I fished in my pocket for my keys, I told them, "So, I live here."

"Like here?" Myles pointed at the van. I nodded. Whatever reservations Jessamine had been holding onto seemed to fade away when she concluded that I was basically as homeless as she was.

"Oh, I didn't realize." She let me open the door and help her up into the front seat. I didn't clarify what she did or didn't really know; I just let her sit with her assumptions as I slid open the side door. I had removed all of the seats but one to make room for my bed. I moved my guitar off the captain's seat to clear a spot for Myles. He got in, and I shut the door behind him. I took a deep breath before I walked around to the driver's side. This was not at all how I saw my day going, yet I felt a hum of something inside of me. Almost like the reverberations of music that you could feel before you could hear it. Something that felt like hope.

I DROVE them to the nearest hotel and had them wait in the van as I went inside and got a room for two nights under Jessamine's name, as I couldn't risk putting my name on it. They let me use a prepaid Visa card, too, which was very helpful. When I went back to get them, Jessamine's tired eyes met mine.

"I don't mean to pry, but I feel guilty letting you pay for this." She gestured to the van. "I know you work hard for your money, and I don't want to take..."

I cut her off.

"I won a fight last week, so I'm good on cash right now."

"A fight?" She sounded confused.

"I box," I explained. "I compete once a month."

Curiosity shone in her eyes.

"I want to see that," she said as I helped her get out of her seat and closed the door behind her. I got the bottle of Xanax out of the side of my carry-on bag and slid it into my pants pocket.

"I don't think you'd like it." I rejected her idea of coming to a fight.

"I really want to." She was so fragile looking all huddled up in my coat, her cheeks pink from the cold air. Her hair was cascading around her in a tangled mess, and her eyes were shiny with fever. I could only imagine how the fight environment would eat her alive. With her having made it on the streets this long, she obviously could hold her own, but I could almost hear the inappropriate comments she would get from the fighters. Forget about the pimps trying to recruit her and the strippers looking at her like some sort of outside competition. I didn't even know if I would be able to focus on the fight, knowing she was sitting, vulnerable, in the crowd somewhere.

"Let's get you up to your room," I said as we crossed the parking lot. The ride up in the elevator was quiet and a little awkward. I didn't yet know her all that well, so although my instincts had led me to jump in and help, we weren't really in a place where quiet felt comfortable or small talk felt natural. When we got to their room, I took the keycards out of my pocket and unlocked the door. Myles went in first, surveying the room, and then fell dramatically onto one of the two queen beds.

"Holy shit, that feels good." He moaned. Jessamine giggled, and I could see the sheer happiness on her face.

"He hasn't slept in a bed in three years, so this is very exciting."

I would have expected to see shame on her face or hear embarrassment in her tone, but I didn't. She just wholly embraced herself and her situation and didn't seem hard-pressed to make any excuses for it. I was growing more and more impressed by her confidence every time I was around her.

"How long have you been living in your van?" she suddenly asked.

"A little over a year." I didn't offer any other details as I placed her bag on one of the chairs. I then took the prescription bottle out of my pocket and counted out a few pills. As I handed them to her for safekeeping, I could see Myles watching, but he remained silent.

"Alright, well, rest up." I awkwardly started to head for the door when she stopped me.

"I get two questions a day."

I sighed.

"Okay, hit me with it."

"Will you come back for dinner later?" She had taken off my coat and sweatshirt and was standing there in a tight, long-sleeved shirt. I swallowed quickly as I got my first good look at just how sizable her chest was in comparison to her small waist. I averted my gaze and answered the ceiling.

"What's for dinner?" I sounded hoarse.

"Room service."

The room was closing in on me as images of her taking her shirt off flooded my mind. I could see her wild hair falling over her body and her dusky nipples peeking through the strands.

"Let me see how the day goes." I swallowed heavily again. "You sleep; if I can make it back, I will."

"Okay." She smiled and watched me back up to the door and waved as I left. I ran as fast as I could back to the safety of my van and hit the gym early when I realized she had only asked me one real question.

I HAD NEVER SKIPPED a day of busking since I had started, yet today called for an emergency workout. I felt so much guilt that I was able to help Jessamine when she needed it, but I had failed others so catastrophically. It seemed unfair that now I was able to be there for someone, yet when it had really mattered, I was unable to step up to the plate.

I ALSO COULDN'T IGNORE how attracted I was to her anymore. I was almost glad that she was tan, dark haired, and curvy because she couldn't be more different from the dainty blonde that haunted me, and somehow, I found comfort in that.

THE GYM WAS QUIETER during the day than it was at night, and it made it easier to do my chaotic workout without so many eyes on me. I pummeled the bag until my arms weighed heavy at my sides, and my knuckles throbbed in protest. Sweat poured down my face, and I could taste its salty path at the sides of my mouth. I took a long drink of electrolytes and then hit the showers. As always, my cock stood proudly, and although I had been ignoring him for over a year, today I finally palmed the length and had to hold back a groan when I did. I moved my hand hesitantly, as if to give myself a chance to back away and stop. The weeping head of my cock kept me going. I leaned against the wall, holding myself up with one hand as I dragged my fist down my erection and then back up. I began to move frantically, slick with my own precum. I imagined Jessamine flat on her stomach, me lying fully on top of her, caging her in and fucking her. She'd be soaking and moaning. I could feel her wetness seeping around my balls and making a mess of the sheets.

"Yesss," I hissed between gritted teeth. I imagined her ass shaking with my every move, and I could see the slightly bruising bite marks I had left there earlier. I could still taste the tang of her pussy on my lips. She had come so violently on my face and had gotten my beard all dirty. I should make her clean it up. I grabbed a handful of her hair and tugged. I knew the bite of pain would hurtle her over the edge.

"Fucking come," I ordered, and she did. Brilliantly and loudly. She shouted, cursed, and cried as I drove into her over and over, her tight channel choking my cock as she orgasmed all over me. I followed my invention of her seconds later, spurting all over my fingers and dripping cum onto the shower floor. My chest heaved as I stared down at it, my cock softening against my thigh. I shook my head as if to clear it, and then held my hand up to the water to wash it clean. This is what it had come to. Fake scenarios in my mind because I had fucked up so badly in real life that all I would allow myself to have now was my imagination.

T woke up with a start. A soft pillow was beneath my head, my body was surrounded by silky sheets, and I felt utterly confused. Where was I? I cleared my throat and then coughed, which made my head hurt. I turned and saw Myles sleeping in the bed on the other side of the night table. It was then that I remembered where I was. It was so nice waking up in a bed; I hadn't even realized how much I missed it. It was so comfortable that, for a moment, I wished that I could keep it. How amazing would that be?

I SAT up gingerly and saw the bottle of ibuprofen sitting next to the lamp. I glanced at the clock and saw that it had been four hours since I had taken it last. I slipped another two pills into my mouth and washed them down with the last of the water. Then I got myself out of bed quietly and went over to Myles. He looked so young and innocent when he slept. I watched him for a moment, making sure that his chest was moving, and then I padded to the bathroom, the carpet soft beneath my feet. I locked the door, brushed my teeth, and then stripped out of my sweat-soaked clothes.

As I TURNED the bath on, I got a glimpse of myself in the full-length mirror on the back of the door. I hadn't shaved in a while —why bother when it was impossible to get laid when you lived in a tent with your brother. I also hadn't done it since it was winter, and I lived in pants literally all day and night. Yet it was obvious that it was getting out of control so I searched in my bag for my razor and got into the water. I had added the little bottle of bubble bath from the hotel, and I could have cried from how delicious it felt all over my body. I leaned back against the tub wall and closed my eyes. I could not even remember the last time I had taken a bath.

I MUST HAVE FALLEN asleep because when I woke up, the water was dangerously high but not yet spilling over. I quickly opened the drain to let it go down a bit and got to work on shaving. I started with my toes, worked my way up my legs, and then all the way to my thighs. Then I did my arms, my armpits, and the little bit of fluff that grew between my boobs. It was for sure the Italian grandmother on my mom's side who had given me that. Then I tackled my pubic hair. As I finished up and felt the water splashing my now-bare lips, I put the razor down and ran a finger through the wetness that had pooled there. I hadn't masturbated in way too long. Again, living in a tent with your brother wasn't exactly conducive to self-pleasure. I wasn't going to go "flick the bean" in the bathroom at work either. So it had been a while. I knew that my brother was in the other room, but I had the water going at full blast, the door was locked, and I figured the endorphins from coming could only help my immune system. Right?

I slid my fingers up to my clit and rubbed it as I held back a moan. Muscle memory had me moving exactly how I knew I needed to in order to come quickly and come hard. Images of muscly arms holding me down assaulted my mind's eye. I loved it a little rough, and I needed a dominating man. I had to be so responsible all the time in life that in bed, I just wanted to be told what to do and when to do it. My hand was splashing the water as I imagined him holding me down forcefully, kissing me with that bearded mouth of his, and fucking me into the mattress.

It didn't take long for me to come, and damn if I didn't feel a little better already. I washed my body with the fancy bottles of hotel body wash and then wrapped myself in the soft, fluffy robe that hung on the hook on the back of the door. I heard a rap on the door as I worked on detangling my hair, which had grown knotty from being shoved into the shower cap. I opened it to find my brother looking well rested and relatively sober.

"How many pills did he give you?" he asked me, his eyes darting around the room.

"How many do you need?" I replied. "Love the person, hate the disease" was a quote they said at family meetings all the time. I didn't really hate the disease; I hated the things that had happened to him that had led him to feel the need to be numb all the time.

"IF I SNORT IT, I'll only need two right now." He kept his eyes downcast because he didn't like talking about this. He almost preferred to pretend he didn't need to be high all the time just to exist. I didn't know if it was uncomfortable for him because he was embarrassed by his actions or if he didn't want to bring attention to it because he knew how much it hurt me. Myles wasn't getting high for anything other than numbing out his constant emotional agony. He didn't really do uppers, and he wasn't out there looking for a good time and partying. He stayed home most of the time and read my ratty copy of *Harry Potter*. He drew and he planted flowers. He rehabbed baby birds that fell out of the nest too young. In fact, he was so careful to only do enough to numb the pain and not more than that. Knowing what a dangerous game of roulette he was playing, he willingly followed the rules that we had come up with together. He would never buy more than two days' worth of product at a time to lessen the risk of him taking too much at once, and he would only buy it from Ricardo, whom we called "the pharmacist" on the streets. He didn't sell tainted product, and he didn't sell heroin, meth, or cocaine. He stuck to pharmaceuticals, weed, or psychedelics. I figured if I couldn't get Myles clean, at least I could try to keep him safe. I leaned over and wrapped my brother in a hug. He felt jittery beneath my hands, so I didn't hold him for long.

"I love you," I murmured.

"I love you too, sis." His voice sounded pained, but he was too sweet to push me away. I walked out of the steamy bathroom and found the pills that Kian had given me. I wordlessly handed Myles two of them and watched as he took a medicine grinder out of his pocket. He ground the pills into dust and then poured it onto the glass top of the night table. Using the key card, he formed two lines. He didn't look at me as he closed one nostril with his finger and snorted both of them. He took a deep breath in and let out a sigh.

I HAD NEVER DONE drugs other than smoke some weed here and there, but I had watched my brother flirt with its toxic love for years. I watched it torture and tease him. Drugs promised him paradise and instead gave him heartbreak. I watched as he slid back down under the covers, and I wished I could give him a life that came with a bed and peace and sobriety. It broke my heart that I couldn't. I took a deep breath in and focused on being grateful that today we had a room. Right now, we were off the streets, and it was only for a moment, but it was a moment all the same.

I WENT BACK into the bathroom to finish combing my hair and then put on a pair of boxers with a thick fleece hoodie that someone had left at work the other day. When they never came back for it, my co-workers told me to keep it. It was black, and in white letters, it said,

"He who does not lick the clit should not get to hit. Coochielations 1:69." Myles rolled his eyes when he saw that I was wearing it.

"Mom would be mortified if she could see you in that," he told me as I crawled back into bed after taking some more elderberry.

"Well, what she can't know won't hurt her." I winked. My dark humor was likely what got me through the hardest of times. He gave a half-hearted laugh.

"I'M GETTING HUNGRY." He was talking slower than usual. "When's your man coming back?"

"For one, he is not my man; I barely know him. What he has done for us is completely unexpected, and I can never repay him. I hope he knows that. Honestly, I don't even know his last name, and I just found out that he lives in a van." I laughed. "Second, I don't know if he will come back, so why don't we order something and if he comes, then he comes." I was very realistic in my expectations of people. I expected very little, so if they did something, it was already above and beyond anything I had hoped for.

I PULLED up the room service menu on the TV that hung on the wall and told Myles to order whatever he wanted. He asked for a burger, fries, and a milkshake. I got soup, a slice of cheesecake, and a drink made of ginger, orange juice, and lemon. At Kafe, we had a drink called a flu bomb that consisted of mint green tea, peach tea, steamed lemon, and honey. So I figured something with vitamin C and lemon in it couldn't hurt. I fell back to sleep while we waited for the food to come, until I was awoken about forty minutes later by the sound of knocking on the door. I had never gotten room service before, and I was feeling very excited to experience it for the first time. Out of habit, I held my finger under Myles's nose to check that he was still breathing and then went over to the door and looked out the peephole. Instead of a hotel worker, there stood a very sexy-looking Kian. I stood there for a moment, pondering how I felt about him actually showing up before turning the lock.

I OPENED the door as I remembered that all I was wearing was a sweatshirt. Kian immediately noticed and averted his eyes.

"They're just legs." I laughed, moving aside so he could come in. He was still not looking at me as he asked,

"Are you feeling better?"

"A little bit. I didn't know if you were coming, so we ordered without you," I told him regretfully.

"That's fine; I can order now."

I got back into bed as there was another knock on the door.

Kian went to open the door while telling me to stay in bed. This time, it was our food, and I gently woke Myles up so he could eat. Kian watched as I blew on a spoonful of soup and then hummed when I tasted it.

"You're not shy with your emotions," he observed out loud.

"Jessa is the most real person I know," Myles piped up. "She's also brave and smart. She's almost always in a good mood no matter what life has put her through."

"Shush." I laughed it off. "Eat your burger and stop running your mouth."

Myles took a bite but I could see the smug look on his face that he had managed to get those compliments in before I shut him up. After a few moments of quiet, Myles piped up again.

"What do you think of her sweatshirt?" He pointed to it when my mouth was full of more soup. I made a noise in protest, but Myles just laughed. Kian shifted in his chair, almost looking uncomfortable.

"I mean, it's a valid statement," he finally replied. Myles raised his eyebrows at me as if to say, "He may be a keeper."

"So when is your next fight?" I asked Kian, pointedly changing the subject.

"It's at the end of every month."

"Where is it?"

"The location changes with each fight, so I don't know yet." Kian got up when there was yet another knock on the door, indicating that his food was now here as well. I watched as he sat down on the one chair in the room and took off his beanie. Oh good god, his hair was better than I had even imagined. It was a light brown at the base, like his beard, but he had natural streaks of blond throughout, and it was long enough to be pulled into a small bun at the back of his head.

"A man bun, huh?" Myles commented. I didn't know what

had gotten into my brother tonight; he was usually so docile and quiet. Kian absentmindedly ran his hand over his hair.

"Yeah, I had a buzz cut my entire life, so I figured it was time for a change, but I may cut it shorter soon."

"I like it," I blurted. Kian's gaze met mine, but he didn't respond, which I was finding to be pretty common for him. What was that quote about a quiet man being the strongest man in the room? I wondered to myself.

AFTER WE FINISHED DINNER, Kian leaned forward in his chair and said, "So I spoke to the hotel, and apparently, there is a program that they participate in that provides a long-term stay for free to help people get off the street, and they happen to have one available now. So I told them about you, and they want to give you a two-bedroom with a kitchenette for as long as you need it."

My brain was having a hard time processing what he had just said.

"No there isn't. I know about all of the available programs out there, and I have never heard of one that does this." I was skeptical. He shrugged.

"I guess it's not public knowledge, but they do it."

I scoffed.

"No way."

He was watching me with those green eyes that seemed to know and feel so much more than he let on.

"Take the room, Jessa," he said softly. I made a motion with my hand to dismiss his words.

"So we're friends now?" I asked sarcastically, reminding him of how he said we weren't friends yet, which was why he was sticking to calling me Jessamine until we were. His slip of Jessa belied his aloof behavior. Kian's eyes darkened for a moment, but he didn't say anything back, as usual. Myles grunted as he stood up and took a cigarette from my pack that I hadn't touched since yesterday due to feeling so crappy.

"I'm gonna go smoke. I'll be back in a few."

I heard the door close behind him, and I looked back at Kian.

"Something feels weird about this," I admitted. "I feel like you're not telling me the whole story, but I really don't even know you well enough to know if you're hiding something."

My own room? With a bathtub and little bottles of bubble bath to use whenever I wanted to? A kitchenette? It sounded like a dream come true. I knew what I would bake first. My mom made the best chocolate chip cookies in the world, and I had her recipe written in her handwriting on the back of an envelope. I would make those, and I would eat them all just to tell her hi. I felt a tear slip out of my eye and run down my cheek, dropping off my nose and into my lap. I heard Kian get up from his chair, and the bed shifted as he sat down on the edge of it.

"I want you to take the room, Jessamine Bardot."

I nodded, still not looking up at him.

"I'll take the room even though it feels weird, but I'm only doing it for Myles." I sniffed.

"I know you are."

I could hear something akin to admiration in his tone.

"I'm going to play your song, and you're going to sleep."

I felt the bed shift again as he got up and went to the door to retrieve his guitar. I laid my head on the soft down pillow and closed my eyes as he began to strum and sing. I fell asleep to the chorus.

When I woke up, the lights were off, the food had been cleaned up, and Myles was snoring softly in the bed next to me. I was burning up with fever. I felt cold on the inside but boiling hot on the outside. I shifted to sit up, and as I shivered, I took two more ibuprofen and looked at my phone. It was ten a.m. I had never had the luxury of sleeping in. Hotel life was treating me nicely, although I really needed to get better because I could not afford to keep missing work.

ERIC HAD TEXTED me last night before I ate dinner, asking how I was feeling, and I told him I still had a fever. He told me to feel better and to take another day off. I knew my job wasn't in jeopardy, but we didn't get paid sick days. He had also said he still wasn't convinced that Kian wasn't a murderer, and I had said he was probably right and to watch his back. Eric had sent me the middle finger and the rolling eye emoji. I got up to pee, and after changing my underwear, I pulled on a pair of sweatpants. As I was looking over the breakfast menu, there was a knock on the door. My heart skipped a beat as I wondered if maybe Kian had come back, but it wasn't Kian at the door; it was someone from the front desk coming to switch us to our new, permanent room.

IT TOOK me a minute to wake up Myles, but once he was awake, we grabbed our bags and followed the hotel worker down one floor. He led us to the new room and gave us our key cards. He left as we entered, and I played it cool until we shut the door.

"Holy shit, My," I whispered.

"Why are you whispering?" He laughed.

"Because if I don't, I'm going to fucking scream." The happiness I was feeling was almost overwhelming me.

"Which room do you want?" Myles asked as he walked into each of them. "Never mind, I'm taking the room with the queen bed, and you take the king."

"Why? I'm perfectly happy with a queen," I protested. Myles stared at me long and hard, then went into his claimed room and shut the door. I guess that conversation was over. It made me laugh as I made my way into my room and marveled over the size of the bed and the attached bathroom. I itched to take my phone out and text Kian to say thank you, but I had never gotten his number. Come to think of it, I had never even seen him holding a phone.

I STILL FELT a flicker of unease when I thought about this supposed program, which I was ninety-nine percent sure did not exist, and I sincerely hoped that he had not spent his own money on getting it for us. But that was absurd because a busker living in his van could never afford this. I coughed, reminding myself that I still needed to rest. I climbed into bed and ordered French toast with orange juice for both of us. The room was so quiet without Myles. Since we had slept side by side for so many years, I was so used to hearing his breathing as I fell asleep. Being alone would definitely take some getting used to.

I HAD a moment of panic and got back out of bed to check on my brother. I knocked on his door, but he didn't answer. I eased it open quietly and saw that he was in bed. I tiptoed over to him and hovered my hand gently on his chest to confirm, yet again, that he was breathing. I gave a sigh of relief as he cracked an eye open.

"Can't sleep without hearing me snore?"

"Something like that." I nodded.

He pulled back the blanket from the other side of the bed. I climbed in and promptly fell asleep.

I busked outside the hotel for the next two days, which turned out to be an amazing spot for good tips, but I did not go back inside to see her. I needed to process what was happening, and I could not think straight around her, her sweet brother, her sarcasm, and her thick thighs. Fuck. I conjured up the image of her thighs that was now branded in my brain. I used to think a toned body was what I was most attracted to, but I had been so wrong. Jessa's thighs had rubbed against each other as she walked in front of me, making her way back to her bed. And when she sat down, they squished, widening on the sides slightly. I would hold onto them so tight as I fucked her, I thought. Now I was hard. I didn't even try to fight it.

I KNEW she didn't believe me when I said there was a program that had given her a free hotel room. She was too smart for that, but she also thought I lived in my van out of necessity, so I didn't think she would presume I was behind it. There was so much that she didn't know, and I hoped it would stay that way. I was cognizant I may have caused some problems for myself in that sense, because I had to use my real credit card for a continuous stay in the hotel. I hadn't used my card since I had disappeared. The people looking for me would see the charge, and it wouldn't take them long to track where it had been used, but I figured I would take care of that problem when the day came. For right now, I just wanted to stay focused on my mission. My mission of self-punishment, forcing myself to stay in fighting shape, and being one with my music because that had always been my life's greatest joy. I realized, with a jolt, that now my mission included one more thing—to keep Jessa and Myles safe, even if that meant keeping them safe from me.

I PULLED my beanie lower on my head as snow started falling again. I had finished my last song as the sun began to set in the sky. I gathered up my gear and headed straight to the gym. As I sat in the locker room after my intense workout, I connected my phone to the Wi-Fi for the first time in a week. Messages that could be sent over Wi-Fi flooded in, and as usual, I ignored them all. I had disconnected my actual number, so I assumed all of those texts were going into no man's land. I went online and ordered a new pick for my guitar since I had misplaced my spare. I also bought more protein bars and then ordered some clothing that had a one-day shipping option. I had to guess their sizes but I thought I did a pretty good job. I had it all delivered to a PO Box under a different name. The picture in my wallet mocked me as I opened it to get my credit card. I couldn't even look at it like I normally did. My actions showed that I was moving on while my heart screamed for me to stay stuck in my pain as my last way of honoring what no longer was.

THE NEXT DAY, I played by the sports bar near Jessa's work, hoping she would feel well enough to return. I still couldn't bring myself to go to her hotel room, but I also wanted to see her face. Hear her voice. Smell her scent.

"Hey, sexy." I was shaken from my thoughts by the sound of a woman's voice. I looked up but continued playing my guitar. I nodded politely but didn't respond. The blonde threw a fifty-dollar bill into my guitar case.

"Thank you," I murmured. She kept standing there in a way that exuded money and privilege. She was from a world I knew very well and wanted nothing more to do with at the present moment.

"Did you get those muscles from playing your guitar?" She giggled.

"Nope." I was hoping she'd get the point and leave. She didn't. I switched to another song, and a few more people gathered around.

"Isn't he gorgeous?" I heard her say to another girl who was moving slightly to the music. The second girl blushed and shrugged.

"I think he can hear you," the girl said, moving away.

"I hope he can hear me. I can be even louder if he wants." The woman winked in my direction.

I grimaced at her innuendo. I figured I knew what she meant, and I had no interest in finding out for sure. I stopped playing and announced that I would be back after lunch. The crowd dispersed, but the blonde stayed.

"I know a place. Do you want to get lunch together?" she asked, following me as I locked my mic into its case.

"No thanks." I didn't even look up. I could tell that she wasn't used to being told no. Yet, to my relief, she actually walked away with a loud *humph.*

I HEADED toward the coffee shop, hoping to shake off the gross energy the woman had left in her wake and felt my pulse kick up a bit when I saw Jessa standing outside, in my coat, smoking. Her face lit up when she saw me. I was growing obsessed with how open she was with her feelings. She didn't give a fuck if you knew that she liked you, was happy, felt sad, or was even enjoying her food. It was such a breath of fresh air, and I respected her confidence so much.

"I guess you're feeling better." I gestured to her cigarette. She frowned at it.

"I finally am. And before you say it, I know it's gross. This is actually my first one since I got sick; I really could have quit." She snuffed out the cigarette after one more long pull on it.

"Why don't you?" I leaned against the brick wall, sticking my hands in my pockets.

"I like the endorphins," she admitted.

"There are other ways to get endorphins," I told her without thinking. I could see that her mind went directly to sex because she started laughing. I could hear the leftovers of her cough in it. I shifted uncomfortably as I let my thoughts drift to sex as well, and my body became fully aware of how many boosts of endorphins I could give her.

"Aw, is my music man shy?" she teased.

"I'm not your music man," I replied stiffly. She cocked an eyebrow but didn't say anything. I was her music man, wasn't I? I was getting fed up with oscillating between my desire to live in a time capsule and my desire to explore my intense attraction to her. Not only to her voluptuous body but also to the kind of person she was. Or at least the small amount that I had picked up on in the short time I had begun to get to know her. I respected her inquisitive mind, her sharp sense of humor, and her obvious self-confidence.

"How's Myles?" I asked, changing the subject abruptly, almost as if I was worried she could read my thoughts.

"He's enjoying living inside."

I heard her happiness and could see the gratitude swimming in her eyes. I liked that I had put it there.

"I bought some more stash for him because I can keep it locked up in the safe," she offered. "Oh, we're baking cookies tonight. You can come bake with us if you'd like."

I didn't sense any anger coming off of her as she said it, but I could feel her unasked question of why I never returned since the other night. I shifted uncomfortably.

"What kind of cookies?"

"Chocolate chip." She was watching me like she was trying to figure me out.

"I'm a bit of a mess," I blurted out, fidgeting with the guitar pick in my pocket.

"I know." She grinned with a flash of her dimple. I felt a strong desire to just lay it all at her feet and let her really choose if she still wanted to invite me over to make cookies. She had a way about her that made me feel like she would accept me and my mess with no desire to try to change me. It felt freeing in a way.

"What time will you be baking?" I went back to the previous topic instead of shedding all of my secrets.

"I get off at six today, so when I walk home, we'll start." She began to walk back to the door to go into work.

"I'll drive you," I called to her.

"Maybe, not my music man." She left with a tinkle of the bell on the door. I stood there for a moment, watching her return to work. She took off the coat revealing her hair that was gathered in a braid today. I was so happy that she was feeling better that I suddenly felt the urge to follow her in, lean over the counter, and smack a kiss on her full lips. But instead, I turned around and walked away. Not because of the ghosts haunting me this time but because we were nowhere ready for that yet. This was a new feeling for me since usually, my body completely rejected the idea of any form of companionship. I wasn't sure if that made me happy or if it made me feel like I was abandoning the part of me that was holding onto the past because I thought it was all I had left.

AT SIX P.M., I was waiting outside Kafe, freezing my ass off. I watched through the window as Jessa put her coat back on. I noticed she wasn't lugging her life around in a backpack anymore, and that little detail warmed my thawing heart. I pulled the door open as she approached it, holding two coffee cups with no covers.

"Careful," I cautioned. She flashed me a grin as she handed me my cup. I stared dubiously at the whipped cream that had a dash of cinnamon on it.

"I'm not so much of a whipped cream kind of guy." The coffee was warming my hands.

"Stop being so hot and bothered by everything and take a sip," she teased me bossily. I rolled my eyes and took a gulp of the hot liquid.

"Hmm." I made a noncommittal sound and went in for round two. I locked eyes with her as she waited impatiently for me to tell her if I liked it.

"It's good," I admitted with a half smirk.

"I told you!" She took a sip of her own drink and ended up with a dollop of whipped cream on her top lip.

"You have a little..." I leaned forward and wiped it off with my finger. We both froze before she interrupted the weird feelings swirling inside of me by saying, "It's one of my favorites on the menu, it's a chai tea latte with milk. No water. Then I added in two pumps each of cinnamon dolce syrup and white mocha syrup. After that, I just topped it with whipped cream and cinnamon."

I LET her chatter as we walked toward my van. Had I ever touched her on purpose before? I didn't think so. I would have remembered the frisson of energy that had run up my arm as my finger passed over her lip. I squeezed my hand into a fist to stop myself from doing it again, this time sans the whipped cream. What was it about this girl that had me in a trance? Up until now, I had done such a good job at keeping my head low and my focus strong. I should be in the gym right now, fucking myself up, preparing for the next fight. I should be writing sad songs and lamenting all I had lost. I definitely should not be opening the van door to let a coffee-and-cinnamon-smelling girl jump in so I could drive her to the hotel room I was paying for to bake cookies. I really shouldn't be here trying not to watch Jessa's ass jiggle as she sat down. I quickly turned and firmly shut the door.

MYLES TURNED to look at us from where he sat on the couch when we walked in.

"Oh, hey," he offered and turned back to the TV.

"He started watching *Friends*," Jessa explained as she opened the fridge.

"I'm up to season two," Myles interjected.

"I never watched it," I admitted.

"It's really funny." Jessa handed me the eggs that she told me she had bought at Family Dollar. I watched as she went to the small counter by the sink and took flour and chocolate chips out of a shopping bag. I placed the carton on the table and sat down.

She had cleaned the metal ice bucket to use as a bowl, but she had gotten cookie pans and a spoon from the dollar store as well. Forty minutes later, we had made a mess, but it was worth it as I was now biting into a hot, gooey cookie. I couldn't remember the last time I had eaten a cookie, let alone a home-made one.

"Better than sex, for sure." She moaned around the cookie, her eyes closed as she savored it. I swallowed thickly.

"Then you haven't been having good enough sex," I mumbled.

"Hmm?" She opened her eyes and stared at me. I shrugged.

"What did you say?" she demanded.

"He said you haven't been having good enough sex," Myles called from the couch again. He seemed surprisingly clear-headed today, and I snickered as she threw him a dirty look.

"Yes, I have," she protested as she grabbed another cookie.

"Okay, ew." Myles pretended to throw up over the side of the couch. I looked around the small hotel kitchenette, taking in the scene and trying to calculate what I was feeling. A struggling addict whom I barely knew sat on the couch, laughing as Chandler cracked a witty joke. A beautiful girl stood in front of me, licking melted chocolate chips off of her non-manicured fingers, and the cookies we had baked together warmed my belly. I was feeling joy, I realized. That was not an emotion I was well acquainted with. There were only a few moments in my life I could recall that had given me this feeling of simplistic joy. Joy that wasn't dependent on anything but living in the moment. Joy that wasn't due to something I had achieved. This didn't happen to me very often, and my heart felt funny as it tried to figure out what to make of it.

I helped Jessa clean up the kitchen when I remembered the packages I had picked up from the PO Box earlier and had left by the door when we came in.

"So..." I sounded awkward. "I wasn't sure what you both needed, so I just picked a few things." I fiddled with the pick in my pocket to calm my nerves.

"What do you mean?" Jessa was wiping down the counter as I brought over the bag. I shrugged, never having been a man of many words, but especially when I felt awkward. I ripped open the packages and slowly laid the contents on the counter—boxers for Myles, underwear for Jessa, and socks for both of them. Then I took out a set of pajamas, some T-shirts, pants, a sweatshirt, a hat, gloves, and a pair of shoes each. Avoiding eye contact altogether, I emptied the contents of the last box, which was sweatpants for both of them, leggings for Jessa, jeans for Myles, and some toiletries. Myles had paused the show and ambled over to survey my purchases.

"How can a guy living in his van afford to buy all this shit?" he asked, sounding uncharacteristically suspicious. I didn't blame him one bit.

"I don't have many bills," I offered weakly, still not making eye contact with either of them.

"Why?" Jessa waved a hand in the direction of the counter.

"You needed help?" It was supposed to be a statement, but it ended up sounding like a question.

"We've always gotten by okay. I don't want you to think we need handouts." Her usually sunny disposition was clouded by her pride.

"I know that." I defended myself. "I'm not doing it because of anything other than I simply wanted to." I fiddled with the pick again, flipping it through my fingers. "I can return it if you want, but I hope you'll keep it." I headed to the door, not waiting for an answer, and let myself out into the quiet hallway.

BACK IN MY VAN, I texted Beau, asking if he had anyone I could fight. I needed to let this pent-up energy out of me, or it would slowly destroy me from the inside out. I was practically vibrating with it when I pulled up outside the brick building covered in graffiti. Beau ran the monthly fights, but he also trained fighters in his dingy basement gym. The smell of sweat permeated the air as I entered through a side door. Beau was wrapping the hands of one of the fighters while two others sparred in the ring. I nodded at him as he called out in greeting to me.

TEN MINUTES LATER, I was shirtless, in the ring, hands wrapped, gloves on, and my focus solely on the man in front of me. We circled each other for a minute, trying to read each other's weaknesses. I noted that he seemed to be favoring his right side, which meant he was off somewhere on his left. He lunged suddenly, and I felt his glove just barely graze my jaw. I punched back and got him on the shoulder. We dodged and danced around each other, taking punches when we could and otherwise focusing on moving quickly to avoid getting hit. I could feel sweat pooling under my arms; my chest was wet, and my hair was damp with it. My muscles sang with the effort of the fight, and I reveled in it. I let him get in a few solid punches to my face just so I could be reminded of the pain of life and not be distracted by a girl and her cookies. My jaw was sore, and my eye was swelling up by the time I decided to stop fucking around and let loose till my opponent was on the floor, bleeding from his mouth.

"Jesus, Kian. Chill a little; it's just practice," Beau snapped at me. I backed out of the ring with a quick apology and then went back to my van without cleaning myself up. I went to sleep sweaty, swollen, and bruised, yet I slept more soundly than I had in weeks.

"It's giving weird vibes," Myles admitted. Our room was on the first floor, so he felt comfortable leaning out the window, keeping half of his body outside since he was smoking a blunt and was trying to avoid setting off the smoke alarm as well as stop any smell from drifting into the hallway. I was getting ready for work and was debating if I should wear any of the clothes that Kian had given us.

"Maybe he's in the mafia or a gang or is secretly an oil tycoon billionaire in the witness protection program." I offered up some absurd explanations as I pulled on one of the black, long-sleeved T-shirts he had left me, admiring how soft the material of a new shirt was. I didn't generally have new clothing. On the off chance I was ever able to buy clothing at all, I always did it at Goodwill because it was cheap, and cheap was the most important thing when life centered around survival, not enjoyment.

"Okay, maybe he is one of those things, though I doubt it." Myles laughed and shut the window. "But what do you think he wants with you?"

He wandered back over to the pile of clothes that we had left in the kitchen, his hair stuck up all over his head from sleeping on it after a shower.

"I don't think he wants anything." I admired the pair of cargo pants that Kian had ordered in a beautiful slate-gray color. He obviously had picked up on my edgier side because they were baggy, and there was a chain hooked onto one of the pockets.

"No one does anything for free," Myles reminded me. The munchies had kicked in, and he was digging into the bag of cookies. I winced. We were both painfully aware of that.

"He barely talks to me. He keeps telling me that we're not friends. He doesn't offer up many details about himself at all, and I think he's only accidentally touched me once." I pulled on the pants noticing that they fit perfectly, and wondering how a guitar player who lived in his van was so on point when ordering clothing because they fit my curvy thighs and ass but also didn't gap on my smaller waist.

"If he wants something from me, he's not very good at showing it. What if he's actually a nice guy who just wanted to help us out?"

Myles shrugged.

"Maybe. I guess time will tell. You know, maybe he is an oil tycoon billionaire; he seems kind of familiar to me." Myles chomped on another cookie leaving a spray of crumbs behind him as he went to sit on the couch to watch another episode of *Friends*. I laughed out loud because where would Myles have met an oil tycoon billionaire?

"Alright, I'm off," I announced as I zipped up my coat and grabbed my phone.

"Could you *be* any warmer?" Myles mimicked Chandler's tone. I laughed and blew him a kiss.

THE WALK to work wasn't terrible, especially since the sun was out today. So, although the weather was still very cold, the warmth from the sun helped balance it out. I stopped at an intersection and waited for the walk signal to turn on. I stuffed my hands into my pockets to keep my fingers warm, and I felt so much gratitude come over me that I hadn't woken up in a frigid tent. That I wasn't rushing to work so I could brush my teeth in a proper sink before my shift started. That I wasn't being woken up by the sound of the paramedics showing up because another person had overdosed.

I SENT some grateful vibes out into the universe because no matter how bad it had gotten, I tried not to focus on the negative. I always chose to fixate my energy and thoughts on the one or two kernels of goodness that I could find in my day. I smiled to myself as I noticed a red sign that had been taped to the pole near where I was standing. It was a notification of the town's free New Year's party that was tonight. They always chose the most random days to throw the yearly party, so the fact that they were doing it a week after New Year's seemed on point for our town. I took a photo of the flier and then crossed the street as the walk sign flashed. I loved attending the local parties. For one, it made me feel normal. Like I was a part of real society. Second, there was free food, and I never said no to free food. I texted Myles the photo, and he texted back, "Maybe."

WHICH MEANT NO, but he was too nice to say it. I didn't mind going alone. I always ended up finding someone to talk to and dance with. Last year I had even ended up fucking a guy in the backseat of his car. I realized, with a shock, that he had actually been the last guy I had slept with. How had I gone an entire year without getting laid? As I rounded the corner, I was met with the beautiful sound of a guitar strumming and the timbre of Kian's voice. His eyes met mine as I stood by the door, clearly wearing the pants he had given me. He nodded at me. Just a quick dip of his chin and a small purse of his lips and my ovaries exploded. Like I had told Myles, I had no idea what he wanted with me. I could not surmise why he was being so nice to me or what he could possibly want in return. But I now knew one thing for certain: I wanted to climb that man like a tree.

No one at work was able to join me at the party. Alanna had no one to babysit her son, and Eric said he was way too old for these things and then scoffed when I reminded him that he was only thirty-four. The store was extra busy this morning, and I got slammed making drinks for four hours straight until I finally stopped for my ten-minute break. I had already made two drinks to take on my break with me. This time, I had put together my favorite recipe for a warm sugar cookie drink, which consisted of a base of the white mocha hot chocolate, two pumps of hazelnut syrup and vanilla syrup, topped with a sprinkle of raw sugar.

As I stepped out into the crisp air, I saw that a crowd of hot girls, who probably attended the nearby college, had surrounded Kian and were all making googly eyes at him. They were doing the typical hot girl behavior, giggling behind manicured hands and acting very obvious about how attractive they found him to be. Kian looked uncomfortable. At first glance, he seemed chill as he sat on his stool, loosely strumming his guitar and singing his song, but I could see a trapped animal look in his eyes. His shoulders looked tense as well, and I wondered why he reacted that way to obvious female attention. Kian was objectively gorgeous. He could have any one of those girls, even all of them, maybe even all of them at once. I snickered to myself as I watched him finish his song and then glance my way. He surprised me by setting his guitar down and standing up to walk toward me. That was new.

"Hey."

"Hi." I handed him his drink, which he took, watching me with a wary look in his eye. I noticed some swelling and bruising around his right eye, and I assumed he had been fighting someone recently.

"So you're not mad?" He pointed to the pants that I was wearing.

"I don't get mad that easily," I informed him. "So no, I'm not mad. I'm a little confused. But I'm also not stupid enough to turn down free clothes." I took a sip of my drink and savored its warm, rich flavor.

"You look good in them."

The words seemed to escape him as if they had to force their way out of his throat. He stared down at his hands for a moment before sneaking another glance at me. I responded by turning around in a little circle so he could get a full view of the pants on me. I laughed when I saw him shift, seemingly uncomfortable.

"I'm sorry if I made you feel weird about it."

He had a little moisture from the drink left in his mustache, and my hormones encouraged me to lick it off. My body clenched at the idea.

"I don't usually do stuff like that, to be honest. You just seem cool..." His voice faltered briefly. "And I felt like maybe you could use some help. That's all. I don't expect anything in return." He took another gulp of his drink as if to shut himself up, and I watched greedily as his Adam's apple bobbed in his throat.

"Well, that's good to hear because, honestly, it takes a lot more than some clothes to get a blowjob out of me," I joked to lighten the mood. Kian seemed to choke on air, and I watched as a slight blush crept its way up onto the area of his cheeks that wasn't covered by facial hair.

"I—" he croaked.

"Shit, music man, it's almost like you haven't heard a joke before."

"I knew you were joking." He sounded defensive, which made me laugh again.

"My ten minutes are up. Let me know what you think." I pointed to his cup where I had written:

"Want to hit up a party with me after shift? There is free food."

I figured if he was anything like me, he wouldn't turn down a free meal, and that way, I would have someone I semi-knew to join me. I also felt like getting him some dinner that he didn't have to pay for would sort of even out the scales for all the nice things he had done for me when all I had given him in return was some coffee. I walked away without waiting to see if he had read my note. No goodbyes. It was easier that way. In my world, maybe I'd see people later. Maybe I wouldn't. Only time knew what would happen. I was just a spectator of what the universe decided, and a long time ago, I had chosen not to fight the current of life.

AT THE END of my shift, I counted down the tills, leaving the excess over two hundred in the till. Then I dumped the brewed coffee, started the rinse cycles, and prepped tea for my coworker, Joshua, who was opening tomorrow morning. I heard the jingle of the bell above the door as I got the cash ready to put into the safe, and without looking up, I called, "We're closed."

"What kind of party?" I heard Kian ask. My head snapped up. That wasn't a no.

"It's a community New Year's party that the city throws every year. The special events department, through the mayor's office, puts it together."

I finished up my work, clocked out, and came around from behind the counter. Kian was so tall next to me, and I liked it because I could see he was strong enough to do what he wanted with me. A shiver ran up my spine, and I busied myself with getting my coat so I didn't make a fool out of myself and lick his bicep or take a long sniff of his delicious manly scent. As we stepped outside, I looked back over at Kian.

"It's not like a date or anything, so don't overthink it, music man." I kept my tone light and airy as he always seemed kind of gun-shy. "I'm gonna go because it's fun, there is dancing, and food and drinks. Sometimes they even give out swag."

"Okay," he said with his jaw tight and his tone terse.

"Okay?" I punched his arm lightly, getting a quick feel of the muscle beneath my hand.

"I said okay." He looked over at me, the confusion evident on his face.

"Don't sound so excited." I laughed as we headed to his van.

"I'm not," he admitted.

"Then don't come. No one is forcing you." I stopped walking, and he had to double back when he realized I wasn't next to him anymore.

"It's not that I don't want to go somewhere with you to hang…"

He was stumbling over his words again.

"Spit it out, big boy," I teased. He shot me a look.

"I think it might be cool to hang out. I just don't like big crowds." He finally finished a sentence.

"I'll protect you from the scary people," I told him, saying the word *scary* in a baby voice.

"I don't need protecting." His tone had grown frosty, making me wonder where I had gone wrong.

"Listen, bro, it's literally not a big deal. I'm used to going on my own." I backpedaled as he seemed so unhappy about the whole thing.

"I'm going." He opened the door and motioned for me to walk. "Get in, Jessamine."

I felt his growl between my legs. If this was how he reacted to being asked to go to a party for some dinner, he would probably run off before I could even seduce him, I admitted to myself. That was unfortunate because I bet he could rock my world for a few hours.

IT TOOK a couple of circles around the block to find somewhere to park the van. As he backed up into the spot that we finally found, I texted Myles, telling him that I would be back late and I would bring him some dinner. He informed me that he was starting season three and if they were serving cannolis to bring him at least five. The party was always held in the large back room of a local Italian restaurant. Everything was covered in gold and black. Black streamers with gold Happy New Year's signs were hanging all over the place.

WE SIGNED in at the entrance, and they handed us a bag that contained a sweatshirt, a container of cannolis, a pamphlet with coupons to some of the local businesses, and, of course, information about the upcoming election later on in the year. After placing our bags on two chairs at an empty table, I made a beeline for the buffet and loaded up my plate with Italian creamed greens, chicken Alfredo, and baked tortellini. Kian still hadn't said anything as we sat down to eat. He had piled food on his plate, too, and I imagined he had to ingest a ton of calories just to keep up with the physique that he had.

THE ROOM WAS DIMLY LIT, and a fake candle flickered on the table between us. A DJ was playing music quietly, but once people were done eating, I knew he would bump up the volume, and the dance floor would be covered with writhing bodies. It was quiet between us, but I never felt the need to fill the silence. Silence never felt awkward for me. I didn't know if it was a confidence thing or if it was weird that I didn't find it awkward. Either way, I happily stuffed my face, enjoying the peaceful moment and the feeling of rapidly getting full. Kian kept shooting me looks until he finally said, "Thanks for inviting me. The food is good."

"It is, isn't it?" I sighed happily and leaned back, having cleared my plate.

"You're different from other girls," Kian observed.

"How so?" It didn't bother me one way or another, but I was curious what kind of girls he usually hung out with that made him call me "different."

"Well, for one, you say what you mean."

He seemed so serious that I laughed.

"Have you been hanging out with a bunch of liars?" I snorted. Kian didn't answer the question.

"You don't seem to care what people think of you," he added.

I nodded. "I don't."

"It's astonishing," he almost whispered. His eyes shone in the fake candlelight, and for a tiny, brief moment, I pretended that it was real. I imagined he was not my music man but rather just my man. My man who had asked me out and told me I looked beautiful. Later, we would hold hands under the table, which would lead to us making out until dessert came, and then we would go home and fuck frantically, right by the front door because he couldn't wait one more second to get inside of me. I shook my head to release the cobwebs of this fantasy inside my brain. Love was not in the cards for me. I knew this, and I had accepted it. Falling in love when you lived on the streets was a recipe for disaster. My main priorities were keeping Myles alive, protecting our overall safety, and making sure I kept saving up for a car or a van to live in. I couldn't add the complication of loving someone to the mix.

"I'm gonna go pee. Wanna grab us some dessert?" I stood, and I saw his eyes drift to my ass and then pop back up to my face as he nodded.

"Sure, what do you want?"

"Surprise me." I flashed a quick grin at him and then went to the bathroom.

AFTER USING THE BATHROOM, I washed my hands and then tried to tame my curls. I noticed that my cheeks were flushed after the quick little sexcapade I had experienced in my mind. I smiled to myself as I stepped out into the long, dark hallway that led back to the party.

"You're so hot." A voice to my right startled me, and I looked over to find a scruffy-looking guy standing there. I didn't answer, just turned and kept walking. I felt a tug on my hair, and I almost fell backward. I quickly steadied myself against the wall, then turned to try and run but found myself caged in by his arms and the overwhelming stench of sweat.

"That was rude." He chuckled. "You could have said *thank you*."

"Fuck you," I spat.

"I'd like to fuck you, actually." He grinned, revealing a mouthful of unhealthy teeth.

"Stop it!" I pushed on him with all my might, but he didn't budge. What this guy lacked in height, he made up for in bulk. Why was no one coming down the hallway? I wondered as I tried to remain calm. I faintly heard that the music had been turned up, and I resigned myself for the worst as there was no way anyone would be able to hear me scream from here. He held me against the wall with one hand as he fumbled with his belt buckle with the other.

"If you're a good girl, I'll make it quick." He leered at me. I felt some spittle land on my chin, and I flinched.

"Don't touch me!" I tried to knee him in the dick, but he moved his pelvis back and then let go of himself to reach up and push me roughly against the wall. I felt the pain reverberate through my back and the side of my head as my body hit the wall behind me.

"You mother fucker!" I growled and again tried to push him away. He just laughed and began to pull himself out of his pants.

HAD it just been this morning that I couldn't believe it had been a whole year since I had gotten dicked down, and now here I was fighting with all my strength to avoid it? I felt some cries bubble up in my chest, but I didn't want him to steal my emotions while he stole my body from me, so I shuddered through the feelings silently as I braced myself for the pain I knew was imminent. I was about to close my eyes to avoid having to look at my attacker's disgusting face when, without warning, the man suddenly fell to the floor with a howl, and I heard Kian shout, "She told you no!"

I felt myself sag with relief as I watched Kian lean over my almost-rapist and pummel his face with his bare hands.

"She said don't touch me!" *Smack*. "She said stop." *Punch*. "So don't touch her." *Jab to the ribs*. "Don't even look at her!" *Kick*. The guy moaned and spat out some blood.

"Kian." I touched his arm, and he reeled on me—the look in his eyes was wild and unfocused.

"You said no, right?" His voice was a little shaky, his chest heaving from the beating he had just doled out.

"Yes." I nodded, my body trembling. "Yes, I said no. I said no." I gulped, and tears threatened to overflow as I felt adrenaline rushing through my body. He had saved me. I had never been saved before. I was always the one doing the saving, but I had never been on the receiving end of it. Without thinking, I threw myself into his arms. He staggered back against the other wall from the force of it but quickly recovered and stood steady as I wrapped my legs around his waist and attacked his mouth with mine.

J *essa is kissing me.* My body was very aware of this sudden change of events. My cock immediately stood at attention; my nerve endings were on fire in the best way possible, and my muscles strained as I held her up against me. My mind was having a harder time catching up.

JESSA IS KISSING ME. The thought rattled around chaotically in my brain. She tasted so good. There was a mix of the red wine she had drank earlier, some herb from the chicken at dinner, and a bite of something musky that I understood was wholly her. Our mouths danced, and her pillowy lips parted slightly as I swiped my tongue against the seam of them. Her body shifted in my hands. I had handfuls of her ass in my palms, her legs were tightly wound around me, and her breasts were smashed against my chest. I heard her give a breathy moan, and any cognitive thoughts I had left fled my brain.

THIS GIRL WAS SEX INCARNATE. Every small move her hips made, every kiss she gave me, every thud of her heartbeat against my pecs felt like foreplay to me. She had her hands up now, one gripping my beard, the other tangled in my hair. She groaned out something nonsensical, and I quieted her with another heated kiss. I nibbled on the sides of her lips, then slipped my tongue into her mouth, drawing out a sigh as she arched against me. I could feel her hips searching for me. I turned her around, pressing her to the wall, and rolled my hips against her pelvis. She gasped into my mouth, not breaking our desperate kiss, and grinded on me, creating the friction she so desperately sought.

SHE WAS WRITHING AGAINST ME, and I pulled away just slightly to watch as her eyes flew open, and she stared at me with glassy, half-lidded blue orbs. Her hair was a messy halo around her, and her chest was heaving. She grabbed my collar to pull me back toward her, and we fell into another round of shared breath, tongues exploring and lips fusing in lust. A few minutes later, I felt her hips shudder, and she gripped my shoulders hard as she broke the kiss, threw her head back, and moaned as she came.

I HAD MADE a lot of girls come in my day, but I had never seen something quite as captivating as Jessa orgasming. She had no reservations. She felt what she felt, and she expressed it. She wasn't timid at all. I had seen girls fake it, and I had seen them get embarrassed. I had seen them try to make noises they thought I would like. I had even been with girls who would not even let me try to get them off; they were just so focused on pleasing me. Jessa, on the other hand, had taken from me without inhibition. I had let her, and the outcome had been cataclysmic. It reminded me of watching the end of a symphony. The frisson of sensation brought on by the music, the soaring notes, the tender chorale, and the last cadence always overflowed me with emotion. The music was so intimate and heartbreaking, and watching her throw all of her fear into a leg-shaking orgasm had given me a similar feeling of triumph and ecstasy.

JESSA STIFFENED in my arms and whispered a quick, "Put me down," so I immediately loosened the grip I had on her body and let her slide down mine until her feet touched the ground. She withdrew a couple of steps back.

"Oh my god." She laughed, her cheeks flushed. "I am so sorry. I just attacked you, and I didn't even ask first. I don't even know if you're gay."

She was talking faster than normal, and she chuckled uncomfortably again, straightening her clothes and running her fingers through her hair. I gestured to the outline of my very hard penis behind my fly and scoffed. "You know I'm not gay."

She didn't answer; instead, she peered out from behind me, and I turned to see that the man I had torn off of her earlier had disappeared sometime, I presumed, during our frantic make out.

"You're not gay. Well, that's good."

She was rambling now, not even mentioning that the guy was gone. She was obviously processing what had just happened, and I gave her the space to do that as it dawned on me that I hadn't freaked out. This was the first person I had kissed since... and I liked it. I enjoyed it. In fact, I wanted more. I looked down at Jessa's swollen lips, her pebbled nipples that were obvious through her shirt, and the beard burn across her chin. I wanted so much more. I reached out to brush some hair from where it fell in her eyes, and she blinked up at me and said, "Dessert?" She didn't wait for me to respond; she just began walking down the hall, back to our table. I willed my dick to deflate and then followed after her feeling a little confused and a lot horny.

BACK AT THE TABLE, she dove right into the plate I had gotten for us to share. It was piled with chocolate biscotti, tiramisu, peach tarts, raspberry jam bomboloni, slices of torta della nonna, and a panna cotta custard dish that was beginning to sag from having sat for so long.

"So good," she said around a mouthful of cake. Her cheeks were flushed as she held out a spoonful of the tart for me to taste. Did I revert back to Kian without a last name, who didn't even want to come to this party, and take the spoon from her? Or did I stay in this moment of Kian, who now knows what her lips taste like and had seen her come from rubbing herself on me and take a bite from the spoon between her fingers?

SHE WATCHED me from under long lashes as if she could see my internal struggle, yet she didn't make a move one way or another to help me choose. I gave in to my more animalistic side, and I took the bite from her hand. As I did, I made sure my lips grazed her finger. She shivered as I sat down across from her. I wanted to fuck her so bad. The things I could do to her—we'd be up all night. I shifted in my seat as my deflating boner came back to full mast. Would she let me fuck her? I wanted to see her face again as she let the pleasure overtake her. I wanted to get her completely naked and have her panting and calling out my name. I wanted to suck on her clit while I had my finger in her pussy...

"Kian?"

My gaze shot up to meet hers.

"Hmm? Sorry, I drifted off for a sec. What did you say?" I wondered if I had been drooling into my beard as my imagination had run wild.

"Do you want some?" She pushed the plate over to me. She had left me half of each option.

"I want you," I blurted. Then I stuffed something, anything, from the plate into my mouth so I couldn't talk anymore. I wasn't used to having to try or ask. In my old life, women came on to me in droves. I actually liked this experience more. It felt real. Something I hadn't had a lot of.

She blinked. "I can give you one night."

My cock loved the sound of that. My brain winced as I knew one night would never be enough to stave off my already growing desperation for her. I nodded, hoping I didn't look too eager. I was almost thirty years old, for god's sake. Chill, bro.

I watched as she pulled out her phone to text someone. Myles, I presumed. Her love for him made me ache with an emotion I couldn't quite name. It was sad to watch her care for someone who was always on the precipice of self-destruction. *Like you?* My inner voice taunted me. I squelched the thought as she pushed her chair back from the table and stood. I took another gulp of the water in front of me and got up as well.

"My place has a brother in it; your place is a van, and I'm kind of loud." She bit her lip as she said it, and it made me want to grab her and kiss her senseless.

"I'll get a room," I said quickly. She cocked an eyebrow at me.

"Had another good fight?"

"I still have more left over from the last one," I muttered, "and I have more fights coming up."

"I'm coming to one," she announced as we stepped out into

the frigid night air. I winced at the thought of her in the crowd, watching my most depraved side emerge.

"We'll see." I motioned for her to switch to the other side of me so I could walk on the side closest to the street.

"Maybe I'll give you a second night if you let me." She gave me such a devilish little grin that I groaned out loud, which made her laugh. I faltered as I opened up the door for her. Did I have condoms? It had been so long since I needed one. I then remembered the three packets inside my wallet that someone had left in my guitar case the other day, along with his number and a twenty-dollar bill. I did not swing that way, but I was instantly grateful he had left them.

I drove impatiently to the hotel she now lived in and got us a room while she went to check on Myles and give him the cannolis and the dinner she had packed up for him. She met me back in the lobby, now wearing a pair of leggings and what looked like a tank top that was slightly revealed from under her partially opened coat.

"We're on the third floor," I told her, showing her the key card. I suddenly felt awkward. I had so many one-night stands under my belt. Most of them, I didn't even remember their names the next morning. I had never given it another thought, and it had never bothered me before. Yet here, with Jessa, I didn't relish the idea of waking up tomorrow and her not being there. She had made it very clear that all I was getting was one night, and somehow, I was the one feeling bad about it. I wanted her to know that I respected her—that I enjoyed our banter and her sarcastic, quick one-liners. I wanted her to know how beautiful I thought she was and that she could trust me with her body. Instead, I said nothing.

We stood in silence as the elevator beeped its way up to the third floor. We exited together and walked with hushed sounds of our shoes on the carpet to find the room. Once inside, Jessa surveyed the bed as she removed her coat. She was, in fact, wearing a tank top and from the looks of it, no bra. Her breasts hung heavy beneath the thin material, and I had to tear my eyes away from them in order to maintain somewhat of a respectable decorum. For the time being, anyway.

"I'm not into vanilla missionary," she suddenly announced. "I need a little spice, but not red room of pain bullshit." She snorted, and I recognized her reference to the popular book and movie. I had actually been at the premiere.

"But I need to be told what to do, held down a little, maybe choke me, slap my ass, make me be a good girl but don't degrade me. I'm not into that. Worship me, but force me to be worshiped. You understand?"

Her confidence in knowing exactly what she needed was making me so hot and bothered I was literally sweating.

"Good news, I'm not into vanilla missionary either." My voice sounded deeper than usual, and I wondered if even though she didn't know me well yet, could she tell how turned on I was by her?

"I told Myles I'd be back by three because I don't have work till the afternoon, so let's do this." She began to remove her pants, and for a moment, I felt cheap. She was using me, and she didn't even try to pretend that she wasn't. On one hand, I loved a progressive woman who wasn't afraid to enjoy sex and not feel like she had to be committed to a man to get it. On the other hand, I wanted to own her. I wanted her to be mine. I was going to give her something more from me than a few orgasms, this much I was sure of, and I wanted it to mean something. *Fuck*. I felt my inner voice get irritated. All I had to do was say no. Leave. Not busk near Kafe ever again. I could still save myself the heartache that I was sure would follow because this girl had the power to break me, and I couldn't fathom why, but I knew I was about to let her.

I UNBUTTONED my shirt and let it fall where I stood.

"Holy fucking shit."

I looked up at the sound of her awed tone. She was staring at my body as she came over to run a few fingers down my six-pack. This was the first time I would be with a woman since transforming my body, and I almost didn't know what to do with it. Almost.

"You like what you see, baby?" I summoned my old personality, and my cocky swag was back immediately.

"I do." She was almost panting as she ran another hand down my defined muscles and then stopped, cupping my package that was imprisoned behind my pants.

"Take these off."

She was bossy. I liked it. I stripped my pants off, leaving me only in my black boxers. I was hoping she wouldn't notice the expensive label on them. They weren't designer by any means, but a guy living in his van would probably not be caught dropping sixty-five dollars for three pairs of boxers.

"Are you clean?" she asked as I reached down to cup her ass, which was covered in a pair of plain cotton underwear. I nodded.

"Are you?"

"I haven't fucked anyone in a year, and yes, I'm always careful —never did it bare," she told me as I walked her backward till she was pressed to the wall with my body against hers.

"So you need this?" I tilted her chin up, forcing her to look at me.

Her eyes glinted in the dark room, and I felt her as well as heard her say, "I really do."

I bent down and slammed my mouth to hers. I felt her moan against my lips, and I forced them to part with my tongue, which danced against hers as I held her face still and made love to her mouth.

I felt her hands by my abs again, tracing them. I pulled away for a moment, gasping as her hands made their way into my boxers, and she grasped my cock with her fists.

"Umph." I leaned my head against the wall from the sheer beautiful torture her hands were inflicting on me. I had forgotten how small and soft a woman's hands were, and I was being strung out to my limit by hers.

With barely any effort, I lifted her in my arms and carried her to the bed. I was going to do this, right? I was finally going to do something that I wanted. I was going to be in the moment. I was going to continue to live my life and stop repressing myself in the prison I had created in my head. I squeezed my eyes shut, knowing that I had a hot, curvy, hopefully soaking-wet woman lying on the bed right under me, and here I was at the start of an existential crisis. I almost pulled back and said never mind when a hot, wet mouth enveloped my cock, and all rational thought fled my mind.

"Oooh fuck." My eyes flew open to look down at Jessa, who had dropped to her knees and was bobbing on my dick with so much enthusiasm that I was left breathless. I canted my hips, and she gagged. I felt myself edging into her throat, and she gagged again, longer this time, and I pulled back just as tears sprang in the corners of her eyes. She hummed around me, and I gathered handfuls of her hair, moving her head, forcing her to take me deeper. I touched the back of her throat again and then pulled out fully, followed by a string of saliva. I was left soaking and painfully hard. She wiped her hand across her mouth, her lips now puffy from the effort she had put into sucking me. She tilted her head to one side, her hair flowing around her body, and seemed to challenge me to make the next move.

"Take off your shirt," I demanded. She pulled off the thin tank top and didn't move, still on her knees. With her shoulders back, she let me peruse her body to my heart's content, showing me her breasts, which were full and tipped a rosy brown color. I took the tank top from her, placed her on the bed, and with a soft push to her chest bone, I had her lie back on the pillow for me.

"Give me your hands," I urged. She immediately held them out to me, watching me curiously. I tied her tank top around her wrists and then lifted them above her head.

"Don't move."

She wiggled her ass against the bed but otherwise stayed still. I put my knees on either side of her chest and shoved my cock back into her mouth.

"Mmph." She made a sound of protest but then recovered from the surprise of my sudden movement and began to suck me. She used her teeth gently on the crown of my dick, and I rewarded her with a groan. She licked up the underside of it as much as she could without full range of movement and then took me back into her mouth fully, opening her throat and letting me fuck her until she gagged again.

I pulled out and slapped her lips with the head of my dick and said, "That's the sexiest sound I've ever heard you make."

She answered by kissing the slit, gathering up the precum that had gathered there. I took my finger and pushed the liquid into her mouth.

"Swallow it," I commanded. She did, and I leaned down to kiss her as I made my way down her body and weighed her breasts in my hands. She was so confident in every area, yet I knew compliments could never be bad, so I said, "Your body is so sexy," as I took her nipple into my mouth. I bit it gently to the point of slight discomfort and then made it better with the swipe of my tongue. She mewled beneath me as I played with her nipple with my fingers. Then I turned to her other breast and nipped my way around her areola until I sucked the whole nipple into my mouth. Her back arched, and she moaned loudly.

"Say my name." I popped off her nipple, leaving it wet and shiny. She shook her head.

"Not yet."

"Not yet?" I kneaded her breast in one hand as I pressed the other one to her ribs, holding her still while I made my way down her body, kissing a trail to her cotton underwear that had a dark wet spot by the crotch.

"Not till you make me scream," she told me slyly.

"Challenge accepted." I usually ripped a girl's underwear off of her, but I was aware that Jessa was limited in her options, so I gently tugged them down her thighs, sniffed the crotch, and then dropped them off the side of the bed.

She continued to watch me but didn't comment. Her thighs could smother me. I ran a hand down one and then slapped it, loving the movement it made as it jiggled from my touch. Girls with no meat on their bones could never catch my attention after this. Not after I had experienced this body with some ripples and dimples on her thighs leading up to her pussy; it was like my own personal playground.

I lowered myself between her legs as I kissed around her belly button, circling her tapered waist between my hands. I moved lower, kissing her pelvic bone and nipping at her hip. She yelped as I licked it. Then I blew on her, noticing that she had been shaved bare, and she shivered, moving her hips as if she could catch my mouth somehow.

"I said don't move," I reminded her. She whimpered as I placed a hand on her pelvis, pushing her into the bed, holding her still, and then I descended onto her pussy like a man starved. Which I was. For her and only her.

His warm mouth enveloped me as he licked my clit and pulled it between his lips. Then he flattened his tongue against it, making moans as he ate me. I was so wet it was trickling into my ass and getting all over his beard. I leaned up to watch him eat me like I was his last meal, but he smacked my stomach lightly, forcing me to lie back down. The sight of his face between my legs was going to be burned in my mind for a very long time.

He moved lower, licking my asshole for a moment, and then swiped his tongue all the way back up to my clit. He did this a few times as he smacked me gently around my pelvis, up my thighs, and across my breasts. I started to feel the rumblings of an orgasm, and I panted, "I'm gonna come!" Suddenly, he pulled away. I lifted my shoulders off the bed to look at him.

"Why'd you stop?" I demanded. I could feel the orgasm slip away, and I fell back onto the bed, feeling let down. Kian chuckled against my leg, where he turned his head and bit the inside of my thigh. He blew some warm air onto my entrance and then stuck his tongue inside of me, lapping at my juices. He flattened his tongue and rubbed it all over my clit as a finger made circles around the puckered entrance of my ass. I wanted to grab his hair, but he had told me not to move, so I kept my hands where they were and lifted my pelvis off the bed, seeking more pressure from his mouth. He pulled his mouth off of me and then spit on my swollen flesh. I didn't know I could grow more turned on, but I did.

"Make me come," I keened. He sucked on my clit, and I felt the wave of an orgasm approaching again. This time, I didn't say anything to warn him that it was happening, but he still knew, and he pulled off of me just in time.

I let out a frustrated "Fuck!" which made him chuckle again. This went on for what felt like an eternity. Every touch was driving me crazy because I just wanted to come so bad, and he was edging me till he could feel my thighs begin to shake, and then he'd pull away only to rev me up all over again. I felt his thick finger push its way into my pussy, and my hips came off the bed as he suckled my clit, making loud wet sounds.

"Let me come," I pleaded. I was on fire, inside and out. My nerve endings were shot—frizzled out from being brought to the edge so many times but not being allowed to go over it.

"Ask nicely." He growled against my lips and pulled back, watching his finger being slurped up into my pussy, shiny with my essence.

"Please, please let me come." I was sobbing now, begging, and my thighs were shaking from the movements he was making with his fingers inside of me. He pulled his fingers out, gripped my thighs, pulling me even further apart, and dove back in, making an O formation with his mouth and sucking my clit inside. The suction and him holding the lower part of my body down so I literally couldn't move blew me apart. My orgasm barreled through me, causing all of my muscles to tighten up and then release. The pleasure over-whelmed my system, and I squeezed my eyes shut as I let myself experience it fully. *Say my name,* I remembered him telling me.

"Kian. Kian," I gasped out as my orgasm kept going, and he didn't stop sucking me. I lowered my tied hands and held his head there as I finally came down from what had to be the best orgasm of my entire existence.

He looked up at me, a very satisfied gleam in his eye. "You made a mess. Come here and clean it up." He was pointing to his face. I shivered but quickly listened and got up on my knees as he loosened the tank top from my wrists. He sat up and I took his face in my hands and kissed him, tasting my flavor in his mouth. He moaned against my lips, and then I kissed my way around his beard, his cheeks, and down his neck, cleaning up like he had told me to.

"Face the headboard and hold onto it." His dominating tone was keeping me slick and wanting. He got up off the bed, pulling his boxers the rest of the way down his legs and leaving them on the floor as he went to get his wallet from his pants pocket. The view was spectacular. His back was corded with muscle and covered with tattoos, and his strong arms also had swirls of ink on them. His defined pecs were bare, but they were their own form of art. His etched stomach muscles led to his cock, which stuck out proudly from his thatch of pubic hair.

HE FALTERED as he opened his wallet, and I saw that same look on his face that I had seen earlier before I had sucked his cock. I turned and placed my hands on the headboard, shaking my ass slightly, looking over my shoulder, and asked innocently, "Like this?"

He looked up at me and away from whatever was putting

that compromised look on his face and dropped the wallet back onto his pants as he almost prowled back to me.

"Good listening." He rewarded me with a slap on my ass. I heard him rip open the condom, and the mattress shifted a little as he climbed onto it.

"I'm going to fuck you, and I'm going to fuck you hard. If you need me to slow down, stop, or be softer with you, let me know. If you don't say anything, I'm going to assume you're okay with it." His mouth was right by my ear, and the husk in his tone and the forewarning of his words drenched me.

"Do your worst, music man," I whispered back at him.

He clenched my hips in a bruising grip, and in one sure stroke, he slammed into me from behind. I bumped up against the headboard and had to catch my breath as he practically hit my cervix. My body clenched at the invasion, and I let out a gasp. He pulled back out, and as he slammed back in, he bit my shoulder. Hard.

Then he forced me to stay upright by holding his arm across my chest, and he fucked me like that, holding me still as he rutted into me. He was breathing heavily in my ear, saying things like, "You're so tight. Your pussy tasted so good. God, your body is hot. Fucking take me, Jessamine. Can you come again like this?"

Suddenly, he let go, and I fell forward, catching myself before my face hit the pillow. He bent over me, continuing to fuck me, never missing a beat. He felt bigger this way, and I moaned. He stuck his fingers in my mouth, holding himself up with one arm.

"Suck," he demanded, biting my earlobe. I sucked, the sensations taking over my body again. He removed his fingers, reached down, and strummed my clit. I exploded. I felt myself grow wetter, and I was certain he could feel me leaking all over his thighs. He pulled out, holding onto the condom, and rolled me onto my back. Then he pushed my legs up so my knees were by my chest, and my pussy was raised and exposed for him.

"Yesss," he hissed. "Hold your legs for me like a good girl."

I immediately responded and held onto my legs with shaking arms. He pushed back into me, and I groaned, feeling overly sensitive as I recovered from my second orgasm. He was thrusting into me, hitting my G-spot as he reached down and squeezed the sides of my neck.

My pulse throbbed beneath his fingers, and I took a deep breath in as he squeezed a little harder. Then he let go and slapped the skin right above my clit, once, twice, three times. I felt my eyes get heavy as pleasure began to assault me again, and he said roughly, "Look at me when you come. Don't you dare close your eyes, Jessamine."

The *Jessamine* detonated me. With no clitoral stimulation, I came again, staring at him as I moaned and groaned and panted out his name.

"Kian. I can't..."

He pinched my clit, sending another shockwave through me.

"Tell me you like it." He gritted through clenched teeth. His hips were snapping against me.

"It's so good. It's so good," I cried as he finally came. He roared with the effort of his orgasm. Sweat was gathering at his temples, some of his hair had come loose around his face, and his eyes were wild with our shared pleasure. He pulled out, letting my legs, which were numb at this point, down gently onto the bed. Then he flopped down on his back, letting out a satisfied sigh.

"Holy fuck."

I looked over at him, and he had a triumphant smile on his face. I knew exactly what he was feeling because I had never experienced sex like this. I had slept with men who bossed me around or held me down, and most of the time, it had been good. But nothing had ever felt like this. This current of my energy flowing to him allowed him to somehow know what I wanted before I even knew. The subtle knowledge that he was in charge but he didn't have to prove it by being an asshole was so hot for me. I also knew I had to leave. My one-night rule was not something I could break. Not with everything else I had to focus on. But a small nap wouldn't hurt was the last thing I thought as I drifted off to sleep.

I WOKE up to find Kian wrapped around me, his legs caging mine, his arm protectively across my chest, and his beard tickling my neck. The light was on in the bathroom, and I could see the tattoos on his arm in the glow. I shifted slightly so I could get a better view. Around his wrist was a staff drawn in black ink, on the left was a black treble clef, and across the rest of the staff were splats of watercolor in blues, pinks, and purple ink that turned into birds in flight along the edges. It was such a delicate choice for such a strong, dominant man.

I looked further up his forearm, where another fine-line tattoo was etched. It was a strand of DNA that was covered in music notes. At the bottom of the strand was an anchor, and at the top was the arrow from a compass. Across his bicep was a fine-line guitar, shaded in some areas to look like the ink had bled off the sides of the drawing. On one side, near the bottom of the guitar, there was half a fingerprint, and at the top were what looked like furls of smoke. These were not cheap tattoos; this much I knew. Who was this man and how did he have such expensive, precise skin art when he also lived in his van? Kian shifted next to me, and I turned to find him watching me.

"Fuck me one more time before I go," I whispered.

He did.

And then I left.

I took the elevator of shame down to the first floor, pausing to wave at the girl at the front desk, who waved back with a knowing look on her face. I tried to be quiet as I opened the door to our room, but Myles sat up from where he was lying under a blanket on the couch as I shut the door.

"What time is it?" he murmured.

"Three a.m.," I whispered. "Sorry I woke you."

He stood, wrapped up in the blanket.

"I tried to stay up for you, but I got tired."

"You didn't have to stay up for me, My."

"I've never been away from you for the night, Jessa. I don't even know how to function without you. I know I'm a loser who doesn't work and is always high..." He paused and looked away from me. "I just, I couldn't go to bed until I knew you were home safe." He leaned over, kissed my temple, and then went into his room, shutting the door behind him.

I stood there in the dark hallway for a moment, trying to process what my brother had just said to me. I sincerely hoped that he didn't really think I saw him as a loser because I most definitely didn't. I didn't mind taking care of him one bit. If people looked at me like I enabled him, then so be it. In the family Al-Anon meetings I went to sometimes, they talked about forcing your addict to hit rock bottom. Some members spoke about kicking their addict out. Cutting off all contact. Shunning them out of their life until they chose sobriety. I absolutely refused to ever even consider treating my brother like that. That behavior sounded like hating the addict to me. Where was the compassion and empathy?

I had read an article that 76 percent of addicts had experienced trauma exposure, and 59 percent were diagnosed with PTSD. My brother had both.

So I would take care of him happily, even if it meant not always having the things I wanted. Like staying asleep in Kian's arms. Like exploring where this attraction could take us. Or even admitting to myself how much I liked what we had done tonight. It had to be one night. One amazing, explosive, leg-trembling night. It was all I could afford right now. Myles needed me, and I had promised my mom I would take care of him. I was a lot of things, but a liar was not one of them, and I would be there for him, no matter what.

THE NEXT MORNING, I woke up sore in all the right places. I stretched, feeling the muscles in my legs protest, and I had a flashback of Kian lying behind me, both of us still on our sides, holding my leg up as he found my entrance and pounded into me from behind. My toes curled up at the memory and I let myself revel in it for a second before I shook myself free and sat up. I smelled like sex, and I needed to shower before work.

I looked at my phone and saw that it was already ten a.m. I opened up a text from Myles that said he had gone to a meeting, and he was going to stop at the local clinic afterward to see if they had any openings with his previous therapist. I had hope that this time he could see sobriety through, but I didn't let myself get excited because I had seen him do this before. I understood the cycle because I knew how damaging this disease was, and I witnessed how tightly addiction kept its grip on its victims. When it came to him trying again, I kept a healthy mix of hope and realism inside of me at all times.

I texted Myles back to say that I was proud of him, and then I headed to the shower. I dreaded the day when whatever magical luck had us in this room ran out because taking a warm shower without having to get dressed, go to the gym, and then shower with other people in the stalls on either side of you was just glorious. Before pulling my hair up under a shower cap, I sprayed in a leave-in conditioner that I had found in the dollar store. I planned to let it sit in my hair during my shower to try to rehydrate my curls, as my hair hated the cold weather.

Once under the water, I quickly ran a razor over my body. I found that I had a bruise on the inside of my thigh, a bite mark on my breast, and a small hickey on my neck. I knew Kian hadn't gotten out unscathed either because the second time we had fucked, my hands were not tied, and at one point, I had scratched my fingernails down his back. I rinsed the body wash off and then got out of the shower to try to put together a cute outfit out of my meager clothing choices. I didn't usually care that much what I looked like, but today, the thought of seeing my sexy busker made me want to try.

No, not *my* sexy busker. He was no one. He had to stay no one. Myles needed me, I reminded myself as I pulled on the bodysuit I usually wore under things to keep warm. Today, I wore it as a shirt because it was tight and showed off every curve. Then I pulled on my dark-wash cargo jeans. I didn't own any light-colored jeans as they weren't allowed in the dress code for work, and since I spent the majority of my time there, it didn't make sense to spend money on something that I couldn't wear that often.

As my hair was air-drying from the leave-in conditioner, I spent some extra time on my makeup, which consisted of concealer for the circles under my eyes, some blush that showed up well on my tan skin tone, and mascara to lengthen my lashes.

Today, I added a bit of eyeliner that I had bought from the dollar store and had never used before and a swipe of tinted lip balm.

I checked the fridge and ate a breakfast of cold gnocchi and chicken cutlets from the leftovers I had brought Myles. Then I checked to see if my direct deposit had cleared, which it had, so I logged into my account to pay for our phone bills and then calculated how much I could use for food and how much I had left to put away for a van. Did I even need a van anymore if I had this room? Too many adult decisions for one day.

I logged out of my bank account and pulled on my coat. My shift was from twelve p.m to eight p.m. today, and I wanted to stop at the gas station for a pack of cigarettes before heading into work, so I had to leave now if I were to get there on time. I had decided that I was going to act like my regular self with Kian. He knew it was a one-time thing. Just some fun between two consenting adults, and now we had to go back to being the coffee girl and the music man. It's just how it had to be.

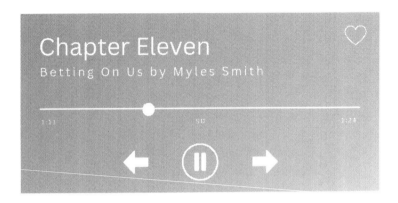

I hadn't slept in a proper bed in over a year, and yet, without her next to me, I tossed and turned for the rest of the night. At eight a.m., I finally called it quits and went down to the hotel's gym, where I ran six miles on the treadmill and then lifted weights for an hour. When I had sufficiently punished my body, I went back upstairs and took a shower. Then I grabbed my keys, my wallet, and my coat and went back down to check out.

I could stay in a room for as long as I wanted. I could even rent an apartment somewhere, but that meant they would definitely find me. That was if they hadn't already. I took advantage of the continental breakfast the hotel offered, and as I sat eating a plate full of scrambled eggs, waffles, bacon, and cut-up fruit, I took my phone out of my zippered coat pocket and connected it to the WiFi. Sure enough, a text had come in the day after I had used my card to get Jessa the hotel room. It was from my manager, and it said, "I swear to god, if you don't tell me that was you using your card and not someone who stole it off your body that was dumped somewhere, I am going to call the police. Jace, this is bullshit. I get it. You're grieving, and I'm so sorry, but how long are you going to just avoid your life?"

Fucking Gordon, I thought to myself. He had always been an asshole—an asshole I loved and appreciated. I typed back a quick, "It was me. Don't call the police, you idiot. And don't tell the boys either. Leave me alone. I need more time."

Three seconds later, I got back a text that read "Too late," which made my heart kick up a notch.

"What do you mean?" I asked him.

"I told the boys that you used your card, but I didn't tell them where."

I felt the eggs I had just swallowed fighting to come back up. I took a long sip of water to wash them down. If the boys knew what state I was in, they would stop at nothing to find me, and then I would lose the slice of peace and quiet that I had built here. Maybe it was time to move on so not even Gordon would know where I was. The thought of leaving so no one could find me was easy, but the thought of leaving and never seeing Jessa again stung a little more than I liked to admit.

My phone buzzed with another text from my cranky manager. "Get a phone number so I don't have to wait for your WiFi to kick in every time I need to talk to you, and I'll stall them for a bit."

I sent him back a "Fuck you" text, but he knew he had won.

I DID two stupid things before going to play music. I went to a wireless store and activated my phone, and I went back to Kafe to busk instead of choosing from multiple other suitable locations. I knew I liked to torture myself; that much was clear from my sessions in the gym and my fascination with boxing without my gloves on, but watching Jessa interact with customers with her boobs bobbing behind her green apron was a new form of abuse.

I played my heartbreak playlist today, which always got me a lot of tips and usually had multiple women hitting on me. Today was no exception.

So far, I had gotten through "Breakeven" by The Script, "Let Her Go" by Passenger, "Skinny Love" by Bon Iver, "Free Fallin'" by Tom Petty, and "Everybody Hurts" by R.E.M. I was singing "Fix You" by Coldplay when Jessa stepped out for her break. I knew the minute she saw me see her, just like the moment when we first met.

She leaned back against the brick wall behind her and lit up her cigarette. As she sucked desperately on her dopamine stick, I continued to sing.

She had her hair down today, and half of her curls fell over her face as she curled over her cigarette, blowing out smoke every so often. She always seemed so perturbed that she was smoking. She did it with jerking movements and never took the time to savor the experience—not like how she drank her coffee or how she had kissed me. No, she smoked like she was mad that the nicotine tempted her day in and day out. I wondered if she knew how much she hated it.

I completed the song just as she finished smoking. The crowd around me dispersed, and she walked toward me holding two cups.

"This is cold," I said as she handed me the latte.

"It is." She nodded.

"It's cold outside," I told her, as if she couldn't feel it.

"It is cold outside." She hummed "Baby, It's Cold Outside" as she took a sip of her drink. I followed suit and was hit with a taste so delicious that I couldn't put my finger on.

"This tastes like Christmas." I realized as I wiped the cold foam off my lip and took another gulp.

"It should." She giggled. "It's an eggnog fluff cold brew."

I waited for her to tell me how she made it, just like she always did.

"It's a simple cold brew base. Then, you add in four pumps of toasted white mocha sauce and one pump of cinnamon dolce syrup. The kicker is adding eggnog into the cold foam and sprinkling on cinnamon dolce topping." She did a little dance as she drank more of her coffee.

"I will keep that in mind when I order my coffee at another coffee shop," I teased her. Her eyes widened, and she stomped her foot.

"You wouldn't dare cheat on me."

We both fell silent at the other ways what she just said could be interpreted.

"Are you gonna answer my questions today?" She just smoothly changed the subject. I didn't think that she'd be leading the conversation in the direction of what happened last night any time soon, so I just nodded, fiddling with the strings on my guitar.

"Where are you from originally?"

I considered lying for a brief moment before I told her the truth.

"California."

Her eyes lit up.

"I've always wanted to live there!"

"Well, why don't you? It's cold here, which kinda sucks."

"I can't leave Myles, and it would be too hard to move him there."

I nodded, realizing more and more how much her life and her choices were so tightly wound up in Myles and his addiction.

"Dogs or cats?"

"Definitely dogs," I confirmed. She seemed satisfied with my answers because she began to walk away without saying goodbye.

"Hey," I called after her. She turned. I lifted my phone up.

"Can I get your number?"

She walked back closer to me.

"You have a phone?" She seemed surprised.

"I reactivated my phone today." I shrugged it off like it wasn't a big deal.

She took my phone and keyed her number in under the name "Coffee Girl." I called her and hung up when I saw my number flash across her screen. She swiped into her phone and saved it in her contacts as "Music Man."

"Use it if you need it," I told her.

She grinned, showing me her dimple, and said, "I've never really needed anything, music man."

It felt like she believed that.

I LOOKED DOWN at my drink to see if she had left me a note. She had and it said, "I like your tattoos." I had to fight a smile when I read it. I knew she had said just one night. I had heard it, and I wouldn't fight her on it either, but her note gave me hope that maybe eventually she would change her mind.

I had so many more things that I could do to her. So many more ways to make her come. So many more sounds I wanted to drag out of her. Having her so close to me just a moment ago without touching her had been torture. I sighed as the front of my pants swelled, and I placed my guitar strategically in front of me to hide it until I could get myself under control. Now that I knew what she sounded like when she came. Now that I was aware of what she tasted like. Now that I could summon up the memory of her curves below mine, I had a feeling my body would be on constant alert around her from now on. The experience we had shared last night was not one I could ever erase from my memory.

NOW THAT MY phone was reactivated and I had logged into all of my apps, my old messages and photos had downloaded onto my phone. Just like I feared they would. I had packed up my guitar, mic, and speaker for the night and had driven to the gym, where I sat outside in the parking lot. Before I could chicken out, I pressed play on one of the voice notes she had sent me. Her voice filled my van, and I clenched the steering wheel as pain erupted in my chest.

"Hi, Jacey baby," she sing-songed. "Come home. I have a surprise for you."

The voice note was followed by a selfie. Her blonde hair gently cradled around her face, her deep brown eyes and long lashes filled the screen. I remembered exactly what she had told me that night.

"Fuck," I yelled to the empty air. "Fuck," I whimpered. The grief clawed its way up my throat, threatening to choke me. Why isn't it getting better? I thought despondently. I am going to be broken over this forever.

I LET it all out at the gym. My muscles screamed from having already been used during my workout this morning, but the truth was that I reveled in the pain. The pain reminded me of all I had lost, and it was a way for me to quantify the emotional agony. I turned it into aching tendons, screaming quads, and busted knuckles. I left the tears and the memories as sweat on the gym floor.

Grief was precisely as bad as people imagined it to be before they experienced it. The inspirational quotes and songs liked to talk about grief getting better, and some days, it did feel less heavy, and that was when I desperately tried to hold onto it. Yet some days, most days, there was nothing that could be done to make me feel better. In those moments, it felt like there was no happily ever after in store for me. What was lost wasn't coming back; that was the fact. It couldn't be fixed so I had to carry it for the rest of my life. I couldn't move on from it. No matter how much Gordon wanted me to. No matter how much the boys needed me to. This is who I was now. Grief was a part of me. It had been absorbed into my bones.

I CRIED IN THE SHOWER, letting the tears wash away with the water. My arms protested with every move I made as I washed my hair and cleaned my body. I had put myself through the wringer tonight. My muscles were swollen, and the veins in my arms were prominent. I was emotionally wrung out, so all I focused on was that I had to eat and needed to sleep. Maybe tomorrow will be a better day. The thought landed flat, but I appreciated my brain's effort.

Robotically, through muscle memory, I dried off, pulled my hair into a low bun, oiled my beard, pulled on my sweats, and made my way to my van. Once I was settled in for the night, I opened three cans of tuna, mixed it with two packets of mayo in a plastic bowl, and ate it with six rice cakes. It was a pathetic attempt at a proper dinner, but it was a good post-workout meal due to the protein and carb content. I fell asleep, without brushing my teeth, alone in the parking lot of my gym. The stark difference between tonight and last night was painfully obvious.

I WOKE up around four a.m. with new music reverberating in my head. I was used to this, and the only way to shut it off was to write it down, turn it into a song, and then my mind would quiet, and I would be able to fall back to sleep. I strummed, then stopped to write. I hummed the tune, then changed it. I played the new notes on the guitar again, and then once I had a fully-formed song, I scratched most of the words out, re-formatted the lyrics, got angry, and threw the whole thing out. Then I started again, completely fresh. The sun was coming up, and the birds were chirping when I finally finished. I was satisfied with what I had created so far. I had written the music and a chorus. I set up my phone and quickly recorded myself playing it one time, and then, utterly exhausted, I laid the song on top of my guitar, and I fell into a deep, uninterrupted sleep.

One day, all you'll have of me
Is my voice
A photo
A memory
And you'll have to make a choice
(My love, My love)
One day, you'll listen to my sound
And me-mo-ries will be found
But you need to promise me
That you'll stop holding on
It has been way too long
And I don't want to stay alive
In you through pain
I'd rather you have nothing left
Than the feeling of a knife in your chest
If the memory of me
Is not making you happy
Then let me drift

Give me a kiss
(Baby, Baby)
And let me drift

I WOKE UP HOURS LATER, my stomach growling and my bladder protesting. Bleary-eyed, I rubbed the sleep out of my eyes, sat up, and yawned and stretched. I had slept until the sun was fully in the sky. I really needed this—a day to just check out and fully feel the pain. I turned my phone to check what time it was and saw, with a flip-flop feeling in my stomach, that I had a text from the boys. It read, "Jace, this is so good. Come home. We'll record it. We miss you. We love you. Come back to us. Where are you, Jace? We're worried."

Frantically, I scrolled up to see what they were talking about. Apparently, in my delusion of being half asleep and completely wrecked from my emotional breakdown last night, I had taken the recording of myself playing and singing the new song and sent it to my old group chat.

I rested my head in my hands, a massive headache threatening to overwhelm all of my senses. I had officially reached my breaking point. Maybe it was time to return. To shed this grief and go back to what I knew best. Creating music. Being around the people who cared about me and stop half existing.

I was no one here, and maybe that wasn't a good thing anymore. I had loved it. I had craved the anonymity—needed it —but maybe that wasn't what I was supposed to be doing anymore. It was just keeping me miserable. My whole goal in disappearing had been to heal and to become someone physically who would never let what happened ever happen again. To punish myself for letting it happen in the first place, but maybe I had paid my penance. Maybe I could be free. Maybe writing that song had finally started my healing.

INSTEAD OF IGNORING their texts like I always did, I finally texted the group chat back. "I'll be in touch soon. Give me a little longer." I had made my decision. I had a little bit more time left of being Kian, the busker. A little more time left to receive coffee cups with notes on them. A little more time left till one last fight, and then I would go back to who I had been. Who I was destined to be.

JACE KIAN WEST.

I wished I were stronger, but I wasn't. I must have looked out the window at work close to fifty times throughout my entire shift on Sunday, and Kian never showed. His number on my phone was burning a hole in my pocket, but I refused to text him. I did not need him or anyone for that matter. He was probably playing music in another location in my little town, and that was okay.

It was okay and normal not to see him every day. Having sex one time did not mean anything. Not at all. My brain was in one hundred percent agreement with me. I was a strong, independent woman. I would be perfectly fine if he never showed up ever again. But my heart was a little sad. I had begun to enjoy our ten-minute interactions. I liked leaving him little notes on the cups of coffee that I made him. I looked forward to hearing what song he had chosen for me. I got a kick out of asking him two questions a day and learning tiny bits of information about him. Meeting him had broken up the monotony of my life. It gave me a little something extra to look forward to in the mornings. It had stretched me creatively by coming up with unique drinks for him. It had given me something more to think about besides what I needed to do for daily survival.

I took a deep breath in as it dawned on me that since I had met him, I had been given the gift of feeling something akin to normalcy, even if was just for a moment. Even if he never came back. I was so grateful for that gift. A new perspective. The knowledge that I was desirable as a human being and not just for a quick fuck behind a tent because we both wanted to come. It was nice to feel like he had enjoyed our little interactions as well. It made me feel whole in a way I didn't even know I needed. I was thankful to the universe for giving me that.

"Are you off tomorrow?" Eric broke me out of my intense train of thought as he moved behind me to grab the tea essence I had just made. I nodded.

"Yes." We were allowed to work six days straight, and then we were required to take a day break. I used to hate my day off because, in the past, it just meant more time in my cold tent, but now I had to figure out how to actually exist as a human again. Did I sleep in? Did I do my laundry? Did I watch TV? Did I go to the library? There were so many options that didn't involve me spending money but also required me to learn to do something out of the pure joy of doing it.

"Where's your boyfriend?" Eric asked, peering out the very same shop window I had been looking through all day.

"He's not my boyfriend." I scoffed. Eric laughed.

"Okay."

I stuck my tongue out at him.

"I've seen the way he looks at you." Eric wiped down the counters as I took off my apron.

"And how does he look at me?" I pretended to be chill about it, but my heart rate had picked up slightly as I waited for my boss to respond.

"He looks at you like everyone pisses him off but you."

That made me falter as I discarded the drink I had made Kian earlier today. Eric's words made me feel a little warm inside. I knew my self-worth. I didn't have daddy issues, even though I probably should. I had received so much love from my mother. I had my brother, who adored me. I even fully loved myself. I was confident in who I was, and I never felt like I needed more than that to edify my worth, yet somehow, what Eric said filled a little hole inside my heart that I wasn't even aware needed filling. I put on my coat and smiled back at him.

"Thank you," I said, uncharacteristically gentle in my tone.

"You're welcome." He nodded at me as I left. Today may have been disappointing with Kian never showing up but it had still been a good day after all.

THE WALK HOME WAS FREEZING. The wind had picked up, and I huddled inside my coat as I walked as fast as I could back to the hotel. I was waiting to cross the busy intersection when I heard my name. I looked up, my eyes tearing up from the cold and there was Kian in his van, waving at me.

"Get in," he called. He didn't have to tell me twice. I would jump at any opportunity to get out of these cold gusts and into my room faster.

"Hi," he said as I climbed into the passenger seat and buckled myself.

"It's fucking freezing," I responded, and he laughed.

"What?" I asked as he pulled back onto the road.

He shrugged. "You're just funny."

"'Cause I didn't say hi back?" I grinned, and he nodded.

"Hi," I said with a sassy tone. His lips twitched, but he didn't say anything. I watched his profile as he drove, and I wondered how someone could possibly be this hot and also be real.

"I hit the gym early, so I'm free for the night and I'm kind of in the mood to watch a movie," he told me as he pulled into the parking lot of the hotel. I raised an eyebrow at him.

"I even got snacks."

"You want to have a movie night with me?" I asked.

"You don't?" he retorted.

"I mean, I have the day off tomorrow, so I can stay up late, but I don't think I've ever had a movie night." I unbuckled as he turned off the van.

"That's basically illegal. How are you twenty-five and never had a movie night?"

I didn't know who this casual, joking-around Kian was, but I didn't mind it at all.

"I'm almost twenty-six," I corrected him.

"When's your birthday?" he asked.

"February twenty-fourth."

"That's pretty soon." He sounded excited. "We'll have a party!"

"I don't need a party," I protested.

"Nonsense. Everyone needs a party." He came around to my side of the van to get the bag of snacks and open my door. I ignored the hand that he held out for me and climbed down myself, which earned me a snort.

"Okay, don't touch me," he joked.

"I won't," I said with an insolent wink. I could have sworn he moaned under his breath.

"My?" I called as I opened the door. There was no answer. Immediately, my adrenaline began to thrum in my veins. Was this the moment I would find him? Was this it? I braced myself as I opened the door to his room and breathed a sigh of relief when I heard the shower going in his bathroom and the sounds of him singing over the water. The relief was obvious on my face as I turned around to find Kian watching me with a knowing look.

"What's wrong?" he asked softly.

"I'm afraid every single day and every single night that one day I am going to find him..." I couldn't finish my sentence as I suddenly felt like I was holding back tears. I wasn't afraid of crying and didn't see it as a weakness. I just didn't want to cry about it right now because crying made the reality that his addiction may take him from me one day feel all that more real.

"That's a heavy burden to carry alone." Kian sounded sad for me, but he didn't make a move to crowd my personal space. He just stood there in the entryway, holding his grocery bag, studying me.

"It is," I admitted. "But right now, he's okay."

I shut down the conversation by taking off my coat and going into my room, calling to him, "I'll be right out." I changed into sweatpants and a sweatshirt and came back out to find Kian putting a bag of popcorn into the microwave. He had also brought licorice, M&M's, potato chips, cookies, beef jerky, and a bottle of vodka.

"Cookies and vodka?" I laughed as I sat down on the couch.

"Why not?" he protested. "It's an adult movie night, so we have adult beverages."

When the microwave beeped, he took the popcorn out and took two of the glasses provided by the hotel and brought them over to the coffee table. He poured each of us a generous serving of vodka mixed with some lime-flavored seltzer and opened the popcorn bag as the smell of melted butter wafted over to me.

"Oh hi," Myles said as he walked out of his room, hair wet from his shower.

"Hi." I grinned at him. "Want to watch a movie with us?"

"I would, but I have a meeting at seven a.m., so I'm gonna hit the sack, but I'll take some licorice." He came over and stuck a piece in his mouth.

"A meeting?" Kian sounded hopeful.

"I am about thirty-six hours sober." Myles sounded so proud of himself. He looked a little worse for wear, as his withdrawals had probably started this afternoon. He was looking a little pale, and the circles under his eyes were more pronounced.

"Bro!" Kian patted my brother on the back, which for him was basically a full-on hug. "I am so proud of you."

Myles grinned at him.

"Thank you," he said softly.

"If you need a ride to a meeting, let me know," Kian offered. "Take some more licorice. The sugar will help. I think."

Myles took another piece and then blew me a kiss.

"Love ya."

"I love you more."

My eyes were wet from Kian's enthusiastic support of my brother's journey.

"Are you crying?" Kian peered at me as I wiped my eyes.

"No." I denied it.

"Mmm hmm."

He turned the TV on and scrolled to look at our movie choices. I bit the ends off of a piece of licorice and used it as a straw to take a swig of my vodka.

"Ooh, make me one," Kian exclaimed when he saw my straw.

I bit the ends off of another vine of candy and stuck it in his cup. He placed his lips on it and took a drink. I had to look away because it was such a simple act, but it was turning me on. Then he poured the M&M's into the bag of popcorn and shook it.

"What are you doing? You're messing up the popcorn." I wrinkled my nose in disgust.

"It's the best way to eat popcorn. Here." Kian held out a

handful. I ate it from his hand, noting the way his breath hitched as my mouth got close to his thumb.

"Mmm, I get it." I licked my lips, liking how the salt of the popcorn and the sweet crunch of the M&M's tasted together.

"Don't question the popcorn master," Kian said playfully. I raised my hands in defeat.

"Never again."

He laughed and then scrolled on the TV.

"Okay, let's see what our choices are. We've got *Harry Potter*, *The Breakfast Club*, *Mean Girls*, or *Good Will Hunting*."

"I vote *Good Will Hunting*!" I vaguely recalled watching it as a kid, and I remembered loving it.

"Matt Damon it is." Kian selected the movie and leaned back on the couch, popping some of his popcorn mix in his mouth. I found myself entranced with the movie. It was about this guy named Will, who is a janitor at MIT. He lives in a small apartment and likes to read or hang out with his friend, Chuckie. Due to getting in trouble with the police, Will agrees to go to therapy but starts mentally harassing the five therapists that he sees until he finally ends up with the therapist played by Robin Williams. Will tries to poke at his therapist's pain points. That is when things started to get emotional for me because the famous scene came on where the therapist, Sean, tells Will that he's too chicken to actually love somebody. The quote, "You don't know about real loss because it only occurs when you've loved something more than you love yourself. And I doubt you've ever dared to love anybody that much." That moment had me sniffling. Then we watched the therapist see the photos of the abuse Will went through as a child. Sean went up to Will and kept saying over and over again it is not your fault, it is not your fault, it is not your fault. When Will finally started to cry, I had tears dripping off my nose. I felt Kian move his arm across the space between us and fold my hand within his bigger one. The movie was so different from my life, yet it hit an ache inside of me till it throbbed like a fresh bruise. When the movie ended Kian flipped the TV off. We continued to sit there in the dark, holding hands and letting the power of what we had just watched really soak in.

The room was so dark that I couldn't really see anything, but I could hear Kian breathing near me, and I could feel the calluses on his fingers from playing guitar. His hand was warm around mine, and it brought me to dangerous places in my mind where I pretended maybe I could somehow manage something real. It was clear that the alcohol I drank was muddling my thoughts.

Suddenly, I blurted, "In twenty twenty-one, ninety-six thousand seven hundred and seventy-nine people died of an overdose."

I felt Kian squeeze my hand, but he said nothing. I didn't need him to. I just kept spewing facts.

"That's 36.1 percent higher than the report in two thousand nineteen. Drug overdoses exceeded homicides by 306.7 percent. Opioids are responsible for 67.8 percent of the overdoses in America, which is three times as many people as cocaine."

I fell silent and just listened for Kian's rhythmic breathing, which seemed to calm the frenzy that had built inside of me. Then I shared so quietly I was almost whispering, "I love him more than I love myself. And I am petrified that one day, he'll just be a statistic... I'm scared that I'm not strong enough to handle losing someone again." My voice was hoarse with the effort not to cry as I spoke into the dark air around me, saying what I had never been able to say to another human before.

"Again?"

I could feel him close to me, but I couldn't see more of him than his silhouette.

"My mom passed away when I was nineteen."

"Oh." He sighed. "I'm sorry."

"Yeah." I felt wrung out from my confession.

"I lost someone," he said suddenly.

"Yeah?"

"Yeah."

"Did you love them?" *Give me your pain*, I thought. I'd rather hold yours than mine. He didn't say anything for a minute.

"I did." His voice cracked. "I wrote a song about it, but it's not done yet."

"I'd love to hear it."

My eyes were assaulted by the light of his phone turning on, and suddenly, a pixelated video of him in his van showed up. It looked like he had recorded it in the dark. Kian propped his phone up against the half-full vodka bottle on the coffee table in front of us and pressed play. His voice was so effortlessly smooth and warm. The words bled with heartbreak and love. I felt his song stuck somewhere behind my ribs, where it stung with a beautiful hurt. When it was done, Kian still had my hand in his.

We sat there again, side by side, not saying anything until he spoke. "I'd like to hold you tonight, if that's okay?"

I stilled. We were in dangerous territory over here. He was obviously dealing with grief, and I was dealing with the anticipation of grief. That didn't seem like the healthiest of foundations to build a friendship on, but maybe it was the perfect thing for now.

"That would be okay," I whispered. I had no sarcastic one-liners left in me tonight. Between the movie, Kian's song, and him holding my hand, I was emotionally wrung out.

WE TOOK turns in the bathroom. I washed my face and brushed my teeth. He showered and came out in his boxers. I averted my eyes from his gorgeous body although I itched to examine the rest of his tattoos that covered his other arm and his entire back. Instead, I climbed into bed and lay on my side, my back to him. I felt the mattress shift as Kian got into bed, and as he pulled the covers up, he hooked his arm over me and pulled me till I was flush against him with my back to his chest.

"Go to sleep, Jessamine. I'm here," I heard him rumble in my ear as I fell asleep in his arms.

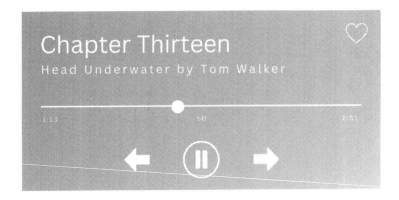

1:13   50   2:01

"**R**ose?" I called, stepping into the foyer from the garage and slipping my shoes off. She was very particular about "outdoor germs" not contaminating the house. She didn't answer, and I wondered if she had fallen asleep. She had texted me a few hours ago asking if I could come home when my show was done instead of going straight to the airport, and what Rose wanted, Rose got. I had booked myself a commercial flight and drove to our house up in Beverly Hills while the rest of my band flew to New York. I stopped in the kitchen and saw that she had left a box of those huge cookies everyone loved in the fridge.

"Don't mind if I do," I murmured to myself, picking one up and taking a large bite. Despite my arguably shitty eating habits, I was thin. Paired with my height, some would call me gangly, but I liked to call myself lean. It sounded nicer. At twenty-eight, I still hadn't really grown into my body. I had the potential to have muscle, but that required eating well and working out. But since I always traveled with security who carried anything heavy for me, and the most strenuous thing I did all day was hold a microphone and strum a guitar, working out wasn't exactly high on my priority list. I wiped the crumbs off my hands and bounded up the stairs to look for Rose. She would be so excited that I hadn't flown out directly from the show.

"Babe?" I peered into our bedroom. It was dark, and the bed was still made with the twenty little pillows on it that she artfully arranged every single morning.

"Rose?" I called out again. Her Mercedes SUV was in the garage; I had passed it on my way in. So where was she? My spidey senses perked up, and I found myself tiptoeing down the hall to my office, which doubled as a recording studio. The door was slightly ajar, and I slowly pushed it open even more. What I saw made my stomach churn.

"Rose?" I whispered in a horrified squeak. Her hands were tied behind her back, a scarf was stuffed in her mouth, and she was on her knees next to my safe. A safe that a man with leather gloves and a ski mask on his face was trying to crack.

"I'll tell you the code. Take it all; just leave her alone," I shouted.

The second man, who was standing to my left, holding a gun, laughed. I felt chills rush up my spine. Rose shook her head at me, her voice muffled behind the scarf. I couldn't understand what she was saying. I was helpless. My security was at the airport. I was weak and defenseless. No way could I take on one of these guys, forget two. I had no weapons, I couldn't reach for my phone, and I couldn't defend Rose. I felt my throat close up with fear. I tried to reason with them again.

"What do you want? I'll give you anything you want. Just please leave," I begged.

"Shut up," the guy at the safe ordered. I heard a click, and the safe opened. He grabbed the cash, the bag holding a diamond necklace and my Patek Philippe watch.

"Take it... and go. We won't stop you." I walked further into the room, and the guy with the gun turned and smacked me across the face. I fell with a pained shout and held my hand to my jaw, which was already feeling like it was beginning to swell.

"Unfortunately for you, this is a classic case of wrong place, wrong time," the guy who had just emptied my safe said to me from behind his mask. "You weren't supposed to be here. She wasn't either."

"Pretend we're not here," I begged. Rose was crying, and tears were streaming down her face into that goddamn scarf.

"But you are, and the bad news is the bitch saw my face." His words reverberated in my head.

"She won't say anything, I swear." I was babbling now. "I'll give you more money."

The two men exchanged a long look, and then the one holding the bag of my belongings shook his head. The man holding the gun pulled down the zipper on his pants.

"What are you doing?" I stood and rushed him in a feeble attempt to stop him, but the masked intruder just turned and smashed the butt of his gun into my head. I fell to the floor as my vision went black.

I woke up to the sound of Rose screaming. I felt foggy, my head was pounding, and when I pulled my hand away from my scalp, I saw blood covering it. I turned my head, and from where I was lying, I saw that he was raping Rose. I started to cry. I tried to sit up, but I was so dizzy and in so much pain all I could do was lie there and beg her to look at me.

"It's okay, baby. It's going to be okay," I garbled through my cries. The man with the gun finished, and then his partner took over.

"Stop it," I pleaded. "Please stop hurting her. She didn't do anything to you." Blood was pouring down my face now, mixing with my tears and dripping off my chin. "Rose, Rose, look at me. I'm so sorry, baby. Rose."

My ears were ringing, and my eyes were getting blurry. Stay awake, I commanded, stay awake. I was half a man, lying here in my own blood, unable to save the woman I loved. I had barely even tried. They hadn't even bothered to tie me up because I was so pathetic. I turned my head, forcing myself to stay conscious. Rose's eyes were full of tears, the horror clear in them, as her body was used, and I, who was supposed to be her man, her protector, couldn't do anything to stop it.

"*Get off of her!*" *I roared in a moment of fury, using all the strength I had left to yell. I stretched out my arm so I could touch the tips of my fingers to hers. They had taken the scarf out of her mouth, I realized. The reason why made me feel incredibly nauseous, and I had to hold myself back from throwing up.*

"*I love you,*" *she mouthed.* "*I love you.*"

"*I love you too, baby.*" *I was sobbing now. The blood was clouding my vision, and I had to keep wiping it away.* I'm going to pass out *was the last conscious thought I had until I woke up again to a dark, empty office, staring into the open, blank eyes of my fiancée.* It's not your fault. *Robin Williams intoned in the background.* It's not your fault. It's not your fault. *I screamed.*

"KIAN! KIAN!" A voice was frantically calling my name, and someone was shaking me. I was having a nightmare that I had already lived.

"You're screaming!" the frenzied voice above me said. My eyes popped open, and I looked around. My boxers and the blankets around me were soaked with my sweat. Where was I? What was happening?

"Kian?"

"Jessa?" My voice was hoarse, and my throat hurt. The lamp next to the bed turned on, and I blinked in the sudden onslaught of light. Jessa peered down at me, worry and confusion evident in her eyes. I lifted my arm and saw the slopes of muscle in my bicep. I let out a sigh of relief. *I am strong now. I could defend myself and those I cared about. I had literally turned myself into a fuck-around-and-find-out meme.*

I sat up gingerly. What had just happened? I had never dreamt of that night. I hadn't gone back there ever since it happened. Why now? Was it my sleeping with Jessa? Was it the movie? Was it my system getting overwhelmed by texting my bandmates? Recording the song? Listening to the voice note? I didn't know, but all I did know was that it had to stay in the past. The worst night of my entire existence could not come back to haunt me. That night had caused me to leave everyone and everything I loved behind and hide. Hide and just languish in my anger, my grief, and my self-loathing. Jessa's warm hand brushed over my face.

"Do you need a drink of water?" she asked.

I nodded. "Y-yes. Water is good."

She got out of bed, and I heard her murmuring to Myles. God, how embarrassing was that? Even the guy who had barely been sober for two days wasn't waking the rest of the place up with his screams. I ran a hand roughly over my face. Jessa came back in with a cup of water and watched me take a sip.

"Want to talk about it?" Her tone was gentle and inquisitive. I shook my head.

"Not now." That wasn't a yes, but it wasn't a no either, and that was progress.

"Should I go?" I felt bad for waking her up and for doing it in a way that probably scared the living shit out of her too.

"Do you want to?" She got back into the bed and hugged her legs to her chest. I ran my hand through my hair as I finished my water.

"No," I answered sheepishly. "But I don't want to bother you if it happens again."

She wordlessly patted the pillow next to her. I lay down and fell asleep with her hands rubbing my temples and her soft words in my ear.

I woke up a few hours later feeling rested and embarrassed over what had happened last night. Jessa was curled up next to me, her insane amount of hair spread out around her. Her long, dark lashes made shadows on her cheeks. She let out a breath, and it made a little whistling sound. I smiled and pushed some of the hair out of her eyes. She shifted but kept sleeping. I didn't know when coffee girl had started to mean something to me, but I felt it thrumming in my veins. I would absolutely go feral on someone for her, and now, with my sculpted body, I could. I genuinely could. That knowledge gave me so much peace.

I leaned over to kiss her dimple and then lay back down, content to just listen to her breathe. Could I somehow have my life back and keep moments like this too? I had six weeks left till the last big fight, and then I had to reconnect with my band. I didn't even know if she liked me enough to listen to my whole story when I was finally ready to tell it, and I only had less than two months left to find out.

I felt her shift, and I opened my eyes.

"Good morning," I whispered.

"I need to go brush my teeth." She slipped out from where she was lying on my arm and started to get out of bed.

"You're beautiful." The words just slipped out, and it didn't hurt as much this time.

"Thank you." She flashed me her dimple. "But I still have stinky breath. I'll be right back."

She was so confident, it amazed me. I was so used to women deflecting compliments or self-deprecating themselves. I didn't think I had heard Jessa say one negative thing about herself yet. She was so different from Rose, and not in a comparison way like one was better than the other. More just an observation. Jessa was simple in her beauty. It shone from within, and it felt warm and inviting. Rose had come across as icy and standoffish because she was shy. She was delicate and small and never wanted anyone to see her without a full face of makeup. I couldn't recall ever seeing Jessa in a full face of makeup yet. I felt guilty thinking of Rose in the same sentence as Jessa, and at the same time, I already knew what Jessa would be like when I told her about Rose. She would not be jealous at all. She would compliment Rose. She would point out all of her attributes and would ask questions to know more about her.

Rose would have been jealous of how easily Jessa loved. Of how confident she was. Of how genuine she was in her feelings and existence. The thought burned in my chest as Jessa came back into the room, pulling on her black bell-bottom jeans that I had come to recognize.

"Myles is at a meeting, then he has one-on-one therapy, and then he has group therapy, which apparently means he is going on a hike today, and he is kind of mad about that." Jessa giggled. "For two people who live outside, we are definitely not always one with nature."

"Lived," I corrected. She placed a hand on her hip and stared at me.

"I love your confidence, but I don't think this room is going to last forever." She didn't seem worried or anxious about it; she just stated it factually. I wanted to tell her I would keep her in the room for as long as she wanted, but I didn't have the guts to possibly make her mad at me before my six weeks were up. I watched as she turned away to change her bra. I got a glimpse of some side boob, which immediately had me aching in my boxers.

I cleared my throat before asking, "Today is your day off, right?" She looked over at me as she pulled on a plain black T-shirt and then a huge black and white plaid button-down shirt over it.

"Yup."

"What are you gonna do?"

"I have no idea. I'd rather be working." She sprayed something in her hair and began combing her curls.

"Let's do something fun," I urged.

"Fun costs money, music man." She raised an eyebrow at me.

"I'll cover it." I got up and stretched. I saw her eyes travel over my body. "My eyes are up here," I teased.

"I know that. I'm not looking at your eyes," she retorted back. I laughed so hard I ended up with tears in said eyes.

"Touché." I ruffled her hair as I went to put yesterday's clothes on. "I have some things to do, but I'll meet you back here in ninety minutes, and then we will have a fun day. On me. Okay?"

She shrugged.

"I'm not a huge fan of you paying for things," she admitted.

"What else am I gonna do with it?" I asked her. "I have another fight soon. I will win, and I'll make it all back. I promise."

"Okay, on one condition."

"I bring you to the fight?"

"You bring me to the fight." Jessa nodded excitedly.

"Fiiine," I acquiesced. "But you have to listen to every single thing I say in regards to you being at the fight."

"Deal." She gave me her hand, and we shook on it.

"I'll be back soon," I told her and left to go to the gym, where I planned to wreck my body and rid myself of last night's nightmare.

I WORKED myself to the bone for sixty minutes, then I cried in the shower for fifteen minutes and made it back to her room exactly ninety minutes later. She was eating licorice when she opened the door.

"That's not breakfast. Let's go eat some real food, then maybe a little spa day? Some shopping?" I inquired as we left the room. She looked at me like I had four heads.

"Who are you?" She laughed.

"Just throwing out girly things to do." I defended myself. She gestured to herself as if to say, *not your typical girl here.*

"Okay, well, what constitutes a fun day for you?" I watched as she stuck another candy in her mouth and pulled her coat closed as we stepped out into the cold air.

"I thought about it while you were gone. I'm down for food. If by shopping you mean Goodwill, I'm okay with that too, and I would love to go to a rage room."

She surprised me with that last one.

"A rage room?" I asked as we walked past the hotel.

"I overheard a customer talking about it, and it sounds fabulous."

"What does one do in a rage room?" I was full of rage all the time; I just didn't know they made rooms for it.

"It's a room that you go into, and you put on protective gear. Then you choose angry music, and you beat the fuck out of a bunch of shit with crowbars and bats. Stuff like TVs, computer screens, mugs, plates, bottles, a stereo... you name it, they got it."

"Are you serious?" I herded Jessa to the side of the sidewalk as someone sped by us on a bike. She nodded.

"Very serious. I looked it up, though, and it's not cheap."

"I don't care. Let's do it." I was feeling spontaneous. Her eyes lit up.

"Yeah?"

I nodded and was rewarded with a smile. God, she was pretty.

AT BREAKFAST, I noticed another difference between Rose and Jessa. Jessa liked food. She wasn't afraid of carbs and wasn't embarrassed to eat in front of me. I had offered to take her to a place called Iron Gate Cafe, where they served eggs Benedict, but she insisted on going to a simple diner called Babe's, where she proceeded to order French toast, a burrito, and hash browns.

Rose was always counting macros or carbs or calories. When we first started going out, she would order a tea and vegetable soup. She'd then take a few spoonfuls and would complain that her stomach hurt. Jessa, on the other hand, was having toast with her maple syrup and had a smattering of confectioners' sugar on her nose. The difference was obvious. I didn't know why my brain was doing this, and it was uncomfortable for me because it didn't really matter. Rose was gone, and I was trying to heal. Yet here my mind was throwing up fun facts about how different this maybe, possibly, new girl was in comparison to my dead fiancée.

AFTER BREAKFAST, we walked from the diner to a Goodwill, where Jessa found me some new guitar picks, a vintage leather jacket that fit perfectly, a pair of baby-blue, high-waisted pants, and a Jimi Hendrix T-shirt. She obviously didn't know that as an adult, I never went shopping for my own clothes, let alone in a Goodwill, and I was loving every minute of it. Of course, she didn't want me to buy her anything, but I insisted that she look, and she finally gave in. She found Myles a green and maroon striped knit sweater, a pair of joggers, and brand-new brown Timberland boots. For herself, she agreed to get two more pairs of cargo pants, one that fit tighter to the leg and one that ballooned around her like a parachute. She also got a black knit sweater, a hat, and a lace black bodysuit that I chose and told her she had to wear to the fight. When she balked, I reminded her that she had agreed to listen to me when it came to the fight, to which she rolled her eyes but didn't argue with me further.

ONCE WE FINISHED SHOPPING, we walked back to the van and drove to the rage room. We entered with a tinkle of the bell above the door. The girl behind the counter had a ton of piercings and the word "Love" tattooed right under her left eye. We filled out our waivers and listened to her spiel about safety. Then she brought us back, where we put on protective goggles, chest protectors, a welding shield, and gloves.

"Damn, look at you, you sexy raging warrior," I teased and was surprised as I said it. I had missed this. This non-grumpy, less closed-off side of me. Jessa gave a little twirl in her safety wear and then picked up a crowbar. The playlist we had chosen began to blare from the speakers, and I felt excitement boil up inside of me. I was going to blast this mother fucking room apart, and it was going to feel amazing.

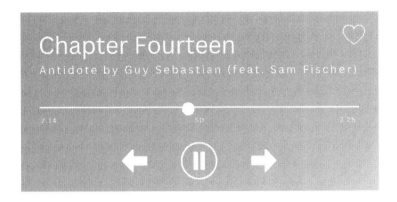

F uck, he looked so good. Kian had taken off his coat, and under it, he wore a tight, long-sleeved shirt that showed off every single peak and valley of the muscles in his arms, chest, and shoulders. Paired with his protective gear, he somehow gave me Viking vibes. I wouldn't consider myself to be a highly reactive person. I generally had a chill personality. At work, I was always the one who helped calm down an irate customer or talked to the delivery people when something got messed up. Yet here I was, feeling primed to go and smash some shit. I didn't have to dig as deep as I thought to access some rage. With a yell, I hit the copy machine with the crowbar. I cracked the top, but it didn't fully break so I kept going, hitting the machine over and over. For my mom, who had died too young. For my dad, who had left us for no reason. For the man who had repoed our car when we were living in it, and for the men who had touched me without my permission. For Myles's dad, who had beat him, and for the girl who had gotten Myles hooked on drugs. For every single night I had gone to sleep cold and hungry. I swung that crowbar until the wires of the machine were showing, the plastic was cracked, and the pieces of glass were scattered around me in smithereens.

Oh my god, that had felt so good. My arms vibrated from the effort, and my heart was going a mile a minute. I turned to look at Kian, who was watching me, his eyes wide, with a glint of emotion in them. I grinned, practically vibrating with excitement.

"Hit something, music man," I encouraged him. He held up an aluminum bat, swung, and began to destroy everything around him. He was so strong that items shattered immediately as he hit them. The muscles in his arms swelled and contracted as he swung, and as much I liked to see it, I had some shit to break.

I turned and attacked several mirrors. They shattered, their wood frames twisting and cracking. Then I took a box of china and one by one I crashed every piece. Some by slamming them to the ground, and others I tossed like a frisbee at the wall. Then I joined Kian in beating the crap out of an old jukebox. I was breathing heavily, standing next to him, swinging my crowbar over and over, feeling any negative emotion completely leave my body. I was so in the moment that I had never felt so exhilarated in my life. Plates were flying, glass was smashing, and I watched as Kian picked up an entire TV, hoisting it above his head, and with a wink, he chucked it across the room, where it crashed into multiple parts.

"Fuck!" I screamed out to the ceiling, laughing as pieces of a mug went flying through the air. Kian turned back to look at me, holding his bat loosely in his hand, his chest heaving from the effort of destroying the room around us. We stood there staring at each other for a second, and then he practically prowled over to me, pushed me against the wall, and kissed me until my knees gave out. I grabbed at his shoulders, and he growled and hoisted me up to hold me in his arms as he attacked my mouth. It was messy, sweaty, desperate, and everything I had ever needed.

"You. Are. So. Hot." He moaned into my mouth. I felt him tug at my hair until it hurt slightly, and I leaned into it, encouraging him. I arched back, baring my neck, and I felt him bite down on my chin, followed by a pinch right over my jugular, and then came a lick to soothe it.

"I have never been this hard in my life," I heard him admit to me, his mouth by my ear. His tongue flicked out and traced the edge of it. "If that girl wasn't right outside this room, I would fuck you right here."

His voice was ecstasy in my ear. I was dripping and grinding myself on him as he fondled my breasts with his free hand and then pulled me down for another searing, heart-palpitating kiss. The music suddenly shut off, and a voice came on over the mic. "Don't you fucking dare make babies in there."

We flew apart. The moment was over. We looked at each other and burst out laughing. Kian let me down gently, and the broken glass crunched under my shoes. He then surprised me by taking out his phone and snapping a selfie of us in the room that we had just demolished before we brushed off all the dust and shards and left the room to remove the gear.

BACK OUTSIDE, we began to walk toward Kian's van. On the corner was a food truck selling churros and waffles.

"Want one?" he asked me. I was getting uncomfortable with him spending money on me. For one, it wasn't like we were a couple and even if we were, I didn't know how I would feel about it. Secondly, the man lived in his van, yet he didn't seem to be that worried about saving his money for important things like gas and basic food. I had never had the luxury of a day like today. I didn't just do things because I wanted to. I didn't buy things on a whim because I was in the mood for them. That was a privilege not afforded to people like me. I was feeling slightly out of my element here. Like I was a little girl who had gone into my mom's closet and came out pretending I was an adult, wearing heels six sizes too big, lipstick smeared on my face, and a fur boa around my neck. I didn't belong here, buying churros in the middle of the day as if I didn't have a care in the world, standing next to a man who could easily be on the cover of *GQ*. Instead of word vomiting all of my convoluted thoughts, I just shrugged. I was usually one to just say what I was thinking, as Kian knew very well by now, yet here, some of my preconceived notions about life and my experiences thus far choked my ability to speak.

"I'm gonna get some. You can watch me eat them, or you can join me." He got in line and ordered way more than one man, even one of his size, could eat. I knew exactly what he was doing, and I rolled my eyes when he came back to where I was standing with an armful of options. Way too many for two people.

"Something is wrong with you." I laughed. He nodded, licking caramel off of his fingers.

"Mmm hmm." He agreed with me. "Are you gonna make me get diabetes by myself?" He held one of the filled churros out to me. I sighed and leaned in to take a bite directly from his fingers. He watched me with those piercing eyes of his, something flashing across them as I left a little swipe of my tongue on his finger. I pulled back and chewed the delicious pastry.

"Good?" he asked, taking a bite where my teeth had just sunk into the warm Nutella and fried dough. I nodded.

"Thank you," I murmured. He gave me a genuine smile as he handed me one of the heart churros; a little bit of powdered sugar sat in his beard, and I reached up to brush it off. His head turned, and he landed a small kiss on my thumb before he took another bite of his food. I didn't acknowledge it, just like we hadn't talked about our soul-igniting make out earlier either.

I found it fascinating how quickly I felt comfortable and at ease around this man. It was easy and simple, something which my soul craved. I hadn't had a lot of easy and simple, and Kian was giving that to me in droves. We kept walking toward his van as we ate when I heard someone say my name.

"Jessa?"

I turned and saw one of the girls who had lived in the tent community at one point, sitting on the sidewalk with a collection cup in front of her and a cardboard sign asking for help.

"Carrie! Hi!" I paused and crouched down to talk to her.

"You look good." She gestured to the man standing a few steps behind me and the food I was eating.

"So do you." I smiled. "Your hair is beautiful as always," I complimented her. Carrie always rolled her dirty-blonde hair into dreadlocks to maintain its integrity and then hooked little charms and bits of ribbon through them. It was difficult to avoid matting with very curly hair while living on the streets. I was lucky that my mom had left me all of my legal documents, so I was able to actually work and afford to take care of my hair. I had also never picked up hard-core drugs, so I still had my wits about me and was able to keep a job. I winced when I thought of Myles telling me that he was a loser. The fact was, being sober and responsible had always given me an advantage. Although I had been living on the streets just a week ago, I had made sure to always work, showered regularly at the gym, and always did our laundry to maintain good hygiene to hold onto some semblance of normalcy. Not everyone was so lucky. I looked down at the heart churro that I held in my hands.

"It's still warm," I told her and held out the pastry bag. Carrie took it and immediately took a bite.

"Good, huh?" I smiled. She nodded. I stood back up. "I'll see you around."

She nodded again, her eyes shifting to the next person walking by. I walked back to Kian, who wordlessly handed me another churro. We didn't say anything more until we got back to the van.

"Do you want to...?" Kian started.

"I need to do laundry," I said at the same time. He started up the van as I laughed.

"What were you going to say?"

He shook his head.

"Laundry sounds like a great idea; I have a load myself."

"I bet you do," I teased.

"Get your head out of the sewer, Jessamine." He pretended to be scandalized as he pulled the van out into traffic. I watched the scenery flash by as he drove, resting my head on the window next to me. Kian was humming, which then turned into full-blown singing, and I closed my eyes, letting his voice and protective energy wash over me.

"JESSA." I woke up with a start.

"You're drooling," I heard him say gently. I lifted my head and wiped at the corner of my mouth. I *was* drooling.

"Sorry, I guess I was tired." I looked around—we were back at the hotel.

"I feel bad about that." He looked ashamed that his screaming nightmare last night was why I had needed a nap in the first place.

"Don't worry about it." I patted his arm and opened the door to jump out of his van. "Thanks for an amazing day off," I said quickly as he came around to where I stood holding the Goodwill bag.

"Thanks for letting me have a day off too." He stood there, his hands in his pockets, his gorgeous, bearded face distracting me from my mission to get back to my room where I could get started on some practical errands like cleaning our clothes and buying some groceries.

"I never get days off," Kian told me.

"From busking?" I asked. Kian took the bag from me and began to walk me to the doors of the hotel. He paused and then nodded.

"From music. The grind is… a lot," he said vaguely. "Today was exactly what I needed."

"Me too," I admitted. "I've never done something like that before," I told him, referencing the rage room.

"Same," he said softly. We stopped at the door to my room.

"Thank you." I leaned over and wrapped him up in a hug. It occurred to me that this man had been inside of me, done dirty things to me, and kissed me like his life had depended on it, yet we had never just hugged. Kian froze for a moment, and then his arms came around me and he held onto me as I rested my cheek against his slab of muscle. I felt him shift as he bent down and pressed a kiss into my hair.

"I'll see you later?" I heard him murmur. I nodded. Why did I feel like crying? I wasn't sure. I didn't look at him again. I just pulled away, unlocked the door, and slipped inside.

I SHUT the door behind me and leaned back on it for a moment. I wanted him to stay. I wanted to invite him in and suck him off until he came all over my chest. We'd shower together and then curl up in bed, and he'd listen while I told him about living on the streets and how it had aged me before I was ready but how staying happy and positive was so important to me.

I stepped away from the door. I could not get attached. My

heart could not get used to warm churros and a man who was stern and uptight with everyone else, but around me, he smiled so warmly that his eyes crinkled up on the sides.

I heard the sound of someone throwing up in Myles's bathroom, and I froze for a second. Wasn't Myles on a healing hike? I heard a groan and realized that Myles was definitely not on a healing hike right now, and I rushed into the room. Myles sat on the floor in just his underwear, holding onto the base of the toilet, his head hanging to the side. The smell of vomit filled the air, and I had to breathe through my mouth. I noticed that my brother's body was covered in a sheen of sweat, his brown hair was stuck to his head with it.

"My?" I knelt down, and he turned his head slightly.

"You don't need to see this, Jess. I got it."

He tried to shoo me out of the room with a weak wave of his hand.

"Shush." I quieted him as I took a washcloth and ran it under cold water. I squeezed out the excess and placed the cold towel on his forehead. He made a sound of protest but didn't move away. His skin was clammy yet sweaty, his arms were trembling, and when he spoke, he sounded slurred.

"I hate this part." He was crying now.

"Come back to bed." I flushed the toilet and took the garbage can with me as I helped Myles get up and practically carried him to his bed. He was so lethargic as I propped him up with his pillows and then pulled the blanket up over him. My plans of doing laundry left my mind as I made a list in my head of items I was going to need to buy to get him through his withdrawals. Ginger tea for the nausea, ibuprofen for the pain, a heating pad for stomach cramps, and chocolate to help increase his body's natural endorphins. I was going to have to use some of the grocery money for this, which would lower our food options. The front desk told me that my room came with three meals a day, so we would stick to the more limited choices from room service until my next paycheck.

"Feeling like shit eventually goes away," I heard Myles mumble. He was curled up in a fetal position with his hands clenched by his face. "But the thoughts in my brain will never quiet without the..." His voice trailed off, and I knew he was referring to the drugs.

"I don't want to be like this, but I have no other way out." He sobbed. "When I'm sober, all I can hear is my dad telling me what a waste of space I am. I can feel him beating me. I know he hates me, and I can't figure out why. It makes me not want to be here sometimes because it's too hard..."

My heart jolted in my chest. I didn't know what to do. I was not a medical professional, nor was I a mental health expert who knew what to say when faced with his difficult thoughts. I wished I could just magically take it all away from him, but this is what trauma looked like. This is why he stayed high all the time, because his brain was a painful place to live in. I reached out and brushed the hair off his forehead.

"Try to sleep. I'm going to get supplies, and I'll be right back." I took his phone and put on some gentle yoga music, and I saw his body relax as he let sleep overtake his troubled mind. Grabbing my wallet and my coat, I slipped back out into the hallway and started the ten-minute walk to the grocery store. There, I bought everything I needed for him plus a bag of mini marshmallows for me. I kept my head down as I walked back to the hotel since the wind had picked up, making it very cold outside. When I got back to the room, I found Myles dealing with a leg cramp as his body revolted against him.

"I can't do it, Jessa, I can't do it." His eyes were bloodshot, his hair was now plastered to his head, and his nose was running.

"You can do anything because you are strong, and you have me, and together we get through everything," I said gently. I was acting calm, but I was really worried. The last time he had detoxed, he had done it in a hospital, but I knew he didn't want to go through that again. The people there didn't treat addicts like humans. They treated them like trash. They humiliated them and spoke down to them. I would never force Myles to go anywhere unless I really couldn't take care of him myself but just in case, a few months ago, I had found a private detox center that cost a pretty penny.

I knew I would have to call if I absolutely needed to. I briefly wondered what he would be like tomorrow, because although I did need to go to work, I would never leave him alone like this. I handed him a cup of electrolyte water with two tablets of ibuprofen. I had guessed that could help somehow and had spontaneously grabbed a bottle off the shelf. He drank them down and then moaned as the leg cramp acted up again. I took the plug-in heating pad that I had purchased and wrapped it around his leg. When he quieted down, I made him a glass of ginger tea and let it cool before I brought it over. He took a couple of sips before leaning back on his pile of pillows. I was so grateful that he was doing this in bed and not shivering in a sleeping bag where the people in the tents next to us could hear him barfing.

I just didn't know what "after this" looked like. I loved him so much, and as much as I would do anything to support him, I was really out of my scope of abilities here. I was a barista. I could make coffee. I didn't know how to keep someone sober. Cognitively, I knew I could never keep him sober anyway. No one stayed sober unless they wanted to. I couldn't beg him, I would never shame him, and there was no reasoning or form of emotion that could convince him. It had to be him and his desire alone that would help him face and beat his demons. I just wished I had more access to choices for him—a fancy rehab or better therapeutic options. I felt stuck. As if he could hear my frantic thoughts, he looked up and said, "I love you."

"I love you too, My," I replied. "I'm going to start the shower for you. Can you manage that?"

He nodded. The ibuprofen had kicked in, and he looked a tiny bit less wrung out than before.

WHEN HE WAS in the shower, I changed into my sweatpants and the black sweater I had picked up from Goodwill this morning, not caring that it wasn't washed yet. Earlier today felt like eons ago, I realized. It was crazy how quickly real life had rudely pushed me out of my good feelings from all the fun I had on my day off. I then ordered room service: a soup with crusty bread for Myles, and lasagna with a side of vegetables for me.

I looked over at my phone, which sat silently on the counter. Although hours had passed, I hadn't received any missed phone calls or texts. Most of the time, I felt proud of myself for being self-reliant, yet sometimes, in moments like these, I could very much feel the chasm in my life due to having been genuinely alone since I was nineteen. Nineteen and raising a younger brother. Navigating the streets and selling a little piece of my soul every time I slept with that man in order to have basic necessities. I truly considered my friends at work to be real friends, but Alanna was raising a son by herself, and Eric had elderly parents he was supporting. As a result, we didn't really talk much in between shifts. I shook myself out of my rare woe is me moment when I heard Myles call for me. He was wrapped in a towel, shivering in the bathroom, eyes downcast as he asked me to help him get dressed since his muscles were too stiff to do it himself.

ONCE HE WAS BACK in bed, freshly made with new sheets that housekeeping had put on when they stopped by, he ate his soup and took some more ibuprofen. I gave him a kiss as he fell asleep. I was happy that his skin was feeling warm and healthy again instead of the clammy flesh from earlier.

"Good night," I murmured. I left the door slightly ajar so I could hear him if he needed me, but six hours later, I hoped that maybe the worst was over. As I got ready for bed, I felt my body begin to give out. I was so tired. Not just physically but mentally and emotionally too. I longed for someone to hold me and carry my burdens with me. I had done such a good job at managing my hardships on my own for so long, and all it had taken to shake me from the monotony of what I had always known was a beautiful busker showing me what it felt like to have someone carry my bag in from the car.

The problem was I could not let myself hope for more. Everything I had loved eventually faded away, and I found it easier to just not want at all. As I got into bed, my phone buzzed unexpectedly, and a text came in. It was from music man. I opened it to find that he had sent me the selfie he had taken of us at the rage room. My hurting heart fluttered at the sight of it. He was standing slightly behind me, his tan arm flung over my shoulder. My hair was a mess around me, held down by the protective goggles. We were laughing, our lips both slightly swollen from the kiss we had just shared. The room around us was destroyed, dust from the plates clung to our clothes, and the wreckage we had created was indicative of the amazing time we had. I looked happy. He looked at peace somehow. The thought "and in the middle of my chaos, there you were" flitted through my brain as I fell into a fitful sleep.

Something had thawed around my broken heart since going feral with Jessa in the rage room. I noticed it when I found myself nodding good night at the security guard at the gym, whom I usually just ignored. I said thank you to the cashier when I went to buy myself some food instead of my usual anti-social grunt. I even looked through some more photos on my phone without completely losing it. I scrolled through images of Rose kissing me on the red carpet, wrapped around me in the hot tub at my birthday party, and a slightly out-of-focus shot of her giggling as I tickled her where she was lying on the carpet of our bedroom. I ended my walk down memory lane by looking at the photo I had taken of Jessa and me. Without overthinking, I texted her for the first time. I didn't say anything; I just sent her the photo. She was absolutely stunning in it, standing next to me with her crazy long curls, her big smile, and her flushed cheeks.

I noticed that I looked happy. It hit me square in my chest, and again, I wondered if I could somehow have both—the life I had to return to and the girl I had found here. For the first time in a long time, I fell asleep in my van without having completely exhausted myself with fury first.

Jessa didn't respond to my text, and she didn't show up to work the next day. I played some music, but it was half-hearted, knowing that I would not be receiving a coffee cup with a flirty message on it. I quit early and went to the gym where I poured all my confused feelings when it came to this girl into the weight room. I didn't leave until my arms were weak and my lungs were burning. I wanted to text her, but I didn't even know what to say. "Wanna fuck?" didn't really express what I wanted to convey. "Miss you" made me sound like a stalker.

But I did. I missed her. I missed watching her love-hate smoke sessions. I missed the sound of her husky voice. I craved the smell of the shampoo that she used. I wanted to have another movie night. I wanted to show her a life where days off didn't have to be a rarity. I wanted to fuck her against the wall until she screamed. She had gotten under my skin with her obvious strength, her sweet laugh, and her snarky one-liners.

I was aware that she didn't know enough about me to actually like me, but I wanted the chance to show her. I was so relieved to feel something other than anger and heartbreak that I was holding onto these new feelings I had for her like they were a flotation device, which made sense because, up until now, I had been drowning.

I settled on texting her "Hi." She didn't answer that one either. Had I read her vibes wrong? She had seemed into me in the rage room. She kissed me back, pulled my hair, and moaned into my mouth. Later, she had wiped something off my beard and had licked my thumb when she had taken a bite of the churro. Had I misread the hug she had given me when I said goodbye to her outside her hotel room? I knew she had said she could only give me one night, but I thought we had bonded somehow over the movie and our licorice straws. I wrote another song before falling asleep. I titled it "Hi."

AWARENESS HIT me as soon as I opened my eyes the next morning. It was an anniversary of sorts—the day I had met Rose four years ago. I rolled over in my van bed, and my muscles screamed in protest. I didn't want to play music today. I didn't want to look at strangers and wonder if they could see the pain I was in. I didn't want to stress about why Jessa wasn't answering me. I didn't want to do anything other than languish in bed. Usually, on an anniversary, people would be out celebrating and pretending that love was the answer to all of their problems. For me, it was the cause of all of mine. The precursor to all of the intense pain I was in.

"Fuck love," I muttered, pulling the blanket back over my face. I had almost fallen back to sleep when my phone buzzed, where it was tucked under my pillow. I felt my heart skip a beat when I saw that it was Jessa, or coffee girl, as her contact name read. I had just got done cursing out love, and here I was, simping over a girl.

"Hi." Her text read. I started to type back, asking if she was okay, when another text popped in. "Wanna fuck?"

I don't know if I should laugh or cry. On one hand, yes, I absofuckinglutely did, but on the other hand, it felt like she was using me again. I would gladly let her, use me all up if she wanted to, please and thank you. But truthfully and painfully, my heart wanted more. I felt a connection to this crazy-haired girl with a funny sense of humor and an affinity for combat boots. I wanted to know what her eyes would look like when I took her to exotic places. I was curious if she liked my music. I wanted to tell her all of the things going on inside my head, even the things I had never shared with Rose. Things like how the music industry had started to burn me out or how money had seemed like the answer to everything in the beginning. But now, I realized it didn't actually make me happy, and even that thought made me feel depressed. I didn't just want to be the busker guy whom she fucked a few times and then left behind. Instead of saying any of that, I just texted back, "When and where?"

A few minutes later, she replied, "My room. Now."

I didn't want to tell her I was so pathetic that last night, I had parked in the parking lot of her hotel, and I was already here, so I just didn't respond. Instead, I threw on a tank top and a pair of jeans, skipping the underwear. Then I sprayed on some cologne, slipped a bunch of packets from my new box of condoms into my pocket, pulled back my hair, grabbed my guitar, and ten minutes after she had texted me, I was at her door, knocking.

SHE LOOKED WORN OUT. All my thoughts of going down on her in the hallway at the entrance of her bedroom left my mind as I took in the circles under her eyes.

"What's wrong?" I asked, stepping in and shutting the door behind me. She hesitated.

"Do not lie to me," I demanded. Bossy Kian was back, I noted. She looked offended.

"I never lie." She almost sneered. "One thing I hate most in the world is liars. I can forgive almost anything else but lying..." She made a tutting sound with her tongue, and my heart sank just a little at her statement. I was one big walking non-truth right now, and I hoped when she found out that she would forgive me.

"Okay, so tell me the truth." I placed my guitar down and stuck my hands in the pockets of my jeans.

"I didn't invite you here to talk." She sighed. "I told you exactly what I wanted from you." She cocked her head and stared at me, but I could see the sadness in her eyes.

"What's wrong? Is Myles okay?" I ignored her attitude. In the short amount of time that I had been getting to know her, I had learned that her defense mechanism was to be prickly in the face of adversity, so something had to be going on, and I wanted to know what it was so I could fix it for her. At Myles's name, her face crumbled, and she started walking away from me. I stepped closer to her, curving my body around hers as she began to cry. I rocked her gently from behind, then once I felt her body start to sag against me, I picked her up and held her like a baby in my arms as I carried her into her room. I didn't let go as I sat down on her bed. I just held her and let her cry. I feared the worst, being that Myles hadn't stuck his head out of his room or let out a laugh from the couch in the living room.

"M-Myles went to a private sober center today to finish his detox. I left as he was getting an IV. He'll be there till Saturday. I paid so much of my savings for it, but he was doing so b-bad here." She hiccuped. "I couldn't leave him in the hospital again. It's terrible there."

"I know," I murmured against her hair. I felt so relieved to hear that he was alive and was getting help.

"He couldn't keep any food down, and he was in so much pain." She sniffed, and her sobs quieted as she sat up in my arms.

"So you dropped him off and then texted me?" I prompted. She nodded.

"Why didn't you text me before? I told you if you needed anything..."

She held her head high. Cheeks flushed, lashes wet from crying.

"I can take care of it by myself. I always have." She wiped the tears off her cheeks and stared at me.

"Yeah, but you don't have to. I can help." I felt her shift in my lap as the look on her face almost turned to disdain.

"I don't even know your last name. Why would I text you to help me bring my brother to a detox center?"

I sighed. She wasn't wrong.

"It's West."

I braced myself in case she recognized it, but she just asked, "What is?"

"My last name."

She shrugged.

"Okay."

I breathed a sigh of relief that I still had time to sort things out and then hit her with the truth as I retorted, "So I'm not good enough to help you, but I am good enough to dick you down?"

"Something like that." She was purposefully being insolent. I imagined she was emotionally exhausted from worry and physically exhausted from playing caregiver for the last two days. I needed to shut her brain off and fuck the attitude out of her.

"Okay." I gave her a look and kept my tone low. With her still in my lap, I reached behind me and pulled my shirt off. I then extracted the string of condoms from my pants pocket as I ordered, "Take off your clothes and lie on your stomach." I didn't even look at her as I stood to pull off my pants, dropping them carelessly off the side of the bed. When I looked back over, I saw that she had listened. She was trembling slightly in what I hoped was anticipation, not fear, but to be safe, I double-checked with her.

"You want this, right, Jessa? You want me?"

She turned to look at me.

"I want you," she confirmed.

"Are you sore?" I asked, referring to what we had done a few days ago. She shook her head, so I promised, "Okay, good because you will be when I'm done with you."

She let out a breathy moan and gyrated her hips against the sheets.

"Don't move," I demanded as I circled her waist with my hands. "You cannot come until I tell you to. Say you understand." I pulled her toward me and then covered her body with mine.

"I understand." She moaned again as I entered her with no warning and bottomed out with one stroke. God, she was so tight like this. I hadn't even checked if she was ready, but I was happy to find her soaking around my cock. I could tell that she had been slick even before I got to her room. I grabbed a handful of her hair and pulled her head back slightly so she was arching off the bed.

"You think you're too good to ask for my help, huh?" I intoned into her ear as I fucked her relentlessly into the mattress.

"N-no," she cried out. My hips snapped against her ass.

"So you just like being mean to me?" I nipped at her ear and then sucked on her neck.

"I'm not," she protested as she tried to look at me, but I pulled her hair harder, forcing her to keep facing straight. She whined but didn't say anything. Gone was her sass. It was a beautiful thing to take a wild woman and tame her with your touch. I let go of her hair, allowing her shoulders and head to fall back to the mattress, and then I shifted so that my body was lying almost completely on her, holding just a bit of my weight up with my hands. I was fucking her so hard that I could hear the sounds of me moving in and out of her with every snap of my hips. She was holding onto the sheets with clenched fists and was panting.

"I need to come," she demanded.

"Too bad." I sat up on my knees, pulled out, turned her to her side, held one of her legs up, and then drove back in.

"Fuuuck." She groaned and slapped her hand against the pillow next to her.

"I told you to hold still." I slapped her chest lightly, and she writhed against my touch. I swatted each breast, her stomach, down her thighs, and then her ass.

"Y-yes. Yes." She grabbed one of my hands and held it to her warmed-up skin as I kept drilling into her.

"Please make me come," she mewled, turning her head so she could beg me with her eyes. I shook my head, and she fell back on the bed with a frustrated moan.

"You've been bad, and bad girls don't get to come." I slapped her ass again, appreciating the jiggle it made from the impact.

"What can I do to be good?" she begged. I pulled out again and dragged her to the edge of the bed. Then I stood up, placed her legs on each of my shoulders, and slid back in. She was so wet it was dripping all over the sides of me.

"You can listen better." I reached down and pinched one of her nipples as I rubbed the other. She nodded frantically.

"I'll listen," she garbled.

"How?" I was panting now with the effort of keeping her on the edge.

"When I need help, I'll text you," she acquiesced. My heart warmed at her submission.

"That's a good girl." I watched as she lit up under my praise. "What else?"

She looked confused. I pushed my luck.

"Am I just a good lay?"

She wriggled her hips under me, and I held her still beneath me. I reached between us and circled her clit quickly. She gave out a breathy groan.

"Answer the question. Do you just see me as an available dick?" I took my hand off her clit. She shook her head, her hair going crazy.

"No?" I confirmed.

"No." Her eyes were getting wild and glassy.

"Suck me." I pulled out, yanked the condom off, and watched as she scrambled onto her knees and sucked me into her mouth. She had to be getting a mouthful of latex, but she didn't falter. I closed my eyes for a moment, reveling in the feeling of her warm, wet mouth all over me. After a few minutes of listening to the sound of her sucking and gagging, I squeezed her jaw gently, but enough to make her stop. I pulled out and leaned down until my forehead was resting on hers.

"At the very least, I want you to know that I am your friend," I told her softly, my cock bobbing hard and insistent between us. She blinked but didn't say anything. "But if you'll let me, I could be something more." I slapped her ass again.

I treaded lightly, knowing she was going through an emotional time right now, and I didn't know her well enough yet to know what would send her running. Although I knew she was strong and could hold her own, everyone had their breaking point. I was painfully well-versed in breaking points. She blinked again. I leaned in and kissed her. Her soft lips parted, and I licked my way into her mouth as I put on another condom and slid into her again. I fucked her slower this time as I slipped my hand between us and rubbed her clit in time with the movement of my hips. I felt her clamping down around me. Between the noises she was making and the erratic movement of her body, I could tell she was close.

"Come, baby," I whispered. She did. She was so loud when she came. Her pussy clamped down on me, and she squeezed my hand that was resting on her stomach. I fucked her through it as I talked to her, saying things like, "You're squeezing me so tight. Fuck. Yes, like that. You're gonna make me come." And she did. I exploded so hard inside the condom that I ended up bending over her from the glorious pressure of it. She turned her head and leaned up to kiss me as I came down from my orgasm. I smiled against her mouth. She hadn't said no, so maybe I had a chance. My brain held onto the kernel of knowledge tighter than the traumatized side of me felt comfortable with.

I PICKED HER UP AGAIN, and she wrapped her legs around me as I carried her to the bathroom. I turned the shower on, and she protested, "It's not a hair wash day."

"What does that mean?"

"My hair is too curly and thick to wash more than once a week, and I just washed it yesterday."

She was distracting me with her curves and her biteable thighs.

"Okay, so wear a shower cap." I picked up the one the hotel left near the soap and began to unpack it from its box.

"That's not exactly an attractive look," she joked, but I finally saw a tiny sliver of her, showing that maybe she did care what I thought of her. She was so flippant, confident, and chill that I could never really tell if she was just having fun with me or if maybe she could actually *like* me.

"I think you already know that I'm attracted to you." I gestured to my dick, which was hardening back up against my thigh. "Wear the shower cap." I handed it to her and watched her twist her hair up into a bun and then place the shower cap on her head. She made a face, and I leaned over to kiss the tip of her nose.

"You've never looked better." I grinned and opened the shower door, ushering her in ahead of me. I sudsed up her whole body with the mini bottle of body wash. Notes of jasmine filled the room, which was now cloudy with steam. My hands ran over her curves, and I grabbed her hips, pulling her closer to me. Her slick stomach and thighs met mine, and I ground my dick against her. She let out a breathy gasp and reached up to hold onto my shoulders. I felt her running her hands up and down my lats and the bulges of muscle in my arms. I heard her murmur something, but I didn't catch it.

"What did you say?" I leaned down as I washed the soap off her body.

"You're so ripped," she repeated. Her hands were now tracing my six-pack.

"You like it?" I asked, shamelessly fishing for a compliment. She nodded, her shower-cap-clad head bobbing.

"Yeah?" I kissed her and then got onto my knees in front of her. "Touch it all you want... I like it, but know that I can also use it to protect you." I kissed a path down her ribs and around her belly button.

"Protect me from what?" She seemed confused. I avoided answering by putting my tongue on her clit and looked up to watch her eyes roll back in her head. If I needed to protect her from anything, I could. I was now a machine. I could defend myself and those that mattered to me. Nothing like what happened to Rose would ever happen again. I had made sure of it. I focused on making Jessa finish in my mouth and ridding myself of my usual distressing thoughts. I didn't have a lot of time left with her before I had to fess up to who I really was. Maybe if I spent a majority of that time in between her legs doing more of this, she'd be willing to be a part of my future too.

My day was turning out a lot different than I had envisioned. I had been so emotionally strung out after dropping Myles off that, without giving it much thought, I had shamelessly texted Kian for a quick booty call. A distraction. A serotonin hit even my cigarette couldn't provide me. I hadn't expected him to pick up on my emotional state when he showed up, and when he did, I had uncharacteristically crumbled in his arms. Check off yet another new experience for me. The sex itself was exactly what I had been craving. It had shut off my brain and forced me to be in the moment. He had been rough enough to turn me into a puddle of need, yet his words belied his demanding thrusts and the bruising hold on my hips. *I could be something more.* It was heart-wrenchingly sweet and paired with the way he threw me around, held me down, and fucked me with abandon—I think I liked the combination way too much for my own good.

I was now sitting on the couch—my feet curled beneath me as Kian paid the delivery driver and brought in our food. Since my room was considered long-term living, I was able to get food delivered directly to me versus leaving it at the front desk, and nothing felt more like a real-person life than having food delivered to where I lived.

Kian had ordered sushi bowls. When he asked me what kind I wanted, I told him I had never ordered a sushi bowl before and to just choose something for me. So much for not letting him spend more money on me. I was getting really bad at that game, I thought, as I took the food he held out for me.

"No work today?" he asked around a mouthful of fish and rice. I shook my head.

"Eric knows what is going on with Myles, so he had me take my day off again today, which means I'll be working the next week straight."

"He seems like a good boss," Kian said, noticing that I needed a napkin, so he got up to get me one. He also brought back a cup of boba tea that he had ordered. I watched as he put the straw in for me before giving it to me. Sheesh, was this what *more* looked like? I could get used to this. *Do not get used to this!* My brain shouted. I was feeling confused since I didn't usually have options in life. Usually, there was one path, one choice available to me, and I took it—with a smile.

There weren't moments that I could remember where I had to ponder which choice was better or what I really wanted. I had always gone with safety as a priority. Sleeping with that guy to give Myles a place off the streets for a while had felt like my only choice at the time. Living in our tent, working every chance I had, eating sandwiches night after night—it was all done out of necessity. Wanting something because it felt good was a privilege I had never been afforded.

I didn't mull this over in an attempt to feel bad for myself. I simply just didn't know what to do with this foreign feeling of weighing out options. I honestly had felt a sense of calm come over me ever since I had begun sleeping in a bed with sheets and a room with heat. I lived with less urgency and a need to watch my back all the time. I even felt like I could handle Myles's struggle better because I was actually well-rested. I was eating warm meals. I didn't have to pee in the bushes at night, and I didn't have to fuck a guy in a public bathroom because we had nowhere else to do it.

I sighed audibly, and Kian looked over at me. A smile broke across his face, and he reached over to hold my hand. My body shivered at the contact.

"I can't eat without my hand." I rolled my eyes, pretending his need to touch me wasn't sweet, adorable, and turning me on all over again.

"I'll feed you," he joked.

"Mmm hmm. Okay." I flashed him my dimple with a laugh, as I slipped my hand out of his to take another bite of my food. I had never fucked a guy and developed feelings. Usually, they didn't hang around long enough for that to happen. Sometimes I didn't even know their name. I had never been in a relationship. I had never sat and watched a movie with a guy while we drank vodka sodas out of licorice straws. I had never had a guy go down on me in the shower, then dry me off and insist on dressing me. I had never had a lazy morning with a gorgeous, bearded man on a random Saturday. It was giving "I like you" vibes, and I wasn't sure what to do with that.

Someone like me didn't usually have situations like this, and if I was honest, I liked it so much that it hurt. The happiness hurt. Because I was afraid of what it would feel like when it went away. The quote, "Better to have loved and lost than never to have loved at all," flitted through my mind. And while I had never loved a man before, I wasn't convinced that I wanted to experience the joy of love if it came with the risk of intense pain through heartbreak.

"Penny for your thoughts." Kian pulled on the ends of my hair slightly. Having him around felt nice. He was like a song I couldn't get out of my head, I realized, in a good way. That song that you listened to over and over and it just got better every time you heard it.

"I'm not thinking about anything," I lied. Kian laughed.

"You're thinking so hard I can practically see it happening inside your head." He called me out as he stood up to clean up our garbage.

"Alright, I am," I confessed. He sat back down next to me, and I leaned against his arm.

"I was just thinking that ever since I met you and then was lucky enough to get this room, I have felt what it's like to live life a little slower, with less of a need to survive each day, and it's been nice."

"My life has been nice since I met you too." He leaned down and kissed me. Softly, briefly. Yet I felt it through every nerve ending in my body.

"'Cause of all the sex?" I quipped.

"Obviously." He ran a finger down my arm, and I quivered from his touch yet again. Something about him was already more than I had ever experienced before. I was physically affected by him. I thought about him when he wasn't around, and when he was, his presence calmed me and revved me up at the same time.

Kian was not wearing a shirt, and I was finally able to get a better look at his tattoos. I examined the arm that I hadn't seen the other day. On his forearm was a fine line tattoo of a music staff surrounded by random circles and the number nine. He had a bunch of dancing music notes stretched around his bicep.

Across his back were multiple tattoos. The biggest one was a G-clef drawn in messy, bold strokes in such a way that it looked like it was turning into smoke and would dissipate if I blew on it.

He had bits of verses from songs and other random music notes all across one shoulder. Along the side of his back, not quite reaching around his ribs, was the shadowy, shaded silhouette of the body of a woman with her hands held up in front of her face. They almost looked like they were pressed up against his skin from the inside out. He had an angry-looking angel playing the violin, a mess of lines and splotches that, fully formed, turned into a face surrounded by smoke, music, and abstract lines. The one that really threw me off was on his right shoulder, and it looked like black and white watercolor. It was a blob with smeared edges at best, but in the middle of it, I could have sworn I saw two tiny feet. I ran my fingers over it and began to ask what it meant when Kian suddenly stood, pulled on his shirt, and went to retrieve his guitar that stood in the corner of the room.

When he sat back down, he began to strum, singing quietly in an almost absent-minded whisper. I curled up on the couch, watching him. He was so beautiful. Originally, I had just wanted him to fuck me, but I had gotten greedy, and now I wanted to hear all about what *more* meant.

He looked over at me from under his long lashes, and I saw the ever-present pain in his eyes that he so obviously held onto like armor, but today, I also saw something new mixed in with it. Something that looked like hope. We could destroy each other with how good it could be; the thought flitted through my mind, unbidden.

Never before had I wanted to say so much yet said nothing. I was not the kind of girl who was afraid to wear my heart on my sleeve. However, this time, as I watched the heat in his eyes and the movement of his fingers on the strings of his guitar, I stayed silent. I pondered all of the ways he could complicate my life and all of the ways we could do the happily ever after thing. As if he could hear my thoughts, Kian smiled at me. His real smile. I smiled back.

I wasn't sure what this was that was happening between us or even what tomorrow would bring, but I liked it. I liked it a lot. He was such an ironic mix of mysterious, rude, sweet, angsty, and sexy. The things that man did to me in the bedroom. I shivered at the memory of him pulling out of me slightly, holding me down with one hand, yet somehow curling me closer to him with the other and then spitting on me *there* before slamming back into me with a groan. As hot as he was when he made me come, he was also so intuitively kind in his ability to pick up on my moods, buying me food and pulling a sweatshirt over my head because he "never wanted me to be cold ever again."

When you threw in his hesitancy to tell me much about himself and his penchants for fighting, he was such a conundrum that I couldn't quite figure out. I closed my eyes, letting his voice wrap me up like smoke, smooth and warm. It felt like, until now, I had gracefully accepted life exactly the way it was, not desiring more. Yet somehow, my heart had still found him, without my permission, but found him all the same.

I MUST HAVE DRIFTED off because I woke up to the sound of my phone vibrating. It was the privately owned detox center that I took Myles to. I answered and was happy to find one of the nurses calling to let me know that Myles was doing well. I was so relieved to hear the good news that I must have said thank you ten times in the whole three-minute conversation. I sat up, rubbed my eyes, and looked around. I found Kian putting his coat on.

"Leaving?" I asked.

"I'm gonna hit the gym," he told me. "Wanna come?"

"To work out?" I laughed. "Nah."

"They have massages and a sauna. It's free if you come on my guest pass."

"Oh, so you're at the fancy gym?" He had piqued my interest. My gym was fine with plenty of areas to work out in and a clean locker-room, but it didn't offer anything fancy like massages. Kian shrugged as if to say, "I guess." I had nothing else to do but sit in my hotel room and worry about Myles, so I got up off the couch.

"I've never gotten a massage before, but it can't be bad, right?"

"Being rubbed all over with oils and creams? No, that doesn't sound bad," he teased. I quickly changed into leggings and a tank top with my one zip-up hoodie on top. The hoodie was something I picked up as a teenager, and it said "Don't worry, be sexy" across the back. Kian laughed when he saw it.

"You are," he confirmed as we left the room.

"I am what?"

"Sexy."

His hand was resting gently near my lower back as he guided me out of the hotel, and I found his protective stance endearing.

"Well, thanks." I remained my usual confident self, but the compliment landed deeper than they usually did. I was used to men finding me attractive in a surface-level way, but it felt like Kian was getting glimpses of my inner self as well, and I hoped he found those parts of me as attractive as he did my body and my face.

UNLIKE THE LAST time we were in his van, this time, I stayed awake and talked the entire time. Kian had asked about my mother, which led to me just word vomiting all over him. I told

him how we ended up homeless and explained how I considered Myles my brother, but we weren't actually blood related. By
the time we pulled up in front of the gym, I was almost out of
breath from my nonstop chatter.

"Whoops, I kinda hogged that conversation." I laughed as I
unbuckled.

"Thanks for trusting me with all of that." His hand ran down
my arm briefly before he got out to open my door. I wanted to
pinch myself as he helped me down and then continued to hold
my hand as we crossed the parking lot. This was not real. I was
the girl whose dreams didn't exceed my love for making people's
coffee and my desire to keep my brother alive. I lived in the
moment because I didn't have the luxury of wondering what the
next moment would bring. I had always been satisfied with that,
and here this gorgeous man was making me wonder if there
could be a fresh reality for me. He was making me hope for
more hand-holding, more talking, more laughter, and more real
moments. That word *more* had certainly been following me
around today. Kian ignored the security guard as we headed to
the front desk.

"Hello." I smiled at him. The guard scowled but nodded.
Kian checked me in with a guest day pass.

"I'll be in the weight room," he told me as he led me to the
massage room and then stopped to press a kiss to my forehead. I
was so overwhelmed by all of it that, for a moment, I felt like I
would pass out from the sheer happiness. This felt so normal.
Almost like I wasn't the girl who lived in a hotel room instead of
a tent, whose dad had abandoned her, and who was one medical
bill away from being completely broke.

"Come find me when you're done," he whispered against my
skin before pulling away, seemingly unaware of the beautiful
chaos he had ignited inside of me.

"Okay." I nodded. I watched him walk away, unabashedly

admiring his ass and strong shoulders, before I turned and entered the room behind me.

APPARENTLY, massages were little slices of heaven that I had never even known existed in all my twenty-five years. I was stripped naked and laid under a soft sheet. The music had me entranced in a deep state of relaxation. The massage therapist kneaded every knot of stress out of me. Not only did she massage my back, arms, legs, and shoulders, but she also rubbed my scalp, which I immediately loved and may have even let out a little moan during the treatment. By the time she was done, I felt floppy and serene. Damn Kian West for showing me a new reality. A reality I could never afford and one he probably would not stick around to see through with me. I wasn't spiteful about it; it was just something I was used to. People didn't stick around much in my world.

Even Alanna and Eric would probably not be around forever. They would move on to better jobs or other areas of town. It would likely just be Myles and me for life. At least, I fervently hoped it would be. My heart felt a little guilty for enjoying such a luxurious day of sex and massages while Myles sat detoxing in a facility, but I chose to focus on it being something to rejuvenate me for when he came home.

After profusely thanking the massage therapist by tipping her ten dollars that I really couldn't afford, I got re-dressed and went to seek out Kian. Almost one and a half hours had passed since he had gone to work out, so I figured he would be close to finished by now. I found him where he said he'd be, in the weight room.

I immediately felt my body flood with desire at the sight of him. He was lying on one of the weight benches, lifting two free weights that looked heavier than I could even pick up one time, let alone do multiple reps with. His shirt was off, and I got a full-on show of the swollen muscles in his arms, his defined stomach, and pecs that appeared etched. He was covered in sweat, and some strands of hair were falling out of his bun. How was he real? He looked up as I walked closer.

"I'm almost done." He grunted, yet he paused to smile at me and asked, "Did you enjoy your massage?"

"I did. Thank you." I ignored the few other people working out in various areas of the room and climbed onto his lap, feeling his thighs strain under my sudden added weight. "Figured you could use some motivation," I explained, grinning cheekily. He let out a breath but didn't protest; he just lifted his weights again. I felt him hardening under my ass.

"It's working," he muttered. I giggled and watched as he did ten more reps, then sat up after putting the weights down on either side of him.

"You're asking for it," he said jokingly as he wiped the sweat off his face with a small towel that he had hanging over the bench.

"I really am," I agreed seriously, gyrating my hips in his lap. I had already come twice today, and yet my body was begging for more. His eyes darkened, and his gaze landed on my lips. I felt my heart rate accelerate as he realized what I wanted. He looked around the room, clocking where the other people were, and then, with his right arm, he gathered me to his sweaty chest and leaned his head down to kiss me. His lips were hot and insistent against mine, and I instantly soaked my underwear at his heady taste. The smell of his sweat was turning me on.

"Not here," he all but growled against my mouth.

I could take him right now. I wanted him so badly that I wouldn't even care, but I didn't want to get him kicked out of his gym, or worse, so I agreed breathlessly, "Not here."

Kian stood up, taking me with him, and swung me over the

bench before gently putting me down. He gathered up his belongings and then took my hand, all but dragging me out of the room.

"Did you check out the sauna yet?" He looked back at me as he asked. I shook my head. He hummed in response but didn't say more. I was certain that the area we were standing in front of was just for men, but he walked me into the locker room anyway, looking both ways to make sure it was empty. He handed me a towel and said in a gravelly tone, "Strip."

I didn't even pause; I took off my jacket, my tank top, and my leggings until I stood there in my plain basic bra and mismatched underwear. He bit his lip and dragged his eyes over me; my skin prickled under his scrutiny.

"You are stunning," he murmured in my ear as he leaned down to kiss his way across my jaw and then down my neck. He had me crowded against the cold locker, but he stopped when we heard voices coming down the hall. He wrapped me up in the towel and then led me to the sauna. The sauna room was currently empty and very large. It was also hot, dark, and foggy to the point that you couldn't see that far in front of you.

Kian led us to the wooden, slatted bench on the far left. He laid his towel down, sat on it, and then pulled me into his lap.

"Can you be quiet this time, Jessamine?" he purred. I could have combusted just from that. From him knowing how loud I usually was to the use of my full name to the fact that he was telling me he would take me here and now. Fuck, everything about this man was so hot.

"I'll try," I panted as he began his perusal of my body with his hands. His large palms worked their way from my hips to squeeze and slap my ass and then work their way down the back of my thighs.

"What do you want?"

I had my eyes closed as I leaned into his touch, and his voice startled me. Between the massage and the smoky aura of the room, I felt drunk and loopy.

"Touch me. Kiss me. Fuck me." I breathed. He lifted my bra to reveal my breasts but didn't unclasp the hooks to take it off, so the pressure compressed the top of my chest, causing the underside to swell up from under the material. He massaged the skin around my nipples and then bent to take one into his mouth, drawing me into a frenzy with his hot tongue and nip of his teeth.

"Have you done this before?" He looked up at me, his face glistening in the steam.

"Fucked a guy in a sauna?"

He clicked his tongue as if to say no and shook his head.

"Fucked a guy in public?" I corrected. He nodded and began to pull my underwear down, forcing me to rise up on my knees so he could drag them down my ass and thighs.

"Yes," I told him without pause, as I had no shame about my sexual history.

"How many men have you been with?" he asked suddenly as he produced a condom from under his towel.

That was random, I thought to myself.

"Including non-consensual encounters?" I asked. I wasn't saying it to put him in his place because I didn't mind the question, and I was happy to answer it, but the truth was my history was complicated, and I wasn't going to sugarcoat it.

Kian faltered at my answer, pausing as he ripped the condom open with his teeth. His eyes met mine, and I saw sympathy in them that I hadn't asked for.

"Don't back down now, music man," I mocked and ground my now-bare pussy around his hard shaft. He moved his hips to make space for his hands, and I watched as he pinched the tip and then rolled the condom down on his cock. I shivered with anticipation. He pulled me down on top of him as he kissed me.

I groaned into his mouth, and he admonished me, "I told you to be quiet."

"It feels too good." I mewled as he began to move me up and down on him in earnest. He had his hands on my hips and was lifting me like I was a set of weights and not a thick-thighed girl with what had to be ten pounds of hair. Hair that was now getting completely wrecked by the wet air around me. The way he had me tilted against his hips had my clit rubbing on his pelvis, and I was revving up for an orgasm so quickly it was embarrassing.

"Yes, yes," I called out, and my voice echoed off the walls. I felt a hand cover my mouth and his voice telling me that I was not behaving myself. I giggled and then moaned as I felt the walls of my pussy begin to squeeze in anticipation. Suddenly, the door to the sauna opened, and someone stepped inside. Kian kept moving, and I felt hot and tingly all over, knowing they would either see us or could at least hear the slick sounds of our bodies moving against each other.

"Get out," Kian called, not missing a stroke inside of me. I heard the muffled voice of people frantically whispering to each other, then a retreat of footsteps and the door closing.

"We need to hurry," Kian told me. "Are you close?"

I nodded, wide-eyed, knowing someone could walk in again at any second. He began to cant his hips and fuck up into me as he moved my body on him. His voice was husky in my ear. Saying things like, "Yes, take me, fuck you're so tight, oh yeah, move like that, kiss me, Jessa, kiss me."

I was so swollen, so slick, and so full of him that I came several seconds later with his name on my lips. He swallowed my cry into his mouth and followed me over the precipice a few moments later. We sat there, my breasts crushed against him, chests heaving. I was close to being smothered from sucking in so much hot, thick air, and I felt emotionally overwhelmed when he leaned down to my ear and whispered, "If you asked me to, I would kill any man who touched you without your consent."

I believed he would, and it healed places in my heart that I didn't know were still hurting until that very moment.

Chapter Seventeen

Love U Like That by Lauv

2:17   50   1:13

I wanted her again. I had just had her, and I was not satiated. I wanted more of the desperate, sloppy kisses. I wanted more of her cries in my ear. I wanted more of her taste on my tongue and her warm body riding mine. God, she was hot. Everything about her tempted me. From the way the corners of her lips were naturally always turned up so she seemed to be perpetually amused, to the way her ass jiggled when she walked, to the shape of her breasts straining against every shirt she wore.

I wasn't just attracted to her body. Her soft, inviting body. Ugh, with that thought, I had to hold myself back from pulling the van over and commanding her to climb back into my lap, where I would lower my fly, push her underwear to the side, and pound into her as her ass hit the steering wheel and the horn with every thrust.

No, I was also growing so fond of her mind. Of her sense of humor. Of her ability to submit to me yet command my attention in every interaction we had. *Don't back down now, music man.* Her words echoed in my head. I had frozen at her casual way of telling me that she had been violated, yet she had immediately gotten me out of my head and kept me focused on the task at hand. I had never had someone in my life who was able to redirect me as quickly as she apparently could. I was known to play the part of the moody musician very well.

In the past, when something happened or triggered me, I would get into my head and let the hard feelings overstay their welcome. My bandmates and my manager hated when I got into one of my moods because it took all they had to snap me out of it. My moods made for great music, as most of my famous songs had been birthed in one of my angrier moments, but it didn't always make me great company when I was in a grumpy mindset.

Clearly, I was a bit dramatic with my emotions at times, as here I was, living an anonymous life, having completely changed my body and left everyone and everything I knew behind to live this self-inflicted punishment. A punishment I had chosen for something terrible that had happened, but I was now realizing that I knew many people who also had awful things happen to them, and they hadn't abandoned everyone they ever knew as a result.

Jessa was a good example of someone who could have so easily thrown in the towel, yet she clearly had never given up, and I respected the fuck out of her for it. I was becoming aware that I may be the dominating one, but she was really the one who owned me. Back to my original thought, *I wanted more*. I wanted more with her. I wanted more *of* her. I wanted whatever more she'd be willing to give me, and I hoped she'd be willing to continue giving it to me once she found out who I really was.

"Penny for your thoughts." Jessa's teasing tone broke me out of my reverie as I pulled my van back into the parking lot of her hotel.

"I haven't seen you smoke all day." I told her a new observation instead of letting her into the storm of my mind.

"I'm not really much of a quantity smoker." She unbuckled and turned to look at me. "I'm more of a *one to two cigarettes max a day* kind of girl."

"For the dopamine?" I winked. She started to say something, then stopped and laughed.

"I see where you're going with this. Are you saying I don't need to smoke because I've gotten so much dopamine from other things?"

"Maybe." I tried to keep a straight face.

"And you're proud of yourself?" She openly laughed at me again.

"I am." I smiled back at her smugly.

The next six weeks were perfect. We spent time together every single day, maneuvering around her work and my gym schedule. We fucked on most of the surfaces in her hotel room, and she even let me go down on her in the elevator that we had taken up to the roof for a picnic beneath the stars. We whispered little facts about ourselves as we were lying under the blanket at night.

She told me about her life on the streets, her favorite color, her dreams of living in California one day, and the resentment she had toward her father for abandoning her and her mother.

I told her things like my favorite food, the dog I had grown up with, and why I thought bananas were the worst fruit in the world. I shared a heavier memory about why I had started voice lessons at the age of eight because my music teacher at school had told my mother that I was a "prodigy." My mother had then pushed me to do it because she saw me as her way to cash out at the bank. I had loved singing but had grown to associate her love of my singing with stress and demands.

I felt guilty for leaving out some major facts about myself. Like the fact that I had been engaged. Or that I was an award-winning, platinum record singer who had a band that was waiting for me to return. I hoped she would forgive me when I finally told her those truths. I planned to tell her after the fight—the fight she and Myles planned on attending.

Three days after our rendezvous in the sauna, I had driven Jessa to pick up Myles from the detox center. We had both been so happy when we saw how alert he looked and the healthy glow in his skin. I had slept over every night while he was away and assumed Jessa would no longer want me there once her brother was back, but when the evening rolled around, I had received a text from her saying that my side of the bed was getting cold. The happiness I felt when that text came in was indescribable. I had run through the parking lot in just my sweatpants and flip-flops to get into bed next to her.

We had gotten into a rhythm of me getting up before Jessa did to drive Myles to his NA meeting. When Jessa woke up, she would order us breakfast. When I got back, we would eat together and then shower, and then I would drive us to work. I enjoyed watching her do her thing inside while I played my music outside. During her breaks, she would bring me drinks with little notes written on the cups. One day, I received a peppermint, white mocha iced coffee with chocolate chips and cookie crumbs on top with the words "You're my favorite plot twist" written on it in her hurried handwriting. Another day, she had brought me a hot chocolate with caramel brûlée sauce and whipped cream that said, "I like when you're happy and naked."

On Monday, she excitedly made me taste a drink that she told me was called a brown butter chai, made from an iced chai latte base with a shot of blonde espresso, two pumps of brown sugar, two pumps of chai, and almond milk. She had written her note across the bottom, and it said, "I find you in pieces of every song I hear." I had kissed her so hard after I read it that she had to practically pull me off her so she could go back to work.

The next day, she simply wrote, "Your voice is my favorite sound" on a cup of coffee that reminded me of chestnuts.

Today, Saturday, was her birthday, and luckily, she was working a shorter shift than usual. I was strumming on my guitar when she brought out a drink that she called a bourbon apple cider. She said it was made from steamed apple juice mixed with two pumps of apple brown sugar syrup and cinnamon. When I made a face, she called me a picky baby, which made me laugh. I was pleasantly surprised to find the drink to actually be delicious versus what I imagined it would taste like —warmed-up applesauce. I impatiently looked to find her note, and my heart rate stuttered when I saw it on the order sticker. It simply said, "What does more look like?"

I licked remnants of the drink off my lip and smoothed my mustache with my fingers as I tried to remain calm and chill. Did that mean what I thought it meant? I had never really had to try to win over a girl. I had never had to wait so patiently to know if someone wanted to be in a relationship with me. Even Rose had been different in terms of how I saw her as a partner and not just a quick lay, but I didn't have to work to win her over. She had already known of me and had set her sights on me long before I knew she existed. So when I decided I wanted her too, it was a done deal between us.

With Jessa, I felt that I had to actually be likable. I had to truly try. I had to win her over. I didn't have fame and money wrapping me up in a desirable package. In fact, with Jessa, I worried knowing that would probably make her like me less.

I also knew I was running out of time, but before she found out more about me, I wanted her to want more with *me*, the real *me*. I was enjoying this slice of real life where I could finally experience the feeling of boy meets girl and has to win girl over. Not fan meets award-winning singer and fucks said singer because he's famous, before slipping out in the middle of the night because the singer's manager made her leave.

JESSA DUCKED her head in an uncharacteristic moment of shyness and smiled at me. I wondered what she meant exactly. Did she want to know what more meant just to understand what it meant to me? Or did she want to know what it meant because she was ready to step into a relationship with me? I was so ready to deliver on that. I wanted to call her mine. I wanted to show her what kind of life I could give her. I wanted all of it with her.

"Can we talk about this later?" I asked, gesturing to the cup. She nodded and started to walk away with her usual omission of a goodbye.

"Happy birthday," I told her again, pulling her back to me. She giggled.

"I think you've said that six times already," she reminded me.

"Get ready for six more." I shrugged. "It's your birthday! Be excited." I put my hands on her shoulders and shook her gently. She responded by pressing her face to my chest and wrapping her arms around me.

"Thank you."

"For what?" I pressed a kiss to her wild hair. She didn't

answer, but she didn't have to. I knew what she wasn't saying because I was feeling it too.

AN HOUR LATER, Jessa's shift was over, and she was holding my hand as I walked her to my van and opened the door for her. Her eyes lit up when she saw the balloons I had put on the front seat.

"For me?" She turned to look at me.

"Do you see another birthday girl around here somewhere?" I pretended to look behind her, and she hit my arm playfully.

"Shut up." She gave a laugh as she climbed into the van and grabbed the balloons. "I haven't gotten balloons for my birthday in forever." She was so excited about them, and it confirmed my hunch that this girl had probably not celebrated her birthday properly since her father left. I was about to remedy that, even if she tried to fight me for spending money on her.

Our first stop was at a nail salon where I had to basically beg her to let them give her a manicure and pedicure. She had told me multiple times that I couldn't spend money on her. I knew she was suspicious about where it was coming from, and rightfully so, but she would soon understand. My fight was in six days, and then I planned to tell her everything there was to know about me.

Jessa finally agreed to do it, but only if I got a pedicure with her, so we sat in two chairs side by side and got our feet buffed, moisturized, and painted. At one point, I looked up to find the nail tech staring at me suspiciously. My heart skipped a beat. I feared she had recognized me, but she didn't say anything and just looked back down to keep cleaning up the cuticles on my toes. Jessa had chosen a deep red polish for her feet and went with a dark onyx black for her fingers.

Interesting choices, Rose huffed in my mind. Her ghost

seemed to be throwing temper tantrums every time my heart acknowledged how much healing Jessa brought me. I ignored her.

OUR NEXT STOP was the hair salon.

"I am not letting anyone touch my hair." Jessa was not happy about the idea of parting with any of her curls.

"You don't have to cut it if you don't want to." I held the door open as she hesitantly shuffled inside. "Kari is a curly hair specialist, and I figured you could just let her wash it and decide what you want to do from there."

She humphed but gave in. Two hours later, she had received a soothing scalp massage, a deep conditioning treatment, and the tiniest trim off the very bottom just to clean up the dead ends.

"Good?" I asked as we walked back to the van.

"I'm loving every fucking second, but I'm mad at you because it's too much money, and you know it." She tried to make herself look mad, but I kissed her all over her face until she gave in and started laughing.

"Kari asked if you were my boyfriend," Jessa announced suddenly.

My heart grew tight in my chest as I responded, "And what did you say?"

"I said you were my music man." She smiled softly; the emotion she was feeling reached her eyes and softened them. I reached for her hand and squeezed it, but we stayed silent for the rest of the drive back to the hotel to get changed and pick up Myles. It was odd to think of her as possibly being my girlfriend when the term couldn't fully encompass what I really felt toward her. She was the girl who had saved me from myself. Was there a relationship status for that dynamic?

BACK IN THE ROOM, Jessa changed into what I called her parachute cargo pants and a black top while I watched an episode of *Friends* with Myles.

"How was group therapy?" I asked when the episode ended.

"It was good. We're learning about regulating our nervous systems and understanding how our trauma makes us prone to addiction," he told me.

I listened silently, soaking in all the knowledge he was sharing. I was so happy for him and his progress thus far, although Jessa had cautioned me from getting my hopes up since she knew firsthand how long a road his recovery journey would be. She had shared with me that she still carried Narcan with her, not because she didn't trust Myles but because she didn't trust his addiction.

It made me sad to watch someone not just addicted to a substance but was also addicted to filling the void within himself with drugs versus his own love. I was coming to realize that so many of us were addicted to something that filled a void. I would readily admit that I was addicted to something—I was addicted to the pain of working out and destroying my body as I built it up so powerfully instead of letting myself just feel the pain of loss. Getting sober or healing really meant learning to love yourself instead of wanting to escape yourself. Accepting what was and allowing yourself to actually feel even the most uncomfortable and painful things. The process was lifelong, hence why so many people relapsed back into their own version of hell.

Exactly, Rose's voice said in my head. Fuck. Why wouldn't she leave me alone?

I was standing in the bathroom, ready to go wherever Kian had booked us to eat dinner, but I couldn't bring myself to leave the room just yet. Today had already been amazing. More than I could have imagined. It had started with birthday sex, and then at work, Eric and Alanna had stuck a candle into a cake pop and sang me "Happy Birthday."

Once work had ended, Kian had pissed me off while simultaneously making me so happy with the two appointments he had booked for me. Now he was taking Myles and me to dinner. I was annoyed at him for ignoring my rule of not spending money on me, but at the same time, I was enjoying every minute of it.

Since homelessness had taken over my life, my birthday had never really been anything more than just having completed another year. Last year, I spent the entire day at work. The year before, I had been sent on a wild goose chase trying to find Myles, who had been high and lost his phone.

Today was already feeling like much more than I was used to and a lot more than I needed to make the day special. I took a deep breath and then grinned when I heard the sound of Myles laughing from the other room. Could this be mine? I wondered. This life with a sober brother, a warm bed, and a hot man who got pedicures with me.

I blinked at my reflection. I had spent more than my usual five minutes on my makeup and had even applied a sticky lip gloss that Alanna had given me. My jumbled thoughts drifted to Kari from the salon. When she had asked me if Kian was my boyfriend, my heart had flip-flopped in my chest. I didn't know what he was. He hadn't yet asked me to be his girlfriend. He had not put any labels on us.

All I knew was that I didn't want to remember what it felt like not to wake up next to him. I wanted to keep the buzz that went through my body when he tugged on my curls and told me to have a good day. I needed more time to keep pulling smiles out of him. Was that *more*? Was *more* laughter and safety and licorice straws and trembling orgasms at two a.m.? I ran my hands down the material of my pants, took another deep breath, and left the room.

"I'm ready," I announced.

"You look amazing, J." Myles stood up, grinning.

"Absolutely gorgeous," Kian agreed, holding my coat open for me.

"Thank you." I let him pull it on me and zip it. Then he placed a quick kiss on the tip of my nose. I looked up to find Myles watching us with a small smile on his face. I cocked an eyebrow at him as if to say "What?" He just shrugged back at me and went to open the door.

"ARE YOU CRAZY?" I stared at the steakhouse that Kian had driven us to and was now standing in front of. I had never heard of it, of course, but I could tell it was way beyond all of our pay grades with its shiny gray exterior, its dark frosted windows, and the gold letters spelling out the name of the restaurant.

"Just go inside, Jessamine," Kian encouraged me. "You only turn twenty-six once."

"Kian, you can't afford this place. I don't care how many fights you've won. This is fancy," I all but hissed at him as I stepped out of the way to make room for a couple that had left the restaurant and were walking down the few steps to get to the sidewalk. She was wearing a fur coat and was holding a shiny black bag with two interlocked Cs on the front of it. In comparison, I was grossly underdressed in my hand-me-down coat and scuffed boots. Kian came to stand in front of me and took my face in his cold hands. He tilted my chin up to look at him.

"Do you trust me?" he asked suddenly. I could all but hear Myles take a deep breath behind me. He had heard me say so many times how I only trusted him because too many people had let us down, and therefore, our trust was not to be given out lightly. The question was a loaded one, and it took me off guard. I didn't answer. Kian's stern face softened as he smiled and gently brought his mouth to mine. He murmured the question again against my lips.

"Do you trust me?"

This time, I barely nodded my answer, and he accepted it as a full yes.

"I got this. You don't have to worry. I know this isn't your usual vibe, and if you hate it, we'll leave. We'll go get bagels instead if you want to. But at least give it a chance. Can you do that?"

I gave in and nodded again. Kian took my hand, looked over at Myles, and then walked us inside. Just as I expected, the ambiance was higher class than any place I had ever been to in all my life. The floor was marble, the lights were low, and instrumental music played gently throughout the room. The entryway smelled of expensive perfume, and the host greeted us from an all-velvet station with a pile of electronic menus on it.

"I have a reservation under Bardot," I heard Kian tell the maître d'. I faltered at the use of my last name, wondering why he hadn't used his, but I was quickly distracted when the man greeted us warmly and then asked us to follow him to the back of the restaurant. As we grew closer, I recognized the people sitting at the table to my left. I looked over at Kian, who was grinning at me.

"You..." I looked back at the table. Eric was smiling at me from where he sat next to his partner, David. Alanna was sitting to the right of Eric. Joseph and Martin, who worked the opposite shift of me, were directly across from them.

"Happy birthday!" Eric whispered loudly. I laughed and went over to hug him. I could tell that all of my friends were feeling a little bit uncomfortable. People like us didn't frequent places like this. Kian pulled out a chair for me, and I quickly sat. After saying hello to all of my friends, I turned back to him.

"You arranged all of this for me?" I asked. It was a stupid question, but I needed to ask it anyway.

Kian nodded, running a calming touch down my arm, and then took my hand in his.

"Happy birthday," he whispered. I held onto his hand for a second longer than necessary, and he squeezed mine in his. I didn't have to say anything. I knew that he knew.

THIS PLACE WAS SO FANCY, the menu didn't have prices. Myles didn't seem too worried about it and immediately ordered mussels as his appetizer and a Delmonico steak for his entree. He seemed perfectly comfortable, while I couldn't figure out why I had so many forks next to my plate. I ended up asking

Kian to order for me because I had no experience to reference to even know what I would want to eat.

"You good?" Kian whispered in my ear. I answered around a mouthful of duck,

"I've never had something so expensive in my mouth before."

Kian let out a genuine laugh and reached over to take a bite of ravioli off my plate.

"Thank you for all of this." I was growing warm from the delicious meal, the wine, and the emotion surrounding the fact that all of these people had come out tonight simply because it was my birthday.

Kian looked at me, emotion softening his gaze, but he didn't say anything. Instead, he ran a finger down the outside of my hand and then linked his pinky over mine. It was a barely visible movement on his part, and yet it meant a lot to me, just like most of the things he did. He may be a man of few words, but him holding my pinky in this fancy restaurant surrounded by my friends for a gathering he had arranged for me made me feel like I was his.

That we were *more*.

DESSERT WAS an eclair birthday cake with sparklers in it as candles. Everyone ooohed and aaahed when the waiter brought it out. They all sang "Happy Birthday" to me, and then they each took out gifts and put them on the table in front of me.

"You guys. No!" I tried to push them back, but Eric stopped me by saying, "Everyone deserves birthday presents, Jessa. Just open them and enjoy yourself."

I ACQUIESCED and opened the gift bag. He and David had gotten me a pair of Uggs.

"I can't accept this," I told him.

"Shush." Eric put his finger against my mouth to quiet me, which made everyone laugh. "Put them on. Let's see how they fit."

So in the middle of this fancy restaurant, I took off my old, laced-up boots and slipped my feet into the chestnut-colored platform boots. The inside was so soft against my toes, and I ran my hand over the Sherpa corduroy material that made up the outside of the boot.

"I love them so much," I admitted. I got up to hug Eric again and then David, who whispered a "Happy birthday, darling" in my ear.

I moved on to Alanna's gift, which was a shampoo and conditioner set for curly hair. When I leaned over to hug her, she whispered how hot Kian was and how lucky I had been to find him. When I sat back down, I saw a smug look on Kian's face, and I presumed he had heard her.

Joseph had given me a Visa gift card because he was a self-proclaimed terrible gift giver, so he wanted me to choose, and Martin had given me a crossbody bag from a popular brand that I recognized. He said it was because I didn't lug my backpack around with me anymore, and I obviously needed a place for the things I brought with me to work.

I tried to protest that I didn't need anything fancy, but Martin interrupted me with a good-natured, "It was literally only thirty-eight dollars, Patricia. Pipe down."

His use of the name Patricia had everyone laughing.

Myles gave me a handwritten card that I told him I would have to open later when I was alone because I was certain it would make me cry.

Lastly was Kian's gift. He handed me a small black box held

closed with a black ribbon. I took it, pulled the ribbon open, and removed the cover. Nestled on black velvet was a gold necklace. It had a thin, dainty chain, and on it hung three small charms. The middle one was a gold handmade circle that had a pressed-in impression on it that looked like a compass. To the left of it was a tiny purple amethyst stone, and to the right of it was a cloudy white moonstone charm.

"It's beautiful." I breathed as I opened the card. Inside, he had scratched out in what I could imagine was a typical hurried musician's handwriting, "You make me feel like I have found true north. Happy birthday, Jessamine Bardot." Oh, I needed to unpack that note when I wasn't feeling so befuddled from the wine and the entire night in general.

Kian had always been attentive, and lately, he had grown more open with me, but he had never said anything that felt like this level of romance before. The beautiful emotion of happiness that I was feeling crawled up my throat in the form of a sob, and I had to swallow to stop myself from suddenly bawling in this fancy restaurant. I would have plenty of time for tears when I was alone and could sort through every amazing moment that this night had offered.

"Thank you, music man," I whispered as I handed Kian the necklace. Of course he was silent as he reached behind me to clasp it in place. It fell right below my collarbone, and I felt it nestled there on my neck, the metal cold against my heated skin. I looked around at the table full of delicious food, my friends, this man, and my sober brother, and in that moment, I could not have wished for anything more in the world.

AFTER SAYING goodbye and multiple thank yous to my friends, we dropped Myles off at an NA meeting and went back to my room, which recently, I had begun to think of as *home*. Kian was carrying the balloons, the remaining cake, our leftovers that the restaurant had packed up for us, and a bag containing all of my gifts, so I held the door open for him and then watched as he put the food into the refrigerator and placed the balloons on the counter. I let the door shut behind me, and I stood with my back pressed against it, my fingers fiddling with the necklace Kian had given me. He was watching me with a quizzical look in his eyes, his face giving away nothing, yet the area around his mouth was softer than usual as if he was more relaxed.

"Did you have a good birthday?" he asked me, shucking his coat and letting it drop onto one of the chairs. He toed off his shoes and began to unbutton his shirt as he walked closer to me.

"I did. Thanks to you." I watched him flick open his belt and begin to thread it through his belt loops with one hand.

"And Myles," Kian corrected me. "He found the restaurant and called all of your friends."

"Did he now?" I was surprised but pleasantly so.

"He did," Kian confirmed. He had now rid himself of his pants and was standing in front of me in just his boxers. He reached out and ran a calloused finger over the necklace, pressing it into my skin until the metal warmed up from my body heat.

"What does true north mean, music man?" I asked softly. Kian fidgeted for a moment, then reached up to tug the zipper of my coat down before he finally said, "I want you to be mine for real."

I stilled, only moving to allow Kian to peel the coat off of me. He let it drop where we stood. I lifted my arms up as he pulled my shirt off over my head. He had to pause to untangle it from my mess of hair before moving onto my pants and shoving them down my legs in one quick motion. I stepped out of them robotically, and Kian kicked them to one side. My underwear was next, followed by his boxers. I felt, rather than saw, him put a condom on. Before I could even process what was happening, I was up in the air, my back against the cold door, his arms holding me up, and his cock was nudging against me until he had fully seated himself inside of me. I had not been prepared, and the invasion burned a little due to his sheer size and my lack of natural lubricant.

"Ouch." I let out an involuntary groan. He stopped and looked at me.

"I wasn't ready," I told him.

"I'm sorry." He lowered me gently until I was standing again, and then he was on his knees in front of me. He had one hand up against my stomach, keeping me pressed against the door, and the other was between my legs, spreading me for his tongue, which was immediately on me. It didn't take long for me to be slick and grinding myself against his mouth, which was sucking, licking, and biting me full force toward a knee-trembling orgasm.

Once I was fully dripping, he hauled me back up in his arms and slid his way back in, still standing in the hallway; this time, his back was against the door. He lifted and lowered me as he would his bell bar at the gym, working me up and down his length, breathing heavily and barely looking at me. I squeezed my knees shut so he couldn't move me anymore, and I tapped his chest.

"Hey."

He finally looked at me.

"What are you doing?" I asked gently. I could still feel him pulsing inside of me.

"Fucking you," he grumbled.

I cocked my head and stared at him as if to say, "Why here? Why like this?"

He frowned, then made a grunting sound as he shifted and

pulled out of me, leaving me empty once again. I wrapped my legs tighter around his waist and peered into his eyes. He huffed again, and then his posture seemed to deflate slightly.

"If I fuck you in that bed while you wear that necklace, I'm going to fall in love with you and..." He held me up with one hand and ran the other one through his hair, leaving a mess in its wake. He wouldn't look at me again. I leaned down and kissed his chest.

"Tell me why that's bad, music man."

I heard him sigh, and then he said, "I'm a mess. And there is a lot I still need to tell you. But at this point, I'm hoping you'll want me to be your mess. I m-mean I want to be your mess if you'll have me."

I could feel his heart beating quickly, and I heard him stutter over his words. I wasn't sure if it was from the effort of talking so much or if it was from him baring his soul to me.

"My mess, as in boyfriend and girlfriend?" I asked.

He shrugged. "I'll be whatever you want me to be."

"Fuck me in our bed, Kian," I responded, and it was all he needed to hear. He did. He wasn't gentle, and he wasn't sweet. He was messy and frantic and desirous and intense, and he was all mine.

Chapter Nineteen

On My Love by Zara Larsson & David Guetta

2:19   SD   1:23

T blinked as sleep left me and looked up at the ceiling. I could hear Jessa breathing softly next to me, and I could feel her hair spread out across my chest. I reached down and absentmindedly rubbed a curl between two of my fingers. Her leg was hooked over one of my thighs, and I was aware of her soft skin pressed against mine. It had been six days since I had left the mess that is me at her feet. Six days since I had enjoyed seeing her so happy at her party, only to awkwardly reveal how much I liked her and wanted her.

We hadn't talked about what true north meant to me yet. We hadn't acknowledged how much we had still left unsaid, but what I did know was now she was mine, and I was hers. Tonight, after the fight, I planned on laying the rest of me all out on the table for her to be able to truly choose me. At least, I hoped she would.

I turned to look down at this woman, who had quickly become a source of calm for me. A lighthouse. A silver lining. I could see the necklace I had commissioned for her against her tan skin, and I hooked the charms over my finger. The moonstone was my birthstone, and the amethyst was hers. I presumed she thought this was a cute twenty-dollar necklace from a local store, but it was actually made from pure gold with real gemstones. I had the same jeweler who made Rose's engagement ring create the necklace. He hadn't said anything to me in the email other than a thank you for the opportunity and a discussion regarding the design, but my anxiety created a whole story in my head about his judgment on how quickly I was moving on.

Did he think about how it hadn't even been two years since my fiancée had been murdered, and I was already making expensive jewelry for another girl?

"Probably," Rose mocked in my head. I shifted my body slightly and let my head fall back deeper into the pillow. I was not going down that road of crazy today. I had to stay focused and sharp for my fight tonight. A lot was riding on me winning. Not only were the stakes high because I was going up against another undefeated fighter, so the pot was bigger than ever, but, more importantly, my girl was going to be there watching me. I needed to prove to her that I could protect her before I told her the story of how much I had failed others in the past.

I was shaken from my thoughts when I heard the sound of Myles making coffee in the kitchen area. His sponsor was coming to pick him up for a meeting. Jessa was not working today, so we were both sleeping in. Well, she was sleeping, and I was stressing. I was stressing because I had received a text from the guys last night about how excited they were for me to come back, and did I need them to send the jet, or should they come meet me?

I texted them back that I would message them once I tied up some loose ends here. Loose ends that were the biggest fight of my short-lived boxing career, a girl who made my heart swell up in my chest every time I thought about her, and a very recently clean addict who had quickly become what I would consider a friend.

My brain shifted gears, and the words "*If I fuck you in that bed while you wear that necklace, I'm going to fall in love with you*" rang loudly in my head. She hadn't flinched. She hadn't asked me to put her down. She hadn't gotten mad at me for not prepping her before sliding in and finding her more dry than wet. She hadn't pushed me away or asked me to explain myself or demanded more or better or less from me.

She had just held her ground as she accepted me with all my broken pieces. Then she allowed me to pour all of my jumbled, confused feelings into her as I fucked her like I hated her while hoping she knew that what I was feeling was the exact opposite.

Afterward, we sat in bed while she ate a slice of her birthday cake, and I gave her another hint of who I really was as I strummed my guitar. I had played the song she'd requested of me, what felt like eons ago, "Calico" by Pointing West. The writer of that song was me. The band who sang it was mine. She hadn't noticed. It didn't click in her head that this muscly man in her bed was once the thin, glasses-wearing, buzz-cut sporting lead singer of a famous band. I had once been him, but I was never going to be him ever again. No matter what the boys, the paparazzi, or Gordon had to say about it. I was now Jessamine's, and even when I went back to singing, I was going to remain hers first.

If she would have me.

I HADN'T FUCKED Jessa since that night. I had tried to explain to her that all the pent-up testosterone from not coming was good for my fight. So, for the last six days, she had been driving me crazy and purposely testing my resolve by walking around our room in various states of undress. Last night, after she showered, she had come out in her full naked glory. I had to literally leave the room because she kept bending down to "pick things up" and I couldn't stand one more minute of it. Her husky laugh followed me all the way out to where I sat next to Myles on the couch.

"What's wrong?" he inquired, munching on a bowl of cereal.

"Don't worry about it," I muttered.

He caught on quickly and didn't ask any further questions.

This morning, she was looking particularly edible as she was lying curled up in the bed, her curves spread out like a buffet just for me. I had to pack up my shit and escape to my van, where I could practice my pre-fight rituals in peace. I texted her that I would be back in time to pick her up.

I never went to the gym on the day of a fight. Instead, I busked for two hours in the same spot I always did beforehand. I was superstitious with my rituals, and since I kept winning, it solidified them even more. After playing some music, I went back to my van and stared at the photo in my wallet for a while, feeling both happy and sad that my usual rage and fury hadn't ignited the way they usually did. I sighed and put it away.

I took out my ratty notebook and scribbled out the first stanza of a new song that had been bouncing around in my head. Then, I drove to the same grocery store I always did to buy an entire rotisserie chicken that I ate alone in the quiet solitude of my van. Except this time, I could feel the essence of Jessa floating around in my veins, spurring me on to win the fight— not due to the frenzy of my temper but rather my craze of emotion for her. It felt like the emotion came from the same place, but it also felt vastly different.

As the sun set, I drove back to the hotel and waited for Jessa and Myles to come down. She was wearing the lace black bodysuit we had purchased at Goodwill. That day at the rage room felt like it had been a year ago when, in reality, it had only been less than two months. I felt like I had evolved so much since meeting her that it seemed like a lifetime had passed.

As she grew closer, I saw that the bodysuit left little to the imagination, and I felt my protective feelings for her rear up inside of me. I almost regretted encouraging her to let me buy it. Objectively, I could see how stunning she looked, and obviously, she felt comfortable enough to wear it. So, I bit my tongue and stopped myself from telling her to zip up her coat and protect herself from the leery gaze of all the degenerates that would be at the fight tonight. Myles hopped into the backseat of my van and grinned at me.

"Let's fucking go, dude!"

His obvious excitement made me laugh. He and I had bonded ever since he had gotten sober. I drove him to his meeting almost every morning and we would talk the entire time. In fact, I had never talked so much in my life. I hadn't known it before, but I needed him and his insights on life.

Some nights, after Jessa would fall asleep, he and I would make food, and we would sit on the couch, and he would tell me about therapy and his meetings. I clung to every word. So much of his healing process was a process I also needed to explore. I may not be an addict in the literal sense, but I was seeking healing all the same.

"Let's fucking go," I agreed in a less exuberant tone, touching my fist to his as he held it out to me. Jessa was much quieter in comparison as she climbed in and buckled herself.

"You okay?" I peered over at her as I shifted the van into reverse.

"I know I insisted on coming, but I've realized I'm not really enjoying the idea of watching you get beat up," she admitted after a moment.

"You assume I'm going to let him touch me, baby." I grinned.

"That's what I'm talking about!" Myles exclaimed from the backseat. Jessa burst out laughing.

"I'll be doing all the touching later," she promised with a wink. I groaned in anticipation, and Myles made a fake gagging sound as we pulled out onto the road to drive to the warehouse where the fight was being held.

BEAU'S EYES almost popped out of his head as I walked in holding Jessamine's hand with Myles trailing closely behind. In all the time he had known me, I had never shown up with anyone, let alone a beautiful woman and her brother.

"When you texted me that you needed two seats for your girl and your friend, I thought you were kidding."

I almost laughed at his confusion. Almost. Instead, I kept a stern look on my face and replied, "When have I ever kidded around with you?"

"Two seats in the front. You got it, boss." Beau rushed off to make sure I had those seats, and I found myself a spot in the corner of the room to prepare for the fight. A lot of money exchanged hands at these events, yet the buildings they chose to host these underground matches in were decrepit at best. Jessa didn't flinch at our dilapidated surroundings—she just stood next to me, watching as I wrapped up my hands.

"When you go out there"—I jerked my head in the direction of the ring where everyone was sitting—"I need you to watch her."

Myles nodded.

"It can get a little crazy, and she..." I didn't finish my sentence because it was weird to tell your girlfriend's brother that I could almost see the shadow of her nipples behind her bodysuit and that, if allowed, the men in the crowd would eat her up and spit her out.

"I got her," he assured me as Beau ran back in to tell me that he had made room for them in the front. I grunted out a thank you and gestured for Jessa and Myles to follow him. I could hear the rumble of the crowd through the open door, and I imagined around a thousand people had already shown up.

"You got this, music man." Jessa grinned up at me.

"You know I do." I grabbed a handful of hair and pulled her face close to mine so I could kiss her. Then I spun her away.

"Stay safe."

She winked. "I always do."

I watched her follow Myles through the doorway and then turned back to finish getting ready for the fight. I saw my phone light up with missed calls from Gordon, Ash, Nile, and Mika.

"Impatient much?" I muttered. I shoved my phone into my coat pocket and ignored it when I heard it buzzing again. Nothing, not even my band being overly zealous about my getting back to California, could distract me right now. It was my last fight as Kian West; in fact, it was my last day as Kian West, and I intended on going out with a win.

I WAITED, no I skulked impatiently near the doorway until I heard my name being shouted over the loudspeaker, and the music started up.

"Let's fucking go," I said to myself, repeating Myles's words from earlier. My heart rate accelerated, and I took some deep breaths to calm my system before removing any bit of a reaction from my face and walking out into the ring to face the bright lights and the tightly wound chaos that lived and breathed between these walls.

As I entered the ring, I could hear my name being shouted,

and I could feel the crowd's frenzy. Although it boiled within me, I didn't let a single emotion cross my face. When the fighter couldn't read me, they never knew what I would do next. It's how I kept winning. Well, that and my never-ending well of anger that spurred me on.

However, I couldn't fully access my usual anger tonight. It hadn't completely dried up, but the calm and happiness that Jessamine offered seemed to have soothed my system, quieting the usual hole of rage inside of me.

A shock of what could only be explained as fear shot through me. My fury was what kept me going during these fights. I needed my fire to keep me focused and locked in on winning this thing. I gulped down the saliva that had pooled in my mouth and shifted my neck from left to right to loosen myself up as my mind raced. I stood in my corner of the ring as they called out the next fighter, and the crowd went wild again.

My opponent was a big, lumbering twenty-something-year-old with a nose that had been broken one too many times and fucked up ears. He leered at me from over the ref's shoulder as he caught me stealing a glance at Jessa and taunted loudly, "That's your girl? When I win, can I fuck her?"

I growled under my breath as I flinched, knowing that Jessa had to have heard him. I didn't risk another glance at her. But, oh, the beautiful savage outrage flared up inside of me just as I needed it, and I sucked in a breath as I let the heat of it fill and fuel me. I could practically taste it. I was finally ready to taunt this fighter into showing me his weaknesses so I could fuck him up and win. This time my anger wasn't due to all that I had lost, but instead was coming to me from everything that I wanted to keep.

THE BELL RANG, and he came out swinging. I dodged out of pure instinct and felt his glove pass right above where my head had just been. This mother fucker was crazy. I now understood how he was undefeated. He had no rhythm, no game, and no strategy; he was just a brawler.

I bobbed and weaved all around the ring. I was almost bored as I let him jab messily at me until I finally let him hit me just so I could get the crowd going wild. My cheekbone stung from where he had punched me, and I could feel blood dripping down my cheek.

I grinned at him as the next round started. I got him down almost immediately with a check hook. It was the perfect move for an aggressive fighter like him.

In the next round, I caught him unawares with a lead right hit. He was fading quickly for such a big guy. I could see it in his stance and the ever-so-sluggish movements of his jabs.

I let him continue to try and lay it on me, and I just kept picking off the punches, letting him wear himself out. I weaved and bobbed, staying just out of his reach. I could see how frustrated he was growing with me. I feinted to the left and then got him with a few jabs and hooks to his abdomen. He was so focused on protecting his head and face that he had left his midsection completely exposed.

In the last round, I was feeling the ache in my legs and arms, but I knew he had to be hurting even worse. My cheekbone had finally stopped bleeding, and it burned uncomfortably, yet I reveled in it. Finally, I had him on the ropes, and I knew I had the win when I knocked him across the chin with an uppercut punch. The crowd went wild as he stumbled against the ropes and was down for the count. I could see the stunned look in his eyes. He thought he had me, I noted smugly.

Beau was in the ring in a flash, holding up my hand and

proclaiming me the winner. The crowd roared. The men were howling. The winners were ecstatic. The women were screaming my name. Yet all I saw was Jessa.

There she was, standing still amongst the mayhem, simply grinning at me, my lighthouse in the fog, and immediately, I knew that I was falling in love with her. I had felt this feeling before. I knew what this emotion crawling up my throat and choking me was. I was falling in love with her because she had returned me to myself. She showed me that hope existed. She helped me enjoy making music again. But most of all I was falling in love with her simply due to the crescendo my heart did inside my chest every time I saw her face.

"Fuck," I muttered. "Let's fucking go."

BACK IN THE PREP AREA, Beau pressed a pile of cash in my hand.

"You sure you won't fight again next month?" he inquired.

"I don't know if I'll be around," I admitted. "I'll let you know."

"Aight, bro." He slapped a hand on my back and then rushed off to prepare for the next match. I unwrapped my hands and then turned my phone over as Jessa and Myles burst through the doorway. Fifteen more missed calls. What the fuck? Worry wormed its way into my brain. Had something bad happened? I picked up my phone to call Ash back when Jessa jumped into my arms, and I forgot everything but her.

"So, so hot." She groaned against my mouth.

"Yeah?" I smirked, holding her up against me with one arm.

"Still here," Myles pointed out uncomfortably. I laughed and Jessa leaned back with her legs still wrapped around my waist.

"I love seeing that." She ran her hand over my lips and then lower, grabbing bits of my beard between her fingers.

"What?" I gently deposited her back down as I grabbed my coat.

"You laughing." She took my hand as we prepared to leave.

"I..." I wanted to tell her everything. I wanted to tell her how much life had hurt before her. I wanted her to know how much she meant to me. I wanted her to know that I wanted both Myles and her to come to California with me. I needed her with me. I wanted more of *more*. I enjoyed having her as my muse for the music. She was my anchor in the waves and my compass when I was lost. I had to have her understand that she was my true north. "I have to tell you more about me." I tripped over my words as we pushed the door open.

"Okay." She nodded. "Back at home?" She turned and kissed my bicep as I nodded.

"Yes, at home." I breathed. My eyes were suddenly blinded by flashing cameras. The air filled with the sound of shutters and shouts of, "Jace. Why did you disappear?"

"Jace, who's the girl? Is this why you abandoned the tour?"

"Have you been working out?"

"Mr. West, will you be returning to the band?"

"Jace, can we get a statement about the baby?"

I had been found, this much was clear. I turned, in what felt like slow motion, and saw Jessa's face first gaping at the insanity that was the paparazzi and then back at me, confusion and panic flaring in her eyes. I sprang into action as I felt my anonymity go up in flames, and everything good that I had found here began to slip through my fingers.

"Don't look at her," I snarled at the paparazzi vermin as I pushed through the crowd, practically pulling Jessa behind me. She stumbled but followed.

As we got into the van, Myles had his hand up, blocking his eyes from the flashing bulbs as he turned to me, and the words, "What the fuck?" ripped out of him.

I sighed, put the van into drive, and outran the paparazzi just like I had so many times before. I didn't have the words just yet. But I knew I had a lot to say. I just hoped she would listen.

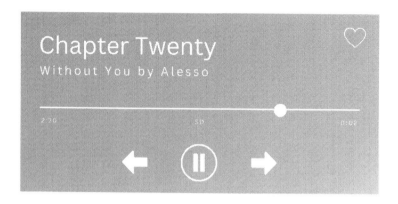

From what I had pieced together, the people harassing us as we left the fight thought Kian was Jace West, the lead singer of Pointing West. I was not exactly up to date on the news out of Hollywood, but I had seen enough magazine covers to know that while they had similar coloring and height, Jace West was not muscular at all. He wore round-rimmed glasses, was clean shaven, and had really short hair.

I peered over at Kian as I followed him into the hotel, numb with confusion. Could he be Jace? With his muscle on top of muscle and his bearded face, it was hard to see any similarities between him and the famous singer. The most burning question in my mind was what baby? Did he have a baby? I watched as he unlocked the door and silently waited for Myles and me to enter. He peered back out into the hallway and then shut the door firmly, locking both locks. He strode to the windows, where he pulled the curtains shut and then stood there, his back to us, his huge arms folded in front of him.

"Are they going to follow us here?" Myles snapped. I shifted where I stood. I had never heard Myles so angry before. Kian shrugged.

"I think I lost them," he murmured.

"I guess you have a lot of experience doing that." Myles strode over to stand in front of him. "Were we some sort of joke to you?" he demanded. "Was this your little feel-good project that you'll tell the world about one day? The famous Jace West took on two homeless people. I can see it in the headlines now. I just can't figure out why you had to use Jessa, of all people."

That shook Kian out of his stupor.

"I didn't use Jessamine. I would never do anything to hurt her." He was whispering, but it felt like he was shouting. Myles didn't back down.

"I'm impatiently waiting to hear whatever explanation you can conjure up for us."

He sat down, looking over at me, worry clear in his eyes. I could tell that Myles thought this might finally be the thing that would break me. To be honest, I didn't know what I thought; I was still stuck in the moment when the lights had blinded me and the shouts had muddled my mind.

Kian looked over at me, and his face was pale. His phone buzzed, and I saw his fist grip it so tight I worried he might crack it.

"Jessa?" Myles used a softer tone with me. I looked up. "Come sit." He patted the couch next to him. I listened, walking on shaky legs until I collapsed next to my brother. He leaned over to unzip my coat, but I kept it wrapped around me because I felt cold with shock and confusion. Kian stood several steps away, looking helpless. His phone buzzed again, and he suddenly shouted, "Fuck!"

I jolted and then felt Myles's hand come down to touch my knee, grounding me where I sat.

"Baby..." Kian's eyes were pleading with me. "I would never

use you. I'm falling in love with you." He knelt down on the floor in front of me. "Can you say something?" He tentatively reached out a hand but thought better of it and pulled it back at the last second.

"You have a baby?" My voice sounded hoarse from screaming for whom I thought had been my boyfriend back at the fight. The fight that felt like it had been ages ago. Now, I wasn't so sure who he even was, let alone what we were.

Kian visibly collapsed into himself, and we sat silently for a moment until he reached into his pocket and pulled out his wallet. He removed his license and a folded-up piece of paper. He turned the license around for us to see. Jace Kian West.

"Kian is your middle name," Myles read. "So you're not a complete liar."

Kian ignored him and handed me the paper. I opened it tentatively. It was a sonogram printout. "Rose Carr," the name read at the top right. There was a due date listed that would make his baby about a year old now. I looked at the fuzzy black and white photo as it dawned on me that I had seen those little feet before. They were tattooed on his back. I opened my mouth to ask him what his baby's name is when Kian began to talk.

"I told you that as a kid, my mother forced me to take music lessons because she saw me as a windfall. They told her I was a prodigy, and to her, that meant I was ultimately a payday." His tone was sad, and his face was beginning to swell where he had gotten hit.

"I was in some inconsequential kid bands early on, but I really got famous when I recorded my first album at sixteen and posted it online. A label soon discovered me, and they helped me form my band when I was eighteen. I had my first number-one single at nineteen, sold out my first world tour at twenty, won a bunch of awards by twenty-two, and by twenty-six, I was on the covers of magazines, had millions of followers on social media, was sold out in every show we did, and was dating a supermodel. By twenty-seven, she was my fiancée, and I had bought a mansion in Beverly Hills where we lived together. I was twenty-eight when she was killed in front of me in a home invasion, and I lost her and our baby."

I could see how palpable his pain was when he spoke about it. Emotionally just as much as physically.

"She was pregnant?" I wondered out loud.

"She was pregnant," Kian confirmed, his vocal cords sounded strained at this point.

"I'm sorry for your loss." Myles startled me as he spoke. I nodded in agreement but didn't speak. I was anxiously rubbing the material of my coat between my hands, and I felt Myles's hand close over mine to calm me.

"So what...?" I started.

"Am I doing here?" Kian finished.

I nodded, not quite making eye contact with him. I was really feeling out of my element here. I had never planned on letting him get this close to me emotionally, and here I was with the universe rubbing my choices in my face. How could I be falling for a man who I wasn't even sure I knew anymore?

"After she was killed, I..." He gulped, and I could see how hard it was for him to talk about it. "I blamed myself." His voice was strangled, as if he had to force the words out.

My eyes flew to his face in surprise. His head was lowered, and his shoulders were dropped as if showing us that this side of his life was physically too heavy to bear.

"I don't know if you know what I looked like back then," he murmured. "I don't even know if you know who I am."

"Everyone knows who Jace West is," Myles interrupted.

Kian sighed but kept talking.

"So then you know that I was thin and had no muscle. The heaviest thing I ever lifted was my guitar. So when I went into my house that night and found two men holding Rose at gunpoint, there was literally nothing I could do to help her." A tear tracked its way down his face, and I had to hold myself back from going over to him and kissing it away.

"When I made a pathetic attempt to stop them, they hit my head so hard that I passed out, and when I woke up, they were r-raping her." A sob broke free from the deep recesses of his chest, and it almost came out sounding like a low howl.

Myles shifted uncomfortably next to me. We had both had our own experiences with non-consensual situations, and hearing what had happened to Rose was affecting both of us.

Kian rubbed the tears from his eyes and then wiped his nose against his sleeve.

"I passed out again, and when I came to, she was gone. They had shot her."

I felt a knot of emotion build up in my throat.

"After the funeral, I just lost it." He sounded numb now. "I packed up some of my shit, bought a van, and disappeared. I disconnected my number, and I lived the next year and a half punishing myself for what happened to her. I figured I would pay my penance by not allowing myself to live my old life. I pushed myself in the gym so I could become someone who would never let what happened to Rose happen to anyone else. I found fighting because it let me channel all of my anger into something other than not wanting to exist anymore. I was planning on living a life as miserable and as quiet as possible until I met you."

Kian finally looked at me. His eyes were red and shiny. I felt his words hit me square in the chest. Myles squeezed my hand, and I squeezed it back.

"You are my sunshine," Kian gasped out as another tear escaped his eye and tracked down his cheek to where it dropped off his chin. "My anger quiets around you. You soothe the pain.

You are beautiful and wonderful and real. The realest part of my life, and that is why you are my true north, Jessamine Bardot."

I reached up to touch the compass necklace that he had given me for my birthday, which felt like a lifetime ago.

"Why didn't you tell us who you were?" Myles sounded calmer now. "Why use your middle name?"

Kian sighed.

"I have been running from the paparazzi for what feels like forever, and I just wanted a slice of peace and normalcy here. I didn't know I would find the two of you. And to be honest, Kian is who I really am. I don't want to be Jace anymore. I have to go back to finish my contract with the label, but once that's done... I think I'm done... not with music but with the fame. I hate it. I have never felt more at home than I have in this room with the two of you, and I really don't want to lose that. I was planning on telling you everything tonight, and I was going to ask you both if you would come back with me."

"Can we have a second?" I asked suddenly. Kian looked confused but nodded.

"Take all the time you need. I know it's a lot." He ran his tongue over his dry lips and stood up. I stood as well and pulled Myles after me into his room, where I shut the door and sat on his bed. I felt bad abandoning Kian in such a highly emotional moment where he had confessed his deepest secrets, but I needed to unpack all of this heaviness with my brother so I could think clearly again.

"He's been paying for this room the whole time, hasn't he?" I said as Myles sat down next to me.

"That's the most logical explanation." He ran a hand over his face and sighed.

"He loves you, J."

I shrugged.

"It's only been a few months, and I don't really know him."

"No, I think we do know him," Myles disagreed. "I forgive him. He's been through the absolute worst thing a human being could go through. I don't think he was purposely playing us. I actually understand why he did what he did."

I shrugged out of my coat and lay back on the bed.

"He's good to you, and you deserve a real life." Myles had gone from being furious to fighting for me to stay with Kian in a matter of minutes.

"I've always had a real life, My," I protested.

"You know what I mean." He winced at his choice of words.

"Yeah." I sighed. "I need to think." I closed my eyes, willing the building pressure in my head to dissipate so I could arrange my fractured thoughts.

"I'm gonna go check on him." Myles stood, and I nodded without opening my eyes.

"Okay." Myles wanting to check on Kian tugged at my aching heartstrings. My sweet brother had finally found a friend in Kian. A friendship where they had connected on a real level. As much as I wanted to forgive Kian for myself and our relation-ship, I wanted to forgive him so Myles could keep what he had found with Kian as well. My brother left the room, closing the door behind him. I could hear Kian in the hallway.

"Is she okay?"

"I think so. She just needs a minute to process."

I heard them move away from the door. I turned over, using my arm as a pillow. I just needed a minute, like Myles had said. I'd go back out there once I had allowed my brain to fully under-stand what was happening.

I took out my phone, squinting in the bright light coming off the screen, and googled Rose Carr. Oh, she was stunning. She was a few inches taller than me, thin, and blonde. I scrolled and found a photo of her and Kian together. He looked like a sexy nerd with his glasses and buzz cut. Rose was perfect. Her hair,

her pale skin, her makeup, her jewelry... all perfect and everything I wasn't. I was curvy where she was thin. I had a mess of
dark curls where she had a coiffed blonde halo of hair. I was
perpetually tan where she was pale. I was loud and messy and in
your face with my feelings, and by the looks of it, she was quiet,
charming, and mysterious. I didn't like the feelings that were
burning in my lungs right now.

I had never been a jealous person by any stretch of the imagination. In fact, when I thought Kian was a busker, living in his
van, I had been very confident in his attraction for me. But now,
as I lie in the hotel room he had been paying for the entire duration of my living here, I wondered if it was all a lie.

Clearly, he had loved his blonde model fiancée, and he had
only found me because she had been stolen from him. I
squeezed my eyes shut as the intrusive thoughts tried to wood-
pecker their way into my brain. I was finding myself jealous of a
dead girl, and it made me feel uncomfortable to be in my own
skin.

"Mother fucking, fuck." I rolled my body to lie on my back as
I kept scrolling. I saw the article announcing Rose's death and
then more social media posts about Kian disappearing. There
was a video of his band saying that he was taking some time off
for his mental health, and then a talk show host made a
comment asking if they really knew where he was. The guys had
laughed it off, but I now knew that at the time they had actually
no idea where he was.

I scrolled once more and immediately regretted it. A photo
of Kian holding his hand up in front of the camera, his hand
gripping mine as I trailed behind him, had been posted fourteen
minutes ago with the headline, "Jace West Found In Upstate
New York." The comments ranged from girls saying how much
they loved his new body, that they wanted to fuck him, and they
were so glad he was coming back to Hollywood to other

comments questioning why he had disappeared for so long and what was the name of the girl who had obviously stolen him from his band. My heart dropped. This was a tiny town. It was just a matter of time before they found Myles and me, and the thought of that scared me. I could be strong, but Myles was delicate, like a raw egg. He was building up a shell, but I knew from experience that it could crack at any time, and under no circumstances could I allow that to happen.

THE NEXT THING I KNEW, I was being lifted up in the air, strong arms holding me, and the intoxicating smell that was all Kian overwhelmed my senses.

"Mmm." I burrowed my face into his chest. I felt him kiss the top of my head as he carried me from Myles's bed to mine. Ours? Mine? My brain couldn't pick one.

He sat me on the bed and, in a gruff voice, said, "Hands up."

I complied, and he got me undressed. Then he pulled a soft T-shirt over my head and helped me climb under the covers. I cracked an eye open to look at him. He was standing next to the bed, shirtless, in a pair of sweatpants. He was so beautiful with all his broken pieces, and I knew he had shared so much with us out of necessity, but I still felt even closer to him now that I had heard his whole story. I couldn't muster up any feelings of anger toward him. We all did what we had to do to survive. I knew that more than anyone.

"I'm sorry I ran off and wasn't there for you," I whispered. I felt feelings of guilt build up inside of me. He had broken his heart wide open to share his story. He had cried, and I just stood up, walked away, and ultimately fell asleep. I should have comforted him. This wasn't about me, and I had not reacted the way I now wished I would have.

"You didn't run off." His smile was haunted as he ran a finger down my bare arm. "You're still here, aren't you?"

"I'm sorry about your baby." I felt my breath hitch when I said it. I felt overwhelmingly sad thinking of those tiny, little feet tattooed on his back for him to keep forever.

"So am I." Kian ran a hand over his beard. "But somehow, the universe then led me to you, and for that, I could never be sorry."

I felt tears well up in my eyes as he said that, and they dropped, hot and wet, on the pillow next to me.

"Don't cry, Jessa." He was immediately on his knees next to me, his breath warm on my face as he wiped the tears away.

"I'm just so sad for you." My voice was muffled against his chest. He didn't say anything; he just held me.

"Rose was beautiful," I murmured against his skin. He stilled. I looked up, and his eyes were wary. "She was." I shrugged.

"She was," Kian repeated my words carefully. I looked at him. He looked at me.

"I'm not really your normal type, am I?" I despised the uncertainty in my tone. Kian froze.

"Every bit of you is my type," he replied sternly.

"Show me." I was needy for his validation, which was such an odd feeling for me to experience. Kian didn't need to be told twice. The covers were thrown back, my T-shirt was ripped off, and his pants were tossed away, instantly showing me how hard he was.

"This," he said through clenched teeth, "is all for you." He ran a hand down my chest and weighed my sizable breast in his palm.

"I am obsessed with these." He bent down and sucked my nipple into his mouth. I let out a breathy moan. He kept his hand moving, lowering down over the flair of my ribs, squeezing my waist, and then slapping my pubic bone. His other hand found its way lower, sweeping through all the wetness that had gathered between my legs, and then he was licking it off of his finger as I watched him.

"You are delicious." He ran his tongue over his lips and then grabbed my thighs. "I have never been so turned on..." His voice trailed off as he kissed his way around one thigh and then turned me slightly to run his tongue across my ass. He slapped it, and I groaned.

"Shh," he warned.

Suddenly, I was up in the air again and instinctively I wrapped my legs around his waist, and he walked us till my back was against the window.

"Shit." The glass behind the drawn curtains was freezing cold, and the temperature change shocked my system. My discomfort turned into a frenzy as I felt him push into me with no condom on, hot and pulsing.

"Does this feel like you're not my type?" he said against my lips as he fucked me hard, fast, and deep against the chilled surface. He almost sounded angry with me for questioning his attraction.

"N-no," I moaned out. He seemed pacified as he bit my lip and then kissed it.

"You. Are. Mine," he said in rhythm with the tempo of his hips.

"Are you mine?" I gasped out, referring to everything that held pieces of him—the media, his band, his obligations to the label, and his old life. Kian stopped moving for a second and lifted his face up to look at me.

"I've never been anyone else's as much as I am yours," he affirmed, his tone deep and melodic as he spoke.

I combusted with a flash of coiled nerve endings and tight muscles. I felt myself soaking down his legs. It was all I needed to hear to fall completely off the edge into oblivion with him. I didn't know what tomorrow would bring, but as long as he was mine and I was his, I would figure it out.

"Come inside me, baby," I urged.

His hips were shuddering against mine, his arms were shaking, and he was moaning into my mouth as he exploded inside of me. As he laid me back in bed, I felt the proof of his attraction for me warm and sticky, seeping back out of me, across my lips, and down my inner thighs. I fell asleep with him singing softly in my ear, his arms around me, his chest to my back. I had just learned to embrace this *real* life and had decided I wanted to keep it, and now he would have to leave. *Jace*. The unfamiliar name rolled around my brain as I fell asleep.

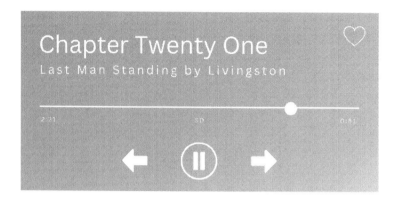

G ordon was sitting on the couch. *In Myles's spot,* Rose's voice in my head pointed out. Ash and Mika were standing behind him. Nile was leaning back against the kitchen counter. Myles had gone to a meeting, and Jessa had insisted on going to work.

"We'll talk later." She had gotten up on her tippy toes and kissed my cheek before she left, just minutes before my band showed up. Apparently, they had been tipped off that the paps had found me and that was why they had been calling me nonstop last night. When they saw that the shit had hit the fan, they flew out to retrieve me, as Gordon put it.

"Holy fuck, Jace." Nile had commented on my new body about ten times now. I rolled my eyes.

"Cut it out, Nile. Please."

"I can't." He walked over and ran a hand across my chest. "It's insane what you've done."

I stepped back, out of his reach.

"Fucking stop."

"Nile, leave him alone," Ash called from where he had sat

down next to Gordon. Gordon, who had finally hung up his cell phone and was typing out a text.

"Okay, the paparazzi are obviously in a frenzy. Big story for them, of course. Apparently, they got a tip from a waiter at a restaurant you had gone to and that's how they found you. So we're gonna have to get you to the airport as fast as possible, and we'll get you back to California, where you belong." He stood and came over to look at me. "Are you gonna keep this new look?" He waved a hand in front of me. I grunted.

"Still a man of almost no words, I see." Gordon groaned. "Jace, we gotta get ahead of this thing. And fast. So I'm gonna need you to start talking. What are we gonna do about the girl? What have you been doing here? Are there any scandals I need to cover up before we get the fuck out of dodge?"

"You're doing nothing about Jessa," I almost hissed. "Don't call her *the girl*."

Gordon backed up a little.

"Chill, Jace." Mika was next to me, guiding me to a chair, where he handed me a protein shake from a local cafe. I took a sip.

"No scandals. I've just been doing my thing. I'm sorry I disappeared. I know that messed up the album and the tour, but I was really fucked up."

"We'll get it all back on track. Don't worry about it, Jace. We're just glad you're back now." Gordon was using his usual tone with me. The one that sounded like he never knew what I was going to do next, and he was sick of cleaning up my messes. My phone buzzed, and I saw it was a text from coffee girl.

"We've got a problem." I stood abruptly from my chair. "The paparazzi found Jessa."

"Okay. You're not going anywhere." Gordon made me sit back down. "I'll take care of it." With strict instructions not to leave the hotel room, he was gone.

I texted Jessa to tell her that Gordon was coming to extricate her as feelings of helplessness crept back up on me. It didn't matter how much muscle I had packed on; once the vultures of the media got their talons into her, there was nothing I could do to protect her. The right thing would have been to leave her alone in the first place, far away from the possibility of cameras and the disgusting world of Hollywood finding her, but I had been selfish, and now I didn't want to go back to my old life if she wasn't coming with me.

"EVEN IF I would consider just hopping on a plane with you and leaving behind the only life I've ever known because you happen to be famous, you know I won't leave Myles." I had a pretty angry Jessa on my hands. We were in the bathroom of our room because it was the area furthest away from the nosy ears of my manager and my band.

I had never actually seen her upset, and as much as I was enraged that the paparazzi had done this to her, an irate Jessa was also turning me on. I certainly was not going to tell her that right now. Not after I had just told her that I thought the safest thing for her to do was leave her job and her friends and come with me to California. She knew I had to leave, whether she came with me or not, due to the label being furious at me. She also knew that I didn't think it was safe for her to be here without me. Not with the media being so hot for this story. It had not taken them long to figure out who Jessa was and where she worked. They had descended upon Kafe, causing chaos, embarrassing her, and asking questions that she had no idea how to answer. I knew her job making coffee was something that gave her joy, and I felt so bad that it had been disturbed this morning because of me.

"I know that where you go, he goes. I wouldn't expect any

different." I was trying to remain calm, but I was feeling frustrated because I should have known they would find her, and I should have done something smarter, like going to work with her to keep her safe. Although I knew Gordon would have quickly pulled the rug out from under that plan. He was keeping a close eye on me as if he thought I may disappear again. She hesitated.

"He's finally sober, and you've always wanted to live in California," I reminded her. "You have nothing keeping you here."

She made an angry face.

"I have plenty here."

"Nothing that you can't leave," I argued.

"That's mean." She scooted away from me.

"I didn't mean it like that," I backpedaled, realizing how that sounded.

"I had a life before you waltzed in. It's not my fault you don't happen to be who you said you were, and I'm somehow caught up in the tailwind of that." She had her arms crossed against her chest. I moved closer to her and took her hand in mine.

"You're right, I'm sorry. I shouldn't have said that. I just want you to come with me. I'll take care of everything." I kissed the tip of her nose. "You know I have to go back, and I'll miss you too much if I can't see you."

"What if we break up, and then I'm stuck in a state where I don't know anyone, but I can't get a job safely because the media knows me?" she asked, ever the practical thinker.

"We won't break up," I assured her. She rolled her eyes.

"You don't know the future."

"With you, I do." I lifted her hand and kissed her fingertips. She was momentarily mollified but not entirely convinced.

"I have to talk to Myles, but I'm just letting you know that if we do agree to come, I don't care how famous and rich you are, I am not changing. I'm not becoming one of your fancy girls."

"I certainly hope you don't." I winced, thinking of Jessa in the fame-hungry, vapid town of LA. I wouldn't be able to keep her completely safe from the paparazzi there, but at least I could do a better job if I kept her close to me than if she stayed here and was on her own.

"I'm afraid I won't know you anymore," she confessed.

"Jessamine." I sighed. "You know me better than anyone in the world does."

She was holding her legs up to her chest as she sat on the floor of the bathroom, and she laid her cheek on her knees as she turned to look at me.

"I know, but I'm scared you won't be able to be that person anymore."

I was scared of that too.

WHEN MYLES GOT BACK from his meeting, he and Jessa disappeared into his bathroom to talk. They had lived the majority of their lives with it being just the two of them, and I knew they would have to make this decision together without me giving my two cents. I gave them their space, but I waited anxiously in the hallway, hovering. It wasn't just that I wanted Jessa to be safe, although, of course, that was a big part of it, but I also selfishly didn't want to leave without her. She had become such a dominant force in my thoughts, in my day, and in my life that I couldn't imagine having to break up or even trying to maneuver through a long-distance relationship. No, I wanted zero distance.

I finally went to sit on the couch to wait for them to finish talking. My band had left to catch some sleep before we flew out, and Gordon was probably off doing some damage control with the press. I closed my eyes and thought about what Ash had asked me earlier.

"Why didn't you let me help you?" He looked hurt. "What's so special about this girl who you met six months ago that she was able to bring you to your senses and get you writing music again? Yet you left me, your best friend of twelve years, without a single word?"

"I'm sorry," was all I could say. "I really am." I couldn't explain Jessa to him. I could barely understand how she brought this calm and clarity to my life. I just knew that she had helped me return to myself when no one else could.

The door opened, and I looked up to find Jessa and Myles walking into the living room. Anxiety sped up my heart rate.

"We'll come," Jessa started. I felt relief flood my system. "But we have a few conditions since this move is really sudden and unexpected."

I nodded.

"Anything," I promised.

"Myles stays out of the spotlight. I don't care what anyone has to do to keep the media away from him, but he doesn't need any stress right now."

"Of course," I agreed. "What else?"

"I can't afford much, but we will not be freeloaders. I don't care how much money you have. We want to earn our keep. So give us something to do." Jessa's eyes met mine. I wanted to tell her exactly how rich I was. I wanted her to know that she would never have to sleep outside ever again. I wanted her to feel safe to just live her life without having to work for any of it, but I knew she would never stand for that, so I didn't argue.

"I'll talk to Gordon and see what you can do."

She smiled at that.

"And lastly, if we don't like it there, we will leave. We're not signing any contracts or NDAs or anything that could keep us there if we don't want to stay. You either trust us or you don't."

Jessa had obviously done some quick googling about the music industry. I held my hands up in agreement.

"If you want to leave, I'll leave with you as soon as my contract is up. Once they don't own me anymore, we can go anywhere you want."

"You don't want to make music anymore?" Myles spoke for the first time.

"I do. Just not like this."

He nodded and scratched his chin.

"So now what?"

"Now we pack." I walked over and engulfed both of them in a big, relieved hug. "I'm so happy," I whispered in Jessa's ear. "It's just for now. In a year, I'll be free, and we can do anything you want."

"Promise?" she said against my cheek.

"I promise," I assured her.

IT SHOULD HAVE OCCURRED to me earlier, but I quickly discovered that neither Jessa nor Myles had ever been on an airplane before. My band watched, amused, as Jessa buckled up like an excited child and peered out of the window as our private plane took off.

"Holy fuck," she exclaimed.

"Just so you know, commercial flying is not really like this." Ash leaned forward in his seat.

"Yeah, this is how the rich fly. I know." She cut him off.

He snorted and leaned back, pulling his eye mask down over his eyes, but not before he shot me a look that showed that he liked what he saw. He was used to my one-night stands. To the giggling models who fucked me just to be able to say that they did it. Even with Rose, my band had just tolerated her. Between being shy and wanting everyone to like her, she had generally stayed quiet around the boys.

I could see that Ash recognized that Jessa was a woman who could hold her own. The fact that she was unimpressed by who they were was definitely a plus as well.

I could tell that Myles was a little nervous, and I watched as Jessa picked up on it and leaned over to hold his hand. Their bond tugged at my heartstrings. Love like that, unconditional, "I will fight all your demons with you" love was not something that everyone was lucky enough to experience in their life. I knew that he was aware of how good she was.

Just last week, he had told me that every single day, he had to fight himself and choose to stay sober and that without Jessa rallying behind him, he would have relapsed by now. It was the longest he had been sober in all of his adult life, and I was hoping that maybe a change of scenery and access to better therapy options would be beneficial for his sobriety.

As if on cue, the stewardess came around to offer everyone a drink. I saw Myles eye the whiskey that Ash asked for, and I held my breath while he ordered a seltzer. He was not an alcoholic, but he knew it was best that he stayed fully sober. I would have to find him an NA meeting and a new sponsor as soon as we got there.

I turned to ask Jessa what she wanted to drink but saw that she had fallen asleep. As I tucked a blanket around her, I got a peek of her necklace hanging out from her collar, and I had a flashback from last night when I had fucked her against the window, her necklace bouncing on her chest with every thrust. It had hurt my heart when my usually super confident girl had questioned if she was my type. She couldn't possibly understand how much of her occupied my waking thoughts. Every day. My feelings for her felt like music that flowed and rippled beneath my skin. I could feel it sizzling in C8s through my veins to my heart.

I took out my phone and began to write my next song. It just tumbled out of me, like it had been written a long time ago and was finally being realized. I felt my love for music thrum through me, and I almost smiled as I looked up to find Ash watching me with a knowing look in his eyes. He knew when a new song bug had bitten me. Jessa shifted next to me, and I ran a hand down her arm to settle her, letting her know I was there. I looked back down at the beginning of my song. I knew it would be a hit. It may even be the most real thing I have ever written.

COFFEE

If my love for you was a melody
You would hear my heart in G7
Like a slice of heaven
Feel it reawaken
My veins strum in G clef
You can see it on a frequency graph
Strum me, baby
Right there
Just like that
Softly, baby
My breath beats in whole notes
Like love codes
It explodes
In a crescendo
All over youuuu
Strum me, baby
Right there
Just like that

Harder, baby
If my love for you was a song
I would sing it in E4
And it will soar
As I pour
All my love into you
Yes, strum me baby
Oh, right there
God, like that
Mmm hmm
I love you baby
Sing it
Louder baby

I slept my entire first flight. I woke up as we touched down, and I felt Kian gently shake me awake.

"We're here, sleepyhead," he said in that gruff tone of his, but his choice of words clearly showed the gentle side of him that had begun to peek through when he interacted with me. When had I turned into such a sap? Warm beds, pillows, and access to running water for this long was softening me. I needed my edge back; I had a feeling this city would eat me alive if I didn't stay on my toes, fully aware and alert to danger. This time, it wouldn't be other homeless people, the police, or the cold that would have me at risk. No, here I knew it would be the ugly underbelly of money hidden by a charade of glitz and glamor that life rubbing shoulders with fame would offer. I rubbed my eyes and unbuckled as I stood.

"Where's my bag?" I asked.

"I got it." Kian had my backpack slung over his shoulder. I felt awkward standing there, not doing anything.

"I can take it." I reached over to grab the strap.

"I got it," he repeated. I saw two of his bandmates exchange a look, and that made me even more uncomfortable. It felt like I had walked into the middle of a family reunion, but I didn't know anyone's names, and they didn't know I existed until yesterday. Add in my lack of worldly experience in many basic areas, and I felt like the odd man out in a way I had never known before.

When working at Kafe, the women who came in reeked of privilege, and they weren't exactly overly friendly, but our differences weren't massively noticeable. They hadn't known I was homeless, so I was just another nine-to-five worker in their eyes. But now, here I was, a civilian amongst Hollywood stars. What made the chasm between our classes even more obvious was I had literally never left my little town or had a regular childhood or even knew what I was going to do after I stepped off this airplane. The playing field was not even, and it was making me anxious.

Put me on the streets with nothing but the clothes on my back, and I would figure it out. Put me on a plane with a man who had just recently become my boyfriend, who also happened to be famous and rich, and I felt all of my emotions clog up inside of me. I felt Myles squeeze my shoulder as he picked up on my inner turmoil.

"It's just an adventure," he whispered in my ear. I recalled our conversation from earlier. I had been inclined to stay. I felt like staying would be better for Myles's sobriety. We were so early on in him being sober for this many weeks straight that it didn't feel like the right move to rock the boat. As much as I wanted to go with Kian and see what would happen, I knew Myles had a solid sponsor here and an NA meeting that he liked going to. I had been ready to hurt my own heart to keep Myles clean, as much as it would suck to do so. I had been ready to chalk the last half a year up to an amazing experience. Such was life. As seasons shifted, we had to learn to say goodbye. I had gotten used to that. But Myles had convinced me to go.

"It will be an adventure, J," he said, sounding excited. "You deserve to stay with someone who loves you like he does."

I had scoffed at the word love, and Myles had just raised an eyebrow at me.

"We always talked about going to California. Fuck this town and the cold weather." He had sounded so emphatic that I had laughed. "I'll find a new support system, I promise. Plus, if anything happens to me, you'll still have Kian," he continued. That had cut off my laughter real quick.

"Stop talking like that," I hissed. "You're doing so good." I felt my heart knot up in my chest at the sad look in Myles's eyes. I knew he was struggling more than he let on. Sometimes, I wondered if he only fought to stay sober for me. Addiction was my worst kind of enemy because I knew that addicts would rather choose an altered state of consciousness from drugs even though their toxicity destroys all aspects of their life because for a moment, a tiny, brief moment, they felt okay.

I WAS SHAKEN from my thoughts as the door to the plane was opened, and everyone began to disembark. Two Cadillac SUVs were waiting on the tarmac, and Gordon was ushering us into them. Already in the car was a driver and a man sitting in the passenger seat whom Kian introduced as Alex, his security guard. Kian and Ash sat in the middle bucket seats, and Myles and I sat in the third row. Other than the private jet, this car, with its leather seats and multiple knobs that controlled who knows what, was the nicest place I had ever sat in. It was a stark reminder of how completely out of my element I was.

"You okay back there?" Kian asked, turning slightly.

"Mmm hmm," was all I gave him. If he sensed anything was

off with me, he didn't mention it. The car glided off, and I leaned back in my seat, watching the palm trees out the window. I half listened to Kian and Ash as they spoke in hushed tones. I understood that Gordon was going to put Kian's house up for sale. The house Rose had died in, I presumed.

"Stay with me," Ash said.

"I'm gonna move into the penthouse," Kian replied.

Was I staying in the penthouse too? I wondered. We hadn't exactly been living together in my hotel room, but we hadn't not been either. But now everything was different. The dynamic had changed, and I didn't know what was normal or what we should be doing in this situation.

"Gordon wants me to do a talk show tomorrow. He says if I play the grieving fiancée card, I can get ahead of the media shit show, and they'll leave me alone faster." Kian sighed.

"You definitely should. They're just hungry for a story. Give them a story, and they'll fuck off," Ash encouraged him.

The words *grieving fiancée* made me shift in my seat; the air suddenly felt warm, and my shirt felt too tight.

"The fans are gonna go crazy over your new look, Jace." Ash laughed. Kian reached up to stroke his beard.

"I'm gonna get a haircut tonight, but you think they'll like the beard?" he asked.

"If they don't, you can always shave it." Ash reached over and pulled a bit of his hair.

"I like it," I interjected. Ash looked over at me, his gray eyes were unreadable.

"Then I'll keep it." Kian reached back, searching for my hand.

"I'm sweaty from the plane." I kept my hands in my lap. His fingers brushed over my knee.

"I don't care," he protested.

I sighed and unclasped my fingers, letting him take my hand

in his big one. He squeezed it and then held it for the rest of the ride, even when I presumed it was uncomfortable for him to keep his arm bent at such an awkward angle.

ABOUT A HALF HOUR LATER, we pulled up to a gated neighborhood in Beverly Hills. We drove up to a swanky-looking building where the security guard got out and held the door open for us. A staff member met us to take our bags and led us into a building and onto the elevator. The elevator stopped on the ninth floor to let Ash off and then continued up to where it opened up directly into the penthouse. I was quickly overwhelmed by the tall ceilings, the huge expanse of marble floors, and the solid glass wall on one side of the main room.

"Let me show you to your rooms." The housekeeper, who had introduced herself as Zara, brought Myles and I upstairs and down a thickly carpeted hallway. She put Myles in a room that boasted a blue carpet, a huge bed with blue velvet-looking linens, and a massive bathroom.

"I'm gonna sleep for a bit," Myles told me.

Please stay with me, I wanted to scream. I hadn't felt this uncomfortable since I became aware that my father hadn't loved me enough to stay. Instead, I smiled and told him to rest up. Zara brought me further down the hallway to double doors that led into a big room that was almost completely white.

"This is my room?" I asked. Zara nodded.

"I'm going to make dinner." She excused herself and then left, closing the doors behind her. I slipped off my Ugg boots because I was afraid of getting the room dirty and walked around to explore. There was a large walk-in closet, a bathroom with all the amenities, and, of course, a California king-sized bed. What was I going to do with a bed this big all to myself? I wondered. My question was answered almost immediately when the doors opened again, and Kian strode in. He was rolling his suitcase, his guitar was slung over his shoulder, and my backpack was held in his hand.

"Sorry to make you wait. I had to make a quick phone call," he explained as he pushed the door shut with his foot.

"You're sleeping in here?" I stumbled over my words. *Get it together, Jessamine*, I said to myself in my head.

"Where else would I sleep?" He cocked his head, looking puzzled.

"I wasn't sure what we were doing," I admitted as I felt a huge rush of relief come over me. Maybe my Kian was still here. Maybe we could keep what we had created back at home. The home that was no longer my home.

"Everything is exactly the same." Kian came over and tilted my chin up so I could look at him. "You're mine, and I'm yours. All that is different is we're in California, and you now know the rest of my story."

"And everyone calls you Jace, I quit my job, your band hates me, and my face is all over the gossip magazines," I added. Kian made a face.

"My band doesn't hate you."

"It feels like it." I pulled off my jacket, not even sure where to put it; this white room felt too perfect for me. He sighed and sat on the bed, pulling me down onto his lap.

"Ash is my guitarist and backup singer. He has known me from the very start and is protective over me because he has seen many women use me."

"I would never!" I protested.

"I know that." He placed a kiss on my forehead. "And soon Ash will know it too. Nile is my drummer, and he doesn't hate anyone. In fact, I'll probably have to keep him away from you because that man will flirt with anything that moves. But he's a very loyal friend, and you will like him. I promise. Mika plays the piano or the keyboard, and if you think I'm quiet, wait till you meet him. He's shy around people whom he doesn't know well, but he's actually hilarious, and he's a great cook. You'll have to make him a coffee."

Kian kissed me again. "It's going to be okay. They'll realize that you're here for good, and they'll get over it. Right now, they're just as shocked as you are. Remember, I disappeared, and none of them had heard from me until recently. So we all just need to acclimate."

He was talking a lot, and he seemed more comfortable here than I had ever seen him back in New York. I guess not having to keep up a lie and hide your identity was a good stress relief.

"Let's shower quickly before the boys show up for dinner. Plus, I want to get to sleep early; tomorrow is a big day. I have to go meet with the label and let them yell at me, and then I'll be doing an interview to hopefully keep the paparazzi off our backs." He stood and took off his shirt. I eyed his etched abs appreciatively.

"Don't change this either." I ran my hand over his muscles.

"Not a chance. There is a gym in the penthouse, and you better believe I'll be torturing myself there daily." Kian flashed me one of his rare grins.

"Okay, good." I followed him into the shower. Maybe I could do this. Maybe I could be a famous singer's girlfriend and find a way to live my life here. It's just an adventure, I told myself. An adventure I could have never imagined for myself, but an adventure all the same.

AFTER OUR SHOWER, I went from standing in front of the mirror, a towel wrapped around me, brushing out my wet curls, to being hauled up on Kian's shoulder as he literally picked me up and walked back into the bedroom. As he began to kiss his way down my neck and open up the towel, I laughed. "I thought you said the boys would be here soon."

"They will be." Kian's voice was muffled against my ribs, his breath tickling my skin and heightening my nerve endings in anticipation. He didn't make me wait long.

"This will be quick," he confirmed.

I watched as he rolled a condom on and then had me rest on my knees on his pillow, my legs spread wide, with my back against the headboard. My arms went around his neck as he got to his knees and then thrust into me. My back was pushed against the headboard with each movement of his hips to the point of pain, but I reveled in it. It was such a strong contradiction to the extreme pleasure happening between my legs that it heightened the experience. I had an unencumbered view in this position, and I watched as he slid in and out of me, where I was swollen and soaking. I was making a mess of his pillow, and I could hear the slick movements of his cock. I groaned just from the added stimulation of the close-up visual of what he was doing to me. I looked up to find him staring at me.

"We look fucking hot together, don't we, baby?"

I nodded and licked my lips, and he leaned in to bite them before kissing me. He pushed me further into the headboard, and I moaned at the bite of the wood against my spine.

"Does it hurt?" he asked, breathless. I nodded.

"Good."

I came. Soaring, falling, burning, exploding. He was watching me; the intensity of his hips against mine belied the lazy look of satisfaction on his face. I was startled when I heard a rap on the door.

"Dinner's ready." I heard the deep voice that was Ash, outside in the hallway with only an unlocked door between us.

"Give us a minute," Kian called back, not hesitating in his movements. Ash didn't answer, but I didn't hear his footsteps walk away either. Kian began to fuck me so hard that the head-board began to hit the wall.

"He'll know," I hissed.

Kian laughed as he groaned. "He already knows." Kian gripped my hip, and I could tell he was close. "Ash likes to listen."

I gasped as Kian unloaded into the condom, his body bowing over mine as he moaned my name. Loudly. Recklessly. I was no stranger to public sex. I had seen everything one could see while I lived on the streets, yet somehow, Kian coming inside me as he told me that his best friend liked to listen to him fuck felt like the filthiest thing I had ever heard.

ASH SMIRKED at me when I walked into the kitchen. I cocked my head and didn't look away. I could see something akin to admiration flash in his eyes, and then they moved their way down my body in a slow perusal. At that I walked away because I was not his to look at. A bark of his laughter followed me. Myles was already sitting at the table, his eyes still holding the tortured look I had seen in them earlier, but he was chatting with Nile, and he had a plate of food in front of him. When he saw me, he pushed his chair back and stood.

"You good?" he asked. I nodded.

"You?"

He nodded his head yes. I blew him a kiss and then joined Kian at the marble island to fill my plate. Zara had made lasagna, Caesar salad, soup, and garlic bread. There was also a cheese platter and two choices of dessert. I took some of every-thing and then sat next to Kian who ran a hand down my arm as I dug in. Nile and Mika sat across from me and made an effort to get to know me as we ate. As we were finishing up, the elevator dinged, and a tall redhead walked out from between the opening doors.

"You mother fucker." She strode over to Kian and hit him over the head with her folder. He stood and gave her a hug.

"I'm so mad at you, but damn, you definitely just made my job even easier." She ran a hand appreciatively over the muscles in his bicep. *Mine,* the word sprang into my mind. I wanted to push her away and make a claim on my man.

As if he could hear me, Kian looked over at me and said, "Jessa, this is our social media manager, Adara. Adara, this is my girlfriend, Jessa."

She turned to look at me and then said without looking back at Kian, "I forgive you for abandoning me without a single word because you brought home this beauty for me to post all over your account. She is going to make your social media look so hot." He laughed as my confused gaze met his.

"Adara is gay and likes pretty things." He explained her familiarity with him, assuaging my jealousy.

"Oh my god, so gay." She leaned in and gave me a hug. "I love your hair so much. Can we do a photoshoot?"

"Umm." I didn't want to, but I also didn't want to disappoint anyone this soon into meeting them.

"Go get some dinner and leave her alone." Kian laughed, pushing Adara away from me gently. "I'll do one instead," he offered. Adara stopped in her tracks.

"Oh wow, you really like her." She looked at me again with more interest than before.

I must have looked confused because Nile said, "Kian avoids photoshoots like the actual plague."

"Oh." I was so painfully out of my element. Eating off of china plates in a multi-million-dollar penthouse, talking about photoshoots while sitting at a table with award-winning musicians. I hoped it wasn't too obvious. Kian reached over and squeezed my hand.

"You made a mess on my pillow earlier," he murmured so quietly that only I would hear him.

"Yeah?" My voice hitched, and I had to squeeze my legs together as his tone turned me on again.

"You'll have to clean it up," he said promisingly. I squeezed his hand, running a finger down his palm.

"Okay."

He grinned, and my discomfort slowly eased into something that almost felt magical. I had woken up this morning existing in one life, and here I was eating dinner in a completely different reality. I had mastered living in survival mode, and now I was opening up my heart to really, truly live.

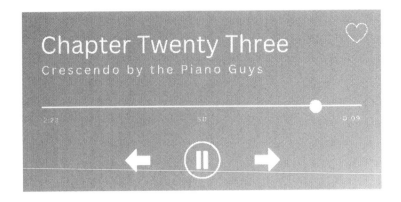

J essa tried to clean up from dinner, but Zara kindly kicked her out of the kitchen, so I took her hand and had her come with me to the recording studio on the opposite side of the penthouse. Myles followed behind, commenting on how different I was now that I was home.

"What do you mean?" I asked, opening the door. My band was already inside.

"You just seem lighter. I mean, don't get me wrong, you're still obnoxiously broody, but you do seem happier here." He observed.

"Fuck off." I grinned and fake punched him in the arm.

"He's attacking me, J. Help!" Myles laughed as he pretended to fall into the large, overstuffed chair that could fit all of us.

"I feel free from all the guilt," I admitted. "Being here with you and being around my friends again feels right."

"Well, thank you for hosting us." Myles had curled up on the chair.

"I'm not hosting you. You live here because you're part of my family now. This is your home too," I said in a serious tone and then walked away so they couldn't argue with me. I saw Jessa sit down next to her brother and say something that I couldn't hear.

"She's so hot, bro," Nile announced as I got behind the glass and closed the partition door behind me.

"Don't look at her," I warned him playfully.

"It's hard not to," he protested. I shot Nile a look as he said, "Are we gonna talk about it or just move on and pretend it never happened?"

"Talk about which part?" Ash had an edge to his voice that told me he was still mad. "The fact that you left without saying a word after your fiancée was killed or that you never even told us that Rose was pregnant. Or maybe that you disappeared and didn't stay in touch with your best friends for over a year."

"Okay, calm down." Mika got in between us since Ash had gotten up in my face.

"We're all hurt, bro," Nile told Ash. "But this new Kian could knock you out in one try. So be careful."

"I would never." I turned to look at Nile, aghast that he would suggest that I would punch my friend.

"Well, you could." He shrugged. I moved past Mika and put my arms around Ash.

"I am sorry. I will say it as many times as you need. I was a total shit for leaving and not telling you where I was. I was in such a dark place I thought I had to leave to save you all from being around me, and I wanted to punish myself for what happened." I said it loudly enough so all of my friends could hear me.

"How do we know you won't go back there? To the dark place," Mika asked quietly, sounding out each word carefully.

"I know you're going to make fun of me for saying this, but it's the truth. I found sunlight." I shrugged, bracing myself for my friends to laugh at my vulnerability. "And that darkness can't exist there."

They didn't laugh. They stood there watching me with relief on their faces, their love for me apparent in the sheen in their eyes.

"Jessa?" Ash asked as he finally hugged me back.

"Jessa," I confirmed.

"Well, then, I guess we better worship the ground she walks on because the label will cut off your cock and stuff it down your throat if you run off again."

Nile came up behind me to hug me as well. "So please stick around and keep your shit together."

"You say the sweetest things," I mumbled against Ash's shirt. Nile laughed. Our little reunion session was broken up by my barber tapping on the glass. I watched as she said hello to Jessa and Myles. Jessa seemed a little quieter than usual, but I was happy to see that she was handling herself better than I had anticipated. I was hoping she would acclimate quickly because I missed her cocky edge. I wanted her to hurt my feelings and tell me she wanted me in the same breath. I returned to the control room and left my band back in the isolated booth as they began to set up their instruments.

"Jesus Christ, Jace, you look... this hair... what the actual fuck?"

My barber's name was Lilith. She had very straight black hair that came to her chin and was cut in a razor-straight bob. She was also covered in tattoos, which reminded me that I had made an appointment with our tattoo artist to finally add some new art to my chest. Lilith cut all of our hair, and until now I had always been the easiest one. A quick shave over my whole head and I was done. Now, I had hair that was almost longer than hers. I came over to her and pulled her into a hug.

"I missed you, you idiot," she whispered in a moment of vulnerability that was not common for her.

"I missed you too." I kissed the top of her head and then turned to introduce her properly to Jessa. Jessa stood to shake her hand and watched as Lilith set up her barber chair and stand with her scissors, razors, and products.

I sat as she wrapped me in a cape. I felt her pull the pony holder out of my hair as she asked, "So what the fuck are we doing?" I pulled out my phone and handed it to Jessa.

"Choose one and show it to Lilith." I showed her the four photos of hairstyles I had saved in my camera roll.

"You want me to choose?" She sounded surprised.

"You're the one who has to look at him," Lilith chimed in as she sprayed my hair with water and brushed it.

"You're the one holding onto it while he goes down on you." Ash had left the isolation booth as well and now stood, leaning against the wall, his arms folded.

"Brother. Right here," Myles chanted as he covered his ears. Lilith burst out laughing. Jessa's cheeks were tinged pink as she looked through my photos, stopping on one and turning my phone to show it to Lilith.

"I like it," my barber confirmed and picked up the scissors. Forty minutes later, I was reminded why I chose to wear a buzz cut for most of my life. It took around five minutes, while this haircut had taken forever. Yet it had definitely been worth it as I looked in the mirror admiring my fresh look. Jessa had chosen a crew cut style that was tapered on the sides and the back with a fade but still left a lot of hair on the top that was layered and still long enough that it fell over my forehead in an artful and messy fashion. She had also cleaned up my beard, leaving it the same length but shaving my neck and cheeks. I loved it. I still looked like Kian yet somehow he had also merged with Jace and I easily embraced how my two selves began to blend.

"This is perfect," I said out loud.

"Of course it is," Lilith retorted as she packed up. "I will see you in two weeks when you get messy again. Ash, you're scheduled with me on Thursday to get cleaned up for the party."

"What party?" I asked.

"The label is throwing a welcome back party. They've spun the story to sound like they told you to take time off," Mika told me as he came back into the main room as well.

"Do I have to go?" I groaned.

"You absofuckinglutely do," I heard Gordon exclaim from the doorway behind me.

"That's my cue to leave." Lilith dashed around Gordon and made a quick exit.

"Okay. Sheesh. You don't have to yell," I muttered.

"With you, I do," Gordon replied as he sat down in front of the channel strip. "Kiwi will be here in a minute, so go set up."

"Aye, aye, captain." I rolled my eyes.

"We're gonna record a quick demo. I sent over a song to the boys a couple of months ago, and they want to get a recording of it so the label is less furious with me tomorrow." I leaned over and kissed Jessa. Myles had fallen asleep next to her. "Are you tired?"

"A little. But I want to hear you play." She smiled up at me. I wanted her to hear me play too.

"Who is Kiwi?"

I laughed.

"He's our recording engineer, and before you ask, I cannot remember why we call him that," I told her. "Let me know if you like the song."

She nodded.

"I will."

As soon as the music started and I had a mic in my hand, it was like I had never left. Ash was singing in the background, and as always, his voice naturally blended with mine. Nile and Mika were right in sync with their instruments, and I immediately remembered why I had fallen in love with playing music with them all those years ago. I felt tears spring to my eyes, and I angrily blinked them away. I could hear my baby's heartbeat in the throb of the drums. I could hear Rose's laughter in the strum of the guitar. I missed her. I missed the little blob on the ultrasound screen whom I had never met. I missed the possibility of a lost future. But it didn't shred my soul the way it used to.

I used to shudder at the thought of losing my fury. Yet here, amongst the music and the rhythm, together with my closest friends and a beautiful girl waiting for me—a girl who didn't know how much she had brought my existence back into tune—I finally felt at peace. I was at peace with my pain. It was a reminder of all that once was, yet the soft edges of the painful memories were a reminder of all that would be. This was harmony. This beautiful place between pain and acceptance. Between looking back and facing forward. Of wishing it had been different but embracing this new existence. It was beautiful and it was broken.

Harmony, after all, was a mix of sounds that form texture. It is both vertical and horizontal, just like my life has been up until now. It is created through melodic movement, and the way each note relates to its previous and its successor creates a subtle harmonic progression. Similar to how my current existence would always be subtly affected by my previous experiences, and my future would be led by my current self, my life was one harmonious note bouncing one off the other. A hum.

I looked up and found Jessa watching me. I loved her, and I couldn't possibly avoid that fact anymore. I loved her with every note inside of me. I hoped she knew that. Kiwi's voice crackled over the speaker, breaking me out of my overly emotional thoughts. "Sounding great, boys, but can I have you start again from the second verse? I think we need to tweak something."

Ash looked over at me and grinned.

"You're back," he mouthed.

"I'm back," I confirmed. It felt good to say. I couldn't wait to tell Jessa my sudden revelation. I looked up to see her again and found an empty chair staring at me. Both she and Myles were gone.

BY THE TIME we had a decent track for the label tomorrow, I was beyond exhausted. Between not having had time to rest my body after the fight, the sudden shock of the paparazzi finding us, having to make a quick life decision with Jessa, and flying for so many hours this morning, I was completely worn out. I took my headset off and said goodnight to the boys. As I walked back into the control room, Gordon looked up.

"Meeting is at eleven a.m. sharp. Your TV interview is at one p.m., and then you're going shopping with your team and Jessa at three p.m."

"What team?" I scoffed.

"Alex, obviously, and one of the stylists that the label is sending over." Gordon stood and grabbed his briefcase. "I have to find you a new personal assistant. I fired the last one."

"Can Jessa do it?" I held the door open for him, and we walked toward the elevator.

"Huh?" Gordon almost laughed.

"She told me that she wants to work," I explained. "I promised I would ask you for something for her to do."

"Jace, she's not going to want to manage your calendar and talk to me all day." Gordon snorted as the elevator doors opened.

"Find something for her to do," I urged. He shrugged,

looking vaguely intrigued that I wasn't dating a gold-digging model this time around.

Hey, Rose protested faintly in my head.

"I'll think of something," he promised. The doors started to shut. "It's nice to have you back, Jace." He looked annoyed that he even wanted to say it, and I felt a smile playing on my lips.

I was practically sleepwalking at this point, but I forced myself to stop at the home gym and got in a quick workout that my body protested the entire time. I wanted to maintain my physique mainly to continue being someone who could protect the people around me, but I also found that the endorphins that flooded my body after a workout were really good for my psyche. However, this was the first time in the gym that I didn't feel compelled to make it hurt to the point of exhaustion.

Is this goodbye? Rose wondered.

"I believe it is," I whispered back.

MY SHIRT WAS COMPLETELY SOAKED through, and my eyes were closing as I took the stairs to go to my room. Our room, I corrected myself. Jessa wasn't there. I saw that while we were in the recording studio, Zara had unpacked Jessa's small bag. Little touches of her were all over the space. Her boots were in the closet. Her small toiletries bag was in the bathroom. Her hoodie was in the drawer. I smiled and then turned to go to Myles's room because I had a feeling I knew where she was.

I STOOD IN THE DOORWAY. At first, I thought they were sleeping because the room was quiet, and all I could hear was their breathing. From what I could see in the dark, Myles was lying under the blanket, and Jessa was lying next to him, on top of the blanket. Their hands were tangled in between them. I was planning to go in quietly and carry Jessa to bed when I heard Myles whisper, "I'm more than an addict, J. Back in New York, that's all I was, but here I can start over. I can be a human being. I don't want to spend all my time at meetings. I want to actually see the beach and figure out my life."

I heard Jessa sigh.

"You can do both. I don't think skipping meetings is going to help you do that."

The blankets shifted as Myles turned from his side to his back.

"I think I can do it without going to NA." He huffed. "I'm sick of it. I want more to life than saying, 'Hi, I'm Myles, and I'm an addict.'"

I sucked in a breath. It sounded like he and Jessa were not seeing eye to eye on how his sobriety would play out here.

"Have you spoken to your sponsor?" I heard her husky voice ask.

"I will," Myles promised quietly.

They were silent for a moment until Jessa said, "For the record, I don't see you as an addict. I've always known who you really are."

It was quiet again, and then Myles responded, "I know you have."

I felt my heart break a little for them. I tiptoed away when I heard Jessa say goodnight, and she started to sit up. She would come to me when she was ready, and I would be there when she did.

THE NEXT MORNING, I worked out early, showered, and put on a suit. When I came down to the kitchen for breakfast, I found Jessa making coffee with the very expensive, large, and fancy espresso machine that usually sat behind an accordion cabinet door on one of the counters. Someone had obviously gone out to get her different kinds of coffee, a variety of milk, multiple jars of tea essence, and mixing cups. Ash and Gordon sat on chairs by the island in front of her, drinking something out of mugs that said "Jessa's Java" on it.

"What is this?" I asked as I came up behind her and kissed the top of her head.

"Ash and Gordon had this set up for me when I came down!" Jessa sounded so happy that I looked over at my grumpy manager and my best friend, who was more known for dicking down girls than he was doing nice things for them.

"You guys did what now?"

"Fuck off," Ash grumbled taking a sip of his drink that left a bit of whipped cream on his lip.

"You made custom cups? How did you get them so fast?" I was handed a travel mug with a cover, and I took a sip.

"It's my twist on the white chocolate cinnamon chai latte," she told me. The light in her eyes made me want to down the entire drink in one gulp just so she could make me another one and tell me all about it.

"I know a guy." Gordon shrugged, referring to the mugs. "You told me she wanted something to do. Well, here it is—keep the team caffeinated."

"Are you okay with that?" I could just imagine what that chaos would look like once we were on tour and everyone wanted a fancy caffeine pick-me-up.

"Are you kidding? It's a dream come true." Jessa leaned up to kiss my cheek and then went back to making another drink.

"Maybe you can learn how to make latte art," Ash offered, leaning forward in his seat to watch Jessa foam some milk.

"I would love that," she gushed. He looked grossly pleased with himself.

"I'll find you a class," I interjected. Ash winked at me. I felt my heart throb slightly with how good it felt to watch them accept her into the fold so easily and willingly.

"Well, I'm off," I announced as Alex walked into the room. "Gonna go get my spanking from the executives." I tried to sound lighthearted, but I don't think any of them bought it. Jessa handed me another cup for Alex.

"Just don't argue with them, and definitely don't say anything stupid," she told me. Gordon made a sound in the back of his throat, showing that he liked that she was just saying it like it is.

"What she said." He nodded. "Call me as soon as you're done, and I'll meet you at the interview." I nodded and left with Alex.

THE YELLING DIDN'T GO AS BADLY as I had anticipated. They weren't happy with me, and they threatened all kinds of legal jargon if I ever pulled a stunt like that again. They told me they wouldn't tolerate any more temper tantrums for the duration of our next tour. They also said they were sorry for my loss, and they liked the demo song that Gordon had emailed them earlier this morning. They shook my hand when we finished and said they were looking forward to seeing me again. I called Gordon as soon as I was back in the car, and he sounded relieved that it hadn't been any worse and that it ended on a positive note. I met him at the studio for my interview, where I sat for a half hour for makeup and hair.

Then we conducted my interview where I stuck to the story the label asked me to tell about how they told me to take time off to process my grief and work on my music. I told them how happy I was to be back, that we were already recording some new songs, and that tour dates would be released soon. The host commented on my new body multiple times, which I answered politely as I tried not to grit my teeth in frustration. My mouth was starting to get dry from all the talking, and my brain was beginning to get annoyed from the typical Hollywood inquiries.

"One last question, Jace," she asked with her blinding, fake smile. "Can you tell us how you met your new girlfriend?"

"No comment," I retorted, shifting in my seat. I could see Gordon frowning where he stood off-camera.

"Nothing? I'm sure your fans would love to know more about her." The host poked once more.

"She's private, and I ask that all of our fans respect that." I was done. I could feel the fake smile beginning to melt off my face and my shoulders started to tense up.

"Alright, well, it was so nice to see you again, Jace, and we cannot wait to hear the new single. Coming to you live from Hollywood, this is..."

I tuned out until they finally cut to a commercial, and an assistant came over to take off my mic.

"I asked you to tell them that I would not talk about Jessa," I told Gordon as he came over to lead me off-set.

"They're already talking about her, Jace," the woman who had interviewed me said from behind me with an icy tone she had not used during filming. "Nice to see you." Her smile didn't meet her eyes as I walked away.

"What does she mean?" I hissed to Gordon, who sighed and took out his phone. Photos of Jessa getting into the SUV at the airport yesterday and walking into the penthouse had been leaked. The article, thankfully, was mainly focused on me coming back, what had happened to Rose, and guessing when the tour would be announced, but they had also written some speculations about my "latest woman," as they called her.

I flinched when I read: "Still nameless, the anonymous knockout was seen leaving the fight with Jace as well as traveling with him on his return to Hollywood. While obviously beautiful, she is not the usual look we're used to seeing him with. She is all curves and boobs, which may be every man's dream but is also every designer's nightmare. Although we do admit, we must get the name of her surgeon because her BBL is to die for."

They had basically called her fat according to Hollywood standards in one breath and then complimented her ass in the next.

I didn't want her to see this, and I definitely didn't want them tarnishing anything to do with Jessa. She was down-to-earth and kind, and while she had seen the harsher side of life, she was still so good, and I didn't want the cruel world of the press cutting away little bits of her until she felt less than whole in who she was.

"Get this offline," I demanded as we got into the car.

"Already on it," Gordon assured me. I leaned back in the seat and closed my eyes. I already couldn't protect her from the vultures Hollywood called the press. For a moment, I wished for the simplicity of when we were back in her hotel room, eating licorice and watching movies.

APPARENTLY, everyone was coming on the shopping trip. Ash claimed he had nothing else to do, Nile made a quip that he went where Jessa went, Mika didn't even explain himself—we just found him chatting with Myles by the elevator, ready to join us.

"Way to keep a low profile." I tried to sound annoyed. "Let's just show up with the entire band."

"You've been gone a long time. They just want to spend time with you." Jessa patted my arm to mollify me.

"Speak for those guys; I'm coming to watch Jessa try on dresses." Ash sidled up beside her and grinned at me when I practically growled at him.

It didn't take Jessa long to choose a dress, although she fought me through the whole process once she found out how much everything cost. Back at home, she hung the dress up in the closet in our room and then met us back downstairs for dinner. Of course, the boys had stayed, and we were all sitting around the table eating homemade burgers and chili fries when Jessa brought up the article. Gordon had gotten it taken offline, but apparently not fast enough.

"What's a BBL?" Jessa asked.

I paused mid-chew as Ash answered, "Brazilian butt lift. Why?"

"Apparently, Hollywood thinks I got one." She stuffed another fry in her mouth as she responded.

"Don't read that shit," Nile told her. "The online space is vile."

"For the record, you have a really nice ass." Ash licked some gravy off his fingers as he tilted his head to look over at her body. I punched his arm when he said it, but he just laughed at me.

"I don't get why it matters," Myles muttered. "A body is a body; why is this place so obsessed?"

"I just think it's funny that they think I would pay to look like this and then at the same time make fun of it." She took a sip of lemonade and shrugged.

"Hollywood is fucked up," Mika agreed.

"Are you guys sick of it?" I suddenly piped up. "What if we stopped playing by their rules once our contract is up? What if we started releasing our own music without the label and stopped going to their stupid award shows or letting them dig into our personal lives?"

"I think Gordon would have our heads," Ash told me.

"Well, in a year, Gordon won't have a say," I muttered.

"As long as we're together, I'll do whatever," Nile announced.

"We certainly have enough money to support any choice we make."

"I'm down." Mika announced around a bite of food.

"I go where you go." Ash sounded serious, which was so unlike him.

"I love you guys." I looked around the table at my best friends. "I think we could have our lives back and love music our own way again."

"I love you all too," Mika said quietly from the end of the table. Ash shrugged.

"Let's talk about it in a year. In the meantime, don't read what they have to say about you," he told Jessa. "Clearly, my guy is head over heels for you, and that's all that matters, okay?" He patted Jessa on the head. I had never heard him be so sincere before.

"I'm not a dog," she joked. He pulled on one of her curls and questioned, "Aren't you a good girl though?" Aaand he was back. I chuckled but pretended to be mad.

"Leave her alone, Ash!" I slapped him harder against the back of his head this time, and he groaned in defeat.

"Okay! Jesus, Mike Tyson, lay off!"

I leaned back in my seat, surveying the room. Mika and Myles were talking as they ate. Nile and Ash were continuing to tease Jessa. I felt physically full from my meal. My muscles burned from my workout earlier. I was home and was recording music again. I finally felt at peace.

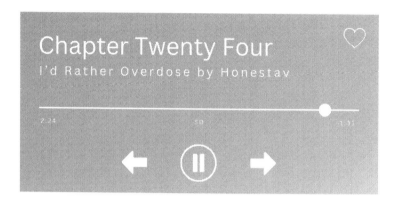

As uncomfortable as shopping with Kian's credit card had made me, standing here in the mirror, I understood why Gordon had insisted we do it. The welcome back party being thrown by his label was tonight, and according to Adara, all of the important people in Hollywood would be there. Kian had rolled his eyes when she had said that. I laughed and told her I didn't know who anyone was to know if they were important or not.

"I love how unimpressed you are." Adara laughed as well. "It's such a breath of fresh air."

An entire glam team had come to the penthouse to get us ready. The boys went first because their hair was relatively quick, and for makeup, all they did was concealer and powder. I, on the other hand, had taken several hours which was so hard since I was impatient and found it difficult to sit still. Yet I now understood the allure of why people did it. I was standing in front of the full-length mirror in our closet, staring at myself.

My curls were still my curls, but somehow better, sleek and

shiny. The stylist had pulled my hair up into a half pony with a braid on the top, and then braided two smaller braids along the side of my head. The rest of my hair was cascading down my back.

My makeup was so beautiful that I was scared to move my face. The makeup artist had almost passed out when I told her I had never had my makeup done before. She kept complimenting my skin as she applied what felt like a million creams. She had put on fake lashes, eyeliner, and eye shadow so my eyes were dramatic and dark in contrast with my dewy, blushed skin. My lips were a soft pink, and I couldn't stop looking at myself.

The stylist had come in with the dress, and had me strip naked so she could help me into it. She hadn't even blinked as I stood there with no clothes on as she chose the right pair of underwear and bra for me, and I figured this must be a fancy people thing. The dress was black lace. It looked sheer, but it had a nude underlay, so all the private bits were actually covered. It had a thin strap on my shoulders and cut down deep between my breasts. It was paired with a thin black silk belt that accentuated my small waist, as the saleswoman had informed me. The rest of the dress was long and flowy and had a slit up to my mid-thigh. It was such a massive contrast to what I had worn my entire life.

The stylist had me put on a nude shaper under the dress that was squeezing my thighs so tight I felt like they would be bruised by the end of the night. I'd honestly rather deal with chub rub than wear something like this again. In the store, I had told them that I had never worn heels before, so they had given me a pair of black, open-toed shoes with shorter heels so I wouldn't fall or walk like a baby lamb in front of all these important, fancy people.

For jewelry, the stylist had put diamond studs in my ears, a bracelet with four-leaf clovers on it on my wrist, and two thin diamond rings on my fingers. I shuddered to think of how much they cost.

I dreaded being a spectacle at this party, but I also wanted Kian to know that I supported him, and although I had been thrust into a life I knew very little about, if there was one thing I was good at, it was acclimating to my surroundings. I had done it my whole life and I could certainly do it now.

I HEARD a shuffle behind me and turned to find Myles standing in the doorway in a suit.

"My! You look amazing!" I hobbled over to him, still trying to navigate walking in heels, and brushed a speck of dust off the lapel of his jacket.

"The one who looks amazing is you. Kian is going to lose his mind," Myles complimented me.

"I can barely breathe in this dress, but they told me that's the point, so I'm just hoping for the best." I shrugged as I laughed at how absurd it was that just a few days ago, I only had a few pairs of pants in my entire wardrobe, and here I was wearing a dress that probably cost the equivalent of a few months of my paychecks from Kafe. I grabbed the tiny purse the stylist had given me, and stuck the extra lipstick the makeup artist had left for "touch-ups" and my phone into it and clicked it shut.

"Ready?" I asked Myles.

"Are you?" He held the door open for me as we walked down the hallway to meet everyone on the main floor.

"No," I answered honestly. I had told Kian I didn't want to be in any photos, so he and the band would be dropped off outside the venue to talk to the press, and the driver had been instructed to drive Myles and me around back to duck in unnoticed. I had told Kian it was because it was his welcome back party, and he deserved the spotlight, and I didn't want to be a distraction. While that was mostly true, I also didn't want too many unnecessary eyes on Myles and me.

I wasn't shy. It was not a low confidence thing either—it was simply just not my vibe and not an expectation that I wanted anyone to have of me. I was happy to be in the background of all this hoopla and chaos. I was pleasantly surprised to find that Kian's friends were funny and much more down-to-earth than I had expected them to be. The coffee gig they had given me had almost made me cry. It had been so nice of Ash and Gordon to go out of their way to give me a gift like that.

But as warm and as welcoming as they had been, and as unassuming and chill as they came across, the lifestyle the band led and the way the people they surrounded themselves with lived was still outrageous to me. It was crazy to think that while people ate steak for lunch, got breakfast spreads delivered every morning, and wore dresses that cost more than most people spent on a month of groceries, there were also people struggling with daily life. Ironically the balance of money felt more off now that I had a tiny taste of luxury than it had when I had struggled to afford basic necessities.

My entire life, every dollar had been spent as carefully as possible, yet now I knew some people had so much of it that it almost became meaningless to them. When I had told Kian I didn't want to spend so much on a dress that I would only wear once he had said, "Babe, I promise I wouldn't even notice if you bought two." I knew he had meant it with the intention to assuage my worry and help me feel more comfortable with the purchase, but it had actually made me sad that the world was the way it was. While so many barely made it, others lived lives of extreme gluttony.

It wasn't the band that made me feel like this and Kian

certainly didn't have any popstar behavior. I had noticed that Ash wore the same shoes everyday so far. I had even found out that Mika drove an old Camry that everyone made fun of him for. My perspective was more shaped from the expectations the label had of them. The haircuts in the house. The expensive cheeses in the fridge that I had yet to see anyone touch. The nightly restaurant deliveries or extravagant dinners that Zara whipped up. The freshly made bed that I came back to every night and the trip to the boutique to buy my dress.

The women there were perfectly coiffed and laughed at all the right moments. They spoke elegantly and wore designer clothes. They were what society looked up to and what I could never and wouldn't want to compete with. I found so much of what these people thought was normal to actually be so over-the-top and unnecessary.

Yet even as practical as I was trying to keep my perspective, over the few days we had been here, Myles and I were definitely enjoying the luxury. Myles had discovered that he really liked sushi, and I could not get enough of the kitchen—the mini coffee shop I had going on, to the always stocked fridge, to the extensive options in the pantry with which I planned to start baking if Zara would let me. I shook myself out of my thoughts as I took the last step down into the main room, being careful not to trip on my dress when I heard Ash whistle.

"Damn, Bardot." He stood to circle me. "You are looking fiiine."

"Get the fuck away from her, Ash." Kian had stood from the couch, practically glowering. Ash winked at me and I laughed. He was just trying to rile up his friend and it had worked. Kian was wearing a black suit that had a tuxedo lapel. His hair was perfectly styled, his beard freshly shaped, and his body strained against the constraints of his clothes.

"You are looking fine, Jessa," Nile called in agreement from where he sat on the couch playing with an unlit cigar.

"I concur." Mika spoke quietly, but he was loud enough for Kian to hear him.

"Jessa, go back upstairs until these hooligans leave," Kian barked, coming closer and drawing me against him with his arm. I took a deep breath, inhaling his scent. His presence never failed to calm me and make me feel safe.

"We're leaving together." Ash snickered as the elevator dinged, announcing someone's arrival.

"You look insane. Outrageous. Incredible," he murmured in my ear, his breath hot against my face, setting all my nerve endings on fire. "Let's stay home. You'll sit on my face, and you can be as loud as you want because no one will be here." He was practically panting and was already semi hard against my stomach.

I had not been in the mood last night. I was tired and still trying to find my bearings. I had never been able to say no in my few past and obviously toxic relationships, so I was apprehensive when I turned Kian down. He had not even blinked when I told him I didn't want to have sex. Instead of complaining or begging like some other guys had, he just kissed the tip of my nose, helped me pull on one of his T-shirts to go to bed in, and held me until I fell asleep. In that moment I felt even more intimately close to him. Yet now I could feel his libido biting at the bit so to speak and every touch between us held a frisson of energy.

"You didn't spend a small fortune on this dress for no one to see it." I ran my hand down his chest, and he flinched.

"Did I hurt you?" I pulled back, concerned.

"I was going to show you later." He had a smirk on his face as he began to unbutton his shirt.

"What are you doing?" I looked around the room. His band

technically did not live here, but I had quickly observed that they were almost always here anyway. It didn't allow for much privacy, but so far, it had been a really fun and loud experience.

"Limo is here," Nile announced.

"We'll meet you down there," Kian told them as they all piled into the elevator, and we finally had some momentary peaceful silence. Kian moved his jacket aside, and behind his unbuttoned shirt, he revealed a fresh tattoo. I leaned closer to examine it. It was a bunch of words... in my handwriting. My heart skipped a beat.

"What's this?" I placed my hand on his chest, avoiding the red, wrapped skin above his right pectoral.

"Look at it." His voice was soft and tender, but there was a sharp edge to it as well as if he was holding back from saying something. I leaned closer and read:

"Jessa Bardot"

"I like that you came back"

"You look hot today, music man"

"I like your tattoos"

"Sing me our song"

"Your voice is my favorite sound"

"Us, music & making memories"

"What does more look like?"

"You are the best thing I never planned"

He had so many of my notes that I had left on the coffee cups tattooed onto his chest. In my handwriting. He had kept them somehow and had permanently etched my flirty words into his skin.

"What did you do?" I whispered, running my finger around the edge of his freshly inked skin.

"All the most important things in my life are on me," he bit

out in that "I really don't want to talk, but I'll talk to you" way
that he had about him. I recalled the sonogram on his back and
the music notes on his arms, and I shivered as the meaning of
his words hit me.

"I put you on me because you have become, arguably, the
most important one." He tilted my chin up so I could look at him
instead of at my handwriting all over his chest.

"I would have never come back if it weren't for you."

I knew he wasn't just referring to California but rather to his
life, his friends, and his peace.

"You are my sunshine, Jessamine Bardot, and I care about
you so much." His voice cracked, and my body shook from the
significance of the moment.

"I need you here, and I want you to stay. I want you to stay
and do things that make you happy. Go to the beach with Myles.
Make coffee. Learn how to do latte art. Swim. Thrift. Whatever
you want. I just want you here where I can enjoy being with you
from close up instead of far away."

"I—" I began.

"It's okay if you don't feel the same way yet." He cut me off as
I wrapped my arms around his waist and pressed my cheek to
his heart. The thump, thump was soothing in my ear. I turned
my head to look up at him once more.

"I want to stay here with you too, music man." I smiled and
then yelped as he bent down to kiss me.

"Don't ruin the lipstick!"

"Fuck the lipstick," he grumbled, but he pulled back and
smiled.

"You'll stay here with me?" His eyes were suspiciously shiny
as we walked to the elevator door, and he buttoned up his shirt.

"I'll show you how much I want to stay later." I winked. Kian
groaned as we stepped onto the elevator.

"Show me now."

"We don't have time."

"I'm holding you to that," he promised.

"I certainly hope so."

Myles was being fidgety. He was usually quieter by nature, but now he was basically mute as he stared out the car window, rapping his fingers on his knee. He kept switching positions and moving every few minutes as if he couldn't quite get comfortable. I felt a lump grow in my throat, and I had to swallow forcibly to make it go away. I knew these signs. I had seen them a million times before. He wanted to use. Well, he always wanted to use, but I could tell that right now, his defenses were even lower than usual. I leaned over, pressing my shoulder to his, and grabbed his hand. He flinched.

"We can go home," I murmured. He shook his head.

"I'm fine," he snapped.

"You don't seem fine." I didn't want to press too hard, but I didn't want to go into a party that would definitely be flowing with alcohol and probably other questionable substances with him in this state.

"Do you need a cigarette?" I could feel my heart rate speed up, and my mind started to race with ideas. I needed to insist that he attend meetings and call his sponsor. It had only been a few days, but he was already melting quickly in his resolve to stay sober. I could feel it. I knew I couldn't force him to want to be sober, but maybe if I could get him to stay clean for a little bit longer, something would change. Or, at the very

least, it would give me some more time to find a good therapist here.

I had also read about neurofeedback and how it helped with
addiction. Back in New York, I could never afford it, but maybe
here, I could make it happen. I could take my earnings from
making coffee for the crew and pay for it. I was starting to slip
back into the fear of losing him as I felt Kian take my other hand
and squeeze it.

"Cigarette stop?" he asked. I nodded.

"We need to make a quick detour," he called out to the
driver. Alex looked back at him from the front seat.

"We need to be there in ten minutes."

Kian shrugged.

"I guess we'll be late then. You all okay with that?" He looked
at his band. They agreed without protest.

I watched from the limo as Alex ran into the closest gas
station and returned shortly with a pack of cigarettes. He
opened the door, and I followed Myles out into the seedy
parking lot of this random gas station somewhere in the middle
of Hollywood. We stepped behind the limo as Alex shut the
door and turned his body slightly to give us privacy. I packed the
box quickly by slapping the bottom and the sides a few times
and then peeled off the plastic wrapping. I slipped a cigarette in
between Myles's lips and lit it while he still refused to make eye
contact with me. I watched as he took a deep breath in and then
blew the smoke out through his nose, the cigarette still hanging
from his mouth.

"You gonna smoke too or just watch me?" He seemed to be
testing me. Was I now this glamorous girl dating a music star, or
was I still the sister he had always known? Had I already
forgotten who we were before this? Was I too good to smell like
tobacco at a fancy party with my famous boyfriend and my
expensive dress?

I didn't answer; I just slipped a cigarette between my lips and lit up. The beautiful, toxic first breath always jarred my system, and I blew out the smoke into his face. That made him laugh, and I felt relief flood me. He was going to be okay, right? He had to be. I might have to ask Kian to help me find someone with a safe, clean supply because I didn't know anyone out here whom I could trust with something as serious as this. I didn't want to buy him product, but I would if it came down to it.

We finished our cigarettes, and Alex came over to take the butts instead of letting us toss them, which made us both laugh again. Myles leaned over and hugged me.

"I'm okay, I promise," he assured me.

"You better be." I tried to sound threatening, but my voice wavered.

"You love him," Myles observed as we walked back toward the car door that Alex held open for us.

"I guess I do." I smiled. Myles squeezed my hand and held the bottom of my dress up so I wouldn't trip as I maneuvered myself back into the car.

"Thank you," I whispered to the band.

"We got you." Ash nodded at me. Kian took my hand and squeezed it tight. It was going to be okay, I told myself. It had to be.

Sneaking in the back had been an amazing idea because as soon as the band stepped out of the limo they were immediately swarmed by the media. They wanted so many photos and stopped each of the guys to do an interview. I had watched from the car and then again through a blacked-out window from inside the venue, and it looked so overwhelming that I couldn't fathom how Kian handled it.

He may come across quiet with little to say, but once I had gotten to know him better, I realized that he was actually always simmering with emotion right beneath the surface. I didn't know how he kept his cool and didn't snap at the ridiculous questions, the yelling, the insane crowd, and the posing for picture after picture. Adara found Myles and me hiding in a corner and practically dragged us over to a table to get food.

"No one eats at these things 'cause they're all on an appetite suppressant, so we can't let it go to waste," she told me as she handed me a plate with fancy-looking pastries on it.

"Why would someone want to suppress their appetite when all of this exists?" I wondered out loud as I licked custard off my finger. Adara laughed.

"More for us" was her answer. She had gotten me a flute of champagne and handed Myles a glass of nonalcoholic cider, which he took but didn't drink. It seemed that the news had been spread around fast amongst the band's staff. Don't give the brother anything; he's sober.

I knew Myles had to be relieved and annoyed at the same time—relieved he doesn't have to explain himself but frustrated that people know his personal business.

By the time the band finally joined us, I was a few drinks and many tiny, expensive cakes in. Adara had pointed out who all the important people were and then told me the tea. I now knew who was sleeping with whom, who had recently gotten their boobs done, who was probably getting dropped from their label soon, and who had just gotten out of rehab. When I asked her how she knew all of this, she very seriously told me that as the head of the band's social media, it was her job to know everything.

Kian came over as Adara bounded off to video some footage of someone doing something. She spoke so fast and with a twinge of an accent that I couldn't always keep up.

"Having fun?" he asked me.

"Oh, so much." I hiccuped.

"Did you drink?" he asked with a laugh.

"Just a little." I made a motion of a small size with my fingers. "I gotta pee," I announced, standing.

"It's right past the elevators to the left," Kian told me.

"I'll be right back." I stood unsteadily on my feet. Heels and champagne were turning out to be an interesting mix.

"We'll come with you," Myles corrected, standing up to follow me. Kian stood as well, and the three of us made our way through the crowd. This proved to be difficult when Kian got stopped every few feet. Everyone kept saying how stunning I was and asking who I was wearing. I let Kian do all the talking because I didn't want to say the wrong thing.

When we finally made it to the bathroom, I went inside, and the boys waited in the hall for me. Peeing in shapewear proved to be almost impossible, but I finally managed it and had my hand on the door handle to pull it open when I heard Kian say, "If you feel like using or if you're out and need help, I don't care if it's the middle of the night, you wake me up. I will come get you or sit with you or do whatever you need."

"I appreciate it," Myles mumbled. I knew he hated feeling like he was a burden and was ashamed to be struggling, so I was happy that he was at least seemingly open to talking to Kian about it.

"Of course, man, you're like a brother to me," I heard Kian say. Tears sprung to my eyes, and I blinked them away.

"I just don't know how long I can fight it for, dude. I'm so tired," Myles confessed. I knew he was struggling. I always knew. I wished I could just take it from him. But this was ultimately a fight he had to battle on his own. All the support and love in the world was helpful, but when it came to beating addiction, it boiled down to one thing: The addict's desire to stay clean had to be stronger than their craving to use. Because that craving never went away. That was the shittiest part of their illness.

"I know you are," Kian said softly. I almost couldn't hear him. I peeked through the crack between the door and the doorway and saw that Kian had Myles wrapped up in a hug. I sucked in a sob and then made some loud footsteps by the door to warn them that I was coming out. I opened the door with a fake, bright smile on my face.

"Sorry, that took so long. This dress is impossible to pee in."

"We thought you fell in," Myles joked, avoiding eye contact with me again.

"Let's go get more of those tarts," I told him, trying to lighten the mood.

"I love you," I told him under my breath, squeezing his arm.

"I know. I love you too," he said and smiled back at me, but it didn't meet his eyes.

BACK IN THE MAIN ROOM, Myles disappeared for a bit, and when I scanned the room, I found him at the crepe station talking to the waiter who was making the dessert. I caught his eye and motioned that I wanted one. He gave me a thumbs-up and kept talking. My feet were starting to go numb from standing in heels for so long, and my thighs hurt from being stuffed into the shapewear. At this point, I was feeling like a sausage.

"You okay?" Ash asked as he noticed me shifting from one foot to the next as I tried to give each of my feet a break.

"Nope," I answered honestly, taking another large gulp of my champagne. "I need to get out of this dress."

"I can help you with that." Ash grinned, slow and seductive, which seemed to be his permanent personality.

"I'm good," I retorted playfully.

"Ash is trying to get his ass beat," Nile interjected gleefully. Ash shrugged lazily.

"Nah, just trying to be a good friend." He winked at me and then strolled away.

"He's an idiot; just ignore him—we all do," Nile told me as he snagged another flute of champagne off of a server's tray and handed it to me.

"Thanks." I took another sip. I had never gotten drunk from champagne before, and I didn't mind it. It was a sweeter and gentler buzz than the heavy sour beer that I usually had access to.

"Jace is a good one." Nile, whom I had never seen act serious in the few days I had been getting to know him, was suddenly sounding sincere.

"I know." I nodded.

"Just making sure 'cause I've never seen him like this with anyone." Nile shifted uncomfortably, sticking his hands in the pockets of his suit pants.

"Like what?" I tried to sound chill, but my heart sped up just like it always did when I thought about the fact that Kian wanted me to stay. That he needed me. That maybe I would get a happily ever after for myself.

I was ready for Nile to say something simple along the lines of Kian looks like I make him happy, but instead, he said, "Like everything finally makes sense."

Suddenly, everything did make sense. I leaned over and gave a surprised Nile a hug.

"Thank you." I smiled. He nodded and then got called away to talk to someone, so I went in search of Kian.

I FOUND him talking to a beautiful blonde with Gordon. Gordon stared at me as I walked up and said, "Wow."

"Hi." The blonde stuck her hand out to shake mine. "I'm Milan. Who are you?" Everything about her was sexy. Her ridiculously long legs, her thick eyebrows, her puffy lips, and even her low voice dripped sex.

"This is my girlfriend," Kian interrupted and pulled me to his side with one strong arm. The girl looked surprised but quickly schooled her face.

"Cute." She pursed her lips at me. "I'll be in touch," she told Gordon, and as she walked away, she waved at Kian but completely ignored me.

"Okaay?" I laughed, feeling awkward.

"Get used to it, hun," Gordon told me. "They all want him, and now their claws are out because they know they can't have him."

"They don't even know me to want me," Kian muttered.

"Can we get a photo of the beautiful couple?" A photographer with a lanyard around her neck stating which famous magazine she was from came up to us, holding up her camera. Kian looked down at me questioningly. I nodded.

"You sure?" He smoothed his beard with one hand, still holding me close to his body with the other.

"You're mine, aren't you?" I stated.

"I've only ever been yours." He leaned down to kiss my lips, and I heard the shutter of the camera purr.

"Then they should know." I kept my tone casual, but I suddenly felt fiercely protective of what we had growing between us. He smiled at my words, and we turned to pose for the camera. She took a few shots and then thanked us.

"You are the most beautiful woman here, Miss Bardot, because I can tell that you are the most real person in this room," she told me in parting.

"Maybe the media isn't all bad," I told Kian as we made our way back to our seats. He chuckled at that.

"No, they're all bad. She's just nicer than the rest of them."

Back at my seat, I found a cooling crepe but no Myles. As I dug into the chocolate and strawberry goodness, I scanned the room again, trying to find him, but since the music had picked up, the dancers were now blocking my view, and he was lost in the crowd.

I couldn't take my eyes off of Jessa. The entire evening, I could barely focus on anything anyone was saying to me because I kept getting drawn back to watching her. Yes, she was physically an absolute knockout; that much was obvious. The Viking vibe she had going on with her hair was making me crazy, and her body in that dress had kept me fighting a boner the entire evening.

But it was more than just her physical beauty that had me desperate for her. Distracted by her. Devoted to her. It was how cute she looked trying to navigate walking in her heels. It was the way she cut up some steak for Myles so when he came back to the table, it was ready to eat. It was her saying thank you to the bathroom attendant and really meaning it. It was the way she had patiently smoked a cigarette with her brother without putting any pressure on him to leave before he was ready to. It was because earlier she had asked Alex how his son was doing since she knew he hadn't been feeling well. It was the way she laughed at Nile's corny jokes, wasn't offended by Ash's ridiculous attempts at flirting, and made time to listen to a melody that Mika had come up with and wanted someone's opinion on.

In the past few days, she had fit right in, to the point that it felt like she had always been a part of our little crew. A family of sorts. She even had Gordon enchanted, although he would never admit it. I could see a future with her so clearly. Moments of me watching her backstage at my concerts, helping her start the little coffee shop I heard her and Myles talking about, maybe adopting a dog, definitely convincing her to get a tattoo with me, showing her the world, sitting on the back patio watching Ash and Nile fuck around in the pool, bringing her to the gym with me so she could taunt me with that ass in her leggings, and ultimately just growing old together. The emotion I had around her one hundred percent of the time was an easy kind of happiness, one I had never experienced before and one I had to keep. As soon as I realized how I felt about her, it was as if suddenly, all the love songs in the world had become about her. I reached over and took Jessa's hand, rubbing my finger over the pulse in her wrist.

"I can't wait to get home," I whispered. She cocked an eyebrow at me as if to ask why.

"I want you." I kissed the side of her face and grew harder as I heard her breath hitch.

"Why do we have to wait till we get home?" she asked me with faked innocence.

I was at full mast in my pants now, imagining myself buried between her legs, hearing her moaning in my ear, and tasting her flavor on my tongue.

"We don't?" I asked it as a question, but I meant it as a statement. She shook her head. I had to bite back a groan. Her hair was everywhere, her breasts were fighting to break free from the confines of her dress, her cheeks were flushed, and I knew she had to be wet from the way she was holding her thighs together.

"Come with me." I stood quickly, willing my dick to deflate so the state I was in would not be obvious behind my fly, and tugged on her hand as she rose from the chair. We walked quickly to the other side of the room.

"Don't make eye contact," she said in that bossy tone of hers. "Or we'll never make it."

I laughed and pulled her closer to me as we walked even faster. I found an empty coat closet past the bathrooms, and we tumbled in, tripping on the carpet, and shut the door behind us.

"I can't see anything," Jessa said huskily. I could sense her near me, and I reached out my hands in the dark, feeling around until I touched her bare arm.

"They say everything feels better when you can't see," I told her, loosening my belt and unzipping my pants. I reached up her dress and came in contact with a thick material that stretched when I pulled on it but didn't rip.

"What the fuck is this?" I demanded, growing impatient. She burst out laughing.

"Someone will hear you," I cautioned. She snorted, which I found endearing, but she quieted, and I heard her clothes rustle.

"It's shapewear to make everything stay where it should under the dress," she explained.

"I don't like it," I almost whined.

"I'm taking it off; hold on, you big baby." She giggled again. I had not brought my wallet to a fancy event like this, but I did have a money clip in my pocket in which Ash had snuck a condom. I reminded myself to tell him that he was my favorite friend. I pulled the condom out of the clip, feeling the money fall free and rustle to the floor. I ripped it open as she announced that she had taken off the offending shapewear, but that I had to help her put it back on afterward. I promised I would, and then I felt for her again, pulling her toward me so I could lift her up against the door as her legs tightened around my waist.

"You've been taunting me all night." I groaned as the tip of my cock slipped into her, and I felt how wet she was. She moaned and shifted in my arms. The slopes of her breasts pressed against my chest, which was encased by my shirt and jacket that was still buttoned. With another push of my hips, I slid into her fully until I bottomed out.

"Y-yes," she whimpered. I leaned in to kiss her, and her lips were soft against mine, but her mouth was desperate, kissing and biting as our breath became one in our frenzy. I slid out of her halfway and then slammed back in, hitting the door as I did and causing it to rattle against the frame.

"Who's making noise now!" she gasped out as she teased me.

"F-fuck." I let out a hiss as my nerve endings lit up all at once, and I felt her clamp down on me, slick and hot. I leaned my head down and pulled back the material of her dress just slightly so I could run my tongue over her tight, beaded nipple. I sucked on her until I felt her grow slicker around me, and I knew she must be bordering on discomfort. I pulled my mouth off and let the dress cover her once more.

"You feel so good." I was fucking her in earnest now, slamming against the door, disregarding the need to stay quiet at this point. I felt her tighten around me again, and I could tell she was close. As much as I wanted to explode inside of her, I pulled out with a groan and gently let her down until her feet touched the ground. She hit my chest with her hand, the bracelet she wore making a jingling sound in the dark.

"I haven't come yet!" She sounded mad, which made me laugh. I knelt in front of her, running my hands up her thighs, letting her dress rest on my arms.

"Do you want to come in my mouth or on my cock?" I asked

my angry, horny girlfriend. The air felt thick around me as I waited for her answer. I couldn't see her face; all I could hear was her labored breathing. All I could feel was her soft skin beneath my hands. I curled my fingers gently into her thighs, squeezing them slightly, and I felt her breath catch again.

"Both," she finally responded greedily.

I slapped her inner thigh, and without any hesitation, I leaned forward and put my tongue on her. She was soaking, and I lapped, letting her taste fill my mouth and overwhelm my senses. I moaned against her flesh, and she gripped my hair in response. It only took a few swipes of my tongue and three or four sucks on her clit until she flooded my mouth and came with a shout, pulling on my hair and clamping her thighs around my head until I had to peel her off of me so I could take a breath.

"Come here," I urged as I pulled on her to come down to where I now kneeled on the carpet. She shifted and lowered her body so she could sit on me. I adjusted her so each of her legs was on either side of me, and I tilted my hips as I held her up against me so I could fuck up deep inside of her. In this position, her clit was rubbing against the material of my pants, and she was panting out things like, "Right there, oh my god, yesss, Kian. Faster, faster..." My heart skipped a beat.

"Say it again," I demanded, fucking her so hard my thighs burned with the effort, and my balls felt ready to burst.

"Kian," she gasped. She said it so effortlessly, so simply, in a way that made me feel like somehow, she had always been mine.

The truth was, at this moment, it felt like I had always loved her. *I love you, Jessamine Bardot. I love you so much*, I thought as I groaned in her ear, and she came again, messily and loudly. Her body gripped mine, and on the next slide into her, I came, gripping her hips and kissing her mouth like the desperate man that I was.

"Holy shit." I leaned back, feeling sweat gathered at my hairline. "So good." I couldn't form any other words than that; my brain had turned to mush.

"Mmm," she agreed against my chest. We stayed like that for a minute, in the dark, our bodies against one another, savoring the moment until we had to leave the closet and go back to real life.

REAL LIFE CAME KNOCKING moments later.

"Jace?" It was Ash. His voice was muffled behind the door, but I heard an odd tone in his inflection that caused my intuition to perk up. I felt uneasy but didn't know why.

"Does he want to listen again?" Jessa giggled, and she felt floppy in my arms. I kissed her cheek, oddly worried that whatever it was Ash had to say was going to disturb this pocket of peace she had found here, with me, but also within herself.

"Hey, baby." I turned on the flashlight on my phone, and she blinked from the sudden onslaught of light. "Let's get dressed."

Ash rapped on the door again.

"Jace!"

"Hold on one fucking second." I stood, zipping up my fly as I tripped over one of her shoes. She stood, eyeing me warily. The moment was over and had been replaced by this odd sense of urgency. I closed my belt and then helped Jessa step into the shapewear unsteadily and quickly pulled it up her body.

"This is barbaric," I muttered.

"Apparently, Hollywood believes pain is beauty or whatever..." Jessa murmured, her hands on my shoulders as I lowered her dress and smoothed her hair away from her face. I took a deep breath in, and despite my desire to stay in our little pocket of peace and passion that we had found in this closet, I opened the door to find Ash, tie askew, face ashen, hair a mess, staring at me.

"Is the party over?" Jessa asked, looking at him, eyes wide, and then back at me. Ash looked over at her; his eyes seemed bloodshot.

"Everyone is gone."

"Okay, let's find Myles, and we'll go home." Jessa began to move away from the doorway when Ash made a strangled sound in the back of his throat.

"What happened?" I meant to ask it calmly, but it came out as a shout. Ash shook his head.

"Asher... don't..." I had to lean against the wall because I knew. At that moment, I knew, but I needed him to say it. Jessa took one look at my face, tossed her shoes back into the closet, and took off running down the hall.

"They found Myles and took him to the hospital," Ash choked out. "Someone found him with one of the waiters outside near the door to the kitchen. He was breathing but..." Ash shook his head, and his eyes grew wet. "It's not good. The paramedics found weed next to him, and they think it was laced with fentanyl."

"Who gave it to him?" I shouted, my blood thrummed through my body, thrilled to be reactivated, ready to fuck somebody up.

"The cops were questioning the waiter, but they didn't arrest him yet. They left with the ambulance but told the staff not to go anywhere because they would be back to talk to them soon." Ash seemed exhausted from having to share this terrible news. *He's going to be okay*; the words reverberated through my mind as I pounded down the hallway back to the now mostly empty room. I threw the doors open, panting as my fury overtook me. I felt my hands shaking as I spotted the waiter that I saw Myles talking to earlier.

"H-him?" I asked, pointing as Ash ran up behind me.

"Jace..." Ash warned.

"Was it him?" I roared. Ash took a step back and nodded. I bounded toward him, my focus on the waiter who may have killed my friend, my girlfriend's brother, and a man I had grown to massively respect. He looked up as I charged him, fear obvious on his face. I felt pride balloon inside of me. I had finally done it. I had become a man who could protect my people. I was going to make it right. I smacked up against him, and he fell. I scrambled on top of him, straddling his body. The first hit of my fist to his face made a popping sound, and blood began to stream from his nose.

"Stop!" I heard someone yell. I ignored them. I kept hitting him over and over until he was lying limp beneath me, breathing but still. His face was bloody and bruised. My arms burned, and my lungs felt empty. I felt hands pull me back forcibly, and I scrambled to my feet. I looked over to find Gordon, Mika, and Nile holding onto me. I wondered where Ash had disappeared to. I growled and tried to throw them off.

"Stop it!" Gordon shouted. "What are you doing?" He sounded furious. The adrenaline was still buzzing in my body, and when the waiter groaned and moved, I tried to lunge forward again, but they held me back—gripping onto me with all their strength.

"The police are back." Gordon stood in front of me and quickly instructed me to put my hands in my pockets. The waiter had pulled himself up to sit on a chair. His right eye was swollen shut, his lip was split, he had a gash on his forehead, and his nose was obviously broken.

"I didn't know there was fentanyl in the weed," he told me as he spat out bloody saliva onto the floor in front of him.

"Shut the fuck up," I roared. "If he dies, it's on you, and I hope that knowledge rots you from the inside out. I hope it haunts you to the point that your life becomes so miserable that you forget what it feels like to be happy, you piece of fucking shit!" I snarled the words and then fell silent as the police walked up to us. They took one look at me and then back at the waiter and his fucked-up face.

"What happened in the thirty minutes that we were gone?" the officer asked sternly.

"He fell," I retorted.

"He fell and broke his whole face?" The cop seemed shocked that I had even dared to say it. Gordon stood in front of me again.

"He fell," he confirmed.

Mika nodded in agreement as Nile piped up, "Yeah, we saw it. He fell."

"Did you fall on your face?" The police officer turned to the waiter, who now had blood dripping off his chin.

He looked at me and must have seen the anger burning in my eyes because he gulped and said through his swollen mouth, "Yeah, I fell."

The cop shrugged.

"If you say so." We could all tell that he didn't believe us but didn't care enough to push for the truth.

"Jace," Mika said softly from behind me. "Jessa."

Jessa. The name thudded through me, and I turned to look for her. My horror had distracted me, and now my guilt threatened to bring all the food I had eaten earlier back up. I had to find her.

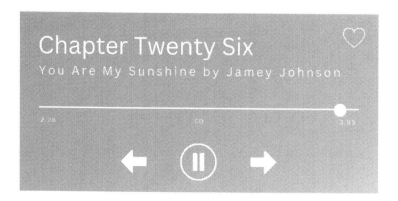

I fell to my knees on the grass outside because my body couldn't hold me up. Not with the heavy knowledge engulfing me that my worst fear had come true.

"Why?" I shrieked. "What happened? What happened? What happened?" I kept repeating myself over and over. My brain and my body felt like it had disconnected. My brain was stuck processing the words that had left Ash's mouth, and my body had catapulted into grief.

What no one had ever told me, warned me, was that grief felt like fear. Like your worst nightmare come to life. Like you had been dunked in a pool of freezing water of cold-blooded fear. My body began to shake, and I chattered, "Where is he?" Had he been alone? Had he known what was happening? Had he been scared? Did it hurt?

I felt hot tears begin to flood my eyes and stream down my cheeks. The sobs that were being torn from my chest were guttural screams, sounds that I didn't even realize I was making. I found myself rocking. I was sitting on the floor, my knees up against my chest, my arms wrapped around my knees, and I was rocking. To self-soothe, to stay distracted from the horror happening inside of me, or to keep myself moving so I didn't stay frozen in this moment forever, no longer wanting to exist. I didn't know why I was doing it; I was just doing it. Ash knelt down next to me.

"I'm so sorry," I heard him say.

Sorry? My brain latched onto that word. How did sorry cut it? How could sorry ever possibly match up against this enormous hole in my heart? I sucked in some air because it felt like I had forgotten to breathe since the words "They found Myles," had left his mouth. My face was sticky with tears, my throat hurt from screaming, and my chest ached from the knowledge that what once was would never be again, and I didn't think I would ever recover.

I had imagined this moment over and over in my head. I had feared it. Dreaded it. Imagined it. Begged the universe about it. Even talked about it with Myles. But not once had I ever even come close to knowing what this would actually feel like. I thought I knew how bad it could be. I feared the sadness. I imagined the pain, but I had been so wrong. I had never touched the depths of this ache before. There was nothing my worst nightmares could have done to prepare me for the depths of hell my grief had pushed me into. From one moment to the next, my entire existence had changed. Nothing would ever be the same. It would all be shadowed by this life-altering, mind-boggling dread for something that had already happened but had changed the literal makeup of my brain. Breathe, I told myself as I sat and rocked. I took a deep breath that burned as it entered my lungs, which were raw from screaming. I felt my heartbeat, dead but alive in my chest. Keep breathing, I thought. For what? At this moment, I did not know.

"Jessa." A strangled voice from behind me startled me out of my numb stupor. I looked up to find Kian standing over me. He fell to his knees next to me, and he gathered me against him as I began to sob—loud and ugly from the deepest recesses of hell inside of me. I would never recover. This ocean of fiery pain would slowly eat away at me until I was nothing.

"What do I do? What do I do?" I was repeating myself again, and my brain kept looping. My tears had soaked right through his shirt, and I felt him crying with me. His chest heaved, and I reached up to find his face wet. My big, quiet man had no answers for me. I peered up into his eyes, tears dripping off of my lashes. These stupid fake lashes the makeup artist had put on me.

"What do I do?" I whispered. Myles would know. He would tell me in his soft, gentle way. He would guide me. He always thought he needed me, but really, I was the one who needed him.

"Let's go to the hospital," I heard Ash offer from behind us. "Gordon finally figured out where the ambulance took him, and the car is here."

Kian looked up at him and then back down at me. "Maybe he's okay." His voice was hoarse, and I saw that his knuckles were bleeding. *He's not okay*, I thought, but I nodded anyway.

Ash offered me a hand, and I grabbed it, standing shakily, feeling like I was about to wake up and find that this was just a horrible nightmare. *You're awake, and this is real*, my brain reminded me. *Fuck you*, I grumbled back to it.

WHILE WE HAD WAITED for Gordon to track down which hospital they had taken Myles to, Adara had run home and brought back a change of clothes for us. I stood in the bathroom shivering as she peeled the dress off me. Next came the shapewear, the jewelry, and the makeup. She left my hair alone and told me to lift my arms. I did, and she pulled a sweatshirt onto me and then did the same with a pair of leggings. She had me put my feet into a pair of soft slippers that I had never seen before, and then she took my hand and led me out of the bathroom as the sobs started up again, and I howled out my pain, completely blinded by the tears.

Ash met me at the doorway of the men's bathroom, where I presumed Kian was changing. He pulled me into his arms, and I heard him whispering to Adara from over my head. My legs buckled, and he caught me, holding me up.

"It will never get better," he whispered to me. My chest shook as I took in a deep, shuddering breath, shocked at what he had just said.

"But it will also get better," he assured me. "Hold onto that."

"H-how do you know?" I asked; my eyes felt puffy and swollen. My throat hurt from crying and screaming.

"I lost someone," he said softly. "And so did he." He looked over as Kian emerged from the bathroom wearing sweats as well. He looked pale and rumpled. *Rose and the baby.* Her face flitted before my eyes, unbidden, followed by two tiny feet. I let out another shuddering sob. Kian was still standing. Ripped in some spots and broken in others, but he was standing. He smiled; he even laughed sometimes. It felt like he loved me. He played music. He drank from licorice straws. If he could do it, so could I. I just couldn't fathom how.

"Let's go," I croaked out. Kian took my hand, his eyes so full of pain that I could hardly stand to look at him.

"Maybe he's okay," Kian said again, holding onto hope.

"We're going to say goodbye," I said firmly. This much I knew. It was time to say goodbye.

THE HOSPITAL WAS GLARINGLY bright and cold. The receptionist pretended that she couldn't see the tears leaking out of my eyes and my lip quivering as I asked where Myles was. Alex was standing behind me. Kian wanted to come in with me, but he couldn't risk the publicity leak. He said he would wait until Alex could secure a quiet and safe entrance for him, and in the meantime, I would have my own time with Myles.

"Ms. Bardot," I heard a voice say. I looked up to find a doctor standing there; her white lab coat said Dr. Green on the pocket. I nodded.

"Are you family?" she asked. I nodded again.

"His s-sister," I stuttered out.

"Come with me." She motioned for me to follow her. We walked down the hallway and stopped outside a room where the privacy curtains were drawn. I could hear the beeping of machines coming from the room. The doctor placed a hand on my arm.

"We did everything we could. We administered Narcan and activated charcoal. We did CPR for forty minutes. Unfortunately, he was without oxygen for too long. He is now intubated, but I need you to listen to me carefully. When you go in there, he will feel warm. He will be breathing. His eyes may flutter, but I need you to have no hope."

I inhaled painfully.

"I do not say that to be unkind," she said softly. "I say that with every ounce of compassion inside of me." She held my hand now as I began to shake with cries. "He is not there anymore. The only thing keeping him looking alive is the machines. So go in there and say goodbye, and when you are ready, we will unplug the machines because that is the kindest thing you can do for him right now. To let him pass peacefully."

"What will happen when you do that?" I asked, trying to compose myself.

"He will stop breathing within a few minutes." She was very matter-of-fact about it, which I appreciated. Don't sugarcoat this shit. I didn't need that.

"Can I stay?" I had to force the words out. My throat felt like it was closing up at the thought of what I was about to do.

"You can." She patted my hand and then walked with me, pulling the privacy curtain aside and allowing me to enter the room.

"Oh, My My." The words flew out of my mouth in a half sigh, half sob. I thought I would run to his bed as soon as I saw him, but instead, I walked slowly. He looked like himself except for the breathing tube shoved down his throat and taped to his mouth. I stood next to his bed for a few long moments, just forcing myself to breathe. In and out. In and out. Tentatively, I reached out and took hold of his hand. It was warm. It felt alive. Like suddenly he would squeeze it, sit up, and this would all be over like a bad dream. But I knew he wouldn't.

What was the last thing I had said to him? I racked my brain. I had told him to go get more tarts and that I loved him. "I know, I love you too," he had said back. They were good last words, I told myself. Solid last words if one had to choose.

I curled my hand around his and watched as hot, heavy tears fell from my eyes into his palm. I wiped them away with the blanket.

"I can't sleep without hearing you snore, My," I whispered angrily. How dare he leave me? My brain was mad at his addiction, not him—I knew this, but it didn't matter because now I was alone.

"You left me all alone," I choked out, blinded once again by the veil of tears.

"You are not alone," I heard Kian say from behind me. I crumbled against the bed, lying on Myles's chest, heaving with sobs.

"Come back," I begged. "Don't go." I could hear his heart beating beneath my ear. *I need you to have no hope*, the doctor's voice sounded in my brain. Hope, the only thing stronger than fear. Fear whose cousin was grief. Grief who was now me. I encompassed it. I breathed it. I was grieving because I could know nothing else when the only thing keeping my brother's heart beating was a machine.

Without even thinking, I crawled onto the bed to lie down next to Myles. I curled my body around him the way I had through so many cold nights when I tried to keep him warm. I brushed the hair off his forehead. I could feel his chest rise and fall, and I pressed a kiss to his cheek and then laid my head on the pillow next to him. I began to hum, singing to him, rubbing his cheek gently, willing myself not to cry, if only for a moment.

I heard Kian's voice rumble something to someone. I didn't know who, and seconds later, the lights dimmed. I heard him walking around the room, but I kept my eyes closed as I kept singing the song, "You Are My Sunshine", that my mother used to sing to us, especially on the nights after Myles's dad would rail on him.

Myles used to make fun of me for being off tune when I sang, but he always sang it back to me, gently, quietly, but he would sing it with me. Now, here I was, singing our song by myself. The bubble of pain in my heart threatened to burst. I swallowed to keep it from exploding out of me.

I opened my eyes and saw that Kian had placed electric candles all over the room casting a calm, gentle ambiance in what was the worst room I had ever been in. They flickered and danced before my eyes, and I felt the tears break free once more.

"Baby." The entire collar of my sweatshirt was now soaked through from the tears flowing down my face and finding their way to my neck. I was a mess. A swollen-faced mess. I felt Kian next to me, and I looked over at him.

"He deserves to go peacefully. Not lying on the ground in a back alley. He'll go here. With the people who love him." Kian's voice was shaking, and I felt my love for him detonate in my chest, breaking me into fragments and piecing me back together.

"He can't sing it back." I spoke quietly because it hurt to talk.

"What?" Kian peered down at me, his face glowing in the fake candlelight.

"I would sing our song, and he would sing with me," I explained hoarsely. Kian took my hand, then held onto Myles's other hand and began to sing. His voice was piercing and ethereal. We sang together. Me off tune, him gorgeous and flowing. As I sang, I stroked his face again.

"Don't take my sunshine!" I wasn't singing anymore. I was sobbing, screaming, crying. Again. Grasping onto his hospital gown and trying to fathom how I could ever figure out how to exist with this pain overwhelming me. Taking over me. Eating me alive. I wailed. I called for him. I begged, and all the while, Kian sang. My one flickering light at the end of this miserable tunnel.

I MUST HAVE FALLEN asleep because it was hours later when I woke up to the voice of a nurse insisting that it was time and then Kian snapping back at her that I would take as long as I damn well needed. I was jealous of my sleeping self because, for that time, I wasn't Jessa who knew that Myles was dead. Or close to it. Sleeping Jessa hadn't known. Sleeping Jessa didn't feel like someone had torn her chest open and stolen her heart. I groaned, and Kian was back at my side in a second.

"Jessamine?"

"Why him?" I croaked out. "It's not fair."

"It's not," Kian agreed. I thought of wispy Rose and his little baby, and I felt the knot in my throat tighten up once more. I heard a rap on the door as someone knocked. Kian squeezed my hand.

"I'll be right back."

When he returned, he was followed by a short, freckled man. A boy, really.

"Jessa, this is Riley. He works for a company called Afterlife Memoires Would it be okay if he works quickly to gather up some items for you to keep as memories?" Kian asked gently. I shrugged.

"Do I need to move?" I asked.

"You can stay right where you are," Riley assured me. I breathed a sigh of relief and laid my head back down on Myles's chest.

"Gather away," I acquiesced weakly.

RILEY EXPLAINED what he was doing as he did it. He took Myles's fingerprint so I could memorialize it. He said some people transferred it onto a necklace, and others would choose to tattoo it. He snipped a small chunk of his hair for a shadow box, and he got a recording of Myles's heartbeat to turn into a song that he would put inside a heart charm necklace that I could wear. It had a button on it that I could press and hear his heart song. Lastly, he took a scan of our hands, clasped together for the last time, that he would turn into a physical 3D printout.

"I am incredibly sorry for your pain," Riley told me as he left.

"I am too," I whispered. "I am too." I turned my face so it rested in the crook of my brother's neck.

"I am so sorry I couldn't save you." I could barely get the words out. "Please forgive me."

"He knew, you know." I heard Kian from above me. I opened my eyes. His were shiny with tears.

"He knew what?"

Kian hummed the tune of the song we had been singing, and then said, "He knew how much you loved him."

I took in a shaky breath and nodded.

"He knew." I wiped my eyes and then told the biggest lie of my life.

"I'm ready."

I was not ready. I would never be ready to return my twenty-four-year-old brother to the wind. But it had to happen, and I was too weak to drag it out any longer. Goodbye had come and gone, and I was just holding onto the vapor of him at this point. It was time to let him go.

The doctor let me keep the lights low and the candles flickering. She didn't make me move from where I was pressed to Myles. I watched as she gently peeled the medical tape from his mouth, but I turned away when she removed the tube.

"It'll be soon," she promised.

Was that good? *How could that be good?* my brain screamed. I wanted to go back in time. I would figure out a way for it to go differently. But in the back of my mind, I knew that every scenario I could come up with would have ended the same way. He had played with fire for so long that it only made sense that, eventually, it burned him.

I was relieved that at least it had happened where people knew who he was, and he hadn't ended up as some John Doe face down in the park. We lay there for what felt like an eternity and a matter of seconds at the same time. I memorized the feeling of the rise and fall of his chest. I traced the shape of his face. I imprinted the feeling of his hair under my palm. I tried to recall the sound of his voice. I felt it all running through my fingers like sand, and the harder I tried to hold on, the faster it fell. At one point, I felt his chest shudder, and a weird gurgling sound came from his throat.

"He's not in pain, right?" I asked frantically. The doctor assured me that he wasn't. I curled back up next to him. My tears had dried momentarily.

"It's okay, My My." I ran my fingers down his cheek again. "You are free now. I love you. I love you. But you can go. Tell Mom I say hi. And when it's my turn, you better be waiting for me." I spoke to him gently. Trying to stay strong for him. "You can go." I kissed his face, held his hand, and finally, excruciatingly, I felt him take his last breath. He breathed out and never breathed back in.

"Time of death..." I heard the doctor announce the time softly. Kian was crying somewhere nearby. After what felt like forever waiting for him to breathe back in, I finally sat up, kissed my brother's forehead, and climbed off the bed.

"I'm ready to go home," I told Kian. My brother was no longer in this room, so there was no point in staying here without him. I wanted to go curl up in his bed, surrounded by his smell, his favorite books, the water bottle on his night table that he hadn't finished, the half-empty pack of cigarettes left on his dresser, and the lingering feeling that maybe he had just gone on a trip and would be home soon. In his bed, I could pretend, but in this room, his death slapped me in the face, and I couldn't take one more second of it.

Goodbye, my brother, I thought as we left the room, *I'll see you later*. I made it five steps out of the room when I saw that Gordon, Mika, Adara, Nile, and, shockingly, Eric and Alanna were all sitting in the waiting room adjacent to the hallway that I had just come from. I took one look at their faces and collapsed. Kian had to carry me out of the hospital as my grief had officially taken over, and I couldn't take one more step.

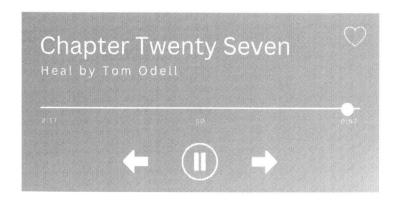

I thought I understood sadness. I had certainly cornered the market on pain for a while. I understood loss intimately. I was not just a bystander to the emotion that was agony and grief. What I had not anticipated experiencing was the utter despair of watching the woman I loved go through it. It wrenched my soul from its foundation and caused it to rattle around inside of me a little more each day.

The first day, she curled up in Myles's bed with Alanna and didn't leave. Not even to pee. She insisted that I send Zara into the room and made her swear on the life of her pug that she wouldn't ever wash the sheets so his scent would linger.

Day two, she got up to use the bathroom, and Eric managed to convince her to let me shower her. She was a ghost before me. She lifted her arm robotically. She turned when I asked her to. She passed me her shampoo, but she wasn't really there. She was too engulfed by her pain to be anywhere but straddling the world of the living and the world of the dead.

Day three, I made the mistake of asking her if she wanted to plan the funeral, and back into his bed she went. This time, it was Ash who took a shift. He watched over her all day, forcing her to eat toast and drink water.

Day four, I found her sitting by the window, chain-smoking, using the lighter she had found on Myles's dresser.

Day five, she cried until her skin was blotchy, and her eyes were so swollen she looked like she was having an allergic reaction.

Day six, she went through his phone and sent herself screenshots of his conversations and their photos to keep as a memory. But she didn't cry. The tears had dried up momentarily.

Day seven, Alanna and Eric had to go home but promised to come back for the funeral.

Day eight, she had me take her and the band to a rage room where she screamed and shouted and absolutely destroyed the contents of the room with her pain, almost to the point of scaring me as her fury overtook her.

Day nine, she wore his sweatshirt and sat in the recording studio listening to us lay down tracks for our new album. Because as stuck as we felt, as much as we wanted to deny it, life did go on. I checked on her between each take, and she almost seemed like herself in rare moments.

Day ten, she had to go back to the hospital to sign paperwork to retrieve his death certificate, and she returned almost catatonic. This time, Mika offered to take a shift. He played the keyboard next to where she was lying curled up in bed for three hours while she sobbed.

Day eleven, Gordon told me I should bring in a doctor, and I almost did until I found her making coffee in the kitchen when I came to get some water for the gym. She had lost weight, and the circles under her eyes were prominent, but she smiled at me, and I held onto that smile all day.

Day twelve, she asked me where I thought she should bury Myles, and I told her about the plot I owned next to Rose and my baby. She stood up and walked away without saying anything. Then she came back, kissed me, and walked away again.

Day thirteen, I found her watching *Good Will Hunting* with Nile, who looked scared and mouthed "Help" to me as I walked by. I made them vodka tonics with licorice straws and stayed to watch the second half of the movie. She cried, but instead of staying on her side of the couch, alone in her pain, she crawled over and let me hold her.

Day fourteen, a package came from Afterlife Memoires, and I saw a shift. I finally saw a glimpse of Jessa instead of the shell of a girl who had been haunting the house for the last two weeks, though no fault of her own. I, more than anyone, understood what she was going through. Well, Ash and I did. I found Jessa sitting by the pool. The penthouse opened up into a pool, a lawn of green grass, and a garden that made you think you were outside of a house instead of multiple floors off the ground. A bowl of watermelon sat on the table in front of her as well as the black embossed box that had come in the mail earlier today.

I had found the company in a frantic Google search as I waited for Alex to get me into the hospital. Shockingly, in a serendipitous moment, they told me that they already had a representative in the hospital on the oncology floor, and when he finished up, he could come down to us. What this company did was beautiful, and I was oddly looking forward to seeing what they had sent. I watched silently as Jessa ran her hand over the box and then proceeded to open it.

She pushed aside the layers of tissue paper to reveal a few more smaller boxes packed inside. The first one contained the print of Myles's fingerprint. She matched up her finger to it and lowered her head for a moment. I waited with bated breath, but she did not start crying, nor did she say anything. She put it to the side and then took out the model of their hands. They had

3D printed it out in a soft white material and then encased it in a shimmering paint so their held hands seemed ethereal and angelic. She ran her finger down the side of their held hands, but still, she did not cry. The next box held the shadow box. The interior was set in black velvet, and there was a light that could be turned on that illuminated it. The clipping of his hair was in a little corked bottle and was hanging from a piece of ribbon hung on a little gold hook. There was a photo of him next to the bottle. There were quotes, dried flowers, and a 3D metal image of the fingerprint with his name engraved on it.

"That is gorgeous," I told her, coming over to examine it.

"It is," she replied softly. She handed the box to me so I could look at it closer while she unpacked the last box. Inside was a black jewelry bag, which she turned upside down to allow the necklace inside to fall out into her hand. It had a thin gold chain with a delicate heart charm hanging from it. There were instructions on a slip of paper on where to find the button to play the "Heart Song". The silence was deafening as I waited for her to press it. Then, suddenly, the sound of Myles's heartbeat filled the air. A few seconds later, it was joined by the beautiful notes of a violin. Then I heard a guitar, and moments later, a piano joined in the background. The heartbeat was constant and played the role of the drum. His song was haunting. It sang of memories, of loss, of pain, of happiness, and of love. She turned the necklace over and showed me the back had been engraved with the words "Myles's Heart Song." It was accompanied by a note that read, "When tomorrow starts without me, listen to the song of my heart and know that love never dies." We listened to the song three times before she turned it off and handed it to me.

"Can you put it on me?" she asked as she lifted her hair. I clasped it around her neck as I heard her say, "I'm ready."

I ran my hand down her neck, relishing the feeling of her

soft skin beneath my fingers. We had not done anything more than hugged or exchange a few chaste kisses since Myles's death. I wasn't sure if it was because she was completely overtaken by her grief or if she also felt guilty that while we had fucked in a closet, her brother had been dying in an alleyway. I hoped she didn't feel guilty about that, but I wasn't sure since we hadn't been doing a lot of talking either, which I was the most concerned about.

Alanna had been checking in on both of us and when I verbalized my concern, she assured me that Jessa just needed time. Something I knew a lot about needing, so I just patiently waited.

"Ready for what, baby?" I kissed the side of her neck and felt her tremble beneath me.

"For the funeral." Her voice was so low I almost made her repeat herself. I had been paying the funeral home to keep Myles's body there until Jessa was ready to bury him, and apparently, now she was ready.

"I'll make some calls." I pulled out my phone as I sat in the chair next to her. She nodded and sighed as if a weight had been lifted off of her. I understood that. Grief was heavy. So much so that sometimes you felt like you couldn't breathe. As each phase of healing came, the heaviness became a little bit lighter. It never left. At times, it even returned to its original intensity. But those little moments of healing, that reprieve from the crushing weight of grief, always made me feel like I could take a deeper breath.

I had learned that grief has no ending. At first, I thought healing was a destination I would get to. A moment when I would finally cross the finish line—when I would have paid my penance and could trade sadness for peace. When I could finally hang up my grief hat and feel happy. The painful truth I had discovered was there is no other side to push through to get to.

It's not a phase to complete. It doesn't just get better. Rather, you endure it. You accept it. You absorb it into the marrow of your bones. The fact was, you never really move on. Instead, your brain rearranges itself to face life with this new reality. A reality that no longer includes someone you love.

"I can leave after the funeral if you want," I heard Jessa say as I texted Gordon to ask him what day the whole team had off so we could all be there.

"Why would I want that?" I put my phone down and turned her around in the swivel chair so she was facing me.

"I'm not really that fun right now." Her eyes met mine, and I saw that hers were full of sadness and confusion but still shone with resilience. I smiled. There was my girl. I liked seeing signs that she was still in there.

I leaned forward and softly kissed her lips. I began to pull back after a moment, but I felt her arm snake up behind my head and keep me there. I deepened the kiss, and I felt her sigh against my mouth. She was still getting used to sharing her burdens with someone. It felt like she was almost surprised that I was here, sincerely sharing in her sorrow. I kissed her once more and then pulled away slightly, keeping my hands on her face.

"I never want you to leave," I told her gently, with a smile. Her posture relaxed. "You don't always have to be fun. I want you any way you want to be. If you need time, I'll hold space for it. If you're happy, I'll be happy with you. If you're angry, tell me how I fucked up."

She gave a short laugh at that.

"If you're excited, take me with you. If you're confused, let me help you figure it out. But one day, you'll get it." I paused and kissed the tip of her nose. "You are it for me, Jessa, and I want you here however you need to be."

She put her hand in mine, her eyes glossy, but no tears slipped free.

"Even if I'm sad for a while?" she whispered.

"Then I'll be sad with you," I whispered back. Wordlessly, she got up from her chair and crawled into my lap. I cradled her against my chest as she molded against me.

"I never told you what true north means," I murmured against her hair. She shifted slightly, and I knew she was listening.

"North is unwavering. No matter how many times you shake up a compass, it will always point north. It's a constant. A guide. A direction that always returns, leading you home. That is what you are to me. You are home." I heard her take a shuddering breath. "There is nowhere you could go that I wouldn't follow." I kissed up her jaw, nipping gently. "So stay here, sweetheart. I got you." I rocked her gently. "You rest. I'm here."

I felt her fully relax for the first time in two weeks, and I relished this shift between us. She was letting me protect her, and I was finally able to be the protector. Her trust in me was not something I took lightly. A breeze rustled across my skin, and the sun shone on my face as if promising better days to come. I looked up at it, letting the rays rest on my face. I heard Jessa let out a slight snore, indicating that she had fallen asleep, as a text popped up on my phone. "Tuesday," Gordon replied. We were all free on Tuesday, so it looked like we would be burying Myles in five days.

WHEN JESSA WOKE UP, she blinked for a second, stretched her body out, and then turned in my lap to attack my mouth.

"What are you doing?" I asked against her lips, mid-kiss. I could hear Zara cooking in the kitchen, the sound of the lawnmower indicated that the gardener was nearby, and I knew my friends were around somewhere.

"You haven't touched me since that night." She was frantic in my lap, trying to drag my shirt off and undo my belt at the same time.

"I was giving you space," I protested as I stood, holding her up as she wrapped her legs around my waist. I was a little confused by her statement. Over the last two weeks, she had not been ready for any sort of intimacy. I hadn't been avoiding it; I had just been respecting her grieving process. Yet now she was lamenting our lack of touch.

"I don't want any space." She was sucking on my neck now, and I had to make a decision. Did I give her what she said she wanted in this moment, or did I insist that she recognize that this may not really be what she wants, and it was possibly due to her emotions being in upheaval for the last two weeks?

Feeling her body pressed up against mine and knowing that I had the ability to shut off her brain and release her from her prison of grief for a moment led me to my decision to let it continue. Mainly to give her a reprieve from her pain, but also, if I was being honest with myself, I missed her like this. I wanted her back.

I walked with her clutching onto me over to the side of the rooftop garden where we wouldn't be visible from the kitchen windows. In a second, I had her up against the stone wall, panting and writhing against me—kissing her neck, palming her ass, rubbing up against the apex of her thighs. She was pulling on my T-shirt, so I reached behind me and yanked it off, holding her up with one hand. She slid down the wall, her hair getting all messy, and stood to pull off her sweatpants. She took a few steps back and walked into the freshly watered garden. I followed, crowding her against a bush. She unzipped her hoodie, and I finally saw that she was completely naked beneath it. I looked around, making sure the gardeners were still not near us, and then I palmed her breasts, rubbing her hard nipples beneath my calloused fingers. She leaned into my hands and moaned.

"Here?" I asked, running my fingers over her lips. She flicked out her tongue and sucked along the side of my thumb. My cock jumped in my boxers.

"Here," she confirmed. I rummaged around in my pants pocket until I located my wallet, praying I would find a condom, which I did, and then shoved my pants down around my ankles. I stepped out and kicked them away. She sank down to her knees, and I watched as she took me out of my boxers. Her mouth was on me in a flash, and I had to steady myself as my leaking dick was enveloped in the warm, wet suction of her mouth. I rested my hands on either side of her hair and began to move her in the rhythm I needed. She gagged, and I let her move off me slightly.

"No," she said, garbling around my length, dripping saliva. It dawned on me that she wanted me to take control. No, she needed me to. I tightened my grip on her head and moved her back onto my length. Her eyes watered, and I could see her gratitude swimming in them. Shut off your brain, I longed to tell her. But instead, I showed her.

I fucked her face in earnest until I was sure that she could not be thinking about anything but my pleasure and her need to breathe through her nose. She licked, sucked, bit, and gagged on me until her knees began to slip in the dirt and mulch. I pulled out, panting, willing myself to last because her exuberance had nearly sent me over the edge. I paused because I could hear voices nearby, but then they faded away, and the sound of the leaf blower started up. I smiled at her as I laid her back on the garden bed. Her hair was tangled amongst the bushes, bits of flowers littered her curls. The sun shone over her body, casting light across her puckered nipples, warming her skin. I ripped the condom open with my teeth and reached between us to make quick work of putting it on. Then I crawled between her legs, feeling my knees sink into the freshly watered mulch and soil. She was lying there, watching me, her lips swollen from our kisses, her pussy wet, her legs trembling. I entered her in one stroke, pushing her deeper into the dirt.

"Kian," she started; tears began to form in her eyes.

"Don't say anything," I ordered. "I love you. Please let me do this for you."

"I love you too," she mouthed, the tears dripped from her eyes, but she tightened her legs around me, and I fucked her into the earth. I had imagined the first time we told each other "I love you" would have been romantic. Maybe while eating chocolate fondue or making love on silk sheets or while having a picnic under the stars. Yet, at this moment, I realized that coffee girl and music man would do it this way. Rutting in the dirt, overtaken by emotion, and living a real, painful life. The perfect moment was this one.

I could tell when Jessa finally let go of what she thought she was supposed to be doing. When she released the stress and pain of the last two weeks. When she allowed herself to have a moment of peace and give herself over to the pleasure, and to truly understand how much I adored her. A moment that she deserved. Her eyes had glazed over, and her cheeks were pink from lust and the sun. She felt pliant and soft in my arms. My hands were muddy, but I reached up anyway and caressed her cheek, leaving dirt across her face in my wake.

I looked down; the condom was slick with her, and mud covered the inside of her thighs. I watched as I fucked into her, hard and punishing. Pushing her against the delicate branches of the bush with every thrust of my body into hers. I could feel her begin to clench me harder, I felt her grow wetter, I saw her legs start to quiver, I heard her breath pick up, and I knew she was close.

I reached over with my dirty hand and closed it around her neck. I squeezed on either side, cutting off some of her oxygen, and I saw her relish in it as she gasped and panted out my name. I fucked her deeper without changing the tempo, and as soon as she began to come, I released my hand from her neck, flooding her with oxygen and heightening her experience. She was calling out now, loudly moaning and saying my name. If the people inside didn't know what was going on before, they certainly knew now.

I clenched her breast as I groaned and slid in and out of her a few more times until I came, filling the condom, feeling the orgasm burst from me, flooding my body with dopamine and love. I rolled off of her with a groan and splayed out next to her, feeling the water and mud seep into my hair and smear all over my back. The mulch was painful under my shoulders. I looked over at her. She had dirt splattered across her chest and around her neck. Her face was smeared with it, and her entire ass and thighs were covered with mud and messy handprints from where I had gripped her. Her hair was a tangled wreck, and I leaned over to pluck a leaf from it.

"You're filthy," I told her, smirking.

"So clean it up." She was propped up on one elbow now, and she widened her legs, showing me what she wanted. I didn't have to be told twice. I ignored the grime the garden had left behind and dove between her legs to make her scream my name again as only a few minutes later, she came loudly on my tongue. So loudly I had to hold my hand over her mouth to quiet her. I looked up from my spot between her legs as she fell back, completely limp on the flower bed, and I felt my heart swell with adoration as I watched her start to laugh. I came up to cover her body with mine and spread a little more dirt across her cheeks.

"You are everything to me." She leaned up to kiss me briefly.

"Trust me, I feel it more," I insisted as we continued this dance of learning to say what we truly felt to one another.

"Kay." She seemed satisfied with that, and she curled up into my body. I held her, covered in dirt and cum, and for a moment, all was the way it needed to be.

It felt weird to put on a new outfit for your brother's funeral. Adara would not allow me to wear my usual black clothes. She insisted on going shopping to bring me some options, and we ended up settling on a black, long-sleeved, thin mock turtleneck top tucked into a pair of black pants paired with a black belt. To complete the look, she had me put on a black suit jacket. She acquiesced and let me wear boots, but she went and bought me a new pair. Of course they were Doc Martens, but I had no energy left in me to fight her on it. I was strangely calm, like I had no more tears left in me.

I had screamed, cried, gone numb, begged for him back, barely slept, and slept too much. I got angry at him, at myself, at his dad, and at life. I had oscillated between the whole gamut of emotions at this point, and now I had settled on acceptance. My sadness was now overbearingly peaceful. I took a deep breath then folded the paper that I had written my speech on into a small square and stuck it into my pocket. I could hear everyone talking downstairs, and I had to prepare myself to face them. Kian had flown so many people in. Of course Eric, his partner,

Alanna, and my other co-workers, but also some of Myles's old friends, his sponsor, people he had met in NA meetings, and some of our tent neighbors.

I heard a knock on the door, and I looked up, presuming Kian would be there in the doorway, but instead, it was Ash. Kian had stood so solidly beside me this entire time that now I couldn't fathom a second of my future without him. What I hadn't expected was how his friends would also step up and be there for me as well. They made me feel like family. They had made space for my sadness. They had not avoided my pain. In fact, in their own way, I believed they felt it too. I now held so much fondness in my heart for a band that I didn't know much about a month ago. At this point, I couldn't imagine not seeing them every day.

"Ready?" Ash held out his arm, and I placed my hand in the crook of his elbow.

"Nope," I responded honestly as he led me down the hallway.

"Yeah, I get that," he sympathized.

He still had not shared whom he had lost, but I could see in his eyes that he understood my pain. Kian stood when he saw me coming down the stairs.

"Limo is here," he announced as he came over and hugged me. I breathed in his scent, allowing it to center me. For two weeks, I had been such a mess. Chaotic, broken, and unable to focus, yet ever since that moment with him in the garden, I had started to feel parts of myself seeping back in. I had lay there in the dirt, bits of leaves and twigs up in places they should never be, my own essence sticky on my thighs, and I had felt joy again. I had worried I would never *feel* again, let alone feel happiness. I had laughed and hadn't felt guilty about it. I had kissed Kian and hadn't felt like I was only supposed to be sad. I had watched my beautiful, sexy boyfriend lower his big body down to the stone floor to eat me out despite the dirt smeared all over me, and I had felt hope for a beautiful future.

I had loved, and I had lost, but I had been brave enough to choose to love again. Nothing could repair the Myles-sized hole in my heart, and I realized that I didn't need to. I had come to accept that I had not died with him that day. I was still here. A bit bruised but still standing. I would learn to live with the pain. I had accepted it as something that would expand and contract depending on the moment of each day. It would never go away, and yet, somehow, I would learn to exist with the pain as a constant reality. Even as I experienced life, opened up a coffee shop, made new friends, went to Kian's concerts, watched a movie, and laughed, it would be there. It was now what made me whole. As odd as it was to say that about the most broken part of my life, it was the truth. It completed me, and I held my grief and my love for Myles simultaneously like it was a fragile bomb.

"How are you?" Kian whispered against my hair.

"I am not good, but we are going to be okay." I leaned up to kiss him and heard Nile pass by and ask if it was okay to go to a funeral with a boner, which made everyone laugh. I grinned against Kian's mouth because I knew even Myles would have found that comment funny.

THE RIDE in the limo had me feeling a little more apprehensive as I began to anticipate what it would be like to watch them lower the casket into the ground that I knew held my brother. Even with all of the people coming, which included my friends, Myles's friends, all of the band, and various people who worked for them who had met Myles in the few days we were in California, we were still a small group, and therefore, I had chosen to go straight to the cemetery. I didn't think we needed to spend time or money on speeches in a funeral home when we could all just gather at the cemetery right away. Neither of us believed in a god or followed any sort of religion, so we didn't need to make a stop at a church or even invite a priest. I was keeping it simple.

The plan was first his sponsor would speak, Kian would speak, I would speak, the boys would sing a song I had chosen, and then we would lower Myles down to his final resting place. The limo turned onto the road leading to the cemetery, and I began to feel even more nervous. I smoothed the material of my pants with my hands as my palms grew sweaty. Alex got out first and opened the door for us. We all filed out of the car and walked silently toward the recently dug grave. Kian was holding my hand, and I almost felt like I was floating instead of walking.

The weather was beautiful. Perfect even. Not too hot. Not cold. Not a cloud in the sky. The sound of birds chirping filled my ears, and I saw a butterfly flutter by. It almost made me want to laugh that life was actively being lived and was so beautiful at the same time that I was preparing myself to say the final goodbye to the one whom death had stolen from me. It would make more sense to me if it had been storming out and the dark sky had cried along with us, but instead, the universe was almost trying to show me more hope as it had sent us the most beautiful day in California since I had gotten here.

As I drew closer to the grave, I saw that the casket was there, suspended above the ground and covered in flowers. My heart thrummed heavily in my chest. We all gathered around the grave in a semicircle. I nodded at Skylar, who had been Myles's sponsor while we lived in New York, and he moved toward the front to stand next to the casket, and the tears finally returned as he spoke.

"Hi, my name is Skylar, and I am an addict."

He paused as one does at meetings and then began to speak again. "I have been sober for seven hundred and thirteen days, and I had the honor of being Myles's sponsor." He paused to blow his nose and then continued. "Every fourteen minutes, someone in the United States dies from a drug overdose. Drug overdose deaths outnumber traffic fatalities and prostate cancer deaths. However, it is hardly talked about because people look at it differently. When losing someone to overdose, it is normal to feel sad and angry and grief-stricken, but what no one talks about is losing someone to overdose also comes with guilt, shame, fear, isolation, and blame. We worry that maybe there is something more we could have or should have done to help them. We wonder if they suffered. We ask ourselves where it all went wrong. It's hard enough to grieve, but it's even harder when your grief is colored by the world's perception of the stigma of addicts. Studies show that when someone dies of other causes, only in two to three percent of those cases does the family receive blaming comments. However, with overdose that number jumps up to 64 percent. This is incredibly sad because these people who died of an overdose were people just like anyone else who passed. You may find it odd that I'm spewing facts instead of just talking about Myles, but I did this for Myles. Because no matter the way he passed, he was a human being, and maybe you know someone like Myles. Maybe knowing these numbers, you will treat the Myles in your life like the human they are versus just seeing them as an addict. Myles was amazing. He was loved. He will be missed. He will be remembered not by how he died but rather that he lived."

I let out a sob as Skylar finished talking. He bent over the casket, almost giving it a hug. I watched as he murmured something, and I had to suck all of my emotion in just to keep it together as I watched him say his goodbyes. He then walked over to me and gave me a hug. We stood there like that for a long moment as his face grew wet. Then he whispered, "I'm so sorry," and went to stand next to Myles's friends. Kian squeezed my hand and then made his way up to the front. Ash moved over to fill the spot that Kian had just vacated but said nothing. Kian cleared his throat as he took his phone out to pull up his speech.

"Some of you may be wondering why I'm up here when I only knew Myles for less than a year, but as much as I wish I had more time with him, that was honestly all I needed to be able to share what a special person he was. We bonded quickly, and he was so essential in my own healing." Kian paused, and I watched his Adam's apple bob in his throat.

"I buried two people right here." He gestured to the two graves to the left of us, and everyone turned to look.

"And admittedly, I was a mess." Kian gave a watery, choking laugh. "Although Myles didn't know exactly what had happened to me for most of the time we spent together, we talked about healing often. He would share his thoughts with me about acceptance and peace. He taught me about serenity and knowing that there were things in life that we could not change. Most importantly, he trusted me with his sister." His eyes met mine, and I let out a sigh that sounded like a whimper as I smiled.

"We watched so many *Friends* episodes together, and on our drives to his meetings, we talked about things that he loved, his goals, his struggles, and his desire to keep Jessa safe. My point is I did not know an addict. I knew a man. I knew Myles. I loved Myles, and I am going to miss you, Myles." His voice cracked, and I had to look away so I wouldn't start bawling right before I had to speak.

"And Jessa..." I looked back at him.

"We all collectively want you to know that when we say we hope you are okay, we don't really mean that we think you could possibly be okay after this. What we mean is we hope the sadness isn't drowning you. We hope you can see the tiny cracks of the light at the end of the tunnel, and we hope you know that even when you feel hopelessly alone in your grief, you are not."

I nodded as another sob clawed its way up my throat, and I watched as Kian laid something on top of the casket and then made his way back to me. I hugged him and felt him kiss my cheek as Ash ran a hand down my back in support, and I heard Eric and Alanna speaking encouragement from behind me. *I can do this*, I thought. I felt my breath hitch as I walked closer to the casket and ran a hand down the wood. I could feel the metal of the heart song necklace against my chest, where it rested next to my North Star charm. I felt suspended in time for a moment, unsure of how I was actually experiencing this nightmare without Myles by my side. Somehow, I centered myself, took a deep breath, and began to speak.

"I was doing some research on the way various cultures grieve, and I came across an interesting fact. The Navajo people have no word for goodbye. Because goodbye means gone, and they believe that when someone dies, they're not really gone since the impact that they had on us lives on. I really like that perspective. What it means to me is we don't love Myles in the past tense; we love him in the present. He is loved. He is special. He is smart and kind and creative and gentle. It's not that he *was* those things, he *is* those things because he will live on in all of us. All of us whom he impacted in his quiet way. I admit that I have been torn up about the way that he passed. For the last two weeks, I've worried that maybe he had been scared or was in pain when it happened, but then I saw a post online the other day that said, 'I believe death is like being carried to your bedroom when you were a child and fell asleep on the couch during a family party. You can hear the laughter from the other room, but you choose to sleep.'" The tears I had kept at bay were now flooding my eyes and tracking down my face. I heard sobs from the crowd, but I did not look up to see whom they were from.

"That gave me so much peace because if death is gentle and loving like that, then I have to believe that he wasn't scared and he wasn't in pain. I know he knew how much I loved and still love him and would have done anything to save him. I want you all to know that this pain of grief that you see me going through is worth it because it means that I got to be his sister and experience loving him. So, just know that I am in no rush to get rid of these feelings because grief is just me holding onto my love for my brother. I'll end off with this: I read a quote that said, 'Where there is deep grief, there was great love,' and that truly encompasses our life together. So I will not say goodbye, My My. I will just tell you, *see you later*."

At this point, I was on my knees in the grass, lying over the casket, sobbing, and as painful and as hollow as it felt, it also felt peaceful and real. Because I now embraced that this sharp-edged pain inside of me was all just love with nowhere else to go. I slowly calmed as I closed my eyes and smelled the flowers on his casket. I felt the sun on my face and the breeze in my hair. I felt my system relax, and I finally mustered up the strength to stand as Alanna came over. She held my hand as we walked back to join the others, and she continued to hold onto me as Kian and Ash began to sing the song I had chosen a cappella. I had asked them to sing a slowed-down version of the song "Symphony" by Clean Bandit. When I received the heart song necklace, I had thought of the lyrics from the song about feeling incomplete and being a part of his symphony.

I had decided it was the perfect song to play at the funeral as it spoke of love, the emotion of music, and the raw energy that was grief. Kian's voice tore another level of sadness through me, and I gently rocked my body to the beautiful melody and meaningful words speaking of not letting go.

Kian held me as we watched the cemetery workers lower the casket into the earth and then begin to fill it in with the dirt that had been piled up on the side. I was out of tears again, and I felt cold and stiff. All I could do was watch them take shovel after shovel full of dirt and slowly deepen the space between my brother and me.

As the dirt filled the entire grave and the crowd began to disperse, a gust of wind rustled my hair and blew across my face. I told myself that it was Myles going off on his next adventure. I sighed and felt the breath fill me with the reminder that I was here. I was alive, and I was going to truly live. For Myles. For myself and for Kian. Kian, who has been my rock since he had grumpily joined my life. Kian, who had cosmically allowed me to achieve my dream of getting Myles to California, even if it had just been for a short time. Kian, who had allowed me to bury my brother just as he asked and not cremate him, which, back at home, would have been all I would have been able to afford. Kian, whom I loved with every fiber of my being for what felt like forever, yet somehow, I had only just verbalized the sentiment to him. Kian, who held me close as we walked back to the car, leaving my brother behind.

BACK AT THE HOUSE, Zara had laid out a spread that rivaled any of the buffets at the local free parties I had gone to back at home. Everyone we cared about was sitting around the house, and I excused myself to get changed out of my funeral clothes. Up in the room, I let them drop to the floor and then put on a pair of leggings and a tank top that had magically appeared in my drawer after one of Adara's many shopping trips. I was plugging my phone in to charge when I heard the door open. Kian came into the room, loosening his tie.

"Hi, baby," he greeted me as he shed his suit jacket and began to unbuckle his belt.

"The song and your speech were beautiful," I told him.

"Thank you." He came over to kiss my forehead and then disappeared into the walk-in closet, returning in a pair of sweatpants. His phone, which he had left on the bed, lit up, and I saw a text from Gordon flash across the screen.

"Terrible timing, I know." It read. "But your single just dropped."

Kian had been working on a song without the guys for the first time in their career together. He wouldn't let me sit in on his sessions, and he had told me I could listen to it when the time was right. I had been so distracted by my grief and the funeral that I hadn't protested at all. I didn't say anything as Kian picked up his phone and read the text. I watched the muscles in his shoulders bunch as he tensed up. He turned and eyed me.

"Ready to go down?" he asked.

"I want to hear your song," I told him, letting him know that I had seen the text. He sighed.

"Today is about Myles. I told the label to wait, but they like to drop music on Tuesdays, so they didn't listen to me."

"Today is about life. I have gone through every single stage of grief in the last nineteen days, and today, I am ready to really and truly live, so play me your song, Kian." I curled my feet under me and waited patiently. Kian hesitated. I smiled as he sat and ran my fingers around the edges of his fresh tattoo.

I was still overwhelmed by his decision to etch me permanently onto him. I planned on getting Myles's fingerprint tattooed onto my finger, and when I went to the tattoo artist, I was also going to get one for Kian. I had already found what I wanted. It was a treble clef outlined in fine line black ink and filled in with watercolor light blues and pinks. The top of the music note ended in a heart, and it was surrounded by more tiny fine line hearts and music notes in a circular design. It was delicate and a perfect way for me to show Kian how deeply my feelings for him ran.

I was shaken from my thoughts by Kian telling me that the title of his new song was "Coffee." My heart skipped a beat as he pressed play, and music filled the air around us. At first, it was just the tender pluck of a violin, but it was quickly joined by the muted tone of a harp, then the thrum of a cello, and the warm timbre of a guitar. The resonant vibration of drums started up, followed by the bright sound of the piano, and then, for a moment, what had to be the thin call of a flute. The horns sounded, and I was quickly surrounded by the notes of an entire symphony. The music died down, and we were left with just the emotive lilt of the guitar, the piano, and the drums. Kian's voice crooned over the speaker. He sang of love, of lust, of music, and of need, all wrapped up in one song. My body recognized what he was saying before my brain did. I shifted toward him, my shoulders curving forward in an effort to touch him and to be touched by him. He gathered me against his chest, my face now against his bare skin, one ear picking up the thump of his heart, the other hearing him tell me he loved me through his music. Something I had known to be true for a while, even though we hadn't actually said it until that day in the garden. We hadn't really needed to. As the song came to an end, the flute and violin played the last bits of the hauntingly beautiful tune that tugged at my heartstrings, and then the room fell silent. I looked up at him as he peered down at me, his eyes swimming with emotion. I reached up and ran my fingers through his beard.

"I love you too," I whispered. "I will never finish falling in love with you." I leaned up to kiss him, and I felt his love and his relief pounding in the rhythm of the pulse in his neck.

"I saw a quote when I was figuring out what to say today." Kian spoke in that gruff, reluctant way he had about him. "It's by Atticus, and it said, 'I lost my way all the way to you and in you I found my way.'"

I took in a deep breath as I allowed his words to seep in. I understood them. I felt them. I knew them.

"You are my true north, Jessamine." He rocked me as he spoke. "It will always be you. If I had to choose between you and everything else, I would choose you. Show me you and all the things I've ever wanted. Still you. Every day. Every time. I know that we've both been through a lot, and we'll both probably always be a little broken inside, but I promise you I love you with every single piece of me."

I felt a tear slip from my eyes and drift down my cheeks. What a beautiful, heartbreakingly perfect day it had been. On one hand, my heart was shattered into a million pieces, and on the other hand, my love for Kian and his love for me were actively putting me back together.

"I love you," I told him again. He smiled and wiped away my tears.

"You have me, baby. Until the very last note in every symphony plays. You have me."

I leaned my head against his chest once more, and I could have sworn I heard the sound of a violin again, playing a song only the two of us could hear.

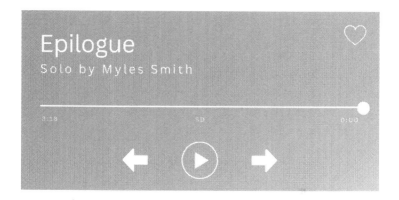

For the first time in my whole life, my soul doesn't hurt. I blink. Blink. I was asking a waiter if he had any weed. Blink. He was telling me to meet him out back. Blink. He was showing me that it's a new strain that he's never tried before. Blink. I'm telling him that I don't care what kind it is, that I just need to numb out the pain I'm in. That I feel like I'm crawling out of my skin every second of every day. Blink. He hands me a lighter. Blink. I think of Jessa. Beautiful, vibrant, sunny Jessa. J. My savior. My sister. She'll be so disappointed. I love her so much; I never want to hurt her, but the agony I'm in sometimes outweighs my desire to be good enough to be her brother. The devil of my addiction claws at my insides until I give in to its evil demands. Blink. I light the blunt. Blink. I inhale. Blink. My eyes stay closed until I open them to this bright space that I'm in now.

"Fuck, I died, didn't I?" I say it out loud, although the room looks empty.

"You did," another voice says next to me. I look over. It's me, but it's not. It's an older version of me. I have some gray hair and a bit of a belly. I feel confused.

"Is this heaven?" I ask.

"No," someone to my right says. I look over. It's me as a teenager. The year I met Jessa. My hair is messy, long, and curling over my neck. I'm wearing that dumb chain. I stopped wearing it when my dad almost strangled me with it. I wait for the fire of pain to light up inside of me when I think about him trying to kill me, but it doesn't. That's weird, I think. The only way I could ever stop the pain was to be high. I never had relief from it otherwise.

"Heaven isn't real," my fifteen-year-old self tells me.

"So what is this?" Do I smell lilac? That was my favorite flowering tree growing up. I could swear I hear a loon yodel off in the distance, and a warm breeze plays on my face.

"This is a good day." My seventeen-year-old self walks up. The age I was when I started heavily using.

"A good day?" I repeat. He nods.

"A good day. Where everything you love is. Everything you enjoy exists, and all of your pain has turned into peace."

I see my nine-year-old self run by, and I feel the urge to go run with him. Blow out dandelions that fluff into wishes. Roll down a freshly mowed hill. Catch fireflies. Make smores and stay up late.

"You can," my twenty-one-year-old self tells me with a grin. "You can do anything you want on a good day." We take off together. I hear a lawnmower, and I smell the grass.

"What was the point then?" I ask as we run.

"The point of what?" my older self asks me. My self who never got a chance to see the world.

"Of life," I tell him.

"Life is music. Our existence is a song," he tells me. "Sometimes life is about the solo. Sometimes it's playful, like fingers over a piano. Sometimes it's sad like the strings on a violin. Sometimes it's hard like composing an entire orchestra. Sometimes it makes no sense, and it hurts like a song with too many verses that never seems to end. And sometimes it's about the crashing chords of love's crescendo leading to the grand finale. The point is not to get to the end. No one goes to a concert just for the last note of the last song. No, people go to be in the moment. To enjoy the tune they're hearing right now. Music is the most in-the-moment moment of all the moments."

I laugh. I can feel my smile all over my whole body.

"What he's saying"—my eighteen-year-old self has joined the chat—"is that music is for right now. And with that comparison, he means that life is meant to be lived today. To enjoy. To be right here. No one knows what happens when the music stops playing, so just choose to dance. Twirl. Skip. You have nowhere to be but right here. Right now."

I hum. Speaking of music, I can hear a song.

"You are my sunshine..." I hear her. J. In my head.

She sounds so close.

"Jessa?" I call. I turn, but I don't see her. All of my selves are watching me.

I begin to sing with her, belting out the lyrics about love and not taking my sunshine away. I hear another voice join her in singing our song. Oh, it feels like pure adoration. Kian. I can taste his voice. It's goodness and strength wrapped in one. She is okay. She still has her song, even though mine is coming to an end. I'm crying. Why am I crying on my good day?

"Good doesn't always mean happy, Myles." My old-man self tells me. I'm wrinkled, I'm using a cane, and I've definitely shrunk. I'm glad J didn't meet this version of me; she would have made so much fun of me for getting shorter.

"Good means peace. Acceptance. Understanding. Even if it hurts," he tells me.

I nod. I get it now.

"You have somewhere to be." My sixteen-year-old self rushes me.

"I thought you said I have nowhere to be." I'm confused.

"Right now, you have somewhere to be." I'm pushed forward. Blink. Tears. Blink. A kiss. Blink. The piano keys in my blood slow. Blink. The strumming of the guitar in my lungs halts. Blink. The beating of the drum in my heart stops. Blink. All that is left is the howl of the violin from my soul, which is love. Because love can never die. I smile and give Jessa's hand a squeeze.

"I will see you later, Jessamine Bardot. I love you," I whisper. I breathe out the last bits of music notes from within me and still.

My song is over.

THE END

ACKNOWLEDGMENTS

As you can imagine, I cried so much while writing this book. Every time I edited the epilogue, I was a literal mess. I hope you were too when you read it. And not in a weird way but in a "I hope you found the sadness this book evoked in you" healing. I hope the pain felt real to you because it is to so many people out there. I hope you saw bits of yourself in the strength of Jessa and the healing of Kian. I hope you have renewed empathy and kindness for every Myles you come across in your life, and I hope you know that on your silent days as you sit with grief you understand that you're just missing them a little louder today, and that's okay.

This story bubbled up inside of me almost immediately after I had published *This Is What It Feels Like*. So I wrote it despite battling bouts of imposter syndrome and self-doubt. Never self-doubt in the beauty of my stories but rather self-doubt in my showing up on social media, my ability to stay consistent, and my strength to keep my eyes forward instead of comparing myself to other authors and wondering if I am worth the investment of continuing to put in the immense of amount of time and resources to self-publish. But I believe that you deserve to read this story. Every Myles deserves to have their story read. As does every Jessa and every Kian. And every Rae... so here you are. Reading another piece of my heart on paper. So please be gentle with it, my readers. It's real, and it beats.

As you read this, I am knee-deep in books three, four, and five, so please subscribe to my email list, and follow me on social media and Goodreads to stay on top of all the new upcoming releases.

Thank you to my husband and my daughters for always cheering me on through this whole process. To my cover designer and my editors, thank you! To my Beta and ARC readers, you are the music to my writing. To all of the readers who take the time to post about my books, who buy my books, who choose to leave positive reviews about my books, and who rally behind me, you literally do not know how much it means to me. I read every word. I glow with every good review. I feel so much joy from every positive message. It literally fuels me in my writing.

And last but not least, to my brother Meyer, whose song is complete; I love you, and I'll see you later.

XOXO,

Rae

If you or someone you know is struggling with Substance Abuse, please find the proper support. One resource is the Emergency Substance Abuse Hotline: 1-800-662-HELP

ABOUT THE AUTHOR

Rae Lloyd is a romance author with a deep passion for the written word. Having been an avid reader since a very young age, she was inspired by the thousands of books she consumed since childhood. Rae's dream of having her writings published has finally come to fruition. She can be found writing in between living life with her three daughters and her husband, as well as hanging out with her many adorable pets, baking gluten-free desserts, or cultivating beauty in her wig salon. With many stories brewing in her mind, stay tuned for more to come.

To stay in touch and receive all book updates, subscribe to get emails at raelloyd.com.

You can also find Rae on TikTok and Instagram @raelloydwrites.

You can join Rae's Facebook group called Rae's Readers.

Made in the USA
Middletown, DE
12 September 2024

60202714R00203